ONCE UPON A KISS

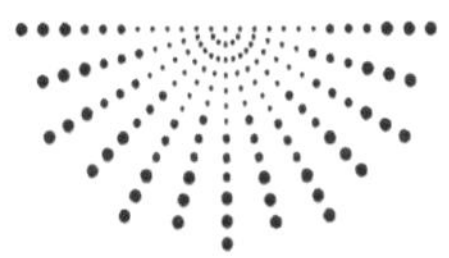

DARA GIRARD

CONTENTS

ISBN 13: 978-1949764543

Once Upon A Kiss: Two Book Collection

Published by ILORI Press Books

ILORI PRESS BOOKS, LLC

PO Box #10332

Silver Spring, MD 20914

www.iloripressbooks.com

Dangerous Curves

Duvall Sisters

The Glass Slipper Project

Taming Mariella

A Reluctant Hero

The Clifton Sisters

The Sapphire Pendant

The Amber Stone

The Emerald Ring

It Happened One Wedding

Unexpected Pleasure

Midnight Promise

Sweet Temptation

Always and Forever

Truly Yours

Novels

Perfect Match

Snowed in with the Doctor

Winterwood Lane

Illusive Flame

Honest Betrayal

The Daughters of Winston Barnett

Remember My Name

THE GLASS SLIPPER PROJECT

DEDICATION

To women who dream.

READER LETTER

Dear Reader,

What does a girl do when she finds her Prince Charming but the shoe doesn't fit?

Isabella Duvall has one big problem. She has three sisters determined to marry a rich man. Enter Alex Carlton, a wealthy man who seems perfect for their plan. Isabella is too practical to enter into their scheme. But her practicality flies out the window when she falls under the spell of Alex's devilish eyes and sexy grins. Unfortunately, he's ready to settle down and she's ready to leave town. What are they to do?

This book is another tale of opposites finding their way to true love. I enjoyed writing about Alex and Isabella, Isabella's relationship with her sisters and their determination to make their plan work.

I hope that you delight in reading about these characters, the plan and its final outcome. If you'd like to hear more about my other books or to sign up on my mailing list, please visit my Web site, www.daragirard.com.

Best wishes,
Dara

PROLOGUE

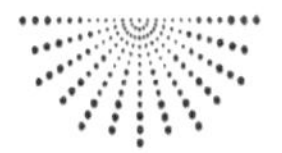

Nestled in the rolling hills and sprawling farmlands of upstate New York was the town of Hydale. It was a place where every season had a distinct character—the late bloom of spring, fierce hot summers, fiery crisp autumns and long frigid winters. It was in this quiet town that Alvin and Caroline Duvall settled and had four daughters: Mariella, Isabella, Gabriella and Daniella.

All, except for Isabella, were known beauties and admired for their looks, grace and charm. But what Isabella lacked in her appearance she made up for with her energy, sense of duty and intelligence. For many years, all was well for the Duvalls until tragedy struck.

With the arrival of an unexpected visitor, their lives were about to change. It started one cold winter day, unlike any other...

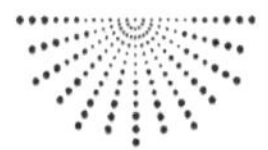

CHAPTER ONE

"When is that woman coming?" Mariella Duvall said checking her reflection in the large ornate mirror, which hung on the main wall in the living room. She trailed one long, beautifully manicured finger along her perfect profile. Nothing had changed in the last half hour since she last checked, but she enjoyed making sure.

Gabby, who preferred her nickname to her full name of Gabriella, sent her eldest sister a stern look from her position on the couch, then returned her gaze to the crossword in her lap. "That woman has a name, Mariella."

"I don't care what her name is. It's so unfair that she's taking over our house."

Daniella, the youngest of the sisters, sat on the rug putting together a puzzle. Her long, frizzy black hair, although pulled back with two silver hair combs, hid her face as she leaned forward and said in a sad voice, "But it's not our house anymore."

The three sisters fell silent, remembering the major losses

the past five years had brought them: first their father died, then their mother and now they had lost their beloved house. Outside, the biting mid-January winds howled through the rafters and swept across the slush-covered lawn, a distant reminder of last week's snowfall. Tiny footprints from squirrels imprinted the surface; inside, the low hum of the radiator buzzed while a grandfather clock ticked away the seconds.

"Well," Mariella said breaking the melancholy silence, "We still get to rent it for the next six months. I just don't see why she and that daughter of hers couldn't wait until then to move in."

Gabby closed her book of crosswords and set it aside. "We should be very thankful the new owner is allowing us to stay here that long until we find somewhere else." She turned her gaze to Isabella, her second eldest sister. Isabella sat hunched over a writing desk in the corner as quiet as a mouse, which many already considered her to be.

She hadn't inherited the Duvall's stately beauty—the elegant neck, the dark flashing brown eyes and skin the color of polished oak. Instead she was of small stature with indeterminate features. But if one were to take a moment's notice, they would see Isabella's attractive soft eyes and her full sensuous mouth, but people rarely took the time to notice. Only seven years older than the youngest, Daniella, she seemed much older. Gabby tilted her head at her sister, curious as to how she felt about their situation. "Don't you think, Izzy?"

Isabella turned around, pushing up the sleeves of the checkered cardigan her father used to wear. "She's coming around noon."

Gabby frowned. "That wasn't the question."

Mariella turned from the mirror, satisfied with the way she looked, and sat on the couch. She picked up Gabby's book, but finding no interest in it, quickly set it down again. "At least she answered my question."

"We're having an important discussion, Izzy, can't you pay attention?"

Isabella sighed and turned back to her desk. "You have two other people paying attention to you, you don't need a third."

Mariella crossed her legs and looked at the clock. "She should be here at any minute."

"Stop calling her *she*," Gabby scolded. "*She* has a name."

"What is it again?"

"Mrs. Carlton," Isabella said patiently.

"Doesn't she have a first name?"

"Probably but I don't remember hearing it. I doubt we'll need to know it anyway."

Daniella put a puzzle piece in place. "Yes. We'd better get used to saying 'Mrs. Carlton,' considering she'll be living with us for six months."

"You mean we'll have to live with her," Isabella said. "This house isn't ours anymore."

"I wish there had been another way. This house is all we had." Gabby sighed and glanced around the grand room that had once housed an impressive array of ornately carved furniture. She felt a sudden sadness, now it had the bare minimum since most of the furniture had to be sold. "Father wanted us to have it."

Isabella swung around and rested her arm on the back of the chair determined not to feel sentimental; although the pain in Gabby's voice echoed the sorrow in her heart. "Gabby, the decision has been made. We agreed that there was no other choice. We had to pay Mom's medical bills and we have just enough to live on. We couldn't afford this house anymore."

"I still don't know why they have to live with us," Daniella said.

"That was the arrangement we made with the new owner. I think it's very kind."

Mariella sniffed. "I bet you it's just a ploy. She's probably a miserable crab apple who stays in her room and bangs on the ground with her cane expecting us to wait on her hand and foot."

Daniella widened her eyes. "Do you really think so?"

"Yes." She uncrossed her legs and leaned forward. "And that daughter of hers is a tired spinster who scuttles to her mother's every command."

"Mariella," Isabella warned.

She sent her sister a look then sat back. "She'll probably be jealous of me."

"Why?" Daniella asked intrigued.

"Because I'm so beautiful, of course. Mom told us that the Duvall women are always envied for their looks." She sent a considering glance at Isabella. "Usually anyway," she amended then returned her attention to Daniella. "It's a responsibility one has to bear. I bet you she will—"

"Let's not look for trouble," Isabella cut in. "Have the rooms been cleared?"

"Yes," Gabby said. "The very best ones as you requested."

Daniella bit her lip. "I hope they are nice!"

Mariella smoothed out her eyebrows. "They don't have to be."

"Mariella, stop it." Isabella smiled at Daniella, hoping to reassure her. "I'm sure they are perfectly fine."

"I think—"

"That's enough Mariella," Isabella said in a tone that would allow no argument. Mariella sent her a look of reproach, but said nothing. "There is no need to imagine the worst. Let's be thankful the house sold. We can think of the sale as a belated Christmas gift."

"The only gift," Mariella said, crossing her legs again. "I don't even know why we put up a tree. We couldn't afford to put anything under it. This is not the life Mom would have wanted for us."

"At least we are all together. That's something, isn't it?" When no one replied, Isabella stiffened her chin. "We can do this as long as we work as a team."

"We won't be together long," Gabby said. "Without this house where will we go?"

"Gabby, it's going to be fine. We'll find another place. You have to trust me, okay?"

She nodded.

Isabella returned to the desk. As she looked over the remaining bills, her resolution faltered. The stack of envelopes included bills from their father's illness. He had died years before their mother became ill. But even after the sale of the house there wouldn't be much money left. She knew they would have to pool their income and find a smaller place to rent for a while. Although their immigrant parents had taught them to buy—never to rent—she knew that, for now, they had no option. She had six months to make sure everyone was taken care of.

Mariella leaned over her shoulder. "What are you frowning about?"

Isabella closed the book of accounts. "Nothing."

Mariella pushed her hand aside. "What is it?"

Isabella sighed then said in a low voice. "We don't have any money."

Mariella glanced at their two younger sisters then Isabella.

Her tone became a sharp whisper. "I thought you said the sale of the house would cover everything."

"I thought it would, but since Mom and Dad didn't have any long term health insurance, and both of them had terminal illnesses, we are still over fifty thousand dollars in debt."

"Fifty thousand? Are you sure?"

"Positive."

Mariella briefly held her head. "This shouldn't be happening to me." She glanced up. "I mean to us," she corrected. "Okay, let me think. I could ask for more time at the gallery. I'm going to be discovered soon Izzy, just you wait. A designer is going to come in and want me to model their clothes. Or better yet, a photographer traveling to the city will enter the gallery and see me and want me to pose for him."

"Preferably with your clothes on," Isabella mumbled.

Mariella narrowed her gaze. "Of course, I'm not naïve."

Isabella only nodded. She knew the likelihood of anyone of any importance passing through their small town was slim. "Perhaps I could ask Mrs. Lyons for more hours."

"Why?" Mariella sat on the edge of the desk and swung her leg. "You can hardly stand your present hours."

"We need the money."

"Why not just ask for a raise?"

Because she couldn't. She wanted to bide her time and convince Mrs. Lyons to take her on the annual European visit she took every May. Mrs. Lyons had always hinted at taking her as a companion and this year she planned to go. However, until she was certain, she didn't want to share that plan with her sisters. "I'd prefer the extra hours. She has a lot of different things that she needs to have done around the house."

Mariella shrugged, not understanding her sister's

reasoning but choosing to accept it. "Then *I'll* ask for a raise. I deserve it."

"You asked for a raise three months ago. You can't ask for another one."

"Then what is your bright idea?"

"Something will come to me."

"Six months." Mariella picked up a pen then set it down again with a weary sigh. "That's all we have. Then we'll be cast out on the street." She made a sweeping gesture with her arm.

Isabella ducked, resisting the urge not to roll her eyes. "Not exactly."

"We'll never be able to afford another house like this. We'll be forced into a hovel, crowded into a one room flat with a landlord that won't allow any male visitors past 10 p.m." Mariella held up a hand before her sister could speak. "Or worse, one who pinches our bottoms and makes lewd comments every time he passes."

"Stop being so dramatic. Our situation is not that bad."

"It's bad enough." She lightly touched Isabella's limp hair wishing there was some way to make her sister look more attractive. Isabella swatted her hand away. She drummed her fingers on her lap thoughtfully. "Perhaps I could persuade Mr. Carlton to give us an extension."

Isabella raised a mocking brow. "How do you plan to persuade him?"

She winked. "How do you persuade any man?"

"He could be eighty years old."

"A man's ego never ages, stroke it and he's putty in your hand."

"I don't think Mr. Carlton needs anything stroked. Six months is plenty of time for us to get things in order."

Gabby approached the table. "What are you two whispering about?"

"The fact that we're broke," Mariella said, checking her nails.

Isabella pounded the desk. "Mariella!"

She shrugged unapologetic. "They have to know the truth. They're not little anymore. Besides, they need to know how important it is for me to be discovered."

"It won't happen," Gabby said. "Things like that only happen in the movies."

Daniella joined the group. "What is everyone talking about?"

"Nothing."

Daniella folded her arms and fixed her face into a pout. "If it's nothing, why are you all talking about it?"

"We need money, Dani," Mariella said. "And we're thinking of ways to make it. Mom always said I was born the most beautiful for a reason, and I think that reason is to make us all rich."

"You're too old to be a model," Daniella said.

"I am not."

"You're over thirty."

"Only by a year. And besides true beauty never ages. People are always shocked when I tell them how old I am."

"And how old do you tell them you are?" Isabella smirked.

Mariella did not reply and went back to studying her nails.

Gabby rested her hip against the desk. "Well, until you're discovered what are we supposed to do?"

"Something will come up," Isabella said, determined to keep their spirits high.

Gabby nodded confidently. "Yes, Izzy always thinks of something."

"That's right," Mariella and Daniella agreed.

"Yes, I do." She returned her sister's confident smiles, trying to quell a growing panic inside.

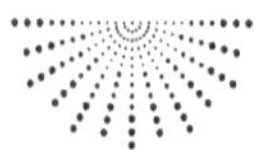

CHAPTER TWO

"**S**top complaining. It's not that heavy."

Alex sent his mother a mocking look. "Which is why I'm carrying it instead of you, correct?"

Velma gestured to her suitcase. "I'm carrying this, aren't I?"

"Yes." He set the trunk on a dolly and pulled it up the pathway. "It still weighs a ton."

"It's an important trunk and it's antique."

"Really?" He studied the trunk a moment. "I didn't know you were that old."

Velma gave her son a stern look, but didn't reply.

"I could help you," Sophia said as she struggled with two suitcases and a large handbag.

Alex looked at his sister's slim build, her face barely visible with her blue knit hat low over her forehead and a matching scarf wrapped around the lower half of her face. "Thanks, Sugar, but this would flatten you."

Alex's assistant and friend, Tony, smiled at her as he

dragged the second trunk, his limp exaggerated by the extra strain on his bad leg. "And that would be a shame."

She lowered her gaze.

"We're early," Velma said. "Perhaps we should wait."

The dolly bumped along the cracked pathway, nearly causing its contents to tilt. Alex grabbed the trunk before it toppled over. "I don't think they'll mind."

"They may not be ready yet."

"They'd better be because I'm not putting this thing back in the truck."

"You're the one who wouldn't hire the movers," Velma said, leaning on her suitcase to catch her breath.

He stopped and shook his head. "I thought you only had a few things."

"Yes, two trunks and our bags."

Alex glanced at the flat bed of his trunk, piled with their belongings. "Twenty bags."

"Eight," she corrected. "Stop exaggerating."

"Are we going to take these things in or freeze out here?" Tony asked, his breathing clear in the brittle air.

Alex started walking again. "You're right."

"Just a minute," Velma said. She turned to the house and clasped her hands together. "I want to look at it first." She stared at the grand Victorian structure silhouetted by the distant sun and pale blue sky.

"You'll have the rest of your life to look at it." Alex passed her, hoisted the trunk up on his back and climbed the stairs of the wraparound porch. He set the trunk down with a hard thud.

Velma gritted her teeth. "Be careful."

"I'm trying."

She walked past him and raised her hand to knock. "Let me speak to them and explain why we're a little early."

Alex glanced upward, trying to remain patient. "You don't have to explain."

"It's really cold out here," Tony said, adjusting his muffler.

"I *want* to explain," Velma said. "I don't want them to think we have bad manners."

"We're only fifteen minutes early, they'll be fine."

"Real cold," Tony said, pushing his ungloved hands deeper into his coat pockets.

"Still, I think I should explain," Velma said. "I don't want things to be awkward between us." She raised her hand again and then stopped. "I wonder if they'll recognize me," she said growing anxious.

Alex slowly smiled, and said in a level voice, "If they do recognize you, they'd better be very nice or I'll let them rent the house for just two months instead of six."

"Wow," Tony said a little louder. "It is *really* cold."

"I'm sure they'll be very nice," Alex said and lifted his hand to knock.

Velma stepped in front of him. "I—"

He rested his hands on her shoulders and met her worried gaze. The anxiety in her eyes accentuated the fine lines and wrinkles on her brown face. He affectionately lifted her hat up from her forehead, exposing a few carefully prepared silver curls. "It's our home now, they can't look down on us."

"But, I'm sure they'll remember what our status was before," she said, her voice reflecting the pain of their past.

"It will be okay."

"Will one of you please knock on the door?" Sophia asked, looking ready to collapse under the weight of the bags. "It's freezing out here."

"Yes, everything will be fine," Velma said. She lifted her chin and rang the doorbell.

A stunning woman answered leaving them all speechless. She looked as though she belonged on a magazine cover: tall, brown like a gazelle with doe eyes, her sleek black hair, cut just below her chin. She stood in the doorway as though she expected flashbulbs to emerge from the bushes.

She smiled at them. "Hello, I'm Mariella. You must be Mrs. Carlton?"

"Yes," Velma stammered.

She held out a beautifully tapered hand and Velma shook it. "It's a pleasure to meet you." She looked at Sophia. "And you are?"

Sophia blinked quickly. "I'm...I'm..."

"That's my daughter Sophia," Velma said. She turned to Alex and Tony. "And this is..."

Mariella suddenly frowned, wrapping her hands around herself. "Brr, it's freezing. You'd better come in and warm up. We have some nice hot cider in the kitchen." She opened the door wider for them to pass through.

"Thank you," Velma said, stepping inside the warm foyer where the scent of cinnamon lingered.

Alex and Tony picked up their trunks and followed. Mariella sent them a cool gaze. "No, you two are to go around the back."

"But—" Velma began.

"It's just around the corner. You can't miss it."

Velma shook her head. "Oh, you don't understand..."

Mariella waved away her attempt at an explanation. "I'm sure these two men have been very helpful to you, but I'm not having slush and mud tracked into the foyer." Mariella returned her clear, dark gaze to the two startled men. "You can leave the small bags here. When you go around to the other entrance, one of my sisters will direct you to the appropriate rooms."

Velma tapped her on the shoulder, desperate to explain. "But—"

Mariella gently brushed her aside as she would a mosquito and continued to address the men. "When you are finished, you can meet us in the kitchen for refreshments."

"You're too kind," Alex said, his voice dripping with sarcasm.

Mariella didn't notice and smiled as though he'd offered her a compliment. "You're very welcome."

"Ms. Duvall," Sophia said in a small voice.

"You can call me Mariella."

"Yes, well—"

"And I'll call you Sophia, and I'm sure we'll all get on well."

Velma raised her hands helplessly. "But you don't understand."

"It's okay, Mrs. Carlton," Alex said in a low voice. "We'll go around to the back and bring in everything else."

"See? There's no problem," Mariella said. She turned and shut the door. An icicle fell and hit the ground from the force.

Alex stood and stared at the door for a long moment.

"Why didn't you tell her you own the house?" Tony asked.

Alex lifted his trunk and headed down the stairs. "Because she'll find out soon enough and regret this moment. I plan to make sure."

THE MEN WALKED around the house through the wet slush

covering the path and finally reached a faded door that, at one time, had been a gleaming maroon. It was now a dirty brown and bowed. Alex set his trunk down and knocked. A young woman barely out of her teens answered. She widened her eyes in surprise looking like a sweet confection one would find at a carnival. She had dark curly hair that floated around her head as if it was soft cotton candy, her cheeks resembling caramel apples. She shook her head and smiled. "No, you don't want this door. You want the next one." She pointed.

Alex narrowed his eyes, feeling the edge of his patience beginning to fray. "Now Miss—"

"Don't worry," she said quickly. "It's not far, only a few feet. My sister Gabby will open it for you." She shut the door before he could reply. Another icicle fell, this time hitting him on the shoulder. Alex stared at the door and took a deep breath.

Tony picked up his trunk. "I'm beginning to hate this house."

Alex lifted his trunk and walked in the direction she had pointed. They finally reached another door that was more than a *few* feet away, as the young woman had assured them. Alex pounded on it.

"There's no need to get violent," a woman said as she opened the door. For a moment the two men stared surprised that three such striking women could all be living in one residence. She tossed one thick braid over her shoulder with the casual grace of the upper class, and glared at them through dark brown eyes that could have melted steel.

Alex shifted his trunk. "Are you Gabby?"

She folded her arms, bringing notice to her ample figure. "Yes."

"Where are we suppose to put these?"

"Let me show you to the rooms."

Alex sighed with mounting dread. "It's upstairs, isn't it?"

She blinked. "How did you guess?"

"I'm having a bad day."

"We have an old elevator."

His spirits brightened. "Yes, that's right. Does it work?"

"Of course."

Ancient may have been a better word to describe the elevator. It creaked and groaned and seemed to sway a little, but eventually reached the second floor. Gabby led them to the far end of the house on the north side where his mother and sister would stay. She pointed to one of the two rooms. "Put Mrs. Carlton's things in there."

"Gabby!" Someone called from below.

"Will you excuse me?" she said.

"Yes."

She left. Tony watched her go. "My God."

"What?"

"They're beautiful. Didn't you notice?"

"Just put the trunk in Sophia's room," Alex said, then headed into his mother's room. He set the trunk down and glanced around the cream-colored room. He looked at the queen-sized wrought iron bed crowned with a carved wooden sculpture of a pot of flowers, draped with a pink coverlet piled high with vintage lace pillows. A large window offered a spectacular view of the front lawn and the long curving driveway.

A rare grin touched his mouth. *Home at last.* The house whispered to him sweetly, like the call of an old friend or a lover he wanted to caress and spend time with. Soon his dream would come true. He would no longer be an outsider. He belonged. He was no longer the poor kid on a bike riding home to another dinner of potatoes and beans. No longer was he standing outside the grand Duvall house looking in and seeing the excited silhouettes or the family gathered around the table for a dinner, knowing the cook had prepared a wonderful meal of succulent chicken stuffed with cheese and broccoli and rice pilaf with almonds.

Soon he'd have his own dinners here with his family gathered in the dining room, Soon he'd be an established figure in the community and everyone would be impressed with how he'd restored the house to its former glory, and the man he had become.

"So Alex," Tony said a few moments later from the doorway.

Alex turned. "Yes?"

Tony looked around unimpressed, his gaze falling on the crooked desk lamp and worn molding. "*This* is the grand house you've been telling me about all these years?"

"You should have seen it years ago."

"I agree."

Alex shrugged unconcerned. "I know it's a little run-down, but with the right attention it will look spectacular."

"It will cost a lot of money." He leaned against the doorframe. "But you don't have to worry about that."

Alex suddenly had a thought. "Let me show you something." He walked down the corridor, with Tony not far behind, until he reached a narrow hall. He walked up a few steps and opened a door to a small room with an overhead landing for storage.

Tony glanced around nervously. "Should we be here?"

"They're all downstairs. Stop worrying."

"Actually, I think you should start," a female voice said from somewhere above them.

Both men halted.

Alex spun around. "Who is that?"

"You'll find out once you tell me who you are."

The men turned in a circle, trying to find out where the voice was coming from. "Where are you?"

The woman scrambled out of her hiding place then leaned over the small landing. "Who are you?"

Alex and Tony glanced up. The look of annoyance didn't help her ordinary features, but both men were transfixed by the fire in her eyes. Slowly the look of annoyance melted into astonishment. "It can't be." She shook her head. "No, it's not possible. I must be dreaming."

Tony grinned. "If men like us fill your dreams, you must have a very uneasy sleep."

She returned his grin—for a moment not looking ordinary at all—then bit her lip and set her gaze on Alex. He stood with a strange anticipation gripping him. Did she recognize him when none of the others had? Did he want her to?

"But you look so much like..." She suddenly disappeared from view.

Tony looked at Alex confused. "Do you think she's the crazy one they keep locked in the attic?"

Before Alex could reply the woman reappeared. She was much smaller than she'd appeared on the landing. Her hair hung limply, as did the long sleeves of her oversized cardigan that fell past her hands. Though there was nothing extraordinary about her face, both men couldn't help but stare at the keen dark eyes. Then a slow smile spread over her lips and lit the brown in her eyes like a touch of honey on choco-late, and for a moment, she looked beautiful.

To Alex's annoyance, unwarranted feelings of lust swept through him as he saw how joy altered her appearance. For a moment he wondered what other 'joys' could do to those expressive eyes. He quickly brushed that thought aside.

She clapped her hands together. "It is you! Lex!"

Tony raised his eyebrows and opened his mouth to comment on the nickname, but one look from Alex persuaded him to decide against it.

"I can't believe it's you. *You* bought the house?"

"Yes."

She threw her arms around him and hugged him. For a moment he was enveloped by the smell of apples mingled with cinnamon as soft cotton brushed against his cheek. He was surprised she felt so thin under the bulky cardigan. For some reason that bothered him. He could lift her in his arms without much effort and had a strange urge to do so, but he was a man of tempered emotions and quickly checked himself, keeping her firmly on the ground.

So many memories filled his head, followed by feelings he didn't want to address. Feelings he hadn't allowed himself to experience in years. He didn't like her ability to bring them— so easily—back to the surface. A quiet anger made him withdraw abruptly.

She staggered back surprised then embarrassed. "I'm sorry. I thought we had parted as friends."

He cleared his throat feeling foolish and angry at himself for hurting her feelings. It was similar to crushing the wings of a moth: "We had. I'm—I just wanted to look at you."

He ignored Tony's odd glance. He already knew how empty his words sounded. She looked so plain and yet there were moments...

She laughed, but instead of putting him at ease, tension grew inside him "I'm afraid there's not much to see," she said holding out her arms. "But look all you want." She playfully spun around for inspection then turned and faced him, her eyes bright with amusement. "Have I changed much?"

"No."

She patted his arm then rested her hand on his shoulder. "Carlton." She gazed at him amazed. "I never would have guessed. What have my sisters said?"

He kept his hands at his side, wishing she would remove hers from his shoulder. He wore a thick jacket and sweater, yet he felt as though the heat from her fingers penetrated both shields. "They don't recognize me."

She frowned. "That's odd. How can that be?" She cupped his chin and moved his head to the side until his profile faced her. "I could recognize you anywhere. Especially from that scar near your ear. It's faint, but it's still there. I remember when you got it. If only my parents could see what you've become..." Her voice trailed off, her dark eyes filling with tears.

Alex touched her shoulder, again amazed by how thin it felt under the cardigan. "I'm sorry about your loss," he said with such tenderness, his friend sent him another curious glance. Alex ignored him.

She blinked back the tears and forced a smile.

"A part of me is relieved. Mom suffered for so long." The brief sadness left her gaze and Alex found himself smiling back. "Oh, but this is not a time for tears." Her words became a whisper. "I can't believe it's you."

"Yes. It's me." For a moment they stared at each other.

Tony coughed.

Alex jumped and remembered his companion. He gestured to him. "Oh, yes this is my friend Tony."

She shook his hand. "Nice to meet you."

"Alex has told me wonderful things about this house."

"I'm glad he had happy memories." An odd expression

crossed her face, but was quickly hidden. She turned to Alex. "Where is your mother?"

"Mariella took her into the kitchen."

"Good, I'll go and see her."

"She's in the kitchen."

"Yes, you said that."

Tony gave him a strange look, he ignored it. "Right."

She raced past him then stopped and turned. "I'm sorry. I didn't even introduce myself. I made a terrible assumption. I doubt you remember me. There are four of us and I just assumed you knew who I was."

"I know who you are, Isabella," Alex said softly, his gaze piercing hers. "I remember you very well. You're not like your sisters."

Tony winced and Alex mentally kicked himself, but Isabella didn't take any offense. "Yes, that's true. It makes me unforgettable, right?"

Alex shook his head. "I didn't mean—"

"I'm surprised you remember me at all. I was a lot older than you."

"Five years."

"Really? You're the same age as Gabby? It felt like a lot more back then." She shrugged. "But now you're all grown up." She turned. "Come on. Let's go into the kitchen. My sisters will be thrilled once they know who you are." She raced down the stairs.

Alex watched her go.

Tony picked up a picture then bent the curling corners back to get a full view. It was a photograph taken years ago of the four sisters in front of the house. "What was that all about? It's not like you to lose your cool."

"I don't know what you're talking about. I just didn't expect anyone up here. That's all."

"So what's so special about this room?"

Alex shoved a hand in his pocket and glanced around at the worn desk and chair, the area rug unraveling at the seams and a large collection of boxes crowded in one corner. "I used to escape up here when Mom was working." He pointed. "From that window I could see people come and go. They used to have a lot of guests and I'd make faces at them without them noticing." He turned and ran his hand along the wall. "And I had a secret panel." He knocked on the wall until he heard something hollow, then slid the panel to the side. "Amazing it's still here."

Tony came up behind him. "What is it?"

"A little hole in the wall I found. I used to hide things inside it. I left behind things such as playing cards, candy, rocks, string, keys."

"Keys?"

"I liked the thought of owning something that could unlock something else. I was always impressed with people who had a lot of keys. To me it meant they owned a lot of stuff and I wanted to own a lot of stuff one day, too."

"Now you do."

He picked up an old silver-colored key and turned it in his hand. "And Izzy used to find keys for me and leave them on the desk along with a snack to eat." He began to smile as he remembered. "She'd also leave a note with no words on it and just a question mark because sometimes we would imagine what the different keys opened. She was really imaginative. She used to..." He abruptly stopped.

"She used to what?"

Alex tossed the key back into the box, it made a loud ping

as it hit the sides. "I don't remember," he said and closed the panel, sealing any more questions about his past. "So that's why I liked this room. It was a place to get away."

"Nice."

Alex headed for the door. "We'd better go before they come looking for us."

Tony nodded, then watched his friend go. He stared at the photograph once more and flashed a sly grin. A man of much older years, Tony didn't miss much and saw more than Alex would have wanted him to. "I think I'm beginning to see why this house means so much to you," he said.

CHAPTER THREE

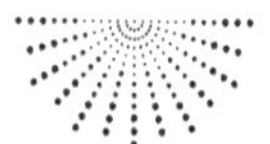

*I*sabella didn't go to the kitchen immediately. Instead, she darted into one of the rooms and shut the door. She sagged against it trying to recover from the shock of seeing Alex again. She knew she shouldn't feel this way, but she couldn't keep her hands from trembling. He looked the same, yet something was wrong. The man she'd just seen was nothing like the young boy she'd known.

She briefly closed her eyes and cringed remembering the way she'd thrown herself into his arms.

It was clear the man "little Lex" had become did not appreciate such familiarity. But how could she have expected him to? They had all changed.

How many years had it been since she'd last seen him sitting on the front steps as his mother offered a tearful farewell? Little Sophia had sat beside him with her hand resting on his knee. She remembered walking down the steps and standing in front of him.

"Aren't you going to say goodbye?" she asked.

"No," he said.

"Very well then, I guess we aren't as good friends as I thought."

He mumbled something.

"What?"

He lifted a gaze filled with rage and tears. "I said I'll miss you!' He turned away.

"I'll miss you, too."

"Will you miss me?" Sophia asked.

Isabella kissed her forehead. "Very much."

Alex looked down at his shoes. "They'll all be sorry one day."

Isabella frowned. "Who are *they?*"

Before he could reply, Velma said, "Bye, Izzy."

Isabella hugged her. "Please keep in touch. Even if it's just a holiday card. We'd love to know what you're up to."

Velma promised she would, then Isabella watched them pile into their Volkswagen and drive away.

Isabella pushed herself from the door, trying to escape the memory. She'd missed them more than she'd expected. They'd been a big part of her life and she hadn't wanted to lose them. She'd waited months for a letter to arrive to tell her they'd settled and what they were up to, but it never came. She never expected to see them again. Why had they come back? Had he come back to make them sorry? Based on the information the Realtor had told them, the new owner was very rich and influential. With his newfound power and wealth, which usually came with a higher social standing, he could make a lot of people very unhappy. Isabella shook her head. She was reading too much into an awkward moment. Just because he didn't remember her well didn't mean he was there to cause trouble.

Isabella walked into the kitchen expecting to hear the

raised voices of surprise and reunion, but instead, she heard the quiet murmur of pleasant strangers. Curious, she peeked around the corner and saw Mrs. Carlton and Sophia sitting primly at the table. Alex and his friend Tony stood by the door, while Mariella profusely apologized for not recognizing him with all the pathos of a staged drama "Again Mr. Carlton, I'm *so* sorry for the confusion. I hope you can forgive me."

The look she sent him offered him no choice, and he graciously responded with a nod of acceptance. Isabella watched his face. Now that she had peeled away the film of memory, she saw the reality of the man who now owned their home. He had a handsome face, which was unnervingly void of any true emotion: It looked as though a painter had created a magnificent portrait without putting any feeling in each brush stroke. Much like Mariella, he knew the power of his looks and used them to his advantage. She could imagine him putting people at ease with a smile that should've put them on guard.

Isabella shifted her gaze to Mrs. Carlton, who she recalled with fondness. She was now dressed in an expensive tailored suit and Isabella decided that she would approach the older woman with caution. She smiled in loving remembrance when she looked at her daughter, little Sophia, who in the past was always getting scolded for getting dirty. Now she sat elegantly in a peach cashmere blouse and dark wool trousers, her hair artfully arranged in curls falling around a slender face with a pert nose and wide hazel eyes. She had her brother's good looks, but more warmth, and provided an obvious contrast to their shabby kitchen.

The tables had turned and Isabella knew the Carltons may not look on the Duvalls with kindness. Although Isabella had loved her mother, Caroline Duvall had been known for her grace and elegance, not for her kindness. Mrs. Carlton would see a faded image of the daughters she'd once dressed for fine high-society parties and events; daughters of a woman who had been stingy with pay but generous with work. They were not grand ladies now, and they were at their mercy. They had six months before they would be out of their lives again.

No wonder Alex had looked at her with distant pity. Like others, he must have been surprised to have to admit she had not developed *any* of the Duvall beauty. Isabella nodded. Now that she had assessed the situation, she was ready to proceed. For some unknown reason, she feared that Alex might not make her sisters aware of their former acquaintance. She would.

Isabella pushed opened the kitchen door and walked up to Mrs. Carlton with her hand outstretched. "Mrs. Carlton, it's a pleasure to see you again." The older woman only stared at her stunned, leaving Isabella's hand hanging in the air with nothing to grasp. She patted her shoulder instead. "You haven't changed." She turned to Sophia. "And little Sophia. You're beautiful. Of course, good looks run in the family."

Mariella stared at her sister, appalled. "Isabella, what is wrong with you? What are you talking about?"

Velma blinked, wringing her hands in her lap. "You remember us?"

"Yes," Isabella said, wondering why she felt on the verge of tears. "I've never forgotten you. I can see why you were too busy to write."

Velma jumped up from her seat and pulled Isabella into her arms. "Oh my darling girl. How I've missed you."

Isabella met Velma's fierce hug with the same emotion,

blinking back tears as her fears ebbed. Mrs. Carlton hadn't changed. She was still the kind, generous spirit she'd loved years ago. The one who had soothed her ego when her mother's harsh words had hurt her, the one who had added a "special touch"—whether it be a layer of silk, or an embroidered hem—to any dress she made for her. "I can't believe it's you." Isabella turned to Sophia. "You probably don't remember me, but give me a hug anyway."

Sophia shyly hugged her, then said, "I do remember you a little bit."

"You used to follow your brother around everywhere." Isabella glanced up at Alex, his intense dark eyes sent a cold chill through her. It was clear that he was *not* in the mood for memories. She swallowed and stepped away. "Well..." she said lamely.

Mariella rested her hands on her hips. "What is going on?"

Isabella maintained a light tone to combat her sister's sharp one. "Mariella. You remember Mrs. Carlton, right?"

She sent the older woman a cursory glance. "Am I supposed to?"

Her tone wavered. "Yes. Mrs. Carlton used to work for Mom as a seamstress, remember?" She nodded at Alex not wanting to meet his eyes again. "And Alex used to run errands and sometimes Sophia would stay with Daniella." She turned to her youngest sister. "You two would play together. Of course you were too young to remember." In an attempt to fill the sudden silence, Isabella said, "And this is Alex's friend, Tony."

Tony smiled. The sisters nodded then dismissed him.

"I don't believe it," Gabby said. "It *is* them." She pointed a finger at Alex. "You stole my bicycle."

Alex rested against the wall looking bored. "I borrowed it."

"You're supposed to return things you borrow."

A faint smile touched his mouth. "I could buy you a new one."

"Good."

Mariella looked at them stunned. "But it can't be. They were poor."

Isabella hit her sister's arm hard.

She coughed and smiled. "It's a delight to see you again. Once more, I apologize about the back door. I thought you were the movers."

"We didn't want too many things in the house just yet," Velma said. "Not until..." Her voice faded away.

"Yes," Isabella said, smoothing over the awkward silence. "Thank you. That was very considerate." When Mariella sniffed, Isabella pinched her. "Don't worry, we'll be out of your way soon enough."

"No need to rush," Alex said. He said the words, but Isabella didn't believe him. She turned and looked directly into his eyes.

"Where will you be staying?" she asked.

"I'm renting a room in town. I'll be busy over the next couple of weeks."

"Doing what?" Daniella asked.

"In two weeks I'm holding a fundraiser for the local nursing home. It will be an upscale event." His gaze fell on each of them then stopped at Isabella. "I hope to see you all there."

"WHAT DO you mean we can't go?" Mariella asked the next

day as the three sisters looked over the invitation. "He gave us four tickets."

"Will you please be sensible?" Isabella said with a tired sigh.

"I haven't attended a party like this in years. It's over two hundred dollars a plate and being held at the Montpelier Mansion. It's my chance to be discovered."

"And I'd like to go," Gabby added. "It's been such a long time since we've gone to something like this. Oh, imagine all the food they'll have."

Mariella winked. "And the men."

Daniella nodded. "It will be so much fun."

Mariella lifted the invitation. "There is no reason *why* we shouldn't go. We have the tickets."

Isabella shook her head. "But we don't have dresses."

"We could charge them."

"We have enough debt as it is."

"You could think of something," Gabby said. "You always think of something."

Isabella bit her lip then slowly said, "I could make you—"

"That's it," Mariella cut in. "Whatever you say, I think it's a perfect idea. You could make our dresses. You're an excellent seamstress. I don't know where or how you learned to sew, but you're good at it. Simple-chic will work. It will be like getting our dresses made in the old days."

"But I didn't say—"

"Oh, Izzy, you're the best."

They all kissed her on the cheek, then left planning for the big event.

Isabella sat at the kitchen table, burying her head in her hands. Outside the leafless trees clapped their branches together in an unheard breeze. She listened to the creak of footsteps above her. It was in quiet moments such as these that the house seemed to speak. In the tranquil hours as sunlight melted into the inky black shadows of night, or when the fingers of dawn brushed the shadows away, the house groaned and moaned as if it were an old woman with a story to share.

Isabella didn't care to listen. She knew all the stories and didn't like any of them. The walls in the solarium reminded her of the night her father told them he had leukemia. The floorboards would gossip about his last days as he stared out the window, half the weight he used to be. The living room would recall her mother's diagnosis given over the phone, while the master bedroom remembered her last words, spoken clearly and firmly as death slowly stole her breath away.

She could still hear the echo of her own footsteps as she paced back and forth in the corridor. She remembered Daniella calling out in the night with a bad dream, and Gabby sneaking up the stairs with food she'd stashed in her pockets because dinner wasn't enough.

Isabella glanced around the kitchen's peeling wallpaper and old stove. She couldn't wait to be rid of the burden of the house. Alex could gladly take it from them. She touched the invitation and stared at it pensively. Her sisters deserved a little fun. But how could she manage to come up with three dresses in two weeks? And not just any dresses. Gowns. She slowly raised her head and looked out into the evening. They deserved to go. There had to be a way. She thought for a moment then tapped the table. She had the perfect idea.

The next day she drove two hours to a designer consignment shop she'd visited several years earlier. Her plan was to find three dresses or gowns to alter. Although it was quite a distance, Isabella knew that she couldn't risk buying something in town that others could recognize.

The Duvall reputation was at stake. She searched through the rack of dresses with the personalities of her sisters in mind. Mariella would want something that would draw attention to her, Gabby would like something more traditional and Daniella would like something nice and pretty. After a three-hour search, Isabella had all the dresses she knew would be perfect.

Back at home, she went into the old sewing room. Because it had been several years since anyone had used it, dust and cobwebs had taken hold. With only two weeks left to alter and remake the dresses, she got to work right away. Isabella spent the night dusting, cleaning and organizing the sewing machine and three wire dress forms hidden in the closet determined to make her sisters' dreams come true.

MRS. LYONS LIVED ALONE in a grand house that had belonged to her dead husband no one had ever seen—and most doubted had ever existed. She had a Siberian mix cat, named Nicodemus, and a companion, Ms. Timmons. She was a formidable woman of seventy-three years who liked to complain of imaginary ailments, but became a martyr when the pain was real.

Although her hair was completely white, she continued to dye it the black it had been when she was younger. The contrasting color only made her pale white skin look almost ghostly, while sharp green eyes were deeply set in a thin, narrow face. She didn't mind growing older or the solitude of her life and welcomed her quiet existence most days, but she enjoyed bossing people around and grew restless when she didn't have the opportunity to do so.

After a weekend of having only Ms. Timmons and her cook to harass, Mrs. Lyons looked eagerly out her window and caught sight of Isabella. She watched with growing anticipation, as Isabella gingerly maneuvered the piles of snow on the side of the road, and patches of treacherous black ice covering the sidewalk.

Mrs. Lyons frowned. Such a dull, ordinary girl, she thought staring at the large overcoat, limp brown scarf and gloves Isabella wore. But she hadn't expected Caroline to loan out any of her other treasures. Isabella suited her needs, she was efficient and punctual. But for a woman who enjoyed finding fault in others and provoking them, Isabella's patient nature became vexing at times.

At the sound of the doorbell, Mrs. Lyons sat back in her chair. She listened to the hushed voices down the hall, then closed her eyes as she heard Isabella's footsteps approaching.

"How are you doing today?" Isabella asked in a bright cheery voice.

"I'm old and I'm sick. How do you expect me to be doing?"

"You're not sick."

Mrs. Lyons opened her eyes, sending a bright green gaze at the young woman. "You're supposed to say I'm not old."

"But then you would accuse me of lying."

"Did you pick up the book?"

Isabella handed her an old volume of poems she'd loaned to Douglas Merchant, a widower trying to win the affections of the local beautician. She'd loaned him the book only a month ago and although she didn't need it back, she liked having Isabella run errands for her. It made her feel important. She set the volume aside next to the cold cup of tea that had been sitting there for the past half hour.

"What should we read today?" Isabella went to the drawn

curtains and pulled them aside, welcoming sunlight into the room. The sun's rays spread across the gleaming Steinway piano, an oak bookcase lined with hardback books and little tea cups Mrs. Lyons liked to collect. She saw a dash of white and orange dart under the couch. "Hello Nicodemus," she said.

Mrs. Lyons shielded her eyes from the brightness. "I don't care what you read. Leave the curtains alone. The sun hurts my tired old eyes."

"Your eyes are fine."

Mrs. Lyons grumbled.

"You complain every time, but within five minutes you are always in a happier mood."

"You've scared poor Nico."

"He'll come out eventually. He likes when I play the piano." Isabella walked over to the bookshelf and ran a finger along the spine of the books. "Now let's see..."

"I don't feel like reading," Mrs. Lyons said in a petulant tone.

"Perhaps I can play something for you." Isabella sat at the piano and noticed a new little figurine: a bust modeled after Michelangelo's David. "This is a beautiful sculpture. It must be from the early 20th century. I bet it costs a lot."

She shrugged. "It wouldn't fetch any more than fifteen hundred."

Isabella stared at it impressed. "Oh."

Mrs. Lyons watched her, a glint entering her green gaze. "If it were real."

Isabella turned to her. "It's a fake?"

"Of course it's a fake. You must learn to develop your eye. A fine terracotta bust would gather some interest. But that," she made a dismissive gesture, "is just a pretty thing of little merit. By now I thought, your years with me would have helped you notice the difference."

"I am trying to understand how to recognize antiques, Mrs. Lyons. I really love them."

"Good. One should respect their elders. By the way, I'm planning my annual trip. This time I'll spend two weeks in Italy along with my regular route. I missed it last year."

"Italy?" Isabella said wistfully.

"Have you ever been?" Mrs. Lyons asked, knowing she had not.

Isabella ran her fingers lightly over the keys then began to play. Nicodemus came from under the couch, jumped up on the bench and began to purr. "No, I've never traveled outside the U.S." She looked at her. "But I would love to."

Mrs. Lyons saw the bright eagerness in the younger woman's gaze and smiled slightly. She'd been hinting at traveling with her for years, perhaps this year she would take her along. "Yes, it would probably do you good. Now play me something festive."

Hours later, Isabella, prepared to leave. "The Saturday after next I must leave early."

"Why?" Mrs. Lyons asked annoyed that there would be any change to her schedule.

"I'm attending a party at the Montpelier Mansion."

"But I only get .a few Saturdays out of you. Mondays, Wednesdays, Thursdays and some Saturdays, that's all I ask."

"I'll make it up to you. There are plenty of Saturdays left."

"I'm sure you're eager to go, I suppose it's to be expected. I forgot to ask you about the new owner of your home. Have you met him yet?"

"Yes."

"Is it true it is one of the Carltons that used to live here?"

"Yes."

Mrs. Lyons raised her brows intrigued. "Interesting. David Carlton's son has returned," she said in quiet wonder then, "and how does it feel to lose your home to him?"

Isabella grabbed her coat. "I have a feeling you expect a certain answer to that."

"Yes, I expect an honest one."

She slipped her coat on. "I can honestly say I am relieved."

"Has he told you his plans?"

"No, and I don't see any reason why he would."

"I've heard things you know. Not that I am into gossip, but it is interesting that they've decided to return *here* of all places."

Isabella agreed, but didn't want to continue the conversation. "I'd better go."

"I'm sure your sisters are throwing themselves his way."

Isabella stopped. "No, they are not."

Mrs. Lyons's gaze danced with delight. "They soon will. Just wait and see. Your mother would have insisted."

"We don't even know him."

"He's rich, attractive and devoted to his family. That's enough."

"Have you seen him?"

She flashed an enigmatic grin. "I've heard things. Of course, I may be wrong. If you would like to describe him for me, I wouldn't mind."

"Your description of him is perfect."

"So is he as handsome as his reputation would like us to believe?"

"I'm sure he is as handsome as he is rich."

"Ah, then he must be very handsome indeed. Perhaps even

you will find yourself throwing yourself in his path in order to catch his notice?"

Isabella buttoned up her coat. "No, I will not."

"Don't speak so soon. It may be a wasted effort, but it might be fun to try."

"Goodbye, Mrs. Lyons." Isabella grabbed her gloves and left.

*I*sabella marched down the front stairs annoyed that she'd allowed Mrs. Lyons to provoke her. What a ridiculous idea! She would never try to catch any man's attention, let alone a young man with eyes as cold as a winter storm and intentions that no one knew. Alex Carlton may have the looks and the charm to make many a lady's heart flutter, but she knew her good sense would keep her heart safe.

Isabella pulled on her gloves and stopped when a familiar burning scent drifted towards her. She turned the corner and saw Ms. Timmons taking a long drag on a cigarette. Her regularly rosy cheeks sunk in as she deeply inhaled. She had a flat face with round eyes like buttons on the face of a big rag doll and wispy brown hair streaked with gray. She heard Isabella's footsteps and quickly waved the smoke away and stomped out the cigarette.

"It's okay, Mabel, it's only me."

"Damn! I just wasted a good cigarette for no reason." She glanced around then lit another one. She exhaled. "Did you leave her in a good mood?"

Isabella laughed. "Is that even possible?"

"I guess not." She took another drag then exhaled. "How are your..." She waved her hand and bits of ash landed on Isabella's coat. "You know."

"Our new owners?"

Mabel nodded.

"They're fine. They seem very nice."

"It must be difficult having them in your house when they used to work there."

"I don't care who owns the house. I'm just glad it's sold."

Mabel didn't hear her. "I would love to get rich and come back and buy this house right from under Mrs. Lyons. Could you imagine her face if she lost this house to me?"

"I'm sure—"

"You're lucky your mother is dead." She pointed, showering Isabella with more ash. "There's no way she'd have allowed this to happen."

Isabella tried to brush the ash from her coat without Mabel noticing. "She wouldn't have had a choice."

"I've heard he's good-looking though."

Isabella began to walk away. She was in no mood to hear about Alex's good looks again. "I'd better go," she said, leaving Mabel to enjoy her last cigarette.

That evening at dinner, Mariella whispered to Isabella as she ate her stuffed eggplant. Because Alex had decided to take his mother and sister out to dinner, only Gabby and Daniella were at the table, but she still wanted to be discreet. "Did you ask for a raise?"

"No," Isabella said. "I told you I wasn't going to."

"Then I hope you're working real hard on our dresses."

"Why?"

"Because it's obvious that making money will be left up to me."

A few days later with the swift, cold descent of the northeastern winter months, matured trees stood tall and naked, while the evergreens endured a second snowfall and chilled breeze from off the Alleghany River. As evening settled over the house, Velma decided to take time to look around. She walked down the expansive oak staircase, her fingers touching the fine detailing at the top of each post. She remembered when she'd moved up and down the stairs at a faster pace.

At the end of the staircase, she turned to her right and entered the main floor study, and for a moment, she remembered the many times she met with Mr. Duvall to discuss her duties and pay. It was during these times that she had allowed herself to fantasize what it would be like to be the "lady of the house".

As she walked from room to room, she felt an overwhelming feeling of pride. Alex had made her dream come true. She knew intuitively that once he had put his architectural expertise into the renovation and remodeling of the mansion that it would regain its grandeur.

She approached a small door off the kitchen and looked inside. She saw Isabella sitting at a sewing machine. The young woman was working on a peach satin dress with two gorgeously adorned dress forms standing by.

In her haste to see what Isabella was doing, she did not see the "Do Not Disturb" sign.

"These are lovely," Velma said, bursting in unannounced.

"I didn't mean to startle you. Please don't stop." She went closer and touched the two displayed gowns.

Isabella glanced up from the sewing machine. "Yes, the blue is for Mariella, the peach for Gabby and the purple one is for Daniella."

Velma looked at the gowns aware that one was missing. "Where is yours?"

"Oh, I'm not going."

"But you must go. Alex gave you all tickets."

"Lex, I mean, Alex, was being very generous. I doubt he will miss me." She looked back at the dresses and sighed, "I didn't do a very good job though. I need to do something more with the blue dress, but I don't know what will work. Mariella will be devastated if she's caught in something that someone might recognize as secondhand."

"You've done very well, Isabella. You've remembered everything I taught you. But there's always a chance to learn more. I'll be right back." Velma dashed out. A few minutes later, she returned with a sewing box filled with an assortment of fine lace, sequins, embroidered patches and expensive gold and silver trim.

Over the next three days, Isabella and Velma worked on transforming the dresses, which they planned to keep under-cover until two days before the party. Knowing her sisters, Isabella made sure that the sign was on the door, and if both of them were not in the room, it was locked with a key. One evening, as they sewed on sequins, Velma turned to Isabella. "You must pick out something for yourself."

"I don't have the time."

"Don't your sisters want you to be there?"

"They'll miss me, but once they are at the party, they won't care anymore."

"Alex is going to have a limo pick all of us up."

"They will love it."

For a moment, Velma saw the young girl with a wide grin who used to greet her when she came to work. Of the four sisters, she was the only one who seemed to notice her. Velma remembered Isabella had loved attending balls as a girl, swirling around in whatever dress Velma had made her. She thought Isabella must have the same hopes and wishes as all other young women, but it seemed that that young girl was very different to the woman she saw hunched over putting trim on one of the dresses. "Why do I get the feeling that you don't want to go?"

Isabella shrugged then said, "Why did you come back?"

"I wanted this house."

She nodded then after a moment said, "Why did *he* come back?"

"To settle down."

She glanced up. "Is that all?"

"That's the reason he gave me. If you want to know the truth, you can ask him yourself."

She shook her head then returned to her task. "It's none of my business."

"I know what you're thinking." Velma smiled when Isabella glanced up surprised. "I know Alex can come off a little...distant, but he really is a kind and generous man. Life has been a little unfair to him and that's made him hard, but he's still a good man."

Isabella quickly nodded, knowing that Velma could be blinded by a mother's love to the true nature of her son. "Of course he is. I'm sure the party will be wonderful." She rested back in her chair and ran her hand over the delicate fabric. "I'm happy you bought this house. It means I'm finally going to be free of it. Free of it forever..." She stood and put the dress on the wire form.

"Won't you miss it a little?"

"I have dreams I want to pursue. My sisters need the limos and parties to make them feel special. I don't."

"And what do you need?"

Isabella pretended not to hear her as she knelt in front of the dress and adjusted the hem, but Velma could have sworn that she heard her say "Freedom."

An hour later, Velma sat in her bedroom crouched over the phone.

"What do you mean she's not coming?" Alex said on the other end. "She has to come. It wouldn't look right."

Velma covered her mouth over the receiver not wanting to be overheard. "She doesn't have a dress."

"Then buy her one."

Velma smiled. "Yes, that's what I thought you would say."

The next day, Velma contacted a friend of hers who found the perfect dress and had it delivered the following day. Late that night, when she thought everyone had gone to bed, she put the dress on the fourth dress form and stared at it, pleased. She couldn't wait to see Isabella's face when she saw it. Suddenly, the door burst open. "It's perfect!"

Velma spun around and stared at Mariella. "You're not supposed to be in here," she snapped.

Mariella didn't notice her as she moved transfixed— toward the dress. "I knew Isabella would get the perfect dress for me."

"Actually—"

"I know I wasn't supposed to peek, but I couldn't help myself. It's gorgeous. It will look stunning on me."

Velma walked up to her. "Mariella—"

"How should I wear my hair? I probably won't need any jewelry." She walked around the display with awe. She knew her sister could sew, but she had never seen anything so beautiful! It was a blue-gray shimmering fitted dress made out of silk and chiffon. The scooped neckline was decorated with tiny black sequins, with off-the-shoulder, fluffed mini-sleeves. The back of the dress fell softly over the shoulder creating tailored folds that were held together with covered sequined buttons. To finish off the look, the hem was scalloped and trimmed with black silver thread pulled up on the side with a high slit.

She looked up at her stunned sister standing in the doorway. "Oh, Izzy, it's beautiful. Thank you so much."

Isabella glanced at Velma and stammered, "But I didn't—"

"I have to go and choose my accessories." She gave Isabella a quick peck on the cheek then dashed out the door.

Isabella folded her arms and sent Velma a knowing look. "Where did you get this?"

Velma's shoulders drooped. "It's meant for you."

Isabella let her arms fall and smiled. "You mean *was*."

"Just tell her—"

Isabella laughed. "Tell Mariella that she can't have the dress? Have you ever seen Mariella in a temper?" She shook her head. "No, she will do the dress justice and I'll wear the blue one. It seems you've accomplished your goal." She winked, encouraging a smile out of Velma. "Now I have no excuse not to go."

❧

"Hold still," Isabella scolded as she pinned Daniella's neckline.

"I am holding still," Daniella replied.

"You don't have to worry about me," Gabby said checking herself in the full-length-mirror.

Mariella shook her head. "She needs to loosen the fabric around your arms."

"The sleeves are fine," Gabby said.

"Yes, except your arms are fat."

"They are not."

"You should diet before the party."

"She looks beautiful," Isabella said.

Gabby lifted her chin. "Thank you." She stared at her reflection running her hands down her wide hips. "Besides, men like a little meat."

"To eat," Mariella said. "Not to dance with."

Gabby poked out her tongue.

"I don't know why we have to get all dressed up now." Daniella raised her eyes to the ceiling and groaned. "The party isn't for two more days."

"Everything has to be perfect," Isabella explained. "We won't have time the night of the party to fuss with details."

"I still don't—"

"I said hold still."

Daniella clenched her jaw and did.

"What about your dress, Izzy?" Gabby said. "Do you need help with it?"

"My dress fits fine."

"And my dress is the best of all," Mariella said. "Which you'll all find out when you see me in it. It's going to be a perfect evening. I can just feel it."

~

Two days later, Isabella wasn't so sure. "What do you mean you can't stay the full time?" Mrs. Lyons demanded.

Isabella kept her voice level. "I told you several weeks ago that I would be going to the fundraiser at the Montpelier Mansion."

"When did you tell me?"

"About two weeks ago."

"I don't remember."

Isabella removed the tea tray. "Just because you don't remember doesn't mean I didn't tell you." Isabella disappeared into the kitchen then returned. "I'd better go."

Mrs. Lyons looked at her closely to make sure she wasn't lying about her activities. "I'm surprised you can afford to go."

"We received an invitation," she said ignoring the blatant hint that they wouldn't have appropriate clothing to wear.

"Yes, I also received an invitation. I wish my health would allow me to attend. Well, I won't keep you long then. I'm sure your sisters are waiting anxiously."

"I told them to go ahead without me. Lex... .uh...Alex hired a limo to take them."

"That's very nice of him."

"Yes, but I'm sure they'll be waiting for me by the door once they get there so I'd better go." She walked towards the hall. "Goodbye."

"Just bring me Nicodemus before you go."

"He's probably hiding."

"But I want to see him. Just look in his favorite place for me." She rang her bell and Ms. Timmons appeared. "Help us find Nicodemus."

A half hour later Nicodemus still hadn't been found.

"Where could he be?" Mrs. Lyons asked, rubbing her hands together. She noticed the front door slightly ajar. "He's escaped! He's so clever with knobs."

Isabella took a deep calming breath. "Mrs. Lyons I'm sure—"

She grabbed her coat and quickly buttoned it. "We must find him."

"But—"

"Do you think your party is more important than my darling cat?"

Yes. "He always finds his way home."

"But it's dark and cold. He's not used to this weather."

"He's lived here all his life. Besides, it will be nearly impossible to find him." Isabella's words were lost as Mrs. Lyons walked outside.

"You might as well go after her," Ms. Timmons said slowly putting on her own coat.

Isabella gripped her hands into fists then followed her employer into the cold, dark evening lit only with the strips of orange light from the descending sun. *Blasted cat!* She searched the grounds calling out his name, her boots sinking into the mud and snow. After another twenty-minute search she went inside determined to leave.

"Mrs. Lyons, you'll just have to wait..." She stopped when she saw Mrs. Lyons sitting in the living room feeding Nicodemus a piece of tuna on the end of a fork as he sat purring on her lap. "I found him hiding under the bed. Go have fun at your little party." She waved her away.

Isabella wrapped her scarf around her neck wondering who she disliked more, the cat or its owner.

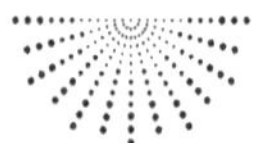

*I*sabella raced home, quickly changed into her evening wear and jumped back into her car, which had cooled considerably. Her car took an hour to heat up. Unfortunately, the mansion was only a half-hour drive. So by the time she arrived, Isabella's hands and feet were frozen. She entered the grand ballroom, her teeth chattering. The event was in full swing and a large crowd had gathered to enjoy the festivities. Numerous floor-to-ceiling windows surrounded the ballroom decorated with colorful, miniature lights and fresh garland. Floating candles in small oval glass holders sat on finely woven satin tablecloths. A wide assortment of food and fine wine filled the main table, fighting for attention with colorful delights such as marzipan sweets and ladyfingers. To one side of the room, a small classical ensemble, dressed in formal attire, provided soothing background music.

Women stood around, some dressed in tight body hugging gowns in an array of colors, with hand-sewn sequin and diamond trimmings. Others wore layers of fabric that scraped the ground and could trip anyone not paying attention. Most of the men wore formal attire, tuxedos with either short or long tails.

Mariella marched up to Isabella who was holding back a sneeze. "Where have you been?"

She blew warm air on her hands and rubbed them together. "Mrs. Lyons lost her cat."

"She's always losing that cat. When will she understand that it's *trying* to run away?"

"She was distraught."

Gabby and Daniella approached them. "You're freezing," Gabby said.

"I'll be warm in a second."

"Go get something warm to eat. They have absolutely fabulous food."

"I'm not really hungry."

"You're never hungry," Gabby said.

"Have you been enjoying yourself?"

"Oh, yes," Daniella said.

Mariella glanced around the room. "This is how I was meant to live."

Isabella folded her arms and bounced up and down on her toes still trying to get warm. "Have you spoken to Le—Alex?"

"Stop doing that," Mariella said.

Gabby hit Mariella on the arm. "Can't you see she's freezing?"

"A lady is never supposed to show distress." She gripped her hands into fists. "I said stop it," she demanded when Isabella began to jog in place. Isabella stood still and hugged herself. Mariella smiled in approval. "That's better."

Isabella rubbed her hands together again. "So have you seen him?"

"We haven't had the chance." She pointed to a man surrounded by women. "Every female in the county is here."

"Hoping to be the next Mrs. Carlton," Gabby said.

Mariella suddenly looked thoughtful. "Imagine being his wife."

"His mother has hinted that he is ready to settle down."

"What a catch."

Isabella shook her head. "And every woman has a hook."

Mariella tapped her chin. "But we have the best bait."

"What?"

"Any wife of his would get to live in our beautiful house, right? Well we already owned it and know everything about this town. We have connections."

Isabella looked at her, suddenly uneasy with the gleam in Mariella's eyes. "What is your point?"

"Think about the benefit of being his wife. You would get to meet fascinating people and wear wonderful clothes."

"Plus, have a husband who is handsome," Daniella said.

"Intelligent," Gabby added.

Mariella grinned. "And rich." She clapped her hands together. "Sisters, I have a brilliant idea. One that will solve all our problems."

Isabella touched her arm with growing apprehension. "Mariella, I'm not sure—"

She shook her hand away. "You're going to like my idea."

Gabby moved in closer. "What is it?"

Mariella paused, studying her sisters' faces then said, "One of us should marry him."

Isabella laughed. "You're not serious."

"I'm very serious. In a way he owes us. He's bought *our* home and is casting us out on the streets."

Isabella groaned. "Not that again."

"Besides, we've known him for years, sort of. We grew up with him. He already knows us and likes us."

Gabby nodded. "It's not a bad idea."

Isabella stared at her stunned. "You're more sensible than that."

"Poor and sensible. Not the best combination." She frowned as she glanced at the large number of ladies surrounding Alex. "But what would make him consider one of us?"

Mariella held up a finger. "First of all, we're the most attractive women in the room."

"Well, that distinction doesn't seem to be working for us right now."

"That's because we haven't used it yet. We have to get him to know of our intentions."

Isabella shook her head. "Mariella—"

"This will work," she cut in.

"How?" Daniella asked.

"Strategic planning. You can get whatever you set your mind to."

Isabella glanced at Alex then her sisters. "I'm certainly not interested in getting married to a stranger or staying in that house."

Daniella smiled. "I am."

"Dani, you're too young for him."

"I am not."

Mariella ignored her and looked at Gabby. "So that leaves the two of us."

"He is nice." Gabby sent him a pensive look. Then turned to Isabella and frowned. "Don't look at me like that Izzy. Women have married for worse reasons. We have debts. Do you want to spend the rest of your life struggling?"

"No," she said, surprised by her sister's determination. "But—"

"Then help us. It's our best hope."

"I just don't—"

"It's a wonderful idea," Mariella said. "What could possibly go wrong?"

Isabella shook her head. "Many things like—"

Gabby grabbed her arm. "We can't do this without your support. Please help us."

Isabella stared at her sisters then sighed. "Very well."

Gabby clapped her hands. "Good." Her brows came together in concern. "You're looking a little pale. You need food."

"No, it's not food." She briefly touched her forehead. "I've just lost my mind."

"But it's a good plan," Daniella said.

Isabella shook her head. "You don't even have a plan yet."

"Tonight we'll study him," Mariella said. "Find out his likes and dislikes."

Daniella surveyed the crowd. "I'll go talk to Sophia. She'll tell me what we need to know."

"Don't be too obvious."

"I won't," she said annoyed. "Give me some credit."

Mariella adjusted her dress strap. "I'll approach him first."

"Why you?" Gabby asked.

"Because I'm the eldest. I make the way easier for you."

"Fine," she said, knowing it was impossible to argue. "I'll go get you something to eat, Izzy."

"I'm really not hungry," Isabella began but her sister had already disappeared into the crowd. She turned to Mariella who watched Alex like a predator.

"Mariella, I hope you know what you're doing."

"I always do. Don't worry, Izzy. Our fortunes are about to change."

"Yawning in public is very bad manners."

Alex sent his mother a glance. "I'm tired of having good manners. Why did I make this evening so long?"

"People are enjoying themselves and enjoying you. We've raised a lot of awareness and... umm... money."

"All for a good cause. I don't know why you have such an aversion to speaking about it when you spend it so freely."

"I'm only helping. You have so much of it. I wouldn't want you to become spoiled."

He grinned. "Ah, always looking out for my best interests."

Velma looked around the grand hall pleased that everyone was having a good time. She saw Sophia talking to Daniella, happy that the two girls were getting on. Then her gaze fell on Marilyn Tremain and her gut tightened. They'd met earlier in the evening. She had once worked for the Tremains as a house cleaner before she'd set up her business as a seamstress. She and Marilyn were of the same age and good looks. Both had husbands who decided to leave them, and had they been of equal status, they may have been friends, but the chasm of class and innate social prejudice made that impossible.

Marilyn had greeted her coolly. "You seem to have done well for yourself, Velma," she said. Years had done little to her exquisite copper skin. She'd let her short dark hair go gray, but had maintained her lithe figure. Velma fleetingly wished she'd done the same, but women in her family always tended to get round as they aged.

"Yes, I'm very proud of Alex."

"I'm sure David would have been too if he'd stayed around."

"Yes."

"I'm actually surprised to see you back here."

Velma nodded. "So am I."

"I hope Alex isn't here to cause any trouble."

"No, he isn't and neither am I. We just wanted to come home."

"As long as that's all," she said in a low voice.

"That's all. You have nothing to worry about."

Marilyn sent her an uncertain look then smiled. "Good. Perhaps we'll get together sometime. I see that Sophia is friendly with Daniella. Which is considerate, she's such a sweet girl, but hardly beneficial considering their present circumstance."

"The Duvall girls are a fine group of women."

"I'm not criticizing them. It's just a shame that their parents didn't have better sense than to up and die and leave them penniless. Very careless if you ask me. We tolerate them now of course. One can't help but be sympathetic, but they aren't regarded in the same way as before."

"By you or by everyone?"

"You'll find out soon enough." She shrugged. "As you know, your friends are your allies and it is wise to choose them well. Excuse me." she said and walked away.

Velma frowned at the memory and focused her attention on the present, glancing at Alex. She knew that they needed the right connections. She had to make sure that Alex understood that. "We have a lot of money now, but money isn't everything you know."

"Money is enough."

"You have to associate with the right people." He flashed a

look of mock, surprise. "Oh, dear. Has my mother become a snob?"

She moved her shoulders annoyed by the accusation. "No, it's just that we left in a hurry and now that we're back people might wonder about our intentions."

"I know. I always wondered why we had to leave."

"I told you that someone wanted us gone."

"And you still refuse to tell me who."

"Because it doesn't matter anymore. Besides, I explained to you that we'd have a better opportunity elsewhere."

"Yes. Dad said the same, but he didn't come back."

"He was a good man."

"Just a little inconsiderate." He forced a smile. "Relax, I don't hate him anymore."

Velma didn't believe him, but didn't wish to argue. "It will take a lot more than money to erase people's memories."

"Of course."

"Most of the ladies come from very important families. I know you're ready to settle down." He nodded. "Yes."

"It's good to have standards."

He raised a brow. "I'm sure you've already set them for me."

"I'm not one to meddle, but it wouldn't hurt if her family is well-established."

He nodded again.

"A woman like that at a man's side is a great asset."

"Don't worry," he said surveying a group of young women who took care to catch his eye dressed in expensive gowns and wearing both bold and shy smiles. He watched them with cool detachment. "I'm a few steps ahead of you. Now go and enjoy the party."

Gabby looked at the selection of food on the banquet table trying to remember which dishes she had enjoyed the most. She wanted to make sure Isabella got to taste the best ones before they were all gone. She grabbed tarts and asparagus drizzled with cheese, and grilled shrimp.

"Coming for a second helping?" Elaine Tremain said watching Gabby with a smirk.

Gabby didn't glance up, ignoring Elaine's slender build and haughty expression. "No."

"Not that it would be unusual for you to do."

Gabby continued to pile her plate.

"Everyone knows that times are really tough for you nowadays, so I suppose it's understandable."

"Isn't this food great?" a male voice said from behind.

The two women turned to see Tony who was also stacking his plate. He noticed them looking and grinned. "I know I've been back here twice, but I'd hate to see the food go to waste."

"Well," Elaine said. "When Gabby's around, food rarely does."

"Then she sounds like my kind of woman." He winked at her. "I don't like people who waste anything. Especially other people's time."

He said the words so amiably that for a moment Elaine didn't know she'd been insulted, then she glared at him and left.

Gabby smiled at him gratefully. "Thanks, I thought she'd never leave. This plate isn't for me, by the way, it's for Izzy."

"You don't have to explain. I don't care if you piled two plates for yourself."

"I would." She sniffed. "I'd end up looking like a pig."

His serious gaze met hers. "You couldn't look anything less than as beautiful as you are."

She ducked her head. "You're embarrassing me."

Tony turned his attention back to the table as though suddenly remembering himself. "I'm sorry."

Gabby began piling her plate again, stealing glances at him. He was better looking than she'd remembered, though he was much older. She had let his graying hair and rugged features distract her from his beautifully sculpted profile, kind mouth and gentle eyes. "You'll like those," she said pointing to a row of fruit tarts.

"How do you know?"

She shrugged and turned, smiling coyly. "Because I did." She walked away unaware of how long Tony continued watching her.

Gabby searched the ballroom for her sister, but when she couldn't find her, she went to look in the hallway. Behind one of the pillars she found Isabella warming her hands over a heating vent. "What are you doing out here?"

"It's warmer."

Gabby frowned. "You're hiding."

"I'm not hiding. I'm trying to warm up."

"You should be warm by now."

"Well, I'm not."

Gabby handed her the plate. "Here's your dinner."

"Thank you. Mmm, everything looks delicious." She glanced around looking for a place to sit.

"It tastes delicious, too," Gabby said following Isabella to the couch. "Tony agrees with me." "Tony?"

"Alex's friend."

"Oh." Isabella sat. "Thank you for doing this." She grinned

when she caught her sister looking longingly toward the ball-room. "You don't have to join me."

"Promise me you won't stay out here all night."

"I promise. Now go." She shooed her sister away. "I'm fine."

Gabby hesitated then left.

Isabella enjoyed her meal and slowly began to feel human again. She was about to come out of her hiding place when she heard two familiar voices.

"I'm entertaining myself with these empty headed peacocks for one reason. Strategy," Alex said. "I take their money and smile and promise to date their eligible daughters, sisters, aunts or cousins."

"The Duvalls are the most beautiful women in the room," Tony replied.

Isabella paused.

"They always are. But they don't have the benefit of money anymore so they probably want to get their hands on mine. Not that I blame them. That's how they were brought up. Their father was a decent man, but their mother was the biggest society snob. She would work my mother all hours," he said, his tone tinged with scorn. "Mariella hasn't changed. She still thinks the world revolves around her, Gabby will still eat anything that has icing on it, and Daniella is just a baby."

"And Isabella?"

"Nobody thinks about Izzy. She's probably stuck to a wall somewhere completely invisible." Isabella gripped the plate in her hands.

"But I'd marry any one of them if they'd have me."

Tony laughed. "You've just described one as vain, another as greedy, one as a baby and one as invisible. Should a man be so disapproving of his life partner?"

"We'd both be grateful. They'd be grateful for my money and I'd be grateful for, ahem, their evident charms."

Tony clicked his tongue. "If a feminist were to hear you, you'd be roasting over a fire."

"I admit. I am only human. Anything that good-looking could warm a man's bed and look good at his side."

"But her mind, her interests—"

"I wouldn't need her for that. I have you if I don't want to be bored. Why do you think you're my assistant?"

"Hmm. Sounds like a fair plan."

"I thought so. Now this is what I plan to do..." Their voices drifted away.

Isabella left her hiding place, no longer trembling from cold. This time anger filled her. She now knew Alex's true nature and she would not allow her sisters to become a part of his scheme. She had to warn them. She disposed of her plate and went in search of her sisters. She saw Mariella surrounded by men, pretending not to notice their attention. Daniella giggling with Sophia as if they were two children in a playground, and Gabby at the dessert table.

She hated her sudden hypocrisy. Hadn't she just agreed to a similar scheme with her sisters? Weren't they just as cold and calculating as Alex and all the other greedy women? They didn't care what he was like as a man. Just what he represented and she'd agreed to help them. She'd just condoned a similar heartless bargain. When had marriage become a business contract rather than a vow combining two souls? Was she too much of a romantic? Had their desperation made them short-sighted? Didn't love matter anymore?

She raced up to Gabby and grabbed the éclair she was about to eat.

"Hey!" Gabby cried.

"You've already had two of those."

"So?"

"Do you want that dress to last the night? Soon you'll be bursting at the seams."

Gabby's sweet eyes dimmed with hurt. "It's not like you to be so cruel, Izzy."

Isabella was instantly contrite. "I'm sorry." She handed the éclair back. "I'm just so angry." Gabby set the éclair on her plate. "Why?"

"We can't go with Mariella's plan. Le-Alex is not what he seems."

"You mean condescending and distant?"

She blinked. "So you noticed?"

"Of course." She grinned, licking a cream stained finger. "I also noticed that he's rich. Very rich."

"We can make our own money."

"It will take us decades to pay off our debts. We have no benevolent aunt or uncle, there's no grand inheritance. And we're not clever enough to run a business and make millions."

"If you give me time—"

"How much time? Izzy, we've lost our home and we have no money. We've sold everything we could and we're still in debt."

"I can get a second job."

"It still won't be enough. We used to be somebody, the revered Duvall sisters, invited to all the parties, had bright futures. But do you know what we are now? Mariella is a book-keeper at a gallery, she didn't get to put her accounting degree to use looking after her own money as planned. I'm an administrative assistant at an insurance firm, my liberal arts degree was useless anyway. You're a lady's companion. Daniella works part-time as a receptionist, hoping one day to return to college. How far do you think that will take us?" She held up a finger. "I know what you're going to say. One of us could go back to school. But could we afford the time it would take to get through three to four years and the extra debt? No, this is not an option I would have chosen for myself, but presently our future looks pretty grim and I would do anything to change that. Mom emphasized looks and money and I plan to make one of those work to get the other."

"But freedom is—"

"Costly. If we succeed with this plan, we'll be all set."

Isabella glanced at Alex who now stood across the room as a lone dark figure. He looked as if none of the bright festivities touched him. "How could you marry someone who's so cold?"

Gabby studied him. "I could warm him up a bit."

"He doesn't have the highest opinion of us or anyone."

She turned to Isabella her gaze sharpening. "Did he say something?"

"Many things he shouldn't have."

"Like what?"

She didn't want to repeat his hurtful words. Yes, Gabby loved her desserts, but she was also kind and smart. "He hurt my pride. He said I was a wallflower."

"Well..."

Isabella made a face. "That's not the point."

Gabby smothered a laugh. "You're right. That wasn't very nice of him. Did I tell you how pretty you look?"

"You don't have to." She looked around. "It doesn't matter anyway."

"I'm sorry he hurt your feelings. You deserve better than that." Gabby squeezed her hand. "Don't worry, Izzy. Once he's family I'll make sure he apologizes."

ALEX STIFLED a yawn while a man as thin as paper and nearly as pale tried to convince him of the benefits of investing in his lawn mower repair company. He nodded absently then a shock of blue caught his eye. It amazed him that in the crowd of rich purples, brilliant reds and exquisite blacks, such an ordinary color should demand his attention. He watched curiously as Isabella marched toward one of the exit doors. *What was she up to?*

"Excuse me," he said, cutting the man off in midsentence. Then he followed her.

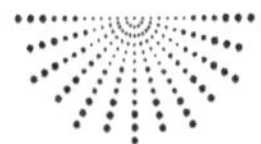

"Where are you going?" he called after her. His voice echoed down the hallway despite the sounds from the ballroom.

Isabella spun around, giving him a full view of her dress. Blue suited her. The color complemented her skin, as did the delicate embroidered detailing in spun gold thread around her neck. Her hair sat piled high on her head, held in place with a jeweled hair comb, but a few tendrils had escaped. Alex wondered how they would feel curled around his finger. "Why do you want to know?" she asked.

He shoved a hand in his pocket. "Curiosity. It's too cold for an evening stroll." He smiled, an engaging expression that usually made a woman smile back, but Isabella only stared.

"I'm leaving," she said in a cool tone.

His smile fell. He stared surprised that she showed none of the warmth she'd displayed before. "Alone?"

"My sisters will find their way back in the limo you provided." She turned and began walking toward the coat check.

He followed as though propelled. "You're leaving too early. Didn't you enjoy yourself?"

"As much as I expected to."

He jumped in front of her. "That's not an answer."

She halted before she bumped into him. Alex felt a little regret that she hadn't, he wouldn't have minded. She met his gaze. "I found everything very amusing. Excuse me." She walked around him leaving him with the faint scent of vanilla and orchids.

"At least let me walk you to your car."

She stopped in front of the coat check and handed in her ticket. "That's okay."

"I thought we were old friends."

She sent him a quiet, superior smile that confused him.

Alex leaned against the wall and studied her unsure of her strange mood. He didn't understand her composed features with eyes that revealed nothing but a polite acknowledgement of his presence. He also was unsure of why he cared. "I haven't seen this town in a while," he said managing a casual tone. "It would be nice to have someone to show me around."

"Of course."

"Someone who knows the place well."

"Yes." She smiled at the clerk as she retrieved her coat then handed it to Alex. He frowned at being turned into a valet then held it out for her to slip into. He let his fingers brush against the back of her neck, amazed by her soft, warm skin. He reached to touch a loose tendril when she spun around and sent him an odd look. Before he could say anything, the look disappeared and she began buttoning her coat. He liked watching her quick, efficient fingers. She could probably unbutton things just as quickly, the thought made his breathing shallow. *What was wrong with him?*

He folded his arms. "Are you trying to be obtuse or don't you want to go out with me?"

Isabella stopped buttoning her coat and looked up at him. "No, I do not want to go out with you."

He stiffened, for a moment he felt as if his heart had stopped. "You're turning me down?"

"Yes." She completed buttoning her coat.

He watched her, stunned. "Why?"

"Let's just say that I'm not on the market."

"You're involved with someone?" he asked doubtfully.

"No, I'm just not interested." She moved to walk away, but he blocked her path determined to get the answers he wanted.

"Let me understand this." He paused trying to gather his chaotic thoughts. Her refusal made no sense. "You're not seeing anyone, but you don't want to go out with me because..." He stopped, allowing her a chance to fill in the blanks.

She smiled with a patient indulgence that infuriated him. "You really don't understand?"

He swallowed his gathering anger and said in a tight voice, "No."

"Come on." She slipped a warm, slender hand in his and led him to the ballroom as though he were a little boy. Alex didn't mind the intent, he planned to prove that he was otherwise. She stopped behind a pillar where they could watch everyone undetected. Isabella began to release his hand, but Alex tightened his hold.

She turned to him and narrowed her eyes; he blinked looking innocent. Then she smiled, with the knowing wisdom of a lion watching a kitten trying to outwit it. The expression annoyed Alex, but he still didn't release her hand. She returned her gaze to the crowd.

"They all look wonderful, don't they?" she asked.

Alex nodded not trusting himself to speak.

"But do you know what I see?"

He shook his head.

"A group of children bragging about who has the biggest toys and who their friends are."

He rested his free hand on the pillar, his eyes darkening to onyx. "And you see me as one of those children?"

She kept her gaze on the crowd. "Right now you're the one with the most toys. Everyone wants to play with you. However, I'm too old for this." She turned to him and the coldness in her gaze matched his. "Find someone else to play with." She sent a significant glance at their locked hands.

Alex ignored the hint and smiled cynically. "Life is all about strategy. I'm not sentimental. I'm not a romantic. I'm practical. I'm also rich and handsome. Do you know what that makes me?"

"Arrogant?"

He gripped the pillar a moment then let his fingers relax. "No," he said in a cool, controlled tone. "It makes me eligible. It gives me leverage. Trust me, I know. I've been without leverage before."

"This isn't business."

"Don't fool yourself. Everything is business."

"Relationships are more complicated than that."

"Only if you let them. People should say what they mean, and mean what they say."

She stared at him in a thoughtful manner, which made him uncomfortable. He released her hand, but his action only made her examination more intense. "What are *you* trying to prove?"

"I'm not trying to prove anything."

"You could live anywhere in the world. Have any woman you want, why did you come back here?"

He glanced away.

"Could it be revenge?" she whispered.

He met her gaze but said nothing.

"You've proven your point. You've succeeded, we haven't. Congratulations. But you want something else besides applause."

He rubbed his, chin and forced a light tone, uneasy with how close to the truth she was. "Why do I get the feeling you don't like me anymore?"

Her gaze searched his face, and for a brief moment sadness entered her eyes, but the emotion quickly disappeared. "Because you're very clever. You always were."

Alex watched her leave, taking rein on his temper. He didn't like being told he was acting childish. He returned to the ballroom annoyed rather than angry. He hated rejection. He hadn't been rejected in a long time—especially by someone like Izzy. She should be thankful he even considered her. He took a deep breath. Izzy wasn't important anyway. He didn't even know why he'd asked her in the first place.

It had been impulsive and he knew better. She had a romantic view of life he couldn't afford to entertain. He wouldn't have gotten this far if he did. Ideas were nice in theory, but not in practice. Which was why he was rich, and she was not.

No, Izzy was of no importance to him, Alex convinced himself, erasing the memory of her standing in the hall and the feeling of her slight hand in his. He had plenty of women to choose from, and one in particular was trying very hard to catch his attention and he was more than willing to give it.

"Hello, Mariella," he said approaching her. "You look stunning."

"Thank you."

"It's nice to be back here in town."

"We're glad to have you back."

"I'm sure there are many places that have changed."

She measured him with her eyes. "If you would like a tour, I'd be more than willing to give you one."

"Thank you. I'll pick you up."

"Of course." She smiled seductively. "You know where I live."

VELMA WALKED up the stairs of her new home glad that the party was over. Her head continued to ache from the high-pitched squeals of the young women who had shared her limo ride. When had she gotten so old? All she wanted was peace. Once she reached the top of the stairs she walked toward her room and then stopped. One young woman had been conspicuously absent from the ride and she wondered how her evening had been. She knocked on Isabella's door.

"Come in."

She entered the sparsely furnished room with posters from around the world on the walls and saw Isabella sitting crossed-legged on her bed wearing jeans and a large T-shirt.

"You look exhausted," Isabella said, leaping from her bed. "Please sit down." She went over to her side table where she had a hot pot of tea and four cups with saucers. "My sisters and I usually eat here," she explained. "I'm sure they'll have a lot to tell me." She handed Velma a cup and poured her some lemon-ginger tea she'd just brewed.

Velma held the warm mug, sighed contentedly and took a sip. She briefly shut her eyes. "Mmm, I needed that." When she opened them she noticed Isabella's wary gaze. "Is something wrong?"

"Did anything happen?"

"What do you mean?"

She shrugged nonchalantly. "I left early. I was just curious if anything interesting occurred." "Not really."

"Did you enjoy yourself?"

"Yes, Alex was pleased."

"I'm sure he was," she said in an odd tone.

"He doesn't tell me everything though, I can only guess."

"I'm sure you understand him perfectly."

Velma took another sip of her tea then mumbled, "Sometimes I wonder."

Someone knocked on the door then it swung open and Isabella's three sisters appeared. "I did it!" Mariella said. "Everything is working out perfectly." She halted when she saw Velma "Oh."

Velma slowly stood. "I was just going. I'm sure you girls have plenty to talk about. Good night."

Once she was out of hearing, the sisters rushed into the room, shut the door and sat on the bed. "It's begun," Mariella said.

Isabella sighed. "What?"

"Our plan," Gabby said. "Did you forget?"

"I'm trying to, but you keep reminding me."

"It's a good plan."

"And it's working," Mariella said. "I've got a date with him."

Isabella nodded impressed. "Fast work."

"I think I should have gone out with him first," Gabby said.

Mariella ignored her. "Soon it will be like before. You should have ridden with us in the limo. It was stuffed with drinks and party treats."

"It's a shame the drive was so short," Gabby said.

Daniella piped up. "It also had heated seats and tinted windows."

Mariella looked pained at her sister's ignorance. "Limos always have tinted windows."

Isabella shook her head. "I'm still not sure about this. We really don't know anything about him."

Mariella rolled her eyes. "We know enough. It's a brilliant plan. You're just upset because it's not yours. But it will work. Nothing will go wrong."

Alex woke up the next morning in a better mood than when he'd gone to bed. He enjoyed a hearty breakfast at a local restaurant called Martha's. It was usually standing-room only in the morning, but he'd managed to get a seat. "Are the eggs the way you like them?" the owner asked. He was a heavy-set man with pale blue eyes and a blinking habit when he was nervous. He blinked fast now.

Alex grinned, putting the man at ease. "They're perfect. I'll be back."

The owner smiled then hurried away.

"These are the best eggs I've ever eaten," Tony said. .

"You say that at every restaurant we go to."

"My tastes are improving."

"Or deteriorating." Alex opened his calendar: "Next month I'll start some minor repairs on the house. The work with the contractor won't start until March."

"Okay."

"Also, at that time you'll have two days free for about eight weeks."

"A reprieve?" He bowed. "Oh, thank you master. And what will you be doing while I enjoy my freedom?"

"Attending this." He handed him a paper. Tony read it then frowned. "A course on antiquing?"

"Yes."

"Do you really need this?"

"No, but I want to learn."

"But what about the um..." He cleared his throat.

"What?"

"The women."

He smiled. "Do you think I'll prove a distraction?"

"It's happened before."

"Only once and that was a different scenario."

"The poor teacher couldn't get any of the female students to pay attention."

"I'll be better behaved this time." He snapped his fingers. "Oh yes, that reminds me. I have a date."

"Had you forgotten?"

He ignored him. "With Mariella."

Tony gave a low whistle. "How did you manage that?"

He held out his wallet. "With this."

"You paid her?"

Alex put his wallet back and scowled. "No. I have money."

"You'll have to be careful."

"What do you mean?"

"Don't take her anywhere that's more beautiful than she is. She won't like the competition."

"TRY TO BE a little interested in what he has to say," Isabella instructed as she fixed Mariella's hair for her date. Mariella's room resembled their mother's, but unlike hers, it had an ornate bed, the scent of rosemary and mirrors positioned everywhere. No matter wherever one looked they would bump into their own reflection.

"I know how to handle men."

"Alex is different."

"Not that different. I notice the way he looks at me. I've seen that look many times before."

Isabella stood back and folded her arms. "His looks can be misinterpreted."

Mariella stood and checked her reflection. "You have nothing to worry about." She held up a hand mirror and checked the back of her hair.

The doorbell rang.

"I'll be down in a minute," Mariella said.

Isabella left the room then sent her sister a look of warning. "Don't keep him waiting too long."

She smiled. "I'll be worth the wait."

Isabella shook her head then went downstairs into the sitting room expecting to see Gabby and Daniella entertaining their guest. Instead, she saw Daniella slouched on the couch, her legs stretched out in front of her with her arms folded and her face in a pout.

"Where is he?"

"Gabby took him into the solarium," Daniella grumbled. "She made me stay here." She stood and whispered, "It seems she's started her campaign early."

"Great. All we need is a tug of war."

Daniella flashed a sly grin. "Is there anything I can do? I can be very distracting."

"No, I'll deal with it."

Daniella fell back onto the couch. "Nobody ever asks me for help."

Isabella left her sister to sulk, and went to the solarium. She heard their laughter before she saw them. They made an attractive couple framed in the picturesque window. It displayed the cool blue of the sky, the white of the snow on acres of land that stretched out to a cottage house in the distance. The house had a lot of property that was rarely used, she was sure the Carltons would find a use for it. She felt suddenly depressed, but quickly dismissed it. She took a step back to knock, but Alex turned and saw her before she could disappear behind the corner.

"Spying on the children?" he said amused. "Don't worry, we're behaving ourselves. We won't play doctor until later."

Isabella entered the room. "Mariella will be down soon."

"Alex was telling me about all the plans he has for the house," Gabby said. "His knowledge of it is amazing. It was built in the 1870s. He can identify the authentic framework and tell what changes our parents made to it. He has wonderful ideas."

"I'm sure he does," she said in a dry tone.

"I'm ready!" Mariella announced from the top of the stairs.

"You'd better go see her coming down," Isabella said.

Alex furrowed his brows. "Why?"

"She won't come down otherwise," Gabby said.

Isabella sent her a look. "No, it's just better that you don't keep her waiting."

He nodded, then turned to Gabby, his tone cordial. "It was nice talking to you. We should do it again."

She slowly lowered then raised her long lashes. "Soon I hope."

His tone deepened. "Yes, it will be very soon."

"Good."

They stared at each other.

"I said I'm ready!" Mariella called again.

Isabella bit her lip to keep from laughing when she saw a flash of annoyance cross his face. "Enjoy yourself, Lex," she teased as he passed.

He stopped in front of her, towering like a maple tree but he didn't offer her shade or comfort, his powerful physique and dark brown gaze made her insides do somersaults. "Don't worry. I plan to," he said then left.

Gabby rushed up to Isabella and grabbed her arm. "I think I know the way to his heart."

"Oh?" she said without much interest.

"Aren't you curious?"

"How you gain his attention is your business, not mine."

Gabby ignored her "It's this house. He loves it. You should see the way his eyes come alive when he talks about it and his voice becomes softer. He really is a very handsome man."

"He could murder us in our beds and the first thing anyone would say is 'Yes, he chopped them up and fed them to the pigeons, but he's such a handsome man.'"

"Don't be disgusting. I only mentioned his looks because they seem to soften when he talks about the house and his family. Those are his two weak spots."

"I see."

Gabby shook her arm. "Aren't you thrilled? I think I've figured out the way to make Mariella's plan work."

"I only hope you know what you're doing."

She kissed Isabella's cheek. "Don't worry. I do. He's nicer than you think, Izzy. I know he hurt your feelings, but I doubt he meant it." She rubbed her hands together in anticipation. "Soon Alex Carlton will be mine."

Five hours later, Isabella sat in the living room trying to pretend that she was not waiting for Mariella's return. When she heard a car drive up to the house she raced up the stairs not wanting to overhear any mushy goodbyes that might occur. She heard the front door open then close. By the time she went downstairs both Daniella and Gabby were peppering Mariella with questions in the sitting room.

"It was wonderful," Mariella said taking a seat as though she were a queen granting her public an audience. "He's a complete gentleman."

Gabby smirked. "Which means he didn't try to kiss you."

Mariella ignored her. "He drove me around an extra two hours because he enjoyed my company so much."

Isabella glanced at the clock. "I had wondered."

"It was wonderful. We drove completely out of town and went on little dirt roads I didn't even know were there. He told me about his travels and all that he plans to do with the house. Now I'd like to rest." She slowly rose to her feet then drifted up the stairs.

Gabby turned to Isabella. "He spent an extra two hours with Mariella?"

"Amazing," Daniella said.

Isabella agreed. "I know."

Gabby shrugged. "We'll see how far he takes me."

Tony tossed his magazine aside when Alex returned to the apartment. "So how did it go?"

Alex fell on the couch and rested his head back. "How did what go?"

"Your date."

He sat up. "Oh is that what it's called? I thought masochistic pleasures might be more appropriate."

Tony winced. "But you were with her a long time."

"I know," he said slowly. "A minor error in judgment."

"Start with the good part."

He sighed and stared at the blank TV.

"Alex?"

He nodded. "Yes, I heard you."

"You mean there wasn't a good part?"

"She is very beautiful."

"Yes, we all know that."

He looked thoughtful. "She would make a great wife."

"Yes."

"If I could figure out a way to zip her mouth shut and keep her from moving, she'd be perfect."

Tony shook his head. "It couldn't have been that bad."

"Do you want to know the first thing she asked me?" He didn't give him a chance to reply. "Where would our second home be? Would I mind if she had a career as a model. And that if I want kids I'd better start now because her skin is still supple." He sighed. "At least I know what she's like and what I'd be in for. I have a date with Gabby next. We'll see how that goes."

Tony nodded, but didn't reply.

That Friday, Alex took Gabby out. He also took her out Saturday and Sunday. When he asked her out again the following Thursday, it became evident that he favored her. Soon they were going out every week. January turned into February. A dozen red roses arrived for Valentine's Day. Mariella was surprisingly philosophical about his choice. "I don't care who he marries as long as it's one of us," she said.

"It's obvious Gabby is his favorite. I don't mind. He's too young for me anyway."

"By only six years," Isabella said thinking of how much older she was than him.

"That's plenty. A man isn't ripe until he's past his thirties."

"He's pretty mature."

"For his age, I guess. He's perfect for Gabby. And they've gone out every week for about three weeks now. Izzy, I think my plan has worked. I think we will have a summer wedding."

As more weeks passed it became clear Mariella's prediction might be correct. Alex preferred Gabby's company to any other woman in town. February disappeared under March's harsh assault, but no one paid attention to the weather. Everyone was excited by Gabby's obvious conquest. One evening while Isabella was coming down the stairs, she saw Sophia and Daniella heading out, arm in arm. They were already acting like sisters.

"Where are you two going?" she asked them.

"Shopping," Daniella said.

Sophia looked Isabella up and down. "Do you want to come?"

Isabella met the kind, but critical look with a smile. "No, thanks."

"I'm paying."

"That's sweet, but I have things to do. Remember this week we have to move out into the cottage so Alex can start renovations. I'm glad he was able to clean it up for us."

"Oh, you don't have to worry about moving. Alex will hire someone. And you don't have to

worry about being polite about money. We're going to be sisters soon."

"You think?"

Both women nodded.

Isabella sent them a curious look. "Do you know something I don't?"

The two young women shared a look then Sophia said, "All I know is that Alex really likes Gabby. He told me so." She opened the door and stepped outside. Daniella turned to Isabella with both fingers crossed and mouthed "It's working" before following Sophia.

Isabella agreed. With her dear sister willingly in his clutches, she felt determined to find out more about him.

Although Isabella felt she should be glad Gabby and Alex got on so well, rumors about Alex's generosity made her cautious. Aside from the fundraiser for the nursing home, he continued to spend his money freely about town. Soon word of how he'd donated funds to the local schools and library reached her. These were two places one had rarely seen him when he was younger. It would have been more appropriate if he'd given funds to the cinema or pool hall. His philanthropy also included the town hall, sheriff's department and community center.

Isabella wondered if he'd suddenly been struck by conscience or if he was trying to buy the town's favor. And if so, why? When she tried asking others, people were too in awe of him to say anything negative, but Isabella finally found someone as suspicious of his actions as she was: Mrs. Grace at the library.

"He just handed us a check," she said, her tiny eyes bright with suspicion and her booming voice filling the quiet room. Aside from her degree in library science, she was completely unsuited for her job as a librarian, with a loud voice and coarse manners. She made Isabella instantly regret her decision to talk to her. Isabella lowered her voice hoping Mrs. Grace would take the hint and do the same.

"That was it?"

"I was curious," she continued in a booming voice, making Isabella wince. "But I wasn't going to say no."

"He didn't say why?"

She shook her head. "He just talked about the importance of the library and how it had been a refuge for him in his youth."

A man in a tweed jacket turned around from his table. "Shh!"

Isabella flashed a sheepish grin, but Mrs. Grace took no notice. "I'm not going to disagree with anyone handing me that much money. If he said the library was a refuge to him, then it was."

Isabella raised her brows. "He said that with a straight face?"

"He's very good at appearing sincere."

"So you doubt his intentions?"

She shrugged. "What I think of him is not important."

"Shh!" the man repeated.

Mrs. Grace turned her beady eyes to him. "Would you mind being quiet? This is a library you know."

The man looked at her, stunned, then slunk away and Isabella decided to do the same.

At Mrs. Lyons's house, Isabella continued to ponder the librarian's words. Alex wasn't doing anything wrong. Generosity wasn't a crime. Perhaps there wasn't anything shady about his actions. Nicodemus forced her out of her thoughts by nudging her with his head and meowing when she missed a note. She decided to concentrate on her playing.

"It seems Alex Carlton is generous with his money," Mrs. Lyons said as though she'd been reading her mind.

Isabella's fingers faltered on the keys, but she quickly righted them. "Yes. He's given money to the town hall, sheriff's department and library."

"His father used to love the library."

That was interesting, Isabella thought. His father had also worked at the sheriff's office. Was there a connection?

"When did Mr. Carlton leave?" she asked.

"I believe Sophia was just a baby or toddler. I remember it was in the spring because there had been a rash of burglaries. Most people suspected him, but the burglaries continued after he left. Nobody knows why he did. But men are undependable creatures so it's to be expected."

Isabella didn't agree, but decided not to argue. "Then Mrs. Carlton left years later with no explanation either."

"She thought she'd get better opportunities elsewhere. However—"

"Yes?"

"It's been rumored that it had something to do with the Tremains."

"How could there possibly be a connection?"

"Well, the Tremain marriage broke up soon after Velma left."

Isabella widened her eyes. "You don't think that they ran off together, do you?"

"Could be."

"But if they had run off together, where is he now?"

"Probably dead, Men have a habit of up and dying on you, too."

"But—"

"Velma was an attractive woman back then. Still is, if you ignore the fact that she's let her figure go. She didn't have a good education and I doubt her son has one, but now they have a lot of money. What does that mean?"

"The Realtor said that the Carltons are very rich."

"But he didn't tell you how they got that way. The Carltons have always been poor. David wasn't worth much and neither were his father or grandfather. They were simple men. Alex may be a little smarter, but tell me how a man with little education and no connections could get to be so rich without anyone knowing what business he's in. Of course there are ways to find out, but I don't like people not being forthcoming about how they butter their bread. And I wonder why, when they can live anywhere in the world, would they choose here?"

Yes, why? How had Alex made his money? Why was he so generous to a town he'd left vowing "to show them"? What was he up to?

When Isabella addressed her questions to Gabby as she cleared the dinner table that evening, she shooed them away. "Izzy, you have nothing to worry about. Alex really cares about this town and he wants to help in any way he can. He truly is a kind and generous man. I wish you could see that."

"So you trust him?"

"He's the type of man I would trust with my life."

Isabella desperately wanted to believe her sister. Gabby was usually a good judge of character. Later that evening, Isabella drove to Martha's, her favorite restaurant, and selected a booth. She liked the worn vinyl cushions and hot coffee. She'd always come here to be alone and think among the distant hum of voices and the comforting scent of apple-peach pie. Right now she had a lot to think about. She scribbled down a list of reasons why she didn't trust Alex. She slowly crossed them off when she discovered a reason why she should.

Question: How did he make his money? Why did he return? Answer: Possible investments. He loved the house? She put a question mark next to it then paused when she felt someone slide into the seat in front of her. She glanced up and froze.

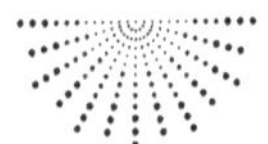

lex stared at her with hard cold eyes that formed slivers of ice in her blood. "You've been asking questions about me," he said.

She met his gaze, though her first instinct was to look away. She knew he would use any show of weakness against her. She should have been more discreet about her inquires. He could make a dangerous adversary. She was about to divert her gaze when she noticed the faint scar on his jaw. She'd been there when he'd fallen off his bike and had to get stitches. She'd wiped the tears he'd been unable to hold back. She stopped a smile and suddenly felt relieved. He may not be that little boy anymore, but she would never fear him. "Stop that, Lex."

He suddenly looked wary, giving her more courage. At that moment she knew that there was no reason to be frightened. "Stop what?" he asked.

"Don't look at me as though I'm an opponent you want to annihilate. I was there when you were sick all over our kitchen floor when you caught the flu."

He glanced away embarrassed, then resigned. His features

didn't soften, but somehow he seemed less menacing. He sighed, tapping his finger against the table. When he looked at her again the hard look was gone replaced by a dark unreadable glint. "You've been asking questions about me," he repeated.

She didn't need to ask how he knew. "Yes."

He tapped faster. "Why?"

"I'm curious about the man who's showing so much interest in my sister."

He stopped tapping. "Your sister wants me to be interested in her and I'm happy to oblige."

"And you've been extremely generous to everyone."

This statement produced a cynical twist of his lips that could have been mistaken for a smile, though it wasn't meant to be. "Feeling left out?"

"I want to know what you're up to."

"I think you already know what I'm up to."

"You want people to trust you."

"Yes."

"Why?"

He shrugged. "Why not?" He glanced down at the menu then called the waitress over and ordered. After handing the waitress his menu, he met Isabella's assessing gaze. This time he smiled with genuine amusement that made her face feel hot. She now understood why Gabby found his company so enjoyable, and if she wasn't careful she would, too. There was something a little *too* appealing about him. "It's all a game, Izzy." He leaned forward and lowered his voice. "Are you sure you don't want to play?"

"Very sure," she said in a crisp tone, annoyed by her traitorous emotions.

"You're missing a lot of fun."

"I doubt it."

He leaned back. "Well, you wouldn't know since you're on the sidelines. You're really good at that."

"It gives me a great view of the whole situation."

"True. Sitting on the sidelines has some benefits. You get to see the whole game and you don't lose anything." He wagged a finger. "But there's one drawback. You don't win anything either."

"The most dangerous games are the ones of the heart."

"I don't play with hearts."

"But you play with people."

"No," he said with deliberate patience. "I don't play with them either. I only play the games people *want* me to play."

"What I've noticed is that people tend not to play the same games."

The waitress came back with Alex's order—a plate full of spinach stuffed mushrooms sprinkled with cheese and a large lemonade. Isabella glanced around wondering if it was a good time to leave.

"Yes," Alex said. "They're all looking at us, but don't worry about it."

She turned to him. "I'm not worried."

"Then why do you look like you're ready to run?"

"Leave. Not run."

He couldn't help a grin. "You looked ready to run to me."

"I just thought you might want to eat alone."

"If I wanted to eat alone, I would have sat at a table by myself."

"You're only sitting here because you want me to stop asking questions about you."

"That, and I'd also like the company."

With me? Isabella wanted to laugh, as she sneaked another

glance at the other young women in the restaurant. She returned her gaze to his lowered head as he cut a mushroom in half, waiting for the rest of the joke.

He suddenly looked up and their eyes met. Yes, his eyes could be dangerous. There was just too much intelligence there and something else that made her skin tingle. A glimmer of humor entered his gaze. "Come on, Izzy, you know me better than that. I don't lie, remember?"

She nodded, not wanting to speak. The warmth of his gaze seemed to fan the heat he'd lit before with his smile. She shifted, awkward.

He pushed the appetizer towards her. "Go ahead and help yourself. You look hungry."

"I'm not hungry."

He pushed the plate closer.

She took a mushroom. "Thanks." She bit into it and was surprised by how good it tasted. She'd come to Martha's for years and had never tried it. "Man, these are good."

"I know."

She took another one.

"Why did you come back?"

"To settle down and get married."

"Is that all?"

"That's all for now."

He was cagey, but Isabella was determined to pin him down. "You've shown a lot of interest in Gabby."

"I like her I always have."

She took another mushroom. "I don't want her to get hurt."

He shook his head. "Nobody's going to get hurt."

"That might be your intention, but being practical is difficult when it comes to people and emotions."

"Fortunately, I don't let them get in my way."

"People or emotions?"

"Both."

"Sounds like a cold way to live."

He shrugged. "Only to some." He glanced down and stared amazed at the empty plate. He looked up at Isabella as she finished her last mushroom. "You really weren't hungry, were you?"

She swallowed then covered her mouth. "I'm so sorry."

"Don't worry about it." He called the waitress over and ordered another plate. When the new order came Isabella watched him eat then asked, "So, do you still do it?"

"Do I still do what?"

"You know." She sent a meaningful glance at the mushrooms.

He finally understood. "Oh you mean this?" He positioned his spoon to face him, rested a mushroom on the handle then hit the spoon, popping the mushroom in his mouth like a catapult. "You mean that?"

"Yes. Show me how."

He frowned. "You used to scold me when I did that."

"That didn't mean I wasn't impressed."

"Okay, I'll show you how easy it is. Scoot over."

To her horror, Alex sat down beside her. She tried to focus on what he was saying, desperate to ignore the feel of his thigh pressing against hers, the scent of wood that clung to his jacket, and most of all, the compelling beauty of his gaze. She would never mistake him for a lifeless portrait again. He was all too real.

"Izzy, you're not paying attention."

She tried to focus. "I'm sorry, this was probably a bad idea."

"No, it's not. I'm going to teach you how to do this."

Alex proved to be a good teacher, but Isabella proved to be a clumsy student. Twice he had to catch a mushroom before it sailed into the next booth and once she nearly poked out her eye. But Alex was patient and determined she would get it and waited until she did; twenty minutes later she accomplished her goal.

"Very good."

"Thank you." She grabbed the ticket for her coffee and opened her wallet. "Let me pay for the first plate."

Alex snatched the wallet from her. "Stop pretending. What are you planning to pay with? Lint?"

She snatched it back. "I have change."

"How much?"

"None of your business. Move!"

"Izzy, I didn't mean to tease you."

"Now."

He reluctantly stood. "Let me pay."

"Why? Is that part of the game?"

His jaw twitched. "I'm trying to be nice."

"But I can't be nice to you? Only you can spend money? Is that how the game goes?"

"I'm trying to help because I know you don't have anything."

"I have my dignity."

"I was being friendly."

"I know. It's just that with you I always wonder why." She stood and walked away.

Alex sat in his booth for several minutes after Isabella left then paid the bill. He shouldn't have teased her. That was unfair. But she bothered him. He'd been thinking about her more than he wanted to and he didn't know why. She didn't interest him. Gabby was the one who did. She would make a perfect wife. He couldn't have Isabella's suspicions get in his way.

Alex walked to his truck and got in. He needed to win Isabella over. He passed the flower shop, then the bakery, and began to smile as the perfect idea came to mind.

SHE LIKED HIM. She wasn't sure she trusted him, but she liked him. A lot. But how could she forget the condescending way he spoke about her family? The calculated manner in which he selected her sisters? Yet he had no pretense. He was honest about everything he did. He did not pretend to be anything, but who he was: an attractive, rich man in want of status in the form of a grand house and a suitable wife. Could she fault him? Had she been in his shoes, wouldn't she have done the same thing? Wasn't her sister also playing the so-called "game"? Yes, she liked him. Perhaps a little too much.

Days after their meeting in the restaurant, Isabella stood by her window and watched Gabby and Alex part. It wasn't the first time she'd stood glued to the window in the attic, gazing down at them. There was always a gentle kiss goodbye. Isabella could see that there was true affection between them. And at the sight of them (Alex caressing Gabby's cheek, Gabby resting her head on his shoulder), Isabella's sleeping heart warmed. They were perfect.

There were no signs of the approaching spring and it seemed clear in a few days they would all have to move through the winter's slush into the cottage so that Alex could begin renovation on the house. Two days before they had to leave, Isabella woke up to a loud pounding noise. She walked into the hall and met Mariella.

"This is unbearable," Mariella said. "Who is that?"

Isabella turned back to her room: "They have work to do."

"It's the morning." Mariella covered her ears then let her hands fall. "Don't they know people have to sleep?"

"It's nearly ten."

"I don't care." She leaned over the railing and saw two booted legs sticking out from under the stairs. "You! Come out of there!"

The hammering stopped.

"Didn't you hear me? I said come out of there."

Alex emerged. Isabella bit her lip to keep from laughing; Mariella looked stunned.

"What are you doing?" she finally asked.

He balanced the hammer in his palm then gripped the handle. "Fixing the stairs They were squeaking."

"Don't you have workers to do that?"

"I don't mind."

"Oh." She gestured for him to continue. "Carry on then."

He gave a low mocking bow. "Thank you."

Isabella laughed. Alex winked before disappearing again.

Mariella made a face. "It's not funny. He shouldn't go around as if he were some blue collar worker."

"He wasn't doing anything wrong. You made an assumption."

Mariella's mood didn't improve the next day when she discovered the cottage only had three rooms and she would be. forced to share with Isabella.

"But I've always had my own room," she said as Isabella unpacked her bags.

"It's only for a few months."

"I can't wait until Gabby gets married. I don't know how much more of this 'roughing it' I can bear."

Isabella agreed. Sharing a room with Mariella was already a chore because she demanded more than half of the room for her clothes and beauty supplies.

When time would allow, Isabella visited different apartments and managed to get two extra hours working for Mrs. Lyons. Although she told Mariella, she wasn't impressed as she sat on her bed staring at her nails. "I just realized that I haven't had a manicure in weeks. And do you know why?" She continued before Isabella could respond. "Because I can't afford it."

"Mariella, there are worse things."

"What could be worse? Look at my hands." She held them out for inspection.

"They look beautiful."

"They look neglected, which they are. He's pushed us out of our homes and he's squeezing us into this sardine can."

"It's not that bad."

Mariella fell back on the bed with an arm dramatically draped over her eyes. "I'm so unhappy."

Isabella was about to reply when Gabby burst into their bedroom with Daniella close behind. "Our problems are solved," Daniella said.

Gabby nudged her. "Let me tell them."

Mariella sat up. Isabella scrambled to her knees. "Tell us what?" She saw the look on Gabby's face and her mouth fell open. "He didn't."

Gabby held out her band and wiggled her fingers, showing off her engagement ring. "He did."

"Isn't it wonderful!" Daniella said.

Mariella clapped her hands. "Didn't I tell you my plan was brilliant? I knew it would work."

Isabella lifted Gabby's hand and stared at the large diamond ring. "Congratulations."

"Thank you," Gabby said.

Mariella tapped her chin. "Of course you must get married as soon as possible so he doesn't have a chance to change his mind."

"I don't see why he would," Daniella said "This ring must have cost a fortune."

Isabella sat back and looked at Gabby. "Are you happy?"

"Of course, she is," Mariella interrupted. "Why wouldn't she be? We're going to be rich. Think of all the privileges she'll have being his wife." Mariella stood. "I'm going to go talk to Mrs. Carlton. Don't worry Gabby, between us you will have a fabulous wedding." She left.

Daniella moved to follow her. "Isn't this wonderful? We won't have to find another place to live after all. I'm going to talk to Sophia." She kissed Gabby's cheek then walked away.

Isabella drew her knees to her chest and kept her gaze on Gabby. "You haven't answered my question. Are you happy?"

Gabby smiled. "Yes, I'm very happy. I like Alex and I'm getting a chance to help my family. What more could I want?"

Isabella shrugged.

Gabby's smile slowly fell. "But you don't seem happy."

"Oh, I am. I...don't..." She paused then said, "There's just so much to think about. So many changes."

"Don't worry about anything. All our problems are solved." She hugged her.

Isabella hugged her back, wanting to believe her.

Isabella hated herself for not being happier. The burden of taking care of everyone was now gone. She could focus on her upcoming class in antiquing and prepare for her trip to Europe. What was there to worry about? Velma and Sophia's excitement about the wedding soon allayed her fears. It was a perfect match. Alex and Gabby were of similar mindsets and interests, and everyone liked to point out what a handsome pair they made. She knew that they would learn to truly love each other.

As the start of her class grew closer, Isabella realized she had a big problem. She hadn't thought through her schedule for work and class. She would have to get a replacement for her Thursdays with Mrs. Lyons. She paced the upstairs as she heard the excited voices of Velma, Sophia, Mariella and Gabby discussing the wedding in the living room. Later, when she saw Daniella sitting alone in her bedroom, flipping through magazines, Isabella came up with a solution.

She knocked on the doorframe. "Dani?"

Daniella held up a magazine and pointed to an entertainment system. "I've always wanted this. Do you think Gabby will let me buy it?"

"I don't know."

Daniella dog-eared the page. "I don't see why not. She'll have the money."

"That doesn't mean you can expect her to give you everything you want. She's marrying Alex, not you."

"I know that. But we've always taken care of each other."

Isabella nodded and entered the room. "Yes, that's a good point. Guess what? I could use your help:'

Her eyes lit up. "Really? Sure, I'll help you. What do you want?"

"I want you to be my replacement with Mrs. Lyons for a few weeks."

Her gaze dimmed. "How many weeks?"

"Eight."

"Could I help you with something else?"

Isabella sat on the bed and gripped her hands together. "I know it's asking a lot, but I will be taking classes that are important to me. I can't work at Mrs. Lyons's on those days *and* get to class on time."

Daniella shook her head. "I don't know."

"It would only be one day a week. All you would be doing is reading or playing the piano or running errands. It won't interfere with your job because it's late afternoon to evening. I'll do my other regular days. Please, help me out."

Daniella sighed. "Okay."

"Thank you. I promise to make it up to you."

"There's one way you can make it up to me."

"How?"

She held up the magazine again. "Convince Gabby to get me this."

Isabella shook her head. "I'll see what I can do." She went to her room relieved that she had been able to convince Daniella. However, convincing Mrs. Lyons proved more difficult. "I don't think I like you foisting your sister on me," Mrs. Lyons said in a condescending tone as she sat in front of the large opened windows, a light breeze toying with the maroon scarf around her neck.

"I'm not foisting anyone on you. You will like Daniella and she will be a good help to you."

She pursed her lips. "While you do what in the meantime?"

Isabella turned her back to her and plumped up a pillow. "I am taking another job."

She nodded, coming to a conclusion. "I see. You want a raise."

"No." She turned to her. "Daniella will be a great help."

Mrs. Lyons's eyes flashed with disapproval. "I suppose I have no choice. The opinions of an old woman rarely bear much weight."

Isabella stopped a grin. "Thank you for being so understanding."

LESS THAN A WEEK LATER, Isabella eagerly drove to the local college where she'd registered for her antiquing course. It was a mini-mester course designed to help students learn about antiques—how to buy them, where to look and how much to pay. Although the course would put a hefty balance on her credit card, she thought it would be a good investment.

Once inside the building, Isabella darted up the concrete steps in awe of the stately pictures and awards on the walls.

She didn't want to linger. She'd never had a chance to go to college and didn't want to feel intimidated. She came to the first door, A-112, and entered. She took a seat in the middle next to the aisle, watching the room quickly fill up. Isabella gingerly took out her yellow notepad and pen, while noticing other students around her booting up their laptops and other electronic devices.

She found it ironic that people interested in the past would be so addicted to present technology. Isabella kept her head down. She didn't want to invite conversation and show how little she knew about the subject.

"Is this seat taken?" a deep voice asked from above.

She glanced up startled then nearly fell out of her seat. "What are you doing here?"

Alex settled into the chair next to her. "I want to learn more about antiquing and improve my mind." He narrowed his eyes and pointed a warning finger at her. "Say one word and you'll regret it."

She grinned. "Maybe."

He lowered his voice. "I'd make sure."

"Then my lips are sealed." She made a zipping motion across her mouth.

"You're supposed to be nice to me." He leaned towards her and smiled. "We're going to be family soon."

"Yes, I know." She inched away, but he didn't seem to notice. The problem with him was his size. He was big and everything about him seemed to invade her space rather than share it. He didn't touch her. He didn't need to. His masculine vitality penetrated the distance between them upsetting her senses in a purely feminine way.

"Are you going to offer me congratulations?"

"I think I'm going to wait."

"Until when?"

"Until after you're married."

He studied her. "Do you think there won't be a wedding?"

She shifted feeling awkward under his gaze. "I'm sure there will be. I just don't feel like congratulating you twice."

He shrugged. "Fair enough." He leaned his chair back until it balanced on two legs. "So what are you doing here?"

"I want to know more about antiques."

He set the chair down, rested his chin in his hand and studied her again. "Why?"

"Why do you?"

"Because I want to. You?" He held up a hand. "And you can't use my reason, it's already taken."

She sighed, resigned that he wouldn't leave her alone. "If you must know, I want to impress somebody."

He blinked surprised, his eyebrows rising. "What's his name?"

"Actually, it's a she."

He blinked again and cleared his throat. "Oh."

"She's an older woman."

He waved his hands. "Hey, no need to explain. I used to go for older women myself."

"It's not like that," she snapped. "She's my employer and I want to impress her with my knowledge of antiques so she'll take me to. Europe with her this year."

Alex grinned. "Why you sly little fox."

"What?"

"You pretend to be against playing games, yet here you are involved in one of your own."

"I'm not playing games."

"Oh really? Then why not just ask your employer to take you with her? Why go through the pretense?"

Isabella opened her mouth then closed it not having a ready reply. When she did finally come up with a response, Alex put his finger to his lips indicating that the class was about to start.

The instructor—Mr. Benjamin Yanders—had no chin, a long, reedy body, thin brown hair and a deep voice that belonged on radio. He readily captured their interest the moment he spoke.

"I'm pleased that you're all here," he said. "I hope you all have the two volumes of *An introduction to the World of Antiquing.* These two books will be your bible in this course, and for those of you who are serious, it will be an excellent lifetime resource. If you don't have these books, they're still available for the bargain price of seventy-five dollars." He lifted several out of a box and set them on the table.

Isabella nearly snapped her pen. *Seventy-five dollars?* She didn't even have two dollars in her purse. When signing up for the class, she'd hoped that the books weren't compulsory. She glanced around. Everyone had their pristine volumes on their desks. She wondered if there was a way she could get it on loan. She was so busy worrying that she didn't notice Alex leaving his seat.

Isabella kept her gaze on the desk until a book slowly moved into her line of vision. She turned to Alex, but Mr. Yanders began the lecture before she could say anything, "If you want to get the most out of this class, you will need to make a 100 percent commitment." Isabella glanced over the syllabus feeling a little insecure. The lecture topics were listed: Understanding the World of Antiquing; Pricing and Labeling of Antiques; and American Antiques. Weekend assignments included visits to antique, shops, assessing period pieces and writing reports about them. The final lesson would involve purchasing an item and presenting it to the entire class. Luckily for those individuals with financial hardship, Mr. Yanders had a personal collection of eclectic antiques he would 'loan' out for the final assignment.

By the time the class finished, Isabella was afraid her hand would cramp from all the notes she had taken. She gathered her things then waited for Alex in the hall, but after ten minutes she grew impatient. She glanced inside the classroom and saw him talking to other students—mostly female. He didn't look as though he would leave soon. She ripped a sheet of paper and scribbled: *Thank you. I'll pay you back Izzy.* Then she went out to the parking lot and searched for his truck. Once she found it she slipped the note under his windshield wiper.

"A love letter?" he said coming up behind her.

She paused then turned.

"No, don't tell me." He took the note and read it then smiled. "It's even better than I thought." He cleared his throat and began to read it aloud. "My dear Alex, words cannot express how thankful I am for your generosity."

She tried to snatch the note. "I didn't write that."

He moved it out of reach and continued. "I was wrong about you and sincerely apologize for my gross misjudgment." He glanced at her. "I noticed' you underlined *gross* twice. Nice touch."

She folded her arms and shook her head.

"If there is any way I can repay you, just ask. Your humble servant, Isabella." He tucked the note in his jacket pocket. "Apology accepted."

"You have an amazing imagination. Do you usually hallucinate?"

He tapped her nose with his finger. "No, that's not how this game works. I'm nice to you then you're nice to me. Try it"

She took a deep breath then said, "Thank you for the books."

"Consider it a peace offering."

"I didn't realize we were at war."

He unlocked his truck and got in. "Not anymore." He closed the door then started the engine. When Isabella knocked on his window, he lowered it. "Yes?"

"Why do you drive a truck? Shouldn't you drive one of those luxury cars?"

"I like trucks. I buy what I want to, not what I'm supposed to."

"No, you never liked doing what you were supposed to."

He raised an eyebrow. "Any more questions?"

"Yes, how did you make your money?"

He grinned then put his truck in gear. "Good night, Isabella."

Gabby glanced at her clock as she drove her car into a space in the parking lot of Alex's apartment complex. She was a few minutes early. She sat and stared at the building, then the ring on her hand. She was engaged. She still couldn't believe she had managed it. She had succeeded in saving her family and her home. She'd made a good decision. Alex was not only rich, but he was sensible. Others might have thought he would rent an expensive condominium or grand home while he renovated his dream house, but he preferred to stay in an apartment.

She got out of her car and headed inside. Alex wanted her to come by and visit him so that they could go over some plans for the wedding. Even though he said his mother and others would take care of everything and she was fine with them doing so, he told her that he also wanted her input. Once at the door Gabby raised her hand to knock, but it swung open and Tony appeared. They both jumped in surprise. Gabby recovered first. "I'm here to see Alex."

"He's not here yet. But he'll be back soon." He glanced inside then at her. "I guess you could wait. Or..." He hesitated.

"Yes?" she urged.

"I'm going for a walk into town. Care to join me?"

"Sure, but can you..." Her words trailed off and her gaze slipped to his bad leg.

"A walk always does me good." Once outside he said, "Congratulations on your engagement."

"Thank you. So where do you need to go?"

"I'm not going anywhere in particular. I just wanted to go for a walk. I hate staying inside when the weather is this nice." He glanced up at the pristine blue sky and inhaled the fresh scent of grass. The hand of winter still gripped March, but spring was slowly prying its fingers away with the arrival of new leaves and blossoms.

"I know a nice path close by."

He gestured with his hand. "Lead the way." She did, taking him to a popular walking path that was close to the river. Gabby slowed her pace when his limp became more pronounced. He didn't say anything, but she knew he was grateful for the consideration. There was a lot he didn't have to say. He had a calm air about him that made her feel comfortable. She understood why Alex had him as his friend.

"So what do you do for Alex?" she asked eager to know more about him.

"Many different things." He rubbed his forehead. "I came home after the war a little lost."

"You were in Iraq?" she asked, thinking about the recent conflict. "When did you come back?"

He grinned at her naiveté. "Many years ago. I was in The Gulf War," he clarified.

"Oh."

"You were probably in elementary school then."

She stared at the ground.

"I did my time willingly and came back a little the worse for wear." He ran a hand over his graying hair. "I should be flattered that you think I'm young and fit enough to fight now."

She stared at him for a long moment, trying to imagine him younger, without the limp and gray hair, but failed. What she saw before her, the man who walked beside her was perfect as he was. "I'm glad you came back."

He laughed.

"I'm serious."

He looked at her, a smile tugging on his mouth. "You don't even know me."

"Do I have to know you to be glad that you lived?"

He turned away.

"Did I say something wrong?" she asked, wondering if there had been others who hadn't felt the same way.

He shook his head, then returned his gaze to her "No, you're very sweet."

"I wasn't trying to be *sweet*. I was being honest."

He moved his shoulders in a manner to dismiss the seriousness of her words and looked away again. "Yes, well, uh...anyway I came back and did odd jobs. I met Alex at one of his construction jobs and we got on well and have worked together ever since."

"Alex has a lot of plans for the house."

"You don't have to worry. He doesn't plan to make too many changes."

"I'm not worried. I trust him. He said that you have some ideas of your own. He really respects your opinion. I'd love to see what you've come up with."

Tony opened his jacket and pulled out a large folded piece of paper. "I have some sketches here."

Gabby took it from him and opened it up. It revealed a layout of the house with the proposed ideas. "That's incredible. It's a perfect blueprint." She looked up at him impressed. "That's wonderful. You're very good." She handed it back to him.

He folded it up, agitated.

Gabby watched concerned. "Did I say something wrong again?"

"No, you're very—"

She held up a hand. "Hold it. I'm not being sweet or kind or cute. I'm being honest. I think you're very talented. Now stop treating me like some child."

He tucked the paper in his jacket. "I'm old enough to be your—"

"But you're not and that makes a difference."

His gaze challenged hers. "What kind of difference?"

Gabby lowered her gaze suddenly feeling flustered.

Tony briefly shut his eyes and softly swore. "I'm sorry. I—" He stopped and turned. "I'm sure Alex has returned. If I'd brought my cell with me we could have called him to find out."

"I don't have one, either. We're too broke for a cell phone and the extra charges."

"Marrying Alex will change all that for you."

He smiled, but to Gabby it felt a little sad. "I'm truly happy for you."

Gabby touched the leaves of an evergreen, wondering why she wasn't ready to go back yet.

When they returned to the house, Tony listened to a voice-mail message from Alex, saying that he would have to cancel his meeting with Gabby and that he needed Tony to prepare dinner for two business associates.

"Do you need help?" Gabby asked him

Again Tony hesitated then said, "Sure." They spent the next several hours planning the menu, shopping for the items, taking the groceries home and preparing the, meal. Alex came through the door as Gabby was setting the table. "Mmm, something smells good," he said. When he saw Gabby he kissed her on the cheek. "I left a message at your house that I had to cancel."

"I know, but since I was already here I thought I would help Tony."

Alex stared at the table and sniffed the air. "You two make a great team."

Tony and Gabby shared a look, then quickly looked away.

Gabby walked to the door. "I'd better go. I told my sisters I'd only be gone a few hours and it's nearly dark."

Alex walked her to the door. "I'll make this up to you next time."

"You don't have to make anything up to me." She glanced at Tony. "I had a wonderful time." He waved then disappeared into the kitchen.

GABBY DROVE home in a mental fog. Twice she missed the

turn to her street and when she finally reached home, she didn't remember getting there. Mariella met her at the front door. "Where were you? We expected you home hours ago. Alex called here to tell us he needed to cancel."

"I know," Gabby said in a soft, distant voice. She walked to the living room where Isabella sat curled up on the couch studying and Sophia and Daniella lay on the floor flipping through a fashion magazine.

"But where were you?" Mariella demanded.

Gabby flopped down into the side chair. "With Tony."

"Why?"

She sat. "I helped him."

"Do what? Find his dentures?"

Gabby glared at her. "No. First we went on a walk and then I helped him prepare dinner for Alex's guests."

"Why? That's his job. You're going to be Alex's wife soon, I doubt he expects to find you in the kitchen with Tony."

"I didn't mind helping him. He's very nice company."

Daniella flipped a page. "I don't see how you two could have much in common."

"He's very smart."

Daniella frowned. "But he's old."

"He's not that old."

"And he's poor," Mariella said.

"He's not that poor."

"And he's plain."

Gabby folded her arms and tapped her foot. "I think he's handsome."

"Gabby, you're being silly," Mariella said. "I know he's Alex's friend, but you don't have to make him sound better than he is."

She set her mouth firmly.

"Leave Tony alone," Sophia said. "He's a very nice guy."

Mariella rested a hand on her hip. "He's a personal servant."

Gabby jumped to her feet. "He's an *assistant* and he makes a good living and he's very talented and kind and..."

Mariella waved her hands. "Hey, there's no reason to get upset. I was just saying—"

"I don't like what you're saying. I don't want you talking about him like that. He deserves better."

Isabella watched her sister closely then said, "You like him."

"I do." When Mariella opened her mouth, Gabby quickly added, "But not like Alex, so don't look at me that way."

Mariella, Daniella and Sophia seemed pleased with Gabby's statement, but her words made Isabella curious.

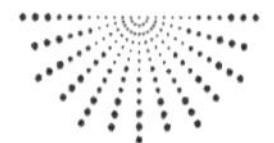

Isabella looked at her quiz grade and groaned. After four classes she knew one thing: She was failing. She looked at the giant red D on her paper and felt like crumpling it up. Mr. Yanders' words echoed in her mind: "I want you to see me after class." He probably thought she didn't belong there. She agreed with him. Why couldn't she grasp anything?

Alex leaned towards her. "Let me see that." She covered the paper with her hand. "No."

"I can't help you if you don't let me see where you went wrong."

"I don't need help."

He clicked his tongue. "We wouldn't want to be *arrogant* would we?"

"It's embarrassing," she grumbled.

"Failing the entire course would be even more embarrassing, plus a waste of money." He kept his hand held out. She reluctantly handed him the paper.

He took it and studied it for so long that her cheeks began to burn.

"Mr. Yanders wants to see me after class," she said, desperate to fill the silence.

"I'll talk to him for you."

"But I don't need—"

Alex stopped her with a stern look. She bit her lip.

He looked at the paper again. "I'm going to offer to tutor you and don't tell me you don't need one." He held up the paper. "This makes it obvious."

"I don't think I can pay you."

He stilled then abruptly stood. "I'm sick of this. I'm trying to be nice to you, but you keep getting on my nerves." He leaned over her, his eyes like flashes of lightning. "What's the point of being so proud that you're willing to fail a class just to spite me?"

She opened her mouth to protest.

"I'm not finished."

She closed it.

"You don't have to like me. That's okay because right now I don't like you very much, either. But I can help you. Close your mouth. You'll know when I've finished talking."

She folded her arms and waited.

"I'm going to be at the library at seven tomorrow. I'll wait for five minutes. No more. I don't care if you come at six minutes past seven, I will be gone. It is your choice to show up or not. Do you understand? You don't need to say anything, just nod your head."

She frowned, but nodded.

"Good." He grabbed his books and left.

Isabella broke from her paralysis and followed him out into

the hall. "You're a—" she began, but the words froze in her throat when he spun around.

He walked towards her, large and intimidating. "I'm a what?"

She gripped her books to her chest. "You're a bully."

"And do you know what you are?"

She boldly met his eyes though her knees trembled. "What?"

He lowered his voice to a whisper. "Desperate."

"I am not desperate. You obnoxious—"

He covered her mouth with his hand then said in an ominous tone, "One more word and I might not show up at all. Now go home." He turned and walked away.

ISABELLA THREW her books in her car and pounded the steering wheel. *Arrogant, pompous jerk* She didn't need his help. She just needed to study harder. She wouldn't give him the satisfaction of showing up at the library. His ego was inflated enough. No, she wouldn't go.

That night she tossed and turned in her bed, debating her decision. She really needed to pass the course. More importantly, she needed the knowledge to impress Mrs. Lyons and knew that Alex could help her. For some reason he knew everything although he spent half of the class with his eyes closed. She remembered a prior class when Mr. Yanders called on Alex.

"Mr. Carlton?" Mr. Yanders had said.

Alex lazily opened his eyes. "Yes?"

"Could you answer the question?"

Isabella watched him with a smug grin certain he'd say,

"What question?" Instead, he surprised them all by stretching and answering the question and adding a tidbit nobody knew.

The teacher stared stunned as did everyone else. "Am I correct?"

"Yes," Mr. Yanders said quickly. "Very good."

"Thank you." He closed his eyes again..

He didn't take notes either, Isabella remembered with annoyance. Yet his papers always came back with high marks. He was arrogant, but he was smart and she could use him. He was going to be family soon anyway so she might as well get used to him.

She continued to debate her decision as she drove to the library. Twice she considered turning back, but the thought of being able to surprise Mrs. Lyons with her knowledge of antiquing would not let her. She arrived at the library two minutes *before* seven, but didn't see Alex anywhere.

She checked the aisles, the magazine and periodical section and even the private study rooms, but still saw no sign of him. She selected a table near the front door and waited. After fifteen minutes she realized the truth. He wasn't coming. To him, everything was a game and she'd come out the loser.

She grabbed her things and stormed out the door.

"Where are you going?" someone called out to her as she raced down the front stairs.

She stopped and saw Alex walking from his truck. "What do you mean, 'Where are you going?' You told me to meet you here at *exactly* seven o' clock."

His eyes lit up with amusement. "Did I?"

"Yes, you did. And I was here on time and you weren't."

"I wanted to see if you would follow directions," he teased.

"Is everything a game to you?"

He placed a brotherly arm around her shoulders and steered her back towards the library. "No. I'm sorry I'm late."

Isabella tried to shrug off his arm, but failed. She wanted to stay angry at him, but his relaxed manner and her relief made that impossible. She fought the urge to move closer. "You were late on purpose."

He held the door open for her, giving no explanation. "Why do I still get this odd feeling that you don't like me?"

"And why do I still get this odd feeling that you're being nice to me because you have an ulterior motive?"

He rested both hands on the door behind her, effectively trapping her in the circle of his arms. "And just what kind of motive would that be?" he asked, his voice cool compared to the heat in his eyes.

"You want me to like you."

"Is that a dangerous request?"

She licked her lips, her mouth suddenly dry. His gaze dipped to her mouth and she felt her entire body grow warm and tense. She hugged herself and his gaze lowered from her mouth to her chest. "It's chilly," she said in a high thin voice. "We should go inside."

"Do you always get cold when you're scared?"

"I'm not scared. What do I have to be afraid of?" He raised an eyebrow, the expression full of meaning, but didn't say a word.

"Do you want me to be afraid of you?"

"It might be wise," his gaze sharpened as his voice deepened.

"Why?"

"Do you really need to ask that question?"

"Excuse me," said a voice from behind them. She carried a load of books and nodded to the doorway.

"Sorry," Isabella said and moved aside, the motion bringing her closer to Alex and the scent of wood polish and faint cologne. She looked at his chest then lifted her gaze to his eyes, expecting them to be amused or mocking. What she didn't expect was the brief heated look of desire so quickly hidden she thought she'd imagined it. She took a hasty step back. "We should go inside." She turned to the door.

He seized her wrist. "Don't run from me, there's no reason to be afraid. I was only teasing."

"Were you?"

"I like you, Izzy," he said as though part of him hated to admit it. "I'm not perfect, but I'm not a bad guy."

She slowly turned to him. "I know."

Alex sighed as though a weight had been lifted. "Come on." He gently shoved her forward. "Let's get to work."

Minutes later, Alex watched Isabella in open amusement as she took out her notebook, and set her pen and colored pencils to the side. She had devised a "color-coded" method to help her remember what period different pieces belonged to.

He rested his chin in his hand and shook his head. "No wonder you're confused."

"What?"

"You've made everything too complicated. Color coding is nice, but you have over sixteen colors here." He picked up a pencil and read its name. "What the hell is *mulberry?*"

"I need these colors. I read that study habits are very important in college. I never went and I want to do a good job."

"I didn't go either so don't worry about it. The key is to do what works, not just what you're told. And color coding doesn't work for you." He picked up the pencils and dumped them in her bag.

"But—"

"And now these." He lifted all her notes. "You're taking a course on antiquing not history. Dates are important, but this is more artistic than intellectual. What areas interest you?"

"I like porcelain."

"Excellent. That's where we'll start. I'll help you identify the different markings." He told her all about the different porcelain marks and the history behind them, how they were used in homes then their discussion slipped into the structures of houses.

Isabella stared at him stunned. "How did you get to be so smart?"

"I stayed out of school."

Her shoulders slumped, wondering if she could get him to be serious. "Oh, Lex."

"Really. I wasn't a good student. I didn't have the patience. I had good teachers, but I was bored. Besides, I knew my life wasn't going to be like the others. Nobody expected to find a Carlton in a fancy white-collar job. We were bricklayers and plumbers. So I didn't see much use for school, but after we left..." He stopped.

"Go on," she urged.

"Mom was able to put me in a great technical high school. It helped me learn a trade and also develop a business background. I had an idea for my own business and my mother helped me with the funding. I spent a lot of time in the library learning what I needed to do, plus talking to people in the field."

"So that donation to the library was real."

"Everything I do is real."

"How much did your mother invest?"

"Enough," he said vaguely, then, "Now let's talk about figurines."

"No, I want to know how you got to be so rich."

"All my money is legal," he snapped.

"I didn't mean—"

"Sure you did. You were curious how some blue-collar, high school graduate could penetrate the walls of the upper-class."

"I want to know because I want to be rich too. If you'd remove that huge chip on your shoulder you wouldn't have to be so defensive all the time."

His jaw twitched then he lowered his gaze and sighed. "You're right. I am defensive." He met her gaze. "I have a lot of money, but I still don't fit in. I don't always do or say the right thing and sometimes..." He rubbed the back of his neck. "I embarrass my mother and sister. They wish I were a bit more refined."

"Gabby will smooth out any rough edges."

He grinned. "That's what I'm planning."

She returned the expression. "So now that your ego has been stroked, will you tell me your

secret?"

"How much is it worth to you?"

She thought for a moment. "Do you still like caramel-fudge brownies?"

"With the thin white icing?"

"Yes."

He leaned forward interested. "Go on."

"How does an entire batch sound to you?"

"It sounds as if it's missing something."

"What?"

"If I remember correctly, those brownies always came with strawberry milk."

"You can buy your own milk."

He sat back and held up his hands. "No deal."

"Okay. A batch of brownies and strawberry milk."

"The way you make it. If you get someone else to make it I'll be able to tell. Is that a deal?" He held out his hand.

She hesitated then shook it. "Deal. Now tell me the secret."

"It's no secret. I started a reconstruction business. Bought some properties and rented them." "You succeeded so young."

"Only to you, I worked very hard."

"I thought you came back for revenge."

"Part of it was that. Mom told me we had to leave because someone wanted us to. I wanted to come back and have whoever that person was try to mess with me." He shook his head. "No more questions. It's time to get back to work."

To her surprise Alex proved to be a patient tutor. Although it took her three tries to identify the proper markings on a porcelain washbowl from the 18th century, not once did he taunt her. He repeated the lesson until she understood. By the end of the session she wondered if she'd completely misjudged him. How could the arrogant, condescending man at the party be this patient, gentle man?

When the librarian, Mrs. Grace, loudly announced the library would soon be closing, Isabella and Alex both jumped.

"Is that woman going deaf?" Alex said.

"No."

"She'd do better in an intensive care unit. She'd have people up and walking in no time."

Isabella stifled a giggle. "That's not nice."

He winked at her. "No, but it's still a funny thought."

"Ten minutes to closing!" Mrs. Grace announced again.

Alex stood. "We'd better leave before she bursts an eardrum."

Isabella felt an odd sense of disappointment as she gathered her things.

"You did very well," he said.

"You're being kind."

"I'm being honest." He placed a finger over her lips. "Stop contradicting me."

"Thank you."

"We'll meet again on Wednesday."

"I have Mrs. Lyons—"

"I know when you have Mrs. Lyons. We can meet before or after."

"Are you sure you'll have the time? I know you're planning your engagement party."

"I have time. I don't plan anything. I hire other people to do that for me."

He held the door open for her and they stepped out into the warm spring evening. The scent of wildflowers filled the air. As they descended the steps, they both noticed an old worn key lying in the corner crack. Alex stopped then began to walk past, but Isabella bent and picked it up. "I wonder what it opens."

Alex stopped and turned. He watched her as she stood under the soft lights of the parking lot, staring at the key. The image seemed to unlock something inside him that he didn't want to acknowledge. "I don't know."

Isabella held it out to him. "I know. Why don't you make up something?"

He took a step back. "I can't."

"Of course you can. You always have a story or response in class."

He shook his head. "No, I can't."

"Oh." She let her hand fall to her side. "I guess when you have everything there's no reason to dream anymore."

He sent her a curious glance. "I don't have everything."

"But you will soon." She took his hand and placed the key in his palm, closing his fingers over it. "You never know. You might think of something later."

"Maybe." He shoved the key in his pocket.

"Next time let's meet at the house. I'm doing some work there."

"Okay."

Alex watched her get in her car and drive off, then took the key out of his pocket and smiled.

At their next meeting, Isabella walked from the cottage to the main house. She saw Alex's truck, but no sign of him. Once inside she heard sawing, and dust and fresh paint assaulted her nose. She walked around curious at what changes had occurred and ended up in the kitchen. Or what used to be the kitchen. It was now a giant hole. No appliances or cabinets had been installed and all of the walls had been painted a nice cream yellow. She heard movement in her old sewing room and went to investigate.

She peeked inside and saw it had been turned into a workroom. Alex was sanding a wood door supported by a workbench. Each deliberate movement strained his tight jeans and accentuated the muscles under his sweat-soaked gray T-shirt. Impressed by his focus she decided to tease him.

"What do you think you're doing?" she said, imitating Mariella's voice.

Isabella bit her lip when she saw him stiffen. "Didn't you hear me?" she continued.

He slowly spun around. When Isabella saw his face

covered in sawdust she burst into laughter. He grabbed a rag and threw it at her. She laughed harder.

He shook his head then chuckled. "Where did that mean streak come from?"

She pointed to her watch. "You're late."

He walked up to her and raised her wrist to read the time. He swore. "I'm sorry."

Isabella rested a hand on her hip. "Yes, well how can a woman compete with a door?" She gestured to what he was working on.

"Just give me a few minutes to clean up."

"No rush. Let me see what you're doing." She walked around to get a better look and blinked amazed at the intricate woodwork.

"Where is this going?"

"It's the door for the back."

She ran her hand lightly over it. "But it can't be, it's gorgeous."

"This house has a lot of hidden treasures." He looked at her, then said, "You don't believe me, do you? Come here." He took her hand and led her to the main staircase. "This woodworking is original."

She touched the railing seeing its beauty, but feeling hollow inside. "I wish I could feel the same way about this house as you do, but when I see these stairs all I wish is that I could see my father come down them one more time. I wish I could hear my mother scolding Daniella for causing scuff marks in the kitchen, and see my sisters playing jump rope in the backyard."

"At least those are good memories. I didn't have a father in my life for long. My mother spent most of her time crying rather than laughing, and Sophia had no place to play. This house means everything to me."

Isabella sat on a step and stared up at him. "What is so important about *this* house?"

Alex glanced away and shrugged. "It's beautiful."

"So? There are many beautiful homes. What drew you to this one? It is just wood and..." "No, it's much more."

"Why?" she pressed.

"Because my great-grandfather helped build it."

Isabella stared at him opened mouthed. "No wonder you want to live here."

"Yes." He sat beside her and although she was acutely aware of him—the feeling of his arm brushing against hers, the scent of sweat and sawdust and his own unique smell—Isabella didn't mind his presence and made no motion to move away. "The Carltons have never owned anything," Alex said. "We've always been laborers and workers who built things we could never afford. I didn't want my life to be like that. We don't pass down much in my family. My grandfather kept some journals where he liked to sketch pictures and he sketched this house and wrote about it."

"Now everything makes sense." She grabbed his hand and turned it upwards. "I'd wondered why a wealthy man would have calluses, You want to honor your great-grandfather by renovating this house, using your hands the way he had,"

He stood abruptly. "No, I'm not that sentimental. I just like working with my hands."

Isabella also rose to her feet and they stood eye to eye. "I see."

He searched her face, his voice deep with regret. "I wish you loved the house as much as I do."

"Why?"

"I don't know."

"Gabby loves it."

Alex dropped his gaze. "Yes, I know."

Isabella squeezed his arm then headed for the door. "Come on, Lex. I have some class notes I want to go over."

He seized her arm and spun her to him. "I want you to call me Alex."

She stared up at him surprised by his serious tone. "Why?"

"Because Lex was a boy. I'm a man now."

She glanced down at his chest then up at his eyes, her mouth quirked with humor. "You think I hadn't noticed?"

"I just want to make sure."

"You don't have to. I know."

"Good. I'm glad you understand."

"I do." She turned and walked to the door. "Come on *Lex*. Let's go over our notes." Before she could get outside she was swept into the air. She cried out in alarm.

Alex held her in his arms and stared down at her. "What's my name?"

She playfully draped an arm around his neck. "You know, you frightened me at first, but this isn't a bad idea. I don't mind you carrying me to the truck."

He tightened his grip and lowered his voice in warning. "Izzy, say my name."

She arched an eyebrow. "What will you do to me if I don't say it?"

"I don't know," he said in a hoarse whisper. "I know what I want to do to you."

"What would that be?" She instantly regretted her bold challenge. Although she didn't know what he wanted to do to her, she knew what *she* wanted to do to him.

She wanted to pull him close and taste his lips and slip her hands under his shirt and feel his chest. She wanted to capture his ear in her mouth and press her lips against the curve of his neck and stoke the heat in his beautiful brown eyes and burn herself on the feel of his hot flesh against her fingertips. She swallowed, not trusting herself to move in case she betrayed her feelings. She could feel his racing heart; it beat in tune with her own.

He bit his lip then unceremoniously released her. "You shouldn't ask questions like that. Just call me Alex, okay?"

Isabella stumbled back her heart fluttering like a trapped butterfly. "Yes, I promise."

"Fine."

She waited for him to move to the door, but he continued to stare at her in a manner that made her insides tremble. "You're angry with me."

He rested his hands on his hips and nodded.

"I won't call you Lex again."

"You think that's the problem?"

"I don't know."

"Are you really that innocent?" He lifted her chin and gazed deep into her eyes. "Yes, you are." He sighed. "I wouldn't want to change that." He headed for the door. "I have another T-shirt in the truck. Let's go."

"Yes, Alex."

The sound of his name on her lips seemed to echo in the silent hall changing something between them. Suddenly, the air felt still as though they were the only two in the world. She didn't know that his name would sound so natural on her lips and he didn't expect to enjoy hearing it so much. But neither addressed how much that moment meant to them, instead Alex nodded and left.

Isabella took a deep steadying breath then followed him.

Their tutoring session that day was short and awkward. Neither wanted to analyze why and deal with what had happened between them. The next time they met at the house they were back to normal and Isabella handed him a plastic container.

Alex stared at it, curious. "What is it?"

"Payment."

He opened the container then smiled, pleased. "Ah, yes the brownies." He looked up at her. "And the milk?"

"I forgot about the milk. You'll get it next time."

"No, I want it now."

"You could make it yourself."

"I want you to make it." Alex left the house and walked toward the cottage. "Don't worry," he called over his shoulder. "We have time."

Moments later, Alex leaned against the kitchen counter watching Isabella stir strawberry syrup in a glass of milk. "Remember to put enough in."

She shot him a glance. "Would you like to do this yourself?"

"No, I'm just supervising. You haven't done it in a while and you may have forgotten."

"I haven't forgotten." She added chopped strawberries, a bit of coconut milk, honey and mixed it all together then handed him a spoon. "Taste it."

Alex ignored the spoon and lifted the glass to his mouth instead. He finished the contents then set the glass down. "Nope. That's not it. Try again."

Isabella stared at him openmouthed.

He laughed. "Just kidding. That was good. Let's go."

WITH THEIR FRIENDSHIP renewed they continued to meet for tutoring and even did their weekend projects together. One weekend in particular, Isabella rushed through the steady drizzle of a mid-April rainfall toward Alex's truck. Although a gray sky hung above, the day seemed bright to her because she got to spend the day with him.

However, on that day, after thirty minutes on the road Isabella grew concerned. "Alex?"

"Yes?"

"We've passed this sign twice." She stifled a grin. "You're lost, aren't you?"

"I know where I'm going. Just hand me that map." He pulled over to the side and parked.

She handed him the map and they looked over it together.

"You're going in the wrong direction," she said.

"Yes, it looks that way."

She looked at him curious. "Couldn't you tell?"

He shrugged. "I got turned around, that's all."

Isabella began to smile as she realized something. "When you took Mariella on that long drive you were lost, weren't you?"

He briefly shut his eyes as though in pain. "Two extra hours with Mariella. For the first time in my life I thought I would burst into tears."

She laughed. "Why didn't you just ask for directions?" When he sent her a look, she held up her hands in surrender. "I forgot, it's a male thing."

Once they found their destination the day was perfect. A little too much so. The rain had given way to sunshine, and the air was clear with a slight breeze whipping up pockets of buttercups. While driving, they discussed their assignment: visit an "authentic" antique shop in the area, and interview the owner. Mr. Yanders had provided a list of certified shops in the surrounding area and each student team had made a selection. Alex, of course, had selected the store the farthest away, at least two hours.

When they arrived at Timeless Antiques, they were greeted by a very friendly middle-aged man who was eager to give them a tour and be "interviewed." Alex had called him several days earlier to explain their assignment and to see if he could put them on his schedule. The store was an antique itself, an old farmhouse built in the early 1800s and remodeled to reflect the Victorian age. It was densely decorated from top to bottom with an array of items, including hand-carved solid mahogany furnishings, marble-top tables, curios, lamps, wardrobes, hardware, furniture and clocks.

Once the interview was over, Alex and Isabella parted to indulge in their own interests then met an hour later at the truck. Isabella leaned against the back of the truck eager to show Alex her surprise for him. When she saw him coming out of the store she could barely contain her excitement. "There's something for you in the back of the truck."

Alex stared at her, barely hearing her words. The full force of her beauty struck him. He'd always been amazed by how joy could alter her face, but he'd never imagined this. She had a look that was timeless. A face that could be carved in maple and displayed in a gallery, but even that would not capture her essence. At this moment, her unattractive clothes and limp hair didn't matter—he saw her beauty as striking as a diamond in the sand.

Alex glanced up and saw he wasn't the only one who noticed. A young man walked past Isabella smiling and stared at her with special interest. When he looked at Alex, his smile disappeared and he hurried away.

"Alex?"

"What?" he snapped, watching to make sure the guy didn't look back. He didn't.

Isabella stared at him confused. "Aren't you curious about what's in the truck?"

Not really. He looked at her and folded his arms so he wouldn't be tempted to remove a strand of hair from her cheek. "Sure."

She gestured to the truck. "Then go ahead."

He opened his flatbed and stared at the large. box. "Another batch of brownies?"

"No, open it."

He lifted the lid and pulled out the object. He studied it a moment then set it down. "How much did you pay for this?"

"You're not supposed to ask that, but you don't have to worry. Your mother helped me. I told her I would do this. It's a nice antique vase to put in your new home."

He leaned on the truck and turned his head away. "Oh, Izzy," he said in a muffled voice.

"What?"

He lowered his head and his shoulders shook with laughter.

Isabella folded her arms hurt. "If you don't like it just say so, you don't have to laugh at me."

He rubbed the smile off of his mouth and sobered.

"I'm sorry. I do like it." He lifted it up again. "It's just that it's not a vase."

"It's not?"

He set it down. "No, it's an urn."

Her eyes widened in horror. "An urn?"

Alex looked at her expression then burst into laughter.

"But it can't be an urn."

He laughed so hard he could barely stand—he leaned against the truck to keep from falling to the ground.

Isabella rested her hands on her hips. "Alex, it's not funny. What's he doing selling urns?"

"Making money obviously," he gasped. "Wait don't be angry. I really do like it. I just see that there are a few more things for you to learn." He draped a brotherly arm around her shoulders. Somehow his touch didn't feel that way, but she didn't move away and neither did he. They both knew it was time to head back, but Isabella didn't mention it and Alex didn't seem inclined to either. He squeezed her shoulder. "I'm hungry." He grinned then patted the side of the urn. Let's take Aunt Lucille to lunch."

Isabella stared at him, shocked. "You can't take *that* with us."

"Why not?" He widened his eyes, appalled. "You can't expect me to leave her in the truck."

She folded her arms and frowned. "You're being silly."

He looked down at the urn with mock embarrassment. "You have to forgive her bad manners. Her mother hadn't taught her any."

Isabella opened her mouth to protest, but stopped when Alex smiled and winked at her. "Come on," he said heading down the street. "I'm sure there are places here to eat," he called over his shoulder.

Isabella glanced around wondering if others were watching him. He made an interesting sight: a tall man carrying a large urn under his arm. When she began to lose sight of him, she sighed and raced after him. "Alex, be sensible," she said ready to beg if she had to.

"What are you in the mood for?"

She threw up her hands, exasperated. "Alex."

He stopped in front of a bistro, glanced at the menu in the window then nodded. "This looks good." He opened the door then gestured for Isabella to precede him.

"I wish I hadn't bought you that stupid thing," she grumbled, sending the urn an evil look.

"So you're not coming with us?"

"No."

"Okay," Alex replied then went inside, closing the door in her face.

Frustrated, Isabella paced in front of the restaurant for several minutes then finally entered. She caught up to Alex just as he was telling the hostess that he wanted a table for three.

"You're being cruel," Isabella muttered as they followed the hostess to a small booth in the back.

Alex set the urn on the vinyl cushion then sat beside it. "Now you won't feel left out," he said to it and picked up the menu. He glanced at Isabella then held the menu up, completely covering his face. "Hold that thought until, after you've ordered. I'm paying by the way. Aunt Lucille insisted. You wouldn't want to make me look bad, would you?"

"As opposed to ridiculous?"

He shrugged then laid the menu aside. "Do I have to order for you?"

Isabella picked up the menu then randomly selected something. "I'll get the Asian salad."

Alex shook his head. "No, you won't. You're allergic to mandarin oranges. Select something else. This time *read* the description."

She blinked, amazed that he had remembered.

"I can have a little," she mumbled annoyed.

He sat back and tapped his chin. "If I remember correctly

the last time you had a 'little' your tongue swelled up like a sausage and you had to eat through a straw for a week."

She snapped her menu shut. "Don't look so smug, I bet I remember more about you than you remember about me."

He leaned forward, a faint light glittered in his eyes, but his tone remained serious. "Is that a challenge?"

It had been, but she decided to withdraw. She lowered her gaze unable to deny that he could be as tempting as a bed to a woman who hadn't slept for days. Suddenly, she was aware that if she moved her leg only a few inches it would be touching his, that the table wasn't as wide as she'd thought. She swallowed, determined to ignore the rush of heat to her face or that he could make her skin tingle by just a glance. She opened the menu instead and ran her finger down the selections. "I'll have this." She pointed to a chicken dish.

Alex pulled the menu to him then shook his head again.

"What now?"

"You don't like asparagus. Don't you read the descriptions?"

"It doesn't really matter to me."

"I can see that. It's probably because you don't take care of yourself." He sighed resignedly as Isabella stared at him outraged. "I guess I'll have to order for you."

"No, you won't."

"Please lower your voice."

"I'm not shouting."

"I meant lower it so that I don't hear you."

She snatched the menu. "You're not ordering for me."

He broke into a wide grin. "Want to try and stop me."

In the end, Isabella decided—she didn't want to think that she had surrendered—to let Alex place the order. The choice was perfect and she enjoyed a succulent dish of red snapper with sautéed seasoned vegetables. She enjoyed her lunch so much that she didn't see what Alex was eating or notice him staring at her until she'd cleared her plate.

Isabella licked her lips. "What?"

A smile tugged on his lips. "You liked it, didn't you?"

She stared down at her empty plate. "No, I hated it." She watched his smile grow and continued to tease him. "I hated it so much that I'm going to come back here and order the same dish just to show you how much I hated it."

The waiter set a large bag on the table. "Here's what you ordered, sir."

Alex took out his wallet: "Thank you. I just need the bill."

Isabella stared at the bag. "What is that?"

"I saw how much you *hated* your lunch so I decided to order more."

"I know I should be ashamed, but I'm not. It was delicious. Thank you."

"You're welcome."

Isabella shot him a glance. "I was talking to Aunt Lucille."

"I'm sorry," he said then leaned his ear toward the urn. He nodded then said, "Aunt Lucille says you're welcome."

Moments later, they ambled back to the truck under the warm, steady gaze of a late afternoon sun. Once inside, Alex handed Isabella "Aunt Lucille" to hold then began their journey back to town. "I wish my schedule wasn't so busy. But after we're married, I think we should spend all day here."

Isabella gasped.

Alex turned to her alarmed. "What?"

"You misspoke," she said unable to look at him, her palms growing moist, and her voice unsteady.

"What did I say?"

"After *we're* married. You meant you."

"Of course," he said quickly. "I meant me...and Gabby. After *we're* married, "I'll—I mean we'll—come back here," he corrected, but somehow his words sounded empty the second time.

"Gabby will love it," Isabella said in a bright voice, hoping to fill the sudden silence, although her words sounded as empty as his. The truth was that, for a moment, what he had said felt right. She'd wanted it to be true. But she soon hated herself for even wanting it to be real. Alex belonged to Gabby, no matter how much she liked to be with him or look at him or talk to him. He didn't belong to her.

Alex nodded not knowing what else to say. *What an idiot!* How could he have made a mistake like that? What the hell was wrong with him? He gripped the steering wheel. It was just a slip of the tongue, nothing more than that. Isabella was right, Gabby would like it there and they'd have a great time. He liked Gabby, he liked her a lot. Then why didn't that make him feel better? The rest of the drive he fought to bring order to conflicting thoughts then felt someone tugging on his arm.

He turned to Isabella who looked at him strangely, "Yes?"

"Are you okay?" she asked.

"I'm fine. Why?"

"No reason. I just wanted to say goodbye."

He frowned. "Why?"

"Because I'm at my house."

He blinked then looked around him. He didn't even remember the drive back. Perhaps it was better that way. "Oh, okay. Goodbye."

"I buckled up Aunt Lucille for you."

He managed a smile. "Thanks."

Isabella glanced at the cottage house where light stood bright against the evening while in the distance the Victorian mansion stood dark and empty like a cave. She turned back to Alex, her hand gripping the door frame. "It was a wonderful day. I had a great time."

"Yes, so did I."

"I'm glad..." she said a little too eager. "That we had a good time," she quickly finished. She waved then dashed into the house. Alex took a deep breath then drove away.

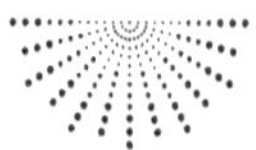

For the next two weeks, Alex's tutoring meetings with Isabella started earlier and earlier. Sometimes they would meet before her appointment with Mrs. Lyons and after, and their sessions became more frequent and longer. Soon others began to notice.

"Do you know what time it is?" Tony said, glancing at his watch as Alex gathered his things prepared to leave.

Alex zipped up his bag. "I'm meeting Isabella."

"How dumb is she?"

He glared at him. "She's not dumb at all."

"Then why do you spend so much time with Isabella?"

"I don't spend that much time."

"You met with her yesterday at six and you didn't return home until nine."

He shrugged. "It was a complicated project."

"How could anything be so complicated that it takes you two hours to figure it out? What do you talk about?"

"Antiques."

"Just antiques?" Tony asked doubtfully.

No, Alex thought. They'd stopped talking about antiques weeks ago. When they met they shared their ambitions and hopes. He felt comfortable with her. Nothing he said was silly or ridiculous. He knew Tony wouldn't understand. Be didn't understand it himself. "Look I'm just helping out a friend okay? She's like a big sister to me."

"I have a big sister and I've never spent that much time with her." He glanced at the urn on the dining table. "How long do we have to look at that ugly thing?"

"It's not ugly."

"Because Isabella bought it for you?"

"It's not like that."

Tony nodded, but didn't look convinced.

Mariella also had her suspicions as she sat in their bedroom and watched Isabella eagerly gather her belongings for her study session with Alex.

"What are you doing?" she demanded.

"I'm going to meet Alex at the library." Isabella sent her sister an odd look. "I told you that."

"No, that's not what I mean."

"Then what do you mean?"

"What are you up to?"

"I'm not up to anything."

"Oh really?" She crossed her legs and swung her foot. "Then why are you spending more and more time with Alex?"

"He's tutoring me."

"He cancelled twice with Gabby because he had a tutoring session with you."

Isabella slowly zipped up her bag. "I didn't know that."

"Well know this." She uncrossed her legs and leaned forward. "I'm not going to let you ruin a perfect plan by confusing him."

"But I'm not—"

"Just listen. It's real easy for a teacher to fall for his student or vice versa." She looked at Isabella closely. "Or has my warning come too late?"

Isabella blushed. "It's nothing." But she knew that wasn't true and it made her heart ache a little. She felt that she could never reveal her true feelings for Alex any more than she could compete with Gabby's beauty.

"It's not 'nothing' if you have feelings for him. He's Gabby's fiancé."

"I know that," Isabella said in a tight voice.

"Then you know what you have to do."

"No, I don't." Isabella sat and faced her. "What do you think I have to do?"

"You can't see him anymore."

The suggestion crushed her. "But he's helping me."

Mariella shook her head with pity. "Izzy, don't make a fool of yourself. You'll only make it worse. Let's face it. It was bound to happen. You're so... uh ...you," she said for lack of a better word. "And he's fun and attractive and young. But it's not what you think. It's not real. He's probably just being nice to you because he wants to help you. You can't see him anymore. You have to tell him that tonight. And if you don't," she said in a low warning voice. "I'll make sure to tell him *and* Gabby how you feel. Now you wouldn't want that would you?"

Isabella swallowed the bitterness in her throat and said, "No."

"Good. It's a harmless infatuation. I've felt it twice in my life. You'll get over it." She turned to leave. "Remember to tell him tonight."

Isabella sat on her bed ashamed of her feelings. Even more

ashamed that they were so obvious to Mariella. Did Alex sense them too? Did he continue to meet with her out of pity? It was ridiculous to have a crush at her age. She walked slowly down the stairs, her hand running along the railing which was a pale imitation of the one at the main house. The one that held so much meaning to him.

Velma met her at the bottom of the stairs. "Off to another tutoring session?"

"Yes, but don't worry," Isabella said passing her. "It will be my last one."

Velma followed. "Wait. Has something happened?"

Isabella opened the door. "No, I've just come to my senses."

ISABELLA WATCHED Alex enter the library. Mariella was wrong. She wasn't infatuated with him. She loved him and that was ten times worse. She could no longer protect herself by remembering the boy he'd been. He was a man now, and every feminine part of her responded to that. As she sat there she wondered what he saw: a poor, plain woman five years his senior who had no education, no money...she was just a name. A Duvall. But that didn't matter. He belonged to Gabby.

"This will be our last session," she announced when he sat down.

He paused and stared at her as though she'd suddenly grown antlers. "Why? What happened?" He smiled. "I know I'm a few minutes late, but—"

"It's not that."

"Then what is it?"

She smoothed out her paper not knowing what else to do

with her hands. "Class is almost over anyway and thanks to you I'm doing so much better. I don't need any more help. And there's so much my sisters and I have to get done planning the wedding and the engagement party."

"You don't have to be directly involved with that."

"Plus, you'll get to spend more time with Gabby. I think it's for the best."

He stared at her, his eyes flat and cold. "Okay."

Their last tutoring session lasted an uncomfortable hour. Then Alex said, "See you in class," and left.

Tony was enjoying a slapstick comedy with a large bowl of popcorn when he heard the front door slam. He turned the TV off as Alex stormed into the room and tossed his bag down. "You're home early," he said surprised.

"She doesn't need tutoring anymore," Alex said in a suspiciously neutral tone.

"You're upset about it."

"I'm not upset about it," he said through clenched teeth. "I have no reason to be upset. So I'm obviously not upset."

"That's good because that would be ridiculous."

"I know that. I'm helping her out and if she doesn't need my help anymore, that's fine. It doesn't bother me."

"Did she give you an explanation?"

"That would have been helpful, but out of nowhere she says we don't need to meet anymore. She wants to give me more time with Gabby."

"How inconsiderate."

Alex scowled. "I spend plenty of time with Gabby."

"You haven't recently."

"I've been busy. She understands. She hasn't complained, but suddenly my time with Gabby is everybody's business."

"It just doesn't look good."

"I don't care how it looks."

Tony stared at him surprised.

Alex held up a hand. "That's not what I mean. Don't try to imply what I think you are implying. There's nothing going on between us. You know I am a loyal man. I made a promise to Gabby and I'll keep it."

Alex made a grand display of his promise to Gabby by showering her with gifts—jewelry, clothes and chocolates arrived at their house at regular intervals. One evening the sisters sat in the living room enjoying his latest present.

"He should have sent you fruit," Mariella said as Gabby bit into a nut cluster.

"He likes me just the way I am."

"Well, no man wants too much of a woman."

Gabby ignored her and took another chocolate.

"You are so lucky," Daniella said.

"Don't worry sisters. Once we're married I'll get you things, too." She handed the box to Isabella. "Go on. Try some."

She shook her head. "They're for you."

"That doesn't mean I can't share. I'll always share everything with you."

Mariella sent Isabella a sly look. "Well, not everything."

Isabella glared at her then looked at Gabby. "Maybe later. After dinner." But she didn't come down for dinner. Instead she stayed in her room.

On the last day of class, Isabella looked at her grade then glanced around the room hoping to show Alex. But he wasn't there. Since their final meeting, he'd started sitting at the back of the class and leaving before she could say anything to him. She left the classroom and headed for her car then saw Alex getting into his truck and called to him. "Alex."

He turned. "Yes?"

She licked her lip then approached him. "I just wanted to thank you." She waved her grade. "You thanked me before." He opened his door.

"Don't be angry with me."

"I'm not angry with you."

"Then why won't you even look at me?"

He didn't move.

"You don't even talk to me anymore."

"I thought that was how you wanted it."

"I don't. I cancelled the tutoring because...I thought it was for the best." When he still didn't look at her she said, "Alex, please."

He reluctantly turned and held out his hand. "Let me see what he gave you."

She handed him the grade like a shy pupil.

Alex looked at it and frowned. "You should have gotten an A."

"I'll stick with my B. I worked hard for it."

"I can go talk—"

She snatched the paper away. "No, I'm happy with what I got. Besides, no one else will know but me."

"And me."

"Yes," she said softly. "And you."

He leaned against the truck, studying her. "Why did you really cancel the tutoring?"

Because I love you. "I told you why."

He shook his head. "I know. I don't believe you." He jumped in his truck. "I'd better go."

Before he closed the door Isabella said, "Friends again?"

Alex paused. "Is that what you want?"

She hesitated, unsure of his tone. "Of course."

"Because sometimes I could..." He held out his hands as though ready to strangle someone. "But sometimes I could..." He let his hands fall then shook his head. "I don't know." That's what bothered him the most. He liked to know things. He didn't like being caught off guard; not being in control. He was usually careful with Isabella. And she'd hurt him—it was stupid, but true–he wouldn't let her do that again.

Isabella shrugged trying to make light of his sullen mood. "I guess we don't have to be friends. We'll be brother and sister soon anyway." She looked away as if something in the distance caught her attention.

Alex drummed his fingers on the steering wheel ready to leave.

She returned her gaze to his hard profile. This wasn't the Alex she'd come to know. She touched his leg in a quick, fleeting gesture. "Alex," she said softly, hoping to break through his hard silence.

At that moment, he bolted from the truck and slammed the door. "What do you want from me?" he asked his voice thick with rage. "Huh? What the hell do you want?"

Isabella took a hasty step back shocked by his vehemence. "Nothing."

"Then why won't you leave me alone?" He tapped the side of his head. "You mess with my mind. Sometimes I don't know whether I'm coming or going. I hate it and sometimes I hate—" He turned to his truck, opened the door then slammed it shut again. The sound seemed to echo in the quiet evening and caused a small night creature to run for cover. He hung his head and said in a flat lifeless voice, "I'm getting married soon."

"I know."

He spun around and caught her gaze with his. "But do you know what that means to me? It means that I'll finally have what I want. I'll finally have a complete family, have someone by my side who can help me get the respect that I need. I can't risk..." He balled his hands into a fist and glanced up at the sky as though searching for answers there. "Gabby loves the house." His gaze fell to her face. "And you don't." Though he said the words as a statement they sounded like a question.

"No, I don't."

He shoved his hands in his pockets. "It doesn't matter anyway. I don't even know what I'm saying anymore."

Isabella's voice was just above a whisper. "I do."

"You do?"

"You want me to leave you alone."

He looked miserable. "No, that's not what I—"

"It's better that way," she said quickly. "You're under enough stress and I have plenty of things to do myself."

"But Izzy..." He reached for her; she moved out of his grasp.

"I'll see you around. We're going to both get what we've always wanted soon. I'm going to Europe with Mrs. Lyons and you'll get married and that's that. I'd better go," she said before he could speak. "Thanks for everything." She raced to her car. When she heard Alex call out to her, she didn't turn around. She didn't want him to see the tears streaming down her face. She jumped in her car and sped away.

Alex leaned against his truck as though sapped of all strength. He watched her go wanting to feel relieved but instead feeling the opposite and not knowing why. He glanced down at the paper that had fallen from her hand and stared at her final grade until everything seemed to blur together. He carefully folded the paper, stuffed it in his shirt pocket then drove home.

DAYS LATER, Isabella stayed in her room trying not to think of Alex, but failing. She heard a soft knock on her door then Gabby entered. "Is everything okay?"

"Everything's fine."

Gabby sat on the bed, her intelligent eyes searching Isabella's face. "Are you sure?"

Isabella drew her knees to her chest, she didn't want to lie to her sister, but knew she couldn't tell her the truth. "Well, to be honest, I still worry about what will happen to us."

"But you don't have to."

"I doubt Alex will want all of us to live with you."

"Why not? There's plenty of room and we all get on so well. It will be wonderful, Izzy. I've told Alex about our debts and he's promised to help us once we're family. And Izzy, you and I can work on the house and make it what we want it to be."

Isabella walked over to the window and stared out at the house in the distance. "I don't want to stay there."

"Why not?"

"I can't." She gripped her hands into fists cocooned in her own misery. "I have to get away."

Gabby came up behind her and rested her hands on her shoulders. "You'll get your chance. Trust me. You'll get everything you want."

Isabella turned to her and forced a smile. "Thank you."

Gabby soon left and Isabella buried herself under the covers. She hated herself for her feelings. Alex had achieved nearly all of his dreams and she hadn't achieved any. She remembered when she was fifteen she'd once bragged that one day she'd move away and travel the world, and yet, she was still here.

She hated herself even more when she lingered on the memory of his smiles, his humor, intelligence and the light that entered his dark eyes when he teased her. Even though the class had ended, her feelings for him continued. She remembered the touch of his hand against hers, the subtle scent of his cologne and the way he spoke about the house. She shouldn't feel this way. He was engaged to her sister; her dear sweet sister who deserved better than her jealousy.

As the engagement party grew closer, Isabella fought a violent battle with her emotions. She was determined to show joy she didn't feel, smile when she wanted to weep and laugh when she wanted to scream. She endured Gabby and Velma's excited plans for the house and the wedding, wishing she could be somewhere far away.

CHAPTER THIRTEEN

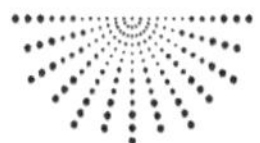

Isabella never thought she would be glad to be in Mrs. Lyons's company, but she was eager to get away from all the engagement and wedding preparations. And with Alex's help, she had amazed Mrs. Lyons on a number of occasions with her now extensive knowledge of antiques. So it was no surprise when, while Isabella sat playing the piano, Mrs. Lyons said, "I've decided to take a companion with me on my travels this year."

Isabella kept her fingers smooth over the keys as her heart began to race. At last her dream would be coming true. She could finally escape. "Really?"

"I don't usually take someone with me besides Ms. Timmons, but I thought about this carefully."

"I'm sure you did."

"So I'd like you to know that I've decided to take Daniella with me."

Isabella's heart cracked; she felt as though her throat would close and choke her, but she managed to say, "Daniella?"

"Yes, and because she would need a companion of her own I thought I would also take someone else."

Her heart began to heal. Of course she would take someone else. She knew Mrs. Lyons wouldn't let her down. "Yes?"

"I'm also planning to take Sophia."

Isabella bit her lip to keep from crying. She missed a note and Nicodemus nudged her and meowed in protest. She focused on the piano keys though they had become blurry.

"I think those two young women will be wonderful on the journey I've planned."

"Oh, I see." Isabella moved her hands over the keys feeling no connection.

"I know you probably had your heart set on going, but I'm sure you can wait until next year."

Isabella continued to play.

"Your sister wasn't sure you would approve. She hasn't said 'Yes' yet. I hope you can convince her and tell her what a wonderful opportunity this will be for her and her friend."

Isabella gave a curt nod.

"Good. I knew you were a sensible girl. Now play me something fast and light. I'm in the mood for Chopin."

When the day ended, Isabella went straight home ready to disappear into her bedroom, but Daniella met her at the front door, anxious. "She told you, didn't she?"

Isabella shut the door with a snap, but kept her tone light. "I would have preferred hearing it from you."

"I didn't want to hurt you and I thought it would be better coming from her."

"Oh." She pushed past her sister and went up the stairs, pleased by how she had maintained her composure although inside she wanted to scream.

"I won't go."

Isabella stopped at the top of the stairs, welcoming the solid railing as needed support, and turned. "Of course you'll go. You'll go with Sophia and have a marvelous time. There's no reason for two of us to be stuck here feeling miserable. And you know what? You have to go because even if you didn't she wouldn't take me anyway."

Tears streamed down Daniella's cheeks.

Her tone softened. "There's no reason to cry."

"But it's so unfair, isn't it? You're the good one."

The good one. She didn't feel good. For one wild moment she hated her sisters. She hated Gabby for winning Alex and hated Daniella for winning Mrs. Lyons, but the feeling soon passed and settled into a deep resigned sadness. She looked at her youngest sister and noticed a subtle change. She dressed more fashionably now and always made sure her hair was carefully styled. Sophia had made a strong impression. A trip to Europe would add a cosmopolitan polish that their mother would have wanted for them. "Promise me you'll write from every country you visit."

"Mrs. Lyons wants to leave before Gabby's wedding. She said she'd planned her trip long before they'd planned their nuptials."

"I'll take pictures."

Daniella ascended the stairs and hugged her. "I love you, Izzy, and don't worry, with Gabby marrying Alex we'll all be happy soon."

"Yes," she said, but her words sounded empty.

Days later, Isabella sat in Martha's restaurant with a cup of coffee and a pastry. She let the coffee go cold and cut the pastry into tiny pieces.

"I thought I'd find you here," a familiar voice said.

She glanced up and watched Alex slide into a seat. She showed a look of surprise at the slick dark suit and tie he wore. It should have given him a quiet commanding presence, but somehow it made him look younger. The thought further depressed her. She didn't want him to be here. Her feelings were too raw and tender. Just the sight of him hurt. The way he sat with broad confidence and vitality made her feel even smaller and insignificant. Alex noticed her attention on his suit and ran a self-conscious hand over his tie. "I just came from a meeting."

She looked down. "Oh. I hope it went well."

He was silent a moment then said, "Daniella told me what happened. I'm sorry."

"It doesn't matter."

"Then why are you sulking?"

She cut her pastry even more.

He pulled the plate away. "I told you that you should have just told Mrs. Lyons that you wanted to go."

"Yes, you're right. You're right about a lot of things," she said dryly. "Congratulations."

The waitress came and placed a plate of stuffed mushrooms in front of them. "I ordered this for you." He pushed the plate towards her.

She pushed it back. "I'm not hungry."

"Gabby said you've barely eaten anything for three days."

"I'm still not hungry."

His dark eyes sharpened. "I'm not going to allow you to punish yourself and your sisters because of the decision of some spiteful old woman. Your sisters love you and you're hurting them by starving yourself. It won't change anything."

She boldly stared back. "I'm not hungry."

"And I don't embarrass easily. So if I have to put you on my knee and force feed you I will."

She folded her arms in defiance; he stood up ready to meet her.

"All right, all right," she said quickly. "You big bully."

He sat. "Say that while you eat."

She reluctantly bit into a mushroom.

He watched her, a smile tugging on his lips. "You're as spoiled as Mariella."

She glared at him. "I am not spoiled. I am not sick and I'm not depressed."

"I know," he said, quietly. "You're angry."

She swallowed hard, fighting the sting of tears.

"Yes, I'm angry. She knew how much I wanted to go. I've worked for her for five years and after only eight weeks Daniella gains her good favor. *Eight weeks!* While I have toiled for hours trying to learn different types of porcelain marks. I've spent money wanting to please her and none of that means anything because she wants a nice, sweet, pretty companion. And I don't fit the bill." She brushed tears away in a quick, vicious manner. "I hate myself for making it matter. But it does. I'm angry that she didn't choose me and I'm angry that you're here. I don't like to be bullied."

"Really? Then why didn't you ever stand up to your mother when she was alive? I saw the way she bullied you around. Why didn't you stand up to your sisters or Mrs. Lyons? You're not angry with me or them. You're angry at yourself. Because the game you're playing isn't working."

She let her hands fall. "I don't play games."

"Of course you do. I know why you cancelled the tutoring sessions with me."

She froze. "You do?"

"You'd outgrown me weeks ago, but didn't want to tell me the truth because you were afraid of hurting my feelings. So you abruptly say it's over and say I should spend time with Gabby."

Isabella didn't reply determined not to show her relief that he was ignorant of the truth.

He continued. "You like to pretend you're pious and patient and sweet with hopes that people will be kind in return. Well here's a news flash, they won't be. If you want something you don't just sit around waiting and hoping for it to happen. You go out and grab it. And if you fail you fail, but at least you tried.

"Do you think I'd spend years hoping to butter up some old woman to get what I wanted?" He laughed cruelly. "No one thought I was good enough for anything. So I had to fight for what I wanted. I had to fight for every scrap. Every cent I own is stained with my sweat and blood. Where do you think I'd be if I'd waited around this town hoping for something to change?"

She was silent a long moment then said, "Do you know the biggest problem with me?"

"I have a few ideas—"

"I'll tell you," she interrupted. "The biggest problem with me is that I'm invisible. Completely invisible. I might as well not exist."

"Don't say that."

"Why not? It's true."

"But—"

She sat back and rolled her eyes. "Don't start with those

'sweet words' you're so good at spreading. I heard what you thought of me at the party."

"That's what happens when you eavesdrop."

"So, you meant what you said?"

He speared one of the mushrooms with his fork. "I don't even know what I said."

"You said I was invisible."

He ate the mushroom then nodded, "Yes, that sounds like something I'd say."

"You were right. But one day I'm going to escape this place and be somebody people notice. Go ahead and snicker."

"I'm not snickering. I'm just curious to know what you're waiting for."

"What?"

"Why wait to leave? Why not be somebody now?" He shook his head before she could speak. "No excuses. You know what the problem is with you?"

"Yes, I just told you."

"No, what you said was wrong, but here's the truth. You're invisible because you *want* to be. Now, before you bite my head off remember you haven't finished your food."

"I don't want to be invisible."

"Then why do you dress the way you do?"

"Because it's comfortable."

"Is that why you always put your sisters first?"

"Someone has to look out for them."

"Or maybe you don't want to appear to be in competition." She stood. "No."

He grabbed her hand, forcing her to stay. "Don't walk away from me."

"Lower your voice."

"I will when you sit down."

She glanced at the door.

He rubbed his thumb against her wrist; his silken voice held a cold edge. "I told you that I don't embarrass easily. But if you don't believe me, try walking away."

Isabella met his gaze feeling the impact of his resolve and knew she couldn't fight it. She sat. "You're infuriating."

Alex released her hand, his tone deceptively casual, and speared another mushroom. "I know." He leaned back and raised an eyebrow. "I also know something else."

She blinked, bored. "What?"

"You're just as attractive as Mariella, just as sensible as Gabby and just as sweet as Daniella. I don't care what anyone else thinks. You don't have to be invisible anymore if you don't want to."

Isabella rested her chin in her hand. "You think it's that easy?"

"Yes. Your mother was wrong. There are many beautiful women in the world and you are one of them. I used to hate watching her with you. You could never do anything right, you always got the second or third best clothing and she treated you like an assistant instead of a daughter. And your father never said anything."

Isabella let her hand fall to the table, offended by his description. "My father was very considerate and my mother had her faults, but she loved us."

"Do you think she loved you?"

"I just said—"

"No, you said she loved *us*. Do you think she loved *you*?"

"Yes."

"Then would she want you here feeling sorry for yourself?"

She held back tears. "No."

Alex stood, shoving the rest of the mushrooms in front of her. "That's something to think about." Isabella sat in the booth trying to make sense of her conflicting emotions. A part of her resented Alex's insight into her life, but another part knew he was right. She had to stop being invisible. She had to stop pretending things didn't bother her when they did. She had to change and she had no time to waste.

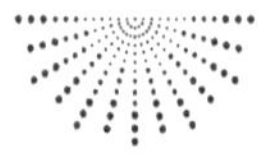

"What do you mean you're giving me two weeks' notice?" Mrs. Lyons demanded.

Isabella drew back the curtains. "Just as I said."

"Oh, I see," she said with a smirk. "You're upset because I'm taking your sister instead of you and this is your childish way of getting back at me."

"No, I'm doing us both a favor. I've never liked you and you've felt the same way about me, so I've decided that it is time for me to leave."

She sniffed. "I've never said I didn't like you."

"You didn't have to. Besides it doesn't matter now."

Mrs. Lyons waved her hands in distress. "How am I supposed to find someone else at such short notice? I'm leaving at the end of the month."

"I know. So it's not a problem. When you return, Daniella could come and help full-time."

"She's still young," Mrs. Lyons grumbled.

"But you two get on so well. There. The problem is solved."

"You're trying to be assertive, but it doesn't become you."

Isabella only smiled.

Mrs. Lyons waved an impatient hand. "Do you want more money? Is that it?"

"No, thank you, Mrs. Lyons."

"But you're the best companion I've ever had. How about if I promise to take you with me next year? I can't cancel on your sister and her friend at this late notice."

"I don't want you to."

Mrs. Lyons nodded satisfied. "So it's settled then. I'll take you with me next year. Now I would like you to read—"

"Mrs. Lyons I don't need more money or a promise of a trip. I'm giving you my two weeks' notice."

"And you've made up your mind?"

"Yes."

She lifted her chin and her eyes grew cold. "Then you can leave right now."

Isabella nodded. "If that's how you feel."

Mrs. Lyons stiffened her chin when it began to tremble. "That's how I feel."

"Very well." Isabella quickly gathered her things.

"I thought you would be more grateful. I was there when you had no one else. I paid you a decent wage. Less than twenty hours a week and you received a full salary and this is how you repay me?" She covered her eyes. "It's unbearable."

"If those tears were real, I'd be deeply moved. Goodbye."

Mrs. Lyons listened to Isabella's footsteps then heard the front door close. She stood and went to the window and watched Isabella walk to her car. This time the tears that flowed down her face were real, filled with the bitterness of regret. She wiped them away and held her head high. No, she didn't care. However, something else did. She caught sight of a lone silhouette as Nicodemus sat like carved wood on the porch railing watching Isabella go.

Ms. Timmons ran after Isabella before she got in her car. "Isabella don't go."

"I have to."

Ms. Timmons gripped her hands together. "She'll forgive you, if you apologize."

"But I haven't done anything wrong."

Ms. Timmons hung her head. "You were always too good for her." She sighed resigned. "Somehow I knew this day would come." She looked up and smiled sheepishly. "I hate to see you go but I understand. Good luck."

"Thanks, I'll need it"

At dinner that evening, Isabella listened to her sisters talk about the upcoming engagement party. Velma and Sophia were out shopping. "I can help a lot more now," she said.

"You won't have time," Mariella said. "I know your class ended, but you still have Mrs. Lyons."

"Not any more."

They all stared at her.

"I quit my job with Mrs. Lyons."

"What!" Mariella said. "Now? You're supposed to quit *after* the wedding not before."

"Well, I did it anyway," Isabella said.

Gabby frowned, "Why?"

"I realized I didn't like her."

"You never liked her," Mariella said. "But that didn't bother you before."

Isabella strategically cut her potatoes into measured pieces. "Well, it bothers me now."

"So what are you going to do?"

"I'll find something."

"Do you know the difficulty of finding a job when you don't have another one?"

"I'll handle it."

Mariella sat as inflexible as marble. "I think it was very thoughtless of you. Fortunately, everything will work out. With Alex as a brother-in-law I'll be able to meet important people." She studied her sister. "I don't know what has gotten into you, but I hope you come back to your senses in time for the party."

Unfortunately, Mariella's hope for her sister to come to her senses didn't come true. A week later Mariella stood in The Orchid Boutique staring at her sister, astonished. "But you can't wear that," Mariella cried. "You'll look ridiculous ."

Isabella looked at herself in the mirror. "I don't think so."

"It has stripes."

"I like stripes."

"Everyone will be looking at you."

She lifted a sly brow. "That's never seemed to bother you."

Mariella rested a hand on her chest. "I'm different. I was born to be admired. You on the other hand..." She faltered.

"What about me?" Isabella pressed.

"You were not born to wear *stripes*," she finished lamely. She turned to her other sisters. "Dani, Gabby say something."

"It's not like you Izzy," Daniella said carefully. "But if you like it..."

Isabella ran her fingers along the neckline "I do."

Mariella rolled her eyes. "Gabby, you're the sensible one. Say something."

Gabby smiled at Isabella. "Promise you'll let me do your makeup."

The spring engagement party for Gabby and Alex was the most talked about event. A large tent stood in the back of the house, on the west lawn. Delicate china sat on sandy-colored tablecloths along with miniature spring bouquets for each of the guests. The soothing sounds from a harpist drifted through the air along with the light scent of sautéed vegetables, red and white wine and smoked fish.

Alex stood next to Tony and watched the crowd.

Gabby came up to him and he kissed her on the cheek. They suddenly heard whispers from behind them and turned and saw a stunning woman in a zebra-striped dress and large wide-brimmed hat. "Who is *that?*"

Gabby smiled at him. "Can't you guess?"

He shook his head. "She must be new in town."

"I know who it is," Tony said. "It's Isabella."

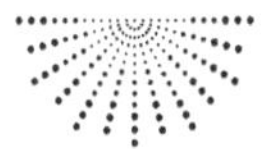

$\mathcal{A}$lex couldn't keep his eyes off of her and neither could anyone else. She seemed as glowing as a spring day. Vividly beautiful. He looked at her in a way that a man shouldn't look at his future sister-in-law.

Tony stared at Alex. "Having second thoughts?" he asked.

"No," he said, sharper than he meant to. "I told you I don't care which sister I marry. I'm not particular."

"Perhaps you should be."

Alex turned to him and frowned. "You've been in a bad mood for weeks. What's wrong with you?"

"I don't like how lightly you talk about marriage."

"Marriage is light. People only pretend to take it seriously. I'm not that hypocritical."

"But you are."

"What?"

"I think it's hypocritical to marry someone when you want someone else."

"I don't want anyone," he scoffed.

"Then why can't you keep your eyes off of Isabella?"

"Nobody else can either. I'm only human."

Tony just stared at him.

He cleared his throat, uncomfortable. "I'm extremely fond of Isabella, but it doesn't extend beyond that. I'm engaged to Gabby and I'll keep my promise. You know that."

At that moment Gabby returned to his side oblivious to his lack of attention. "Everything is fantastic."

Alex smiled at her. "I'm glad you think so."

Elaine Tremain approached the trio, holding a glass of wine. She offered Gabby a quick glance then focused her attention on Alex. "I wanted to offer you my congratulations."

Alex bowed his head. "Thank you."

"I find your engagement extraordinary."

"Then you must be easily amazed because I don't see anything extraordinary about it at all."

"Well the Duvalls have always been an... interesting family. Frankly, I find Isabella's outfit very amusing."

Gabby tensed. "I think—"

Alex stayed her. "Elaine?"

She took another sip. "Yes?"

"Go away."

She stared stunned then left in a huff.

"I can't stand that woman," Gabby said "But now that she's gone let me show you this." She shoved her plate under Tony's nose. "Have you tried this?" She used her fork to point to the slice of roasted almond mousse cake. When she lifted up a piece to take a bite, a cream-covered almond landed on the bare skin revealed above her neckline. "Clumsy me," she said wiping the almond up with her finger and putting it in her mouth. "But never mind, it's delicious."

Tony ripped his gaze from her chest. "I'm glad," he said as though he were choking.

"Are you all right?"

"I'm fine."

"Then go ahead and take some."

He swallowed and shook his head. "No, that's okay."

She snapped her fingers. "I know. You think it's too early for dessert. But I saw something on the table that I think you will love. Just wait right here." She turned and left before he could reply.

"Don't worry," Alex said sensing Tony's tension. "Once we're married, I'll get her out of trying to feed everyone."

Tony abruptly turned. "I'd better go."

"Why? It's still early."

"I think I'm coming down with something."

"But—"

"Tell Gabby..." He took a deep breath. "Tell her I'm sorry."

Alex stared at him confused. "Sure. Take care of yourself," he said and watched his friend disappear into the crowd.

TONY DIDN'T REMEMBER DRIVING home. He just knew he needed to escape. He needed to escape the chatter, the food, the people and even the bright day. He sighed. If only he could escape his feelings for Gabby just as easily. At home he took a shower then prepared something to eat. He wasn't hungry, but he needed something to do.

Unfortunately, cooking reminded him of the time he'd spent with Gabby, so he didn't linger in the kitchen too long. He eventually ended up sitting in the living room eating whole wheat toast. He sat with the lights low and flipped on the TV. When someone knocked on the door he ignored it until they knocked again. He got up from the couch and reluctantly answered. He stepped back stunned when he saw Gabby.

"You're supposed to be at the party," he said in a gruff tone.

Her astute brown eyes remained fixed on him. "You left the party early. Alex said you weren't feeling well. I was worried."

He gripped the door handle until he was afraid it might break in his hand. "You don't have to be. I'm feeling better now."

"Then come back to the party. It's not the same without you."

"Nobody will miss me."

"I'll miss you."

He lowered his head. "I can't go back."

"Why not? Is your leg hurting you?"

He absently rubbed his leg. "A little. You'd better go." He turned.

She touched his arm and he spun around so quickly she cried out in alarm.

"I want you to leave," he said. "I want you to go back to your party and your family and your fiancé and forget about me. Is that understood?"

Gabby blinked back tears. "No, I don't understand. I thought we were friends. We use to have good times. Remember when we were tasting the food from the different catering companies and driving into town for paintings for the house because Alex didn't have the time? Lately I hardly know you. You've been so cold and distant. What have I done?"

He sighed as though he felt the whole world was about to crush him. "You haven't done anything."

"Then tell me what's wrong."

He grabbed her shoulders and peered deep into her eyes. "I've fought a lot of battles in my life. I like to think of myself as a loyal friend, but right now I'm questioning myself. For once in my life I *envy* Alex because I can't fight his youth, his looks or his money." He briefly shut his eyes. "And worst of all I cannot fight how much I love you. I want to marry you." He stepped away from her. "There. Now you understand."

She stared at him speechless. Tony hated the silence. He hated not being able to tell if she was looking at him with horror or pity.

He patted her head as though she were a little girl. "I know it sounds silly to you. I'm a lot older and—"

Gabby stopped his words with a kiss. She gripped the lapels of his shirt and kissed him as though if she stopped he'd disappear. Then she pulled away and said in a breathless rush, "I love you, too. I didn't know it until this moment." She caressed his cheek. "Yes, I will marry you."

Tony stood as if he'd been unplugged. "Are you serious?"

Gabby grinned. "Do you want me to kiss you again?"

"No." He slid one arm around her waist. "*I'll* kiss *you* this time." He crushed her soft body to his solid form, his mouth covering hers with all the passion he'd pent up for months. She moaned with pleasure as his hands skimmed her full curves with deliberate enjoyment. "I can't believe this," he said in a barely coherent grumble.

Gabby kissed his chin. "Will you take me as I am?"

"Definitely." Tony unzipped her dress and lowered her sleeves.

Gabby laughed at his eagerness and shook her head. "No, I mean would you run away with me?"

He paused. "Oh."

She drew away from him unsure of what his response

meant. She wrapped her arms around herself as though suddenly chilled. "I can't go back. I can't face all those people. Especially..." She gazed up at the ceiling blinking back tears then returned her gaze to his face. "Especially my sisters. I'm letting them down."

Tony gently cupped her face in his hands. "We don't have to do this."

Gabby turned and kissed his palm, which had felt warm and safe against her cheek. "But I want to." Her tears slowly dried with the warmth of her love as she studied him. "I want to spend the rest of my life with you."

ISABELLA SCANNED the festive crowd with growing concern. She'd managed to escape her new sea of admirers and wondered where Gabby was. She'd seen her slip away over an hour ago and hadn't seen her since. She knew something was wrong, but Isabella remembered her sister being very vague when she'd questioned her at the time.

"Alex said Tony wasn't feeling well," Gabby said, looking like a child who'd just had her favorite balloon popped.

Isabella lightly touched her shoulder. "Don't let that worry you. I'm sure he's okay."

"It's not like him to just leave a party."

"Gabby, he's a grown man. I doubt anything is wrong."

Her shoulders sagged. "You think I'm being silly, don't you?"

"No," Isabella said carefully. "I just think it's odd that you're worried about one person when you have so many people here."

"You're right. It doesn't make sense." She looked at Alex

with the same careful consideration she'd had all those months ago at the Montpelier Mansion. "Alex is very handsome."

"Yes."

"And kind."

"Yes."

"And rich."

"Yes, but of course that's not everything."

Gabby suddenly turned and stared at her as though realizing something. "You're right. I could leave everything behind."

"What?"

She quickly kissed Isabella on the cheek. "Thank you," she said then walked away and Isabella hadn't seen her since.

Nobody else appeared to notice her absence. They were too busy enjoying the fine food and drink, the opportunity to brag about recent accomplishments and gossip about the misfortunes of others. Isabella saw Velma speaking in low tones to Mrs. Tremain. Although the women stood close, there was no warmth between them. Again she wondered about their connection. Could Mrs. Lyons's rumor about Velma running off with Mr. Tremain be true? Was that how she had been able to afford giving Alex money for his business?

"I hope you know that you look absolutely ridiculous," a condescending voice said behind her.

Isabella turned and saw Mrs. Lyons stroking Nicodemus. She wore a shimmering blue blouse that added an odd unearthly tint to her pale skin. "So glad you could come."

"You're parading about as though you're the one who is about to get married. But I know the truth. You're unemployed and soon you and your sisters will be an unwelcome burden to the Carltons. Or do you expect them to cheerfully dole out an allowance?"

"No, I expect them to rent us a cardboard box. What do you suggest?"

Her keen eyes slowly measured Isabella. "I would say that you look like your mother, but I would be lying."

Isabella smiled. "And I would say you look like a rotted fish and I would be telling the truth."

She narrowed her eyes then sighed with disappointment. "I suppose I can't scare you anymore. Shame. I enjoyed it." She looked down at the cat she cradled in her arms. "When I am gone, I will need someone to look after Nicodemus. I think you'll do. He hasn't been the same since you..." She glanced up. "I will pay very well of course. You know how generous I can be. I also know you need the money, so don't be stubborn about it. I will drop him off next week. Ms. Timmons will give you the exact date and time. All I request is that you feed him and play the piano for him, at a minimum, twice a week."

"I don't think—"

"How does this number sound?" She gave her a large figure.

"Sounds very good."

Mrs. Lyons nodded pleased with herself. "I thought so."

"Thank you."

"You're welcome." She looked Isabella up and down again. "I still think you look ridiculous."

"I think she looks stunning," Alex said as he approached the two women.

Mrs. Lyons transferred her cool gaze to him. "Typical. Carltons always appear at just the right time." She turned and left, Nicodemus's tail swishing back and forth under her arm.

Isabella shook her head. "What did she mean?"

Alex leaned close to her and whispered, "Where is your sister?"

"I don't know." When he softly swore she said, "She probably went to get some fresh air."

"We're outside for goodness' sake, how much fresh air does she need?"

Isabella walked towards the parked cars then stopped. "Her car is gone."

"And Tony's gone, too."

"You don't think...?"

"What am I supposed to think? He was fine one minute then sick the next. He's up to something."

"Gabby wouldn't do that. She wouldn't leave without telling us."

"Prove it."

She nodded. "I will."

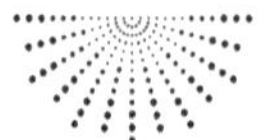

They rushed over to the cottage and Isabella led Alex to Gabby's bedroom. She opened a closet and rustled the clothes hanging there. "See? She hasn't taken anything. Everything is as she left it and—" She stopped.

"What?"

Isabella tossed her hat on the bed and waved a dismissive hand. "It's probably nothing."

"I'll decide that."

"She talked about leaving everything behind." Alex turned and stormed out of the room. Isabella followed him down the stairs. "But that doesn't mean anything."

He walked out the front door. "It means everything." He marched to his truck.

"Where are you going?"

"To prove a hunch."

"I'm coming, too."

Velma came around the corner and called out to them. Alex opened the driver's side ready to jump in.

"At least hear what she has to say," Isabella said.

He sent her a look then slammed the door closed.

Velma approached them breathless. "I'm glad I found you. People are beginning to wonder if the future bride and groom were enjoying an early honeymoon."

Alex leaned against his truck and folded his arms. "There might not be a wedding."

Velma's confused gaze darted between them. "What do you mean?"

"Gabby ran off with Tony."

"We don't know that," Isabella said.

He turned and got in his truck. "We're about to find out."

Isabella squeezed Velma's hand. "Don't say anything until we get back, okay?"

Velma nodded.

AT HIS APARTMENT, Alex found the proof he needed when he walked into Tony's room: Tony's suitcase and clothes were gone. Alex walked back into the living room where Isabella stood waiting.

She looked at him expectantly. "Did you find anything?"

"No, which proves my point. They've gone off together."

Isabella fell into the couch. "I can't believe it. How will they live?"

"They'll probably pawn my ring and live well on that for a while." Alex said in disgust.

"Gabby wouldn't do that. That would be really bad manners."

He stared at her dumbfounded. "Bad manners?" His voice cracked. "You don't think jilting your fiancé at your engagement party and running off with his best friend is bad manners?"

"I didn't mean it like that."

His voice rose. "Then what did you mean?"

"I don't know." She covered her ears. "Stop shouting."

Alex raised his voice louder. "Why? Because a refined rich man doesn't shout?" He kicked over a chair. "Because a refined rich man keeps his feelings hidden?" He grabbed a vase and threw it against the wall where it shattered, leaving a wet stain. "He's not coarse and loud and obnoxious, right?" He picked up a picture and smashed it against the table.

"Alex, stop acting like a child."

He sent her a cutting glance. "What did you say?"

"You heard me."

"You think I'm acting childish?" He gave a mocking bow. "I'm sorry I don't meet the Duvall standard of maturity. I guess that opinion runs in the family considering your sister decided to run off with a man nearly twice her age."

"This isn't about you."

Alex laughed without humor. "Funny, it feels like it's about me since I have to tell a whole bunch of people what just happened." He collapsed into a chair and held his head. Isabella reached for him then stopped. She tapped her foot not knowing what to do or say. She wrung her hands and toyed with her necklace. After five minutes she said, "It's not your fault."

He groaned. "Damn, now you're going to give me the dumped speech."

"The what?"

He looked at her. "The 'it's not you, it's her, it's probably for the best' speech. Things people say that are supposed to make you feel better, but never do." He held his head again. "April 23rd," he mumbled.

"What?"

He sat up. "That was the day my father left. I thought I would die, but I didn't. I survived that and from that day forward I knew I could survive anything and I will."

She stared at him a moment then softly said, "That's, why."

"What do you mean?"

"Every April around that time I used to see you sitting in the alcove staring out the window as though you were expecting someone. You'd be there all day, but I never made the connection with the date. You were waiting for him to come back."

He shook his head. "I wasn't waiting. I never expected him to come back."

"Then why did you go up there?"

He hung his head and was silent for a long time. Then he began to speak, his voice was deep but clear, echoing the pain of his memories. She gripped her hands into fists so that she wouldn't reach out to him. "I wanted to hide," he said. "I always felt that everyone else remembered. People usually looked at me with pity or disdain, but somehow for me that day was different—their looks hurt more. And I didn't want to remind my mother because I was his son. I didn't want to see or talk to anyone except—"

He abruptly stopped, but he didn't need to continue. She knew what he was about to say. He'd only talk to her. Perhaps because she was too young and didn't know the shame or didn't pity him. She never questioned why he was there or when he would leave, they passed the hours away sharing stories, listening to music and playing games. They could be together for hours without tiring of each other's company.

Alex looked at Isabella as though remembering too. He stared at her with such intensity that she grew uncomfortable and stood. "Let me clean up this mess." She went to the closet and grabbed a broom then began to sweep the remnants of the vase and shattered glass from the picture frame.

Alex watched her in wonder as though seeing her clearly for the first time. Why hadn't he noticed before that she'd been the one he'd always turned to, that she'd always been a comfort to him. He had been upset when they'd cancelled the tutoring session because he knew he would miss her and he did—more than he should have, he could admit that now. He knew what he needed to do.

He stood and walked up behind her. "Stop sweeping for a minute."

She kept her gaze on the ground. "I'm almost done."

"Isabella," he said his tone a tender command.

She looked up in surprise. "Yes?"

"I want to ask you a question."

"You can ask me while I sweep."

"No, I can't." He gently took the broom from her. "I need you to look at me."

She met his eyes. "What's your question?"

"I was thinking that we could help each other. You need money and I need... We make a good team and I thought we should get married."

Isabella took the broom from him and began sweeping again, the sound of the shattered glass scraping across the floor, penetrating the silence.

"Didn't you hear me?"

"Yes, I did," she replied in a flat tone.

"Then what do you think?"

"You wouldn't want to know what I think." She bent and lifted the dustpan.

"Yes, I would."

She flashed him a look of such venom that his gut clenched. "I think you're cruel, arrogant and selfish. But I believe we've discussed your faults before so I don't need to go any further than that."

"Cruel?" His voice cracked. "I'm offering you a favor."

"I don't need your kind of favors. Excuse me." She began to move around him, but he blocked her path.

"What's wrong? I'm offering you a great compromise."

"How did you ask Gabby to marry you?"

He glanced up at the ceiling exasperated. "That was different."

"You mean *she* was different."

"Yes."

"What did you say to her?"

"I don't remember."

"Yes, you do."

"It doesn't matter now."

She shoved past him and marched to the kitchen. She dumped the glass in the trashcan.

"I said that she was beautiful," Alex finally admitted. "And that any man would be happy to come home to her and I would like to be that man."

Isabella nodded. "But because you couldn't get your first choice, you'll settle for me."

"That's not what I meant."

"But you have it all wrong," she said bitterly. "You don't have to marry me in order to marry a Duvall. I have two other sisters, in case you've forgotten. And they're beautiful. We can have this conversation again if they decide not to have you. But that's highly unlikely."

"I don't want them."

"Why not?" she challenged. "They have everything you want. The looks, the grace, the name."

"I don't care. I want you."

She shook her head in disgust. "You don't mean that."

"I do." He rested his hands on her shoulders. "I want to marry you."

She narrowed her gaze unsure. "Why?" She held up her hand. "No, I already know why. I'm safe. You'd never have to worry about a man running away with me."

"That's not it."

"Then why? You have so many choices."

"For me there's only one choice."

"I'm sorry about Gabby, but—"

"This has nothing to do with Gabby." His words were barely a whisper.

"I don't understand."

"Then let me explain it to you." His lips touched hers like a light breeze. "Do you understand now?"

The feel of his lips against hers felt oddly flat and void of any emotion. "No."

He brushed her lips again.

Isabella drew away, resting her hands on his chest. "Let's go, Lex." She moved to the side ready to walk around him.

Alex seized her arm, his tone hard. "What have I told you about treating me like a boy?"

Isabella yanked her arm free and glared at him, her voice tense with fury. "If you want me to stop treating you like a boy, then stop treating me like an *old woman.*"

Alex stared at her as if she'd suddenly become a stranger.

In a way she had. He'd placed gentle platonic kisses on her lips as though she were just an old friend. Someone he wanted to form a business partnership or bargain with, not as a woman. He blocked her path when she moved again. "Izzy, I'm sorry."

She dismissed his apology with the wave of her hand. "It's okay. Come on. No more games."

He rested his hands on her shoulders then tenderly slid them down her arms. "You're right. No more games."

Without warning, Alex covered her mouth with such passion Isabella thought she would collapse under the smoldering assault.

"Put your arms around me," he said in a low husky command. When she didn't do so fast enough, he did it for her, pressing her chest against his. She could feel her nipples hardening against the soft lace of her bra.

He deepened the kiss and she shyly darted her tongue in his mouth. He groaned low in his throat, smothering her mouth with a wild, hungry demand until Isabella was pressed against the counter. He unzipped her dress then moved it from her shoulders and let it fall to her feet. "You're so beautiful."

He didn't give her a chance to reply, but she didn't care. She enjoyed the embrace and pressed closer to him, suddenly she felt an odd sensation and pulled away. "I think you're vibrating."

"I wouldn't call it that. I'm certainly on fire."

She laughed. "I mean your phone. I think someone's calling you."

He trailed kisses down her neck. "They can leave a message." Soon the ringing stopped. "See."

But then the home phone rang. "You should probably get that."

"No."

Velma's voice came over the intercom. "Alex, where are you? People are beginning to ask questions."

He broke away and swore. "I forgot about the party."

Isabella pulled up her dress then turned to him. "Please zip me up before you go."

He started to then stopped. "Let's pretend the zipper's stuck. It can miraculously fix itself in five minutes."

"What could we possibly do in five minutes?"

Alex stared at her speechless, very tempted to show her but decided against it. He knew that five minutes with her wouldn't be enough anyway. "Forget it." He zipped her up.

They dashed out the door and raced to his truck. He was about to get in the driver's seat when he noticed a large yellow blossom had fallen on the hood of his truck. He picked it up then looked at Isabella and held it out to her. "Will you marry me?"

She took it and put it in her hair. Then she blew him a kiss and smiled. "Yes."

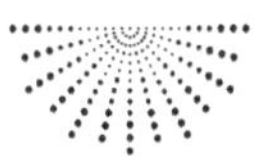

A week later, Isabella stared at her reflection in the mirror with doubts. "Perhaps this isn't a good idea," she said.

"It's a perfect idea and you're going to marry Alex tonight if I have to force you," Mariella said, fixing Isabella's tiara. "I will not let you change your mind. This plan has to work."

"Forget about your plan. What about me?"

"What about you? Your life is perfect now. You're marrying the man you love and he's rich."

"But I'm not sure he loves me."

"Don't worry about the love thing. It's the legal contract that you want. His love won't matter after a few years."

Isabella didn't believe her but decided not to argue. She swatted Mariella's hand away from the tiara. "I don't need this."

"You're going to wear it," she said adjusting the headdress made of Austrian crystals and pearls. She eyed Isabella's simple white gown with regret. "Too bad you couldn't wear the dress, too."

Isabella disagreed. The tiara was enough of a reminder that she was Gabby's last minute replacement; it would have been far too humiliating to have had to wear her dress also. Isabella glanced at the closed door. "At least let me talk to Daniella," she said remembering that her sister was standing outside the door because Mariella had barred her entry.

"You're not talking to anyone until this wedding is over."

Downstairs in the living room Velma and Sophia sat and watched Alex walk around the room checking his watch every two minutes.

Sophia grinned: "You're nervous."

Alex tugged on his watchband then the sleeve of his tuxedo. "I'm not nervous."

"Yes you are," she said in a singsongy voice. "Are you afraid that in the throes of passion she'll look up at you and remember that she used to wipe your nose when you were a kid?"

He glanced at his watch again, Velma nudged her and whispered. "Leave him alone."

Sophia was quiet a moment, but couldn't resist teasing him again. "Or maybe she'll remember how she used to dry your tears."

Velma nudged her harder. "That's enough."

Her grin widened into a malicious smile. 'Didn't she used to change your diaper?"

"Sophia that's enough. Go upstairs and find Daniella."

Sophia reluctantly disappeared around the corner then peeked her head back inside the room and said, "You're nervous."

Alex spun around. "I'm not nervous."

She giggled then left.

Alex turned to his mother. "I'm not nervous."

"Of course you're not," Velma said calmly. "But are you sure that you know what you're doing?"

"Yes."

"Do you promise to be a good husband to her?"

He shrugged. "Sure."

Velma smiled and shook her head. "No, don't be casual about it." She stood in front of him and said in a low voice. "I think we may be the only two people who know you're not marrying Isabella out of pity or to save face. Everyone else thinks it's the opposite, but I hope that I raised a son who will follow his vows. A son who will treat his wife with respect. Isabella has enough people who pity her. I don't want you to give them another reason. Your father was an example of a bad husband. I want you to promise me that you'll be a good one."

He stared back at her feeling the seriousness of her words. "I promise."

She patted him on the shoulder. "Good. Now let me go see if the minister has arrived."

Under a pink and purple sky and in the presence of a stunned audience, Alex and Isabella became husband and wife.

After the minister made the announcement, Mariella grinned proudly, glad that her plan had worked. Then she heard a flash and turned.

"Excuse me," the man behind the camera said. "Have you ever thought of modeling?"

She lifted a brow. "Who wants to know?"

He handed her his card. "I'm a freelance photographer, but I'm also a scout for the Tristan Modeling Agency in the City. Would you mind if sent them your picture?"

She wrapped her arm around his. "No, tell me more."

Less than a week later, Daniella and Sophia flew off to Europe, Mariella signed a lucrative modeling contract and was whisked away into the city, and Isabella moved back into the main house with Alex. Though Velma had helped her pack, she hadn't been able to convince the older woman to move back with them.

"I'd just be in the way."

"But Velma, you wouldn't. There's plenty of room."

She sent Isabella a knowing look. "Not when you're newlyweds."

Isabella carefully folded a blouse, heat touching her cheeks. "It's not like that."

"It will be."

"I didn't expect things to happen this way." She looked at Nicodemus prowling his crate in the corner. Ms. Timmons had dropped him off two days before they traveled. "I almost wonder how it all happened."

"Life doesn't always go as planned, but you have to make the best of it." She zipped up Isabella's suitcase. "You're all ready to go." They each grabbed a bag and Isabella picked up Nicodemus's carrier and headed outside.

"Are you sure you want to stay here?" Isabella asked as they walked toward the main house. "I've gotten used to it."

"But Alex bought the house for you."

"I've grown to love the cottage and Alex will fix it up for me. I'll visit. A house can't have two mistresses."

Isabella stopped and stared at it. It stood tall, proud and beautiful in the bright afternoon. A part of her still detested it and feared that her feelings would never change no matter how much she loved Alex. "A part of me is afraid that I can't measure up. He and everyone else will expect me to be as my mother was."

"Just be yourself, Isabella. I know you'll do just fine." They walked up the front steps together then Velma set her bag down. She kissed her on the cheek. "I know you will."

For a long moment, Isabella watched Velma walk away then she turned to the door ready to face the inevitable. She knocked on the door. Alex opened it as though he'd been waiting. She jumped back startled.

"Let me help you," he said, grabbing her bags.

"Thank you." She followed him inside then stopped, astonished. She was first struck by all the exposed wood trimmings around the doors, windows and walls. Alex and his crew had painstakingly taken off layers of paint to reveal the original dark oak. In addition, with the use of glass blocks and strategically placed dome shaped skylights, the natural lighting immediately made the place appear bigger. It did not look or feel like the house they had lived in.

Alex studied her. "Would you like a tour or do you want to settle in first?"

"A tour would be nice."

Isabella did not close her mouth as Alex showed her all of the changes that had been made. Two stained glass windows had been added to the living room and one of the walls removed. The old fireplace had been renovated to reveal intricate woodworking detail, and colored slates replaced the ordinary white wood frame. In the dining room, a platform ceiling had been added along with an antique crystal chandelier. Off to the side, where her father's office had been, floor to ceiling bookcases had been refinished, revealing the light pinewood and designer trim around the ceiling.

All of the bathrooms were now installed with original

antique finishing, free-standing bathtubs with bronze claw feet and newly installed circular showers and separate commodes.

Her favorite room was the conservatory. Alex had skillfully taken what had been the large family room on the main floor and totally transformed it. He had installed an assortment of built-in shelving, wood molding and exquisitely designed wall lamps. And in the middle of the room, sat a grand piano graciously surrounded by a collection of thin wrought-iron windows.

"It's beautiful," she said at last.

"We can make new memories here," he said.

"Yes," she said quietly, wondering if new ones could erase the old ones imprinted on her heart.

Isabella unpacked her bags and looked around the master bedroom. She'd released Nicodemus and he had disappeared somewhere downstairs. It was evident that Alex had the room decorated with Gabby in mind, which depressed her. The walls were painted a soft lime-green—one of Gabby's favorite colors—with matching bedcovering and curtains. Every day would be a reminder that she was her sister's replacement. She was Alex's last desperate choice to marry a Duvall. Every day she would wake up and remember that she wasn't supposed to be here, that she was meant to be somewhere else.

Isabella brushed the thought aside; nothing could be done about it now. She would make small changes so that in time the room would feel like her own. If she was to be the new mistress of the house she would have to act like it. Isabella jumped when she heard a bell ringing. Dinner was ready. She gathered her courage then headed downstairs to eat with her new husband.

He was coming to get her and Isabella halted on the stairs

when she saw him. "Where are you going?" she asked looking at his three-piece suit.

"To dinner."

"With whom?"

"With you."

She frowned confused. "I thought we were eating in."

"We are. The cook just left."

She covered her mouth to keep from laughing. "You dressed up to eat dinner at home?"

"Yes, I thought rich people did that."

"Maybe some, but not like that. And *we* certainly didn't."

"I remember that your father always looked polished."

He scowled. "What's so funny?"

She bit her lip.

He surveyed himself. "Do you think I'm overdressed?"

Isabella managed to control her laughter, descended several steps and said, "Let me help you. First you don't need the jacket." She pulled it off and hung it over the railing. "Or the waistcoat." She unbuttoned it then stripped it off also. "And you can loosen your shirt." She undid one button on his shirt then stopped when she realized what she was doing.

"Continue," he challenged. "I'm beginning to enjoy myself."

She jerked her hand away. "No, I think you're all right now. There's nothing else to remove."

Alex clicked his tongue in disappointment and rested a foot on the step behind her. "Aren't you even curious?"

"About what?"

"Whether I wear an undershirt."

"I never thought about it."

He brushed his knuckles against the line of her jaw. "You're not even a little curious about me?" His gaze swept her. "Because I'm curious about you." Be gently removed her cardigan. "Very curious." His hands moved to the front of her blouse and undid her buttons in swift deliberate movements and soon her blouse fell away. Tingles raced up her arms spreading like wildfire as his hand skimmed down her bare arm. "It's your turn now," he whispered.

Her voice came out in a breathless rush. "My turn to do what?"

"To be curious." He took her hand and rested it on the front of his shirt. "Don't be shy."

"I'm not shy."

"Neither am I."

At first she fumbled with the buttons of his shirt and twice she glanced up at him to see if he was silently laughing at her. But he wasn't. He continued to watch her with an electrifying intensity that made her more eager to break down the barriers between them. Once she had unbuttoned his shirt she bit her lip then touched the contours of his chest with her fingers as she'd once imagined doing. "You don't wear an undershirt?"

"No."

"I'm glad."

"Show me how glad," he said in a thick, husky voice.

Isabella moistened her lips then pressed them against his bare chest. "This glad." She moved down to his stomach and kissed him there, causing his muscles to constrict. "And this glad." She moved back up and kissed his nipple. "And this glad." Isabella reached up and held Alex's face in her hands, staring at his full lips. "I'm glad that I married you." She kissed his mouth expecting the wild sensations of when they'd kissed before. But this time was different. Somehow his mouth tasted sweeter, softer and the feel of his lips made her senses swirl.

Alex didn't have to say anything, his persuasive mouth

made that point clear. He brought her close and the glorious feel of his bare flesh against hers aroused the sensitive area between her legs and made it grow moist with liquid heat. She skimmed her hands over his defined chest muscles. "Our dinner will definitely be getting cold."

"Who cares?"

"I thought you were hungry."

He laughed. "I am." He cupped her bottom, pressing the evidence of his desire against her. "Can't you tell?"

"We shouldn't do this now." She said the words, but they held no meaning. She didn't want to be anywhere else, but in his arms, feeling his rough, calloused fingers sliding over the contours of her bare skin as though he were examining a fine antique.

"But I want to."

She pressed her lips in the curve of his neck then gently bit down in playful warning. "Didn't anyone teach you to listen to your elders?"

"I'm listening." He took one of her breasts in his hands and rubbed his thumb across her nipple. Just tell me what to do."

"What you're doing right now is nice."

"I can do better than *nice*." He covered the top of her breast with his mouth, teasing her nipple with his tongue.

Isabella sunk to the ground, the throbbing between her thighs growing more intense. "Alex," his name was a primitive plea on her lips.

He gathered her in his arms and said, "I'm not doing this here." He meant to take her upstairs, but when she darted her tongue in his ear, he forgot all about his intentions and rested her on the landing. He struggled to tame the fierceness of his desire, determined to be tender with her. He never thought he could love anything more than the feel of finely sanded wood, but Isabella's body proved him wrong. No piece of wood, no matter how refined, felt like this. Her body made his hands feel as though they were on fire and he couldn't get enough of her. They continued roaming over every part of her, feeding the growing ache inside him.

Alex brought her tiny soft frame close, groaning as her shapely curves seemed to fill the contours of his body, and entered her with a slow, deft motion careful to make her first time as painless as possible. He felt her wince and touched her cheek to soothe her. "Shh, don't tense up on me. Welcome me inside. You're going to like this."

Isabella stared at him, her eyes bright with unease. "Is that a hope or a promise?"

He grinned. "It's a guarantee. I take care of what belongs to me. Trust me."

He moved inside her and watched her face; he watched to see what she liked and what she didn't like. When he didn't get a positive reaction, he began to pull away ready to find another way to please her.

Isabella grabbed his arm. "Don't. Keep going." She arched her pelvis driving him deeper inside the tight warm fit. Her complete surrender was nearly his undoing, but he managed to keep rein on his own passionate desires; he made her enjoyment his ultimate goal. He watched her face flood with pleasure and heard the soft cries of her satisfaction. He never knew what a gratifying activity it could be to watch the rise and fall of her nipples, to notice beads of sweat gather between her breasts, and to see her breathing grow shallow.

"It's okay," she said, trailing a finger along his clenched jaw. "Let yourself go."

They both thought they would explode from the force of ecstasy that cascaded over them. Nothing else mattered—not food, time or place—as they tried to satisfy what felt like an insatiable hunger. They made love until they thought their muscles would turn to mush and Alex nearly collapsed on top of her, but rolled away before he did. He closed his eyes trying to remember how to breathe. "I think we're done."

Isabella clicked her tongue in pity though she was as exhausted as he was. "I've tired you out. I guess I'll have to go out and get a younger man."

He tightened his hold around her waist. "Just try to get away from me," he said, his tone a deep, sensuous challenge.

"I can hardly move."

Isabella rested her cheek on his chest, her body feeling light and free as though it could dissolve into thin air. All her life she'd been surrounded by beautiful things and beautiful people, never thinking she could be one of them, but Alex had changed all that. He made her feel gorgeous, as if she were the most desirable woman in the world. "I love you," she whispered.

He folded her in his arms and held her tightly. She pressed her lips on his bicep then forearm. Alex opened his eyes and stared up at the ceiling then noticed the railing, and swore.

Isabella sat up and looked at him concerned. "What is it?"

He covered his eyes and groaned as though in pain. "I took you on the *stairs*. Your first time and we did it on the stairs." He let his hand fall and gazed up at her. "I doubt this is what my grandfather had in mind."

She rested his hand on her hip then began kissing his chest. "At least we proved this structure was well-made."

He skimmed the length of her thigh with due appreciation. "It's not the only thing that's well-made." He stood then lifted her up. "Let's see if the bed's well-made, too."

They never made it to dinner that night, and nearly missed breakfast and lunch too the following day.

"I'm starving," Alex said. They lay in bed together, the bright afternoon sun warming the room through the large bay window.

Isabella traced a path on his chest. "I'm not."

"You'd better get used to eating." He placed his large hand on the gentle curve of her stomach. "You could be eating for two soon."

"That's not likely."

He stilled. "Why not?"

"I'm on the pill." She laughed as his expression changed. "Don't worry. I haven't been with another man," she said quickly. "I use it for feminine issues."

Alex took a deep breath taking hold of the rush of jealousy that had seized him. "Oh."

Isabella placed her hand on top of his and smiled at the thought of carrying his child. "But I can stop anytime you want."

His eyes darkened and it was clear that the thought pleased him too, and for the rest of the day they forgot all about food.

*A*lex and Isabella spent the next week doing two things: eating and discovering positions in which to enjoy each other. One afternoon, while they were resting, a loud piercing cry invaded the silence.

"What is that?" Alex asked.

Isabella listened then jumped up. "Damn, I forgot."

"Forgot what?" he asked watching her hastily pull on clothes.

"Nicodemus."

"We haven't forgotten about him. We've fed him every day."

"I know, but I haven't played the piano for days." She dashed out of the room.

Alex swore then followed her. He was halfway down the stairs when he remembered he'd forgotten to change. He swore fiercely, returned to the room and pulled on jeans then went downstairs. He found Isabella in the living room opening the piano and talking to the cat beside her who continued to loudly voice his annoyance.

"I know, I promised," she said, trying to calm him. "Just give me a minute."

"Are you sure there's nothing else wrong with him?" Alex said wincing as Nicodemus meowed again.

"No, he likes the piano. It soothes him." She sat down and flexed her fingers.

Alex sat beside her. "Okay, get started."

Isabella looked at him uncertainly. "Umm... you can't sit there."

"Why not?"

"Because Nicodemus likes to sit next to me when I play."

Alex folded his arms "Well, too bad." He looked down at the cat who sat by his foot, staring up at him through narrowed gray eyes.

"You don't want to upset him. He can get really nasty."

"So what?" He stared down at the cat. "What could you possibly do to me?" Nicodemus continued to stare at him, twitching his tail slowly from side to side. Alex turned to Isabella. "See?" he said, flashing a smug grin. "He knows who's boss." At that moment Nicodemus leapt up and locked his claws on Alex's bare chest. Alex cried out and fell off the piano bench.

He tried to pull the cat off, but Nicodemus sank his claws in deeper.

"I'm going to kill him."

Isabella fell to her knees and tried to break them apart. "Lie still Alex! Stop and he'll let go."

But he didn't listen and continued to struggle with the cat.

"Nicodemus get down!" Her words appeared to work like a switch. He retracted his claws, jumped down then walked over to her.

Alex sat up then winced, grabbing his chest. He glanced down and saw the blood on his palm and felt streams of it sliding down.

"You naughty, naughty cat," Isabella said. Nicodemus slowly closed his eyes then opened them again.

"I should put you in your carrier."

"You should put him in that urn," Alex said, gesturing to the object he'd set on the mantel.

She frowned at him. "Don't say things like that."

"Why not? I plan to kill him." He rose to his feet, holding the cat in his line of vision. Nicodemus arched his back and hissed.

"Alex, you're antagonizing him," Isabella said. "I told you he could get nasty."

"Well, so can I."

She picked the cat up. "No more fighting."

Alex stood and stared at her incredulous. "You're protecting *him?*"

A smile tugged at the corner of her mouth. "I'm protecting you."

He narrowed his gaze, insulted.

"Go upstairs and I'll bandage you up."

He pointed to the cat. "Wait until we're alone!"

"Alex," Isabella said.

He headed for the stairs. "I'm going."

Moments later Alex sat on the bathtub rim while Isabella cleaned his wounds and applied ointment. "He got you really good."

"Don't worry. I'll return the favor."

"You can't hurt that cat."

"Why not?"

"Because he belongs to Mrs. Lyons."

"Which is another reason to teach it a lesson!" Alex suddenly stiffened. Isabella looked up and noticed him staring at something in the distance. She turned and saw Nicodemus sitting in the doorway licking his paw. "A big lesson," Alex said ominously.

"Forget about him."

Alex pointed to the cat. "You wait 'til she falls asleep. Then it's just you and me."

Isabella grabbed his face, forcing him to look at her. "I told you to forget about him. I'll deal with him." She bandaged Alex's wounds then stared at her handiwork. "There. Just like new. But you'll have to rest. It seems you'll have to find something else to occupy your time."

He rested his hand on her thigh then began to knead it. "Like what?"

She moved his hand away. "Something besides what we've been doing."

His gaze flashed with outrage then grew dangerously cold. "You know that cat's dead, don't you?"

"Don't say that. I know you don't mean it."

He put his hand back on her thigh and slowly inched upwards. "Do you know what I had planned to do to you tonight?"

She stepped back from him. "I'll find out another time. Come lie on the couch. I'll play for you both." Alex was not pleased with the arrangement, but Isabella managed to convince him to rest on the couch while Nicodemus sat beside her on the piano bench. She played and Nicodemus purred with pleasure. By the time she was finished, Alex was fast asleep.

WITH ALEX RECUPERATING from his wounds, Isabella knew she had to fill her time with something and decided to go into town to shop. She hadn't been around people for so long she wondered if everyone could sense what she had been up to for the past week because she was acutely aware of how her body felt.

"I know what's going on."

Isabella spun around and faced Mrs. Tremain. "I'm sorry?"

"Your sister found out the truth about them, didn't she?"

"What?"

"I thought about warning you, but I wasn't sure it was my place. I knew your parents wouldn't have wanted such a union, but I knew about your desperate situation so I kept my nose out of it, but once I heard what your sister had done, I thought, 'Bravo'."

"Mrs. Tremain, I'm sorry, but I don't know what you're talking about."

She hesitated. "So your sister didn't tell you why she left?"

"No, she didn't."

"And Velma hasn't said anything?"

"Should she?"

Mrs. Tremain shrugged, but looked relieved, "Good. It's best to stay naive."

Isabella's curiosity about Mrs. Tremain and Velma came to the forefront again. Upon reaching home, she saw Velma working in her flower garden and decided to say hello.

"I just bumped into Mrs. Tremain."

"Oh?" she said with polite interest.

"She said hello."

"That's nice."

"I thought, perhaps we could have her over for dinner?" She watched Velma closely, but Velma revealed nothing.

She shrugged. "If you want to. How are things going between you and Alex?"

Isabella shifted awkwardly. "We're getting to know each other."

"That's good. It's important to enjoy each other's company."

Isabella felt her face grow warm, remembering just how much they were *enjoying* each other. "Yes."

Because she couldn't enjoy Alex as she would like to, Isabella busied herself by going on antiquing sprees. One day, when she returned home from shopping, she saw a platinum, silk, nightgown on the couch with a note that said *Look inside the piano*. She did and found a pair of red panties with a note that said *Look in the kitchen pantry*, which she did and discovered a pink lacy bra with another note leading her to the solarium. Ten minutes later she ended up with five panties, three nightgowns, a garter belt, a white teddy, three bras and a note that said *Look in the bedroom.*

Isabella cautiously opened the bedroom door and saw a brand new bedroom ensemble in zebra stripes with curtains to match.

"Do you want to try it out?" Alex asked from behind her.

"It's wild."

"That's how you make me feel. And I remember you wearing something like it before."

"I can't believe you did this."

Isabella walked towards the bed then dropped all her new gifts on it. She wouldn't feel like Gabby's replacement in this room anymore, it was all hers. Isabella touched the finely woven Egyptian sheets. "It's beautiful. When did you manage to do all this? You were supposed to be resting."

He pulled her into his arms and kissed her. "In case you haven't noticed, I'm feeling better."

"I'm noticing it now." She kissed him back. "Thank you for everything."

"You're welcome."

"But you forgot something."

"What?"

"You bought me things for my bed."

"Yes."

"And things I can wear in my bedroom."

"Yes."

"But nothing for when I leave it."

He stared at her with a blank expression.

"You didn't buy me any clothes."

"That's okay. I like you naked anyway."

"I doubt you would like me greeting your guests that way."

He paused, thoughtful; she hit him.

"I'm just imagining the look of envy on all the men's faces."

"Yes, come to think of it. I did catch Roland Quick looking at my butt at the engagement party."

Alex's gaze sharpened. "He did?"

"Yes, and my zebra dress made Matthew Gable think of wild things, too. I wonder what he would have said if he saw me naked. And then there's..."

"We're buying you new clothes tomorrow."

"Thank you."

"For now, try something on."

Isabella began to, but once she stripped down, Alex didn't see a need for her to put anything back on and they missed yet another dinner.

SEVERAL DAYS LATER, Alex woke up to a loud piercing scream. He jumped out of bed and raced down the stairs. Isabella crashed into him as she darted around the corner, gripping the urn against her chest.

He steadied her. "What's wrong?"

"I can't find Nicodemus anywhere and this urn is full."

He shrugged. "So?"

She stumbled back as if he'd struck her. "Alex, you didn't."

He widened his eyes at her accusation. "Of course I didn't. The urn is full of dirt. I was bored one day and decided to see how much it could hold. What kind of man do you think I am?"

"You said—"

"I know what I said," he cut in. "But I'd never do it."

"Then where is he?"

"Causing the devil some trouble if we're lucky."

Isabella hit him. "Stop that. We have to find him."

Alex shook his head then reluctantly agreed. "Okay, I'll look outside." He took the urn from her. "Calm down. I have a bad feeling that he's fine."

Ten minutes later Alex found Nicodemus on the roof. He stared up at the cat with the urge to leave him up there, but knew that Isabella wouldn't like his decision. He went into the top room alcove then climbed out the window. Alex. held out his hand. Nicodemus stared at him, but didn't move. "Come here you dumb animal."

Nicodemus began to arch his back.

"Okay, okay. Let's come to a truce. I won't threaten to kill you and you won't touch me again. I don't believe in hurting animals, but I do make exceptions for demon spawn."

Nicodemus hissed. Alex raised his hands in surrender. "Okay, okay. No more insults. I'll talk to you nicely. Please come here."

Nicodemus turned his head away.

Alex hung his head in defeat. "Fine, I can wait." He leaned back against the house, the wood siding warm against his bare back as the summer sun cascaded over the finely manicured lawn. He laughed at the sight he imagined they made: a cat and a half-naked man sitting on a roof. Five minutes passed, then Nicodemus turned and walked up to him. He sat down beside Alex's thigh and waited.

At first Alex didn't move then he held his hand out and Nicodemus pressed his wet pink nose against his palm then bent his head. Alex scratched him behind the ears. "Ah, so I guess we're friends now, huh? We both pretend to be big bullies but we're softies inside." Nicodemus began to purr.

Isabella peeked her head out of the window. "So this is where you are. I've been looking everywhere."

Alex picked Nicodemus up then crawled back inside. "We had to discuss a few things."

"And everything's all right now?"

Alex kissed her on the forehead. "Everything is perfect."

As more time passed, Isabella started to believe Alex's words. Things did seem perfect. She began to settle into her role as mistress of the manor. It was the same title her mother once had: Mistress of 143 Waverly Lane. And she looked the part. As promised, Alex bought her an entire wardrobe of new clothes and jewelry. After their first dinner party, which, proved to be a huge success, Alex lay on the bed and watched Isabella slip out of a cream dinner gown he'd had made for her. He'd never get tired of watching her. "I told you that you had nothing to worry about."

Isabella pulled on a robe. "I know. It's just that the reputation of the Duvall mansion is so important." She glanced up and saw a strange look on her husband's face. "I mean the Carlton mansion."

He sighed. "I suppose it will take a while for people to get used to that."

Isabella sat down on the bed, resting a hand on his leg and smiled at him. "Don't worry, I'll make sure that they do."

Alex placed his hand on hers and stared deep into her eyes. He had everything that he wanted, but he wondered about her. Are you happy?"

Isabella pulled away from his grasp and stood. "I'm so glad things went well. It was a great party, wasn't it?"

His heart fell, but he kept his voice as bright as hers. "Yes, it was."

HAVING GUESTS SOON BECAME ROUTINE. They held lavish parties and quiet dinners; entertaining the very high to the low. Soon Alex and Isabella were the most talked about couple in the county.

Not only were people impressed with her entertaining skills, but Isabella also became involved with various charities and reconstruction projects in town.

And Isabella found joy in her new role, but restlessness still seized her. There were still times when she didn't want to return to the house although she knew it had changed and

Alex would be there. She told herself the past was over, but the house still seemed to talk to her. Seizing her mind and flooding it with melancholy memories. When Alex was home the voices were silent, but when she was alone she heard the distant whispers.

Isabella thought about her sisters often and missed them desperately. She regularly received letters and postcards from Daniella (with a note from Mrs. Lyons warning her that she'd better be treating Nicodemus well). Occasionally, she got a note from Mariella, but it was usually a photograph or a magazine picture with her face. She still hadn't heard from Gabby and wondered if she ever would. Isabella knew that Alex probably wouldn't want to hear from the couple, but she knew she couldn't live with not knowing what had happened to her beloved sister. The guilt that she might have convinced Gabby to run away lingered and was a heavy pain on her heart.

Autumn soon came and Velma caught a cold that turned into pneumonia. Isabella brought her into the main house so she could take better care of her. A chill of déjà vu went through her as she remembered her mother's 'simple' illness turning into much more. She was determined to do all she could.

For the next two weeks, Isabella took care of Velma, forgetting to take care of herself. She made sure Velma was fed while forgetting her own meals. And as Velma grew stronger, she became weaker and weaker.

Alex noticed the change in her—the dark circles under her eyes and lost weight. "Did you have breakfast this morning?" he asked her as she came out of Velma's room.

"I will."

"You don't have to look after her the way you do. She's getting better. I could have a nurse come in."

"It's okay. I like to help."

He grabbed her arm. It scared him how thin she felt. "You've helped enough."

"I'll know I've helped enough when she's completely better."

"No, you've done enough now."

"I can't just sit around and watch nurses come and go. I have to do something."

His tone became gentle, finally understanding her fear. "She's not going to die, Izzy."

"I know. I'm going to make sure." She walked past him and Alex watched her helplessly.

On a cool autumn day that brought the promise of rain, Daniella and Sophia returned from their travel abroad in Mrs. Lyons's car. Isabella greeted them with Nicodemus already in his carrying case. When the two young women saw Isabella standing in the doorway, they stared at her, shocked by the way she looked. The two were too kind to say anything, but Mrs. Lyons was not.

"Doesn't he take care of you?" she asked.

"Of course," Isabella said surprised by the vehemence of her statement. "He's wonderful."

"Then why do you look like a scarecrow? Is the man so vain he doesn't notice that his wife is about to collapse?" She raised a knowing brow. "I get it. You barely see each other and you love him so much that it's eating you up inside."

"That's not it at all."

"Leave her alone," Daniella said, putting a protective arm

around Isabella. "I'm sure we've just caught her at a bad time. Tell Isaac to help us with our bags, please."

Mrs. Lyons turned on her heel and returned to the car with Nicodemus's carrier. Daniella turned to her friend. "Sophia go say 'hi' to your mom, tell her I'll come see her later." She didn't wait for a response and led Isabella inside the house. She was too concerned by her sister's altered appearance to notice the changes to the house.

"Are you sure everything is okay?" Daniella asked as they sat in the kitchen.

"Everything is fine." Isabella looked at her sister, aware of the change in her, impressed by her marked maturity and refined manners. "I'm truly happy. I've just been busy taking care of Velma."

"She's sick? Why didn't you tell us?" Daniella asked alarmed.

"She's much better now." Isabella grabbed Daniella's hands. "Thank you for all of your letters. I felt as though I were there. Tell me all about the last part of your trip." Daniella did and Isabella listened while her heart ached thinking of the travels she wanted to take. She wondered if she'd ever take them, or if her destiny was never to leave.

Alex glanced at his watch as he waited at the checkout of Martha's restaurant. The owner fluttered around him like an anxious rooster. "Your wait won't be much longer," he said blinking furiously.

"Fine," Alex replied. He knew he was making the man nervous, but was too preoccupied to calm him. His sister and Daniella would be arriving back soon and he wanted to be there to greet them. He also wanted to wave goodbye as Isabella returned that damn cat to Mrs. Lyons. Although there had been a truce, Nicodemus could still be a nuisance when he wanted his way and Alex hadn't always been in the mood to let him have it. He was glad to see him go.

Alex looked at the menu again and wondered if he should haye ordered two appetizers instead of one. He had noticed that Isabella had been looking frail lately and he wanted to treat her. She had a bad habit of skipping meals when he wasn't paying attention.

At last the owner handed him his takeout. Alex opened his mouth to thank him when he noticed that the man suddenly looked thunderstruck. Alex was about to ask him what was wrong when silence fell around him. He turned to see why and saw Gabby and Tony taking a seat. Gabby saw him first, then Tony. Alex felt the flames of temper clawing at him, remembering the embarrassment they had caused him, but quickly got control. He thanked the clerk then approached the table.

Gabby sent him an uneasy glance, but Tony's gaze didn't waver. Alex took a seat and said pleasantly, "This is a surprise."

The couple looked at each other but didn't say anything.

"I know my wife will be happy to see you," Alex continued.

"So you managed to get married after all," Tony said.

"Yes."

Gabby gripped her hands together. "Alex, will you ever forgive me?"

Alex smiled. "Of course. I could never stay mad at you." He stood. "Besides we're family now."

"What?" they chorused.

"Just as I planned, I married a Duvall. The prettiest one."

Tony fell back in his chair and stared at Alex as though he'd turned into an alien. "You married *Mariella?*"

"No."

"*Daniella?*" Gabby guessed.

He shook his head. "No."

They paused. Then looked at Alex then each other then Alex again. Suddenly, as though in slow motion, their eyes widened and their mouths dropped open. "You married *Isabella?*"

Tony shook his head amazed. "I should have guessed."

Gabby blinked. "I don't believe it. She was the only one who didn't want to marry you."

Alex shrugged. "Let's just say she changed her mind."

"Why?"

"Because I can be very convincing."

"You *wanted* to marry her?"

"Of course I did," Alex said offended. "Why wouldn't I?"

"I'm not suggesting that you wouldn't. It's just...I never considered..."

"That a man would find Isabella attractive?"

"No, I just never pictured you two together."

"You shouldn't be so surprised." Tony said.

"I can't help it." She sent him a curious look. "Why aren't you?"

He shrugged. "Few things surprise me." He pointed to Alex. "Especially when it comes to him."

"Oh," Gabby said unsure. "Is she okay?"

"Yes, we're happy," he said, pushing back a nagging feeling of doubt "She's a little thin, that's why I'm buying her these." He gestured to several large plastic bags. "I wanted to surprise her, but I think this will be a better one. Come on."

Gabby and Tony followed Alex home in their car. Once at the house, they stood still staring at it stunned by its transformation.

"It's beautiful," Gabby said in awe. "It's everything you promised."

They began to walk up the stairs, but halted when Daniella raced out the front door and nearly crashed into Tony. "Alex. Thank God you're here. It's Izzy. She's collapsed in the kitchen."

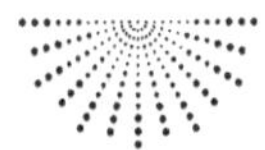

A dangerous case of pneumonia," the emergency room doctor said. "She's a young woman who should be able to fight this, but her immune system is weak because of a rare blood disorder. We can only do so much."

Everyone went into action. Alex hired a private nurse. Velma helped supervise her duties. Sophia and Daniella helped rearrange Isabella's schedule and made apologies for cancelled appointments. Gabby helped in the kitchen organizing Isabella's meals and Tony researched other doctors in the area who could better treat Isabella's condition.

Autumn continued to settle, carved pumpkins made their debut on stairs and porches, copper and red leaves blanketed the ground and families prepared for holiday reunions. But for the house on Waverly, the reunion was anything but joyful.

Mariella had returned from the city once she'd heard the news and demanded answers. "Well, what is being done?" she asked as the three sisters sat in the solarium.

"Alex has gotten the top specialists to look at her," Gabby said.

"And what have they said?"

"They basically all said the same thing. We have to wait and see."

"But that's ridiculous. There must be something we can do."

"She has a private nurse who monitors her every day and Velma's never far behind."

"Do you remember how Mom..." Daniella began.

"No," Gabby warned. "Don't say it. We can't lose Izzy." Her voice trembled. "Not this way."

Daniella's eyes filled with tears. "Maybe this is our punishment. Izzy was the one who always wanted to get away and we forced her to stay and now she'll leave us forever. Now she'll truly be free."

Gabby violently shook her head. "No, stop it. It's not our fault."

"Isn't it? You ran off and I went to Europe and even you..." She pointed to Mariella.

Mariella rested a hand on her chest appalled. "What about me?"

"You left for New York without her."

"She was already married."

"But maybe she just got married because of us."

"That doesn't mean we're to blame. She wanted us to be happy. We did what we had to do."

Gabby wiped away tears. "Maybe Daniella's right. It is our fault."

"Don't you start," Mariella scolded. "She's going to get better. She's young and strong. She'll get over it."

"Have you' seen her?" Daniella shook her head and answered her own question. "No. Just like you never saw Mom sick or Dad. You don't like anything that isn't beautiful."

"That isn't true. And that isn't fair. Just..." Her voice faltered. "I can't see her like that." Mariella voice's broke then she covered her face and burst into tears.

"So, how have things been?" Alex asked as he and Tony sat on the front step on opposite sides.

The late autumn day welcomed the sight of sparrows poking in the ground and squirrels darting to and fro with acorns in their mouths.

"Good," Tony said.

Alex didn't ask him what he meant and Tony didn't offer to tell him,

"Are you planning on staying in town?"

He stared at Alex measuring his response. "We'd like to."

Alex nodded. "If you ever need a job, you know where to look."

His gaze fell. "Thanks."

"You're wel—" Alex stopped when he spotted a small figure in the distance. He stiffened. "What's he doing?"

Tony turned and saw a cat walking towards them. "Looks like he's coming here."

"He'd better not."

The two men watched in amazement as Nicodemus walked past them up the stairs to the front door. He meowed loudly then scratched on it. Alex jumped to his feet and ran to the door. "You're going to ruin the finish. Go home. I'm not letting you in."

Nicodemus glanced up at him with a disdain that came natural to felines then scratched the door again. Alex gripped the doorknob then swore and opened it. Nicodemus calmly walked inside. Alex swore again then slammed the door.

Tony laughed. "I guess you don't like him very much."

"I don't like him at all."

"Then why did you let him in?"

Alex collapsed back into his former position. "Because Izzy likes him."

Tony studied him for a long moment then said, "It's real, isn't it?"

"What? My dislike?" He shot a look of disgust at the closed door. "Sure, it's real."

Tony shook his head. "No. Your marriage."

Alex picked up a red and yellow leaf that had fallen on the step. He held the stem and twirled it between his fingers. "What makes a marriage real?"

"Love. Commitment."

"I'm committed. I've gotten her the best of everything: clothes, food, even the best doctors."

"Right. I'd forgotten you're not particular who you marry. So I guess when Isabella passes on you can move on to Daniella."

Alex stopped twirling the leaf. "Isabella's going to get better."

"And if she doesn't, lots of women have sympathy for a widower."

He crumbled the leaf in his fist. "Stop saying that. Isabella isn't going anywhere."

"Not that it matters of course," Tony said casually. "You could marry anyone. Everyone knows you married poor Isabella because you had to. In a few days you could be free."

Alex lunged at Tony and grabbed him by the lapels of his

coat with the ferocity of a bear. He shoved him against the post, his voice harsh and raw with pain. "I said stop it."

"Why the hell can't you admit that you're in love with her?"

Alex released him, stormed down the steps and headed for his truck. Tony followed him, his limp pronounced as he tried to catch up. "You're afraid to admit it. You're afraid to admit that if Izzy dies *all* the money you have and *all* the things that you own won't mean anything to you. You don't want to face that."

Alex jumped in his truck. Tony stopped him before he could close the door.

"I know how you feel. If Gabby were lying up there in that room close to death, forcing me to imagine a future without her, I would slowly lose my mind."

Alex gripped the steering wheel. "I'm not you. I don't let things bother me. I promised myself I'd never—"

"Hurt the same way as when your father left?" Tony finished. "You survived that so you can survive anything, right?" He glanced away and stared at the grand Victorian structure. "I know that loving things like property and houses is safer, but sometime in your life you're going to have to risk loving people, too." He turned his gaze to Alex. "Before it's too late." Tony closed the door and walked away. Alex started the ignition then roared down the driveway.

News of Isabella's illness spread throughout the town and soon people in the community dropped by with food, gifts and home-brewed remedies. One unexpected visitor appeared late one evening. Marilyn Tremain sat in the room with Isabella and looked at Velma who sat quietly on the other side of the bed.

"I always expected you to say something," she finally said.

"I promised you I wouldn't."

She sniffed. "People are good at breaking promises. I felt as though I had to be better than you, belittle you somehow because you knew something that could destroy my reputation. You still do."

"You paid me to forget and I did."

"And you didn't come back to get more money?"

"Alex has plenty of his own." Velma hesitated then said, "Why did you do it?"

"I guess I wanted to see if I could. I was a bored, rich housewife with nothing to do, so I did some foolish things. Your husband knew. I admit I seduced him and he left in guilt. Letting you catch me was sloppy work on my part. I usually entered buildings undetected, but I should have known that trying to rob the Duvall house would be dangerous. There's something about this house."

Velma's voice became a whisper. "I know."

"When I gave you all that money, I expected you to stay away. I didn't want to see you again and be forced to remember my secret."

Velma nodded. "I wouldn't have come back, but Alex wanted to return here. I've never told him the truth about why we left."

Marilyn looked at the bed. "I don't think she wants to be here."

Velma took Isabella's cold hand and cradled it in hers. "I know that, too."

After Marilyn left, Velma continued to sit by the bed softly humming. She could tell that Isabella had little fight left in her and didn't know what to say. She hated the feeling of helplessness. Alex always asked about her, but he rarely came into the room. It wasn't like him to be skittish of sickness, but she didn't want to force him.

She looked lovingly at Isabella, her face ashen, her frame small and fragile in the large bed. "You know you're not being fair to us. You're not giving us a chance. We aren't perfect but we're nice to know. Your mother wasn't a wonderful woman, but she loved you and so did your father and they wouldn't want this for you."

∾

ISABELLA DREAMT OF FLYING. Like a kite, like a cloud, free. She saw her mother descending like an angel from the heavens, more beautiful than she'd ever been on earth and reached out her hand to her. Then she saw her father, handsome and strong as he had been before illness whittled his vibrancy away. It was so good to see them again. She wanted to be with them always.

∾

VELMA JERKED awake when someone gently shook her shoulder. She looked up and saw Alex. "Go to bed, Mom. I'll stay with her."

Velma looked up at him; although he spoke calmly the darkness in his eyes worried her. He looked older and tired. But she knew there was nothing she could say to lessen his anguish, so she left. Alex sat beside the bed and grasped Isabella's hand and brought it to his lips. "Look, I'll make you a deal. I'll give you anything you want if you'll..."

He took a deep breath then shook his head. "No, I won't play games. We were always honest with each other and I'll be honest with you now. I thought it was just this house that called me back, but it was you. It took me a long time to realize it, but it's true. I love this house, but I love..."

He bit his lip unable to say the words he wished to and caressed her hand then lay beside her and fell asleep.

EARLY THE NEXT MORNING, Gabby sneaked into Isabella's room and saw Alex fast asleep with his arm around Isabella, but what brought tears to her eyes, was seeing her sister awake.

"Izzy?"

Isabella pressed a finger to her lips and pointed to Alex.

Gabby crept up to the bed. "Oh, Izzy."

She held out her hand and Gabby grabbed it. "I can't believe you're here."

"I couldn't stay away."

"I'm sorry I made you run away."

"You didn't. It wasn't your fault. I discovered you were right all along. I was marrying Alex for all the wrong reasons. But I didn't think that you would have to marry him instead." Gabby bit her lip. "Do you love him?"

"I do love him." She looked at the sleeping man beside her. "Very much."

Gabby kissed Isabella's hand. "Then we're all happy now. Truly happy."

"Yes."

Alex moved and Gabby released Isabella's hand. "Looks like he's waking up. I'll leave you two alone." She slipped out of the room as Alex slowly opened his eyes.

When he saw Isabella staring down at him, he blinked, trying to adjust his gaze.

"Hello, Alex."

He sat up, his heart racing. "You're awake."

She smiled softly. "Yes."

He dug in his pocket and pulled out the key she'd given him. "I discovered what the key opens. Can you guess?"

She shook her head.

"No? Then I'll tell you." He turned her palm up and placed the key inside it. He felt worn and broken as he stared down at her hand, knowing what he had to do. "This is the key to your freedom."

"My freedom?" she said her mouth caressing the sweet sound of the words. "You mean that I can leave?"

"Yes," his voice broke, but he didn't lower his gaze. "I love you. I've always loved you and I always will, but I'd rather see you happy alone than miserable with me."

She gripped the key in her hand and held it close to her heart then handed it back to him. "I choose to stay with you."

He took the key, his hand shaking, joy evident in his eyes. "But you hate this house."

"No." She shook her head. "I thought I did, but I was wrong." She searched his eyes which reflected the love she had always felt for him. She lay back on the pillow and reached up to touch his cheek. "I was just waiting for you to come home."

$$\sim$$

WINTER BROUGHT a snow chilled breeze that swept through the town, dusting snow on the hills and clothing the naked trees. That Christmas, presents lay piled high under a Douglas fir, but no one noticed them. The Duvall sisters were all together and happy—that was the greatest gift of all.

MIDNIGHT PROMISE

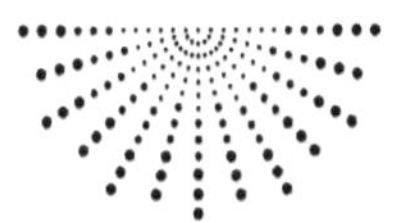

Dear Reader,

Welcome to the second book in the *It Happened One Wedding* series where the best part of the story is after "I do."

Have you ever known someone who just seems unlucky? They lock their keys in the car on the same day they're running late? They get their clothes caught in doors or sharp corners?

Well, Dr. Naomi Mensah is one such woman. She has no time to think romance when her world constantly seems to be falling apart.

Enter Sebastian Scott, a man she resists at first until she learns he's the one person she can't live without.

I hope you enjoy *Midnight Promise*.

All the best,

Dara

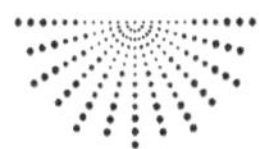

*T*he strange noises in her bedroom should have been her first clue.

The noises should have alerted her to the fact that her life, as she knew it, was about to blow up in her face. But Dr. Naomi Mensah had been so tired after returning from her trip to Costa Rica for a conference, that the strange noises didn't register at first. The flight had been delayed and traffic hellish, but she was still happy to be back, a day before scheduled, to get work done. As much as she liked attending workshops and listening to experts in her field to find out about the latest discoveries and developments, she preferred to be working in her lab.

Her research lab was her haven and every day she looked forward to being there.

As she entered her one bedroom apartment, on the first floor of a remodeled three level apartment complex tucked away in a Maryland suburb, she'd only been thinking of slipping into bed as she dropped her suitcase in the cluttered foyer, stacked with old trade journals, newspapers and books she wanted to donate, but never got around to.

The noises rose and fell in a strange rhythmic pattern. Naomi immediately thought her housekeeper, Maya, was struggling to shift furniture so she could find areas to clean, although if Naomi had been more clearheaded, she would have known that scenario was unlikely. Maya James, a heavyset girl in her mid-twenties with a smile as bright as the moon on a clear night and a walk as slow as a snail stuck in honey, appeared to be allergic to any type of exertion. Especially dusting, washing and vacuuming. It was only after hiring her that Naomi discovered that Maya was the second cousin of the owner of the cleaning service.

But by that time, she'd been fooled by the younger woman's charming smile and didn't want to have to find someone else. Luckily, Naomi wasn't too particular in her housecleaning needs and felt Maya did a serviceable job and since Naomi was rarely home—she spent most of her waking hours at the lab—as long as the basics were taken care of, toilets cleaned, shower and tub scrubbed, kitchen organized, she didn't have any real complaints.

"Maya, I'm back," Naomi called out to her, hoping not to scare her as she headed to her bedroom. "I know it's early, but a main speaker wasn't able to attend, so I decided to come home. I just want to sleep so you can finish cleaning tomorrow." She opened her bedroom door and stopped when she saw two people in a position that made her face burn with embarrassment. "Oh, excuse me," she quickly said before she closed the door and turned back to the hall.

Then she paused and realized she hadn't just entered the wrong room in a hotel, she was in her apartment. There were two people in her bed!

She swung open the door again. She clearly hadn't been loud enough with her first entrance because the couple hadn't stopped their activity. It looked as if they'd increased their amorous interaction.

Naomi's gaze dropped to the dark pair of trousers lying on the wood floor that sat next to a pair of orange and black striped boxers. *Did the man think he was a tiger?* Her gaze shifted to the bright pink bra on the bed post, black fishnets pooled beneath it. Maya's sturdy brown legs were wrapped around the man while he grunted like a boar, beads of sweat glistening on his bald brown head. The room smelled of warm bodies and expensive cologne.

"What is going on!" Naomi said, banging the door with her fist to get their attention. Her actions had the desired effect: The bed stopped squeaking, the moaning and grunting halted and two expressions of surprised disbelief met hers.

The man scrambled out of the bed with an agility that belied his large size. He wasn't exactly fat, but was soft enough around the middle to hint at a decades' long career sitting at a desk. As he pulled on his boxers, Naomi noticed a gold ring on one of his chubby fingers. She hadn't realized Maya was married to a man nearly twenty years her senior. She understood new adventures helped to keep a marriage fresh and alive, but didn't appreciate them finding it like this.

"Sorry," he said breathless. "Didn't realize it was so late." He quickly buttoned up his conservative, light green shirt.

"Just go," Naomi said.

He shoved on his shoes and grabbed his coat. Naomi impatiently waited for him to finish, half expecting him to kiss Maya on the cheek and tell her he'd see her later, but he didn't. Instead he reached inside his coat. It was only when he pulled out his wallet that Naomi finally understood the full picture.

The stranger wasn't Maya's husband, but a paying customer. Naomi snatched the crisp bills out of his hand before Maya could. "Thank you," she said, tucking the money in her jeans pocket. "Now go and forget you ever came here."

He nodded and left.

When Maya didn't immediately follow, Naomi turned to her. She knew the girl could move slowly, but her movements had become glacial. The man had already changed and left, but Maya was just latching up her bra. She still had a cream white blouse and black skirt to put on. "Why are you still here?" Naomi demanded

Maya reached for the blouse. "You haven't paid me yet."

Naomi folded her arms. "That's a joke, right?"

"I cleaned the kitchen. I mopped the floor."

For some wild reason, Naomi imagined Maya with the man making their way across the kitchen floor with every forward thrust moving Maya's bottom across the ground.

Naomi grabbed Maya's fishnets, heels and skirt then headed for the door.

"Hey, those are mine!"

Naomi opened her front door and tossed them out into the hallway. "I know."

"I can't go out there half dressed."

"Don't worry, nobody's looking. And if they are, you've got great legs." Naomi shoved a screaming Maya out the door and closed it while Maya continued her nasty name calling. She leaned against the wall and squeezed her eyes shut. Was this really happening? Did she really just see that?

A few seconds later, Naomi straightened when someone knocked on her front door. She sighed and answered, "What?"

Maya stood there and flashed her bright, beautiful smile. "Could you keep this between us?"

Naomi slammed the door closed.

"And then what did you do?" Naomi's younger sister, Elia, asked at the reception of their cousin's wedding. The two women stood under the large, white canopy being pounded by an unexpected spring rain. The bride, looking as if she belonged on top of a five tiered wedding cake, dressed in an ivory gown with long lace sleeves, sat in the corner, tears streaming down her face. The wedding ceremony had been ruined by the sudden downpour and she refused to dance or be comforted because she felt her marriage was doomed. Three bridesmaids, dressed in matching neon pink and turquoise dresses, surrounded her, trying their best to ease her distress. The groom, dressed in a navy suit and patterned tie, stood to the side with his best man, smoking something that didn't look or smell like a cigarette, but everybody pretended was.

Naomi and Elia took little notice of the groom or the bride since they were used to their cousin's dramatics and knew with enough coaxing she'd soon be taking over the dance floor. So they busied themselves at the make-your-own flower station where guests were given printed instructions and could work with an array of spray mums, different colored roses and colorful ribbons and pins to create their own corsage or boutonniere.

Behind them, other guests ate and chatted at the various purple covered round tables with white decorative accents, or took to the dance floor.

Naomi grabbed another spray of mums, wishing she could forget the incident that had happened three days ago. "There wasn't much to do."

Naomi glanced at the teary bride then the groom. He had a similar build as the man she'd found in her bedroom and soon the image of the man's tiger colored boxers and big brown bottom, bobbing up and down in the air, crashed into her thoughts. She wasn't sure she'd ever be able to close her eyes again. She groaned. "I come back from Costa Rica to discover my housekeeper has been using my apartment as a..." She shivered unable to finish the sentence. "I have to move. God knows how long she's been doing this. How many men have been going in and out of my place?" Naomi grabbed a pin and pricked her finger. She silently swore and sucked on it. "This is a nightmare."

"I'm so sorry," Elia said, expertly tying a ribbon around her corsage. She was good at crafts. Naomi's younger sister excelled at most things domestic or otherwise. She was the kind of woman who could win a beauty pageant, garden prize and baking prize all in the same day. She was a slender woman of refined manners and taste, her black hair was pulled back in a chignon, the blue dress she wore complimenting her dusty cocoa skin.

Naomi, in contrast, could already feel the knot of her braid coming lose; her green dress was too tight and too short. It was a cocktail dress with a flared skirt she'd grabbed at some dress shop, which was more suited for a cocktail party than a wedding. She'd fallen for the shop owners' assurance that it was perfect for her and that the color complemented Naomi's walnut colored skin.

Naomi had none of her sister's refined traits—being all thumbs in a garden, a disaster in the kitchen and although some remarked on the prettiness of her brown eyes, few looked past the serious dark eyes surrounded by heavy frames and her boyish figure to notice.

Naomi checked her finger for blood then grabbed the pin again. "I've already had two men show up at my place."

"You can't stay there."

"I know," she said, pricking herself again. "And I also have to get a new bed."

Elia snatched the pin from her. "What is wrong with you? You're worse than Susan," she said, referring to her four-year-old daughter. "Use the ribbons instead."

"I was following the instructions." She pointed to the elegantly typed card. "It says—"

"I know what it says, but you can't do it. Remember when Mom tried to teach you how to use the sewing machine?"

Naomi cleared her throat, heat stealing into her cheeks as she recalled the incident. "I was young and I only needed a few stitches."

"You were seventeen and Mom wouldn't let me near a sewing machine for *years* because of you."

Naomi grabbed one of the red ribbons.

"Why do you need a new bed?" her sister asked.

Naomi wrapped the ribbon around the stem of her flowers, but one slipped out of her grasp and fell to the ground. "I found a strange man in it," she said, picking the flower up. "Do I need to tell you the story again?"

"No," Elia said, watching her sister struggle to bind the stems together before taking it from her and doing it herself. "I mean you could just change the sheets and…"

Naomi watched her sister's expert hand, refusing to meet her eye. "I got upset so after they left I…" She licked her lip and toyed with her necklace. "I cut it up."

Elia's hands paused; Naomi slowly lifted her gaze to meet her sister's stunned expression. "You cut it up?"

That had been Pete O'Connell's fault. After stripping the sheets, with the ferocity of a zealot eager to toss a witch into a bonfire, she'd gotten a call from her research assistant, Monica, apologizing and telling her that she couldn't be part of Naomi's project because she was going to be working with Pete instead.

The arrogant, two faced bastard had stolen yet another top research assistant from her. Naturally, she didn't let her disappoint show. She wished Monica the best then hung up, grabbed a pair of scissors and attacked the bed as if she'd found Pete with Maya's legs wrapped around him, his annoyingly smug grin wiped clean off his face. He also had a similar build as the man she'd found with Maya. Big and bald with a peppered beard and ruddy cheeks. "Are you happy now?" she asked with each stab. "You couldn't stop with just one?"

Elia snapped her fingers in front of Naomi's face, bringing her out of her memory. "You cut up your mattress?"

Naomi nodded. "Yes."

"Why?"

She didn't want to tell her about Pete, that would sound crazy. She shrugged. "I got angry."

"You know I could have used it."

"No, I didn't actually."

"Because you don't think about things like that," Elia snapped. "I told you that we had to reorganize our guest room for Barry's great aunt and that the headboard got broken."

Yes, she had, Naomi now remembered. She just hadn't paid attention. "I'll help you get another one."

"What a waste. Next time call me."

"There had better not be a next time."

"I didn't mean it like that." She sighed, wistful. "I always loved your bed. You have terrible taste in most things, but it was gorgeous. The oak inlay—"

Naomi frowned. "Terrible taste?"

Elia adjusted a flower in her corsage. "We both know that you spend more time in your lab than anywhere else. You'd be happy with just a cot if you could get away with it."

"Still that was a little harsh." Naomi glanced down at her dress. "I even tried to look nice tonight."

Her sister patted her affectionately on the arm. "I know you tried and it shows."

Naomi paused not sure if that was a compliment or insult. Her sister eventually made it clear when she added, "You're lucky the dress isn't pink or you'd end up looking like a flamingo."

Naomi pulled a face, but decided not to care. Was it her fault she'd gotten their father's skinny legs? "Besides, I only got rid of the mattress not the entire bed so you weren't going to get it anyway."

A woman in a large orange hat, tottering on black heels that were accented with a flower design at the ankle latch, with a gait that made her look as if she were constantly walking on egg shells, approached them. "What are you two doing over here? You should be comforting your cousin. She's in such a state."

Naomi looked at her cousin who was now wiping her tears with a handkerchief. "She just wants the attention, Mom. It's not as if it's her first wedding."

June Mensah kissed her teeth. "Who are you to talk? At least she's had two husbands," she said, holding up two fingers as if it were a crude gesture. "You can't even get one."

"I don't want one."

"Quiet!" June said, then looked to the right and the left as if to make sure no one overheard. "If you speak like that, people will believe you."

Naomi feathered the petals of a mum. "Which is exactly the point."

Her mother patted her cheek, a look of sympathy crossing her handsome features. "Don't worry, my darling, your time will come."

"Mom, you're not listening. I don't—"

"I see you're wearing your aunt's necklace. You finally got the clasp fixed like I told you?"

No. "Of course," she said. She'd intended to, but the task kept escaping her mind and after the housekeeper incident, she had completely forgotten about fixing the clasp before she'd chosen to wear it. It was an expensive gift from her aunt that her mother had warned her about handling with care, but she didn't think it made much sense to keep something locked away that was meant to be worn.

Elia handed Naomi the now finished corsage. "Why did you wait so long to tell me?"

Naomi sniffed the corsage. "Not now," she warned under her breath.

"Tell you what?" June asked, gathering some flowers to create her own corsage.

"Nothing," Naomi said.

"She's traumatized because she found a man in her bed," Elia said.

Her mother's eyes widened. "Was he dead?"

"You watch too many dramas," Naomi said.

"You leave my dramas alone. Am I right?"

"No," Naomi said, giving her sister a fierce look. She hadn't wanted to let her mother know about the situation. She would only worry.

"Did you bring him home and forget his name?"

"Mom—"

June waved her hand. "No, that doesn't sound like you. I can't remember the last time you had a man in your apartment, let alone your bed. Did—"

"It was her housekeeper," Elia said.

"That Jamaican?"

Naomi pointed her corsage at her mother. "Says the daughter of Jamaican immigrants."

Her mother bristled. "You know what I mean. She was completely uncouth."

Elia snorted. "More than you know. Naomi found her baking someone's plantain in her oven."

June blinked then frowned. "You don't want her baking plantain in your oven?"

"No," Elia said with a giggle. "Maya put a man's plantain in her *personal* oven."

Her mother's frown deepened. She turned to Naomi. "What nonsense is your sister speaking?"

Naomi shook her head and feigned ignorance. "I don't know."

Elia released a heavy sigh. "The Jamaican—"

"She has a name," Naomi said.

Elia lifted a brow. "Does it matter now?"

"Yes, because—"

Elia turned to her mother. "She serviced a man in Naomi's bed."

Her mother blinked. "Served him what?"

Elia threw up her hands in exasperation. "Mom, why can't you understand subtly?"

"What's the use of being subtle when you can speak plain?" June shot back annoyed. "That's what your sister is good at." She looked at Naomi, expectant. "You tell me what happened."

"Mom," Naomi said with a sigh and brief shake of her head. "It's nothing."

Her mother set her gathered flowers on the table and folded her arms. "Your sister is spouting nonsense about nothing?"

"Yes."

Elia rested a hand on her hip. "Naomi found her housekeeper having sex with a man in Naomi's bed. Is that clear enough for you?"

June's mouth fell open. "She brought her man to your place?"

"That's where it gets worse. He wasn't 'her man' he was a client. She's a working girl. A prostitute."

"I know what a working girl is," June said, lifting her chin, offended.

"I wasn't sure," Elia said with a teasing grin. "Since you didn't understand my plantain analogy."

"Because that made no sense. How can you use plantains and ovens as a euphemism for sex?" She tapped her chin, thoughtful. "Although, now I can see the connection. But you know what would have been better? If you said Naomi found The Jamaican spreading her guava jelly over the man's—"

Naomi held up her hand, wanting to plug her ears. "Mom that's enough." It was enough to have to try to rid her mind of brown bottoms and striped boxers; she didn't want to add plantain and guava jelly to the mix.

June nodded with a knowing look. "I didn't trust her. Never trust a woman who dusts with her fingers. I once caught her using her palm because she was too lazy to use a cloth and—"

"Well, she's gone now."

Her mother suddenly covered her mouth in horror. "Dear God, to think she likely used that same hand on a man's cucumber. Your house could be covered in seeds!"

It was now Naomi's turn to look around to make sure nobody heard her. "Mom, please keep your voice down."

Elia giggled. "No one will know what she's talking about."

June clasped her hands together, her voice anxious. "You can't go home. What if there are other men there waiting? Did she put your address online?" Her eyes widened with renewed horror. "If so, then your address has gone international and you could have men coming from all corners of the globe!"

"I doubt that will happen."

Elia couldn't stop a grin. "Two men have already shown up."

Naomi glared at her sister. "Will you shut up?"

June pressed her hands against her cheeks, distress covering her face. "This is awful."

"Don't worry, Mom. I've changed the lock and I will be moving soon."

"Just wait until I tell your father. He'll know what to do."

"No, wait..." Naomi said, but her mother hurried away before she could stop her. She turned and hit her sister in the arm. "You're still a little snitch. Why did you have to tell her?"

Elia shrugged unrepentant. "What are little sisters for? At least she's not bothering you about getting married now."

"True."

They both looked at their cousin who was still crying.

"How long is she going to milk the attention?" Elia asked.

"Give her another ten minutes and she'll be fine," Naomi said, looking outside. "Plus it seems that the rain is easing up."

"She better get on the dance floor soon, because I don't know how high her new husband is trying to get," Elia said, nodding at the groom and best man whose mood and appetite appeared to have improved.

Naomi frowned. "Maybe Mom's right and we should go talk to her."

"There's nothing to say." Elia sighed. "Poor thing."

"I don't think it's that bad. The rain didn't ruin everything."

Elia shook her head. "No, I'm talking about your mattress. It finally gets some action and gets stabbed and tossed out."

"I don't need a man."

"It's been eight years. Are you sure it's not because—"

"You ended up marrying the first guy I ever dated seriously? No, I'm fine. I've told you this more times than I can count. You and Barry are perfect together. It never would have worked between us." She knew that people still felt a little sorry for her. That her younger sister ended up with the first and only man Naomi had ever brought home. But she didn't need anyone's pity. She'd met Barry Seagrove at twenty-two after completing her doctorate and saw dating as a new experience to try. He'd been a fellow student a few years older whose interest in biodiversity interested her.

It lasted four months. She felt relieved when they admitted that things wouldn't work out. She wasn't too surprised when a few weeks later he and Elia started going out. They'd hit it off at their first meeting with a passion she and Barry had never shared.

Naomi wasn't sure there was 'The Right Man' out there for her and didn't want to look. Others didn't understand her real passion—microbiology. They didn't understand that she felt alive looking at the life that abounded, which was invisible to the naked eye. They couldn't comprehend that the sight of microbes made her skin tingle, the magnificence of binary fission versus the process of mitosis, made her heart race.

Presently she was researching the correlation between the hepatitis C virus and kidney cancer; her focus being whether a carrier of the hepatitis C virus is significantly more prone to being diagnosed with kidney cancer than those without it. She was also interested in the ranging mutations of elephantiasis. No man could compete with that.

"I'm not like Mom," Elia said. "I'm not saying you have to get married, but you haven't even tried to be with someone."

"I don't need to. I'm not like you. I don't need shopping with the girls, wine tastings, book clubs and family vacations."

"True, but you do need a life."

Naomi pressed two fingers to her neck as if searching for a pulse. "You mean I'm dead?"

"I mean you need a life outside of the lab." She lowered her voice. "You're not taking care of yourself. You have bags under your eyes."

"That's because I haven't been able to sleep since—"

"No, you've had them before. And you've lost weight. Have you been skipping meals again? And without a bed, where do you sleep?"

"I have my power shakes. And I sleep on the couch." She rubbed her corsage underneath her sister's chin. "You're starting to sound like Mom. Don't worry about me," she said, although her sister's concerns reminded Naomi of her mentor, Dr. Vera Conklin, who'd urged her to attend the wedding 'just to be social a bit'. Naomi was known as a 'no show' at most family events, either from lack of interest or forgetfulness. She'd missed an uncle's housewarming party (she'd gotten absorbed in her research and lost track of time), her sister's baby shower (she'd gotten the dates mixed up) and her parent's twentieth wedding anniversary (same reason). Although she wasn't close to her cousin, aside from her mentor's urging, her mother's insistence and her sister's constant reminder, Naomi knew she had to attend the wedding or her mother's middle sister would have given her hell.

"Don't you think it's odd that you're rarely home; that you rarely pay attention to the real world around you, that your housekeeper could use your place for months without you knowing?"

"No, I don't. I love my work. And Maya is just...I should have gotten rid of her sooner." Naomi closed her eyes and groaned. "She worked for me for more than a year. How often do you think she used my place and I didn't know it?" She waved her corsage. "Never mind. Don't answer that. I just need to move out and put this all behind me." She turned to look at her cousin who was now on the dance floor with her new husband. "See? Everything turns out okay in the end. I'll be fine." But even as she offered her sister a smile, her words felt like a lie.

CHAPTER THREE

She shouldn't have come. Her sister wasn't the only one to mention the dark circles under her eyes or her lost weight. She couldn't help that she was built like her Ghanaian born father— Dr. Abraham Mensah—all lines and angles without curves. And if they weren't worried about her appearance they kept reminding her how rarely they'd seen her. Yes, she travelled a lot. Yes, she worked long hours. Yes, she was still single. Was that a crime? Was it wrong to be ambitious?

Not that it was getting her very far since Pete had taken another researcher from her. What was the use of graduating from the University of Pennsylvania at eighteen, getting her post graduate training at the Stanford University School of Medicine if she wasn't making any strides? Why weren't people clamoring to work on her projects? Why was she thought of as second best?

Even the lab she'd been using had been shut down due to a mold outbreak. She was working in an interim facility, which housed seven other organizations—one a crystal healing center and the other an accounting firm. She felt like a failure compared to her father, who like his father before him, had graduated with honors from Oxford University, had served on several boards, won prestigious awards and wrote on subjects such as tuberculosis, elephantiasis and the mechanisms of acquired immunity. Although he had retired he was still a much sought after speaker.

Naomi spent the remainder of the night assuring her father that she'd be fine and he didn't need to escort her home, telling her cousin she made a beautiful bride and twice avoiding a man who thought her doctorate meant she was a physician and who wanted her to look at the suspicious mole on his neck.

By close to midnight she was ready to leave and happily made her escape into the cool spring evening, walking briskly through the parking lot. The rain had stopped, leaving the ground wet, the reflection of the moon shining in the puddles. She was looking at one such reflection when her heel caught in a grate and she stumbled forward.

She caught herself before she fell, but felt her necklace slip from her neck. She scrambled to reach it, but it slid through her fingers and clattered down the grate.

No, no, no. Please no!

Just what she needed. A bad week turned worse. She dropped to her knees, the cold, wet asphalt pressing against her skin.

This couldn't be happening.

Naomi touched her neck again, her heart sinking. The necklace was gone. Truly gone.

She pulled out her cell phone and used the light to peer into the dark black pit, hoping to see a glint of the gold chain reflected, but she didn't see anything. She tried to lift the grate, but it was heavier than expected and bit into her skin, causing her to yank her hands away and flex her sore fingers.

Naomi squeezed her eyes shut as her mother's voice rose in her mind, "I thought you said you finally got the clasp fixed like I told you. Do you know how much that necklace cost? Why are you so irresponsible?"

It wasn't that she didn't treasure it, she'd been careless, but it wasn't the first time. She'd ruined a silk blouse, a gift from her grandmother; a silver tea set she'd received from an uncle. But her aunt's necklace had been special. It had been a gift she'd given to Naomi when she'd gotten her first job. "A gift for all your accomplishments and the many more to come," she'd told her that day. And now she'd lost it down a sewer.

"Want me to get it for you?"

Naomi looked up and saw a man in shadow, the lamplight illuminated behind him. She squinted, trying to make out his features. "I'm sorry?"

"You just dropped something, right?" he asked, his voice as deep and dark as the shadows around him.

"Yes."

"What was it?"

Naomi touched her throat again half hoping it would magically reappear. No, it was still gone. "My necklace."

"Do you want me to get it for you?"

Naomi pointed to make sure he understood the situation. "It fell down the grate."

"I know." He shoved his hands in his pockets. "Do you want me to get it for you or not?"

She wouldn't be too proud. She wasn't going to pretend she didn't need help. "Yes," she said feeling relieved. "Please."

"But I'll need a favor in return."

"Anything." She paused. She couldn't be too grateful. She

didn't know who this man was. "As long as it's not illegal, immoral and it's within my power."

A smile entered his voice. "What's your definition of immoral?"

"I won't sleep with you."

"You think sleeping with a man is immoral?"

"Only when it's in exchange for certain favors," she said, her former housekeeper fresh in her thoughts. But she wished she hadn't mentioned it. *Why were they having this conversation when she just needed his help?* She stood to her feet, but still couldn't make out his features with the light behind him, the darkness still masking his face. "Those are my conditions otherwise you can leave."

He shrugged. "Fair enough. I'll get your necklace, if you promise to hire me as your assistant."

That didn't make any sense. "What kind of assistant?"

"Someone who helps you with your day-to-day duties. A personal assistant."

He needed a job that bad? She didn't need a personal assistant, and even if he'd wanted to be a research assistant, she wouldn't want to hire someone she'd just met in a parking lot.

Naomi shifted her gaze to the grate. But she did need her necklace back. "Okay."

He held out his hand. "Promise?"

She recoiled for a moment. His hand was enormous. She looked at what she could make of his shabby tux. Maybe he needed money. At least he was asking for a job. She would give him a good reward instead. She held out her hand. "I promise."

"Good." He lifted the grate as if he were lifting the lid off of a paper box and descended inside.

Naomi adjusted her glasses and paced. She chewed her nails and paced some more. Could he find it? Was it gone forever? How would she explain the loss of the necklace if he didn't? Her mother would never let her hear the end of it. "Can you see anything?" she called down to him, seeing the light from his cell phone.

"There's a lot of water, the rain didn't help."

She groaned. He wasn't going to find it. It was hopeless.

"But I'll get it, Mensah. Don't worry."

Mensah? He knew her last name? She didn't remember telling him. It didn't matter. He just needed to find the necklace. Naomi paced some more and as time passed her hopes faded. Soon she heard his feet on the metal ladder. She crouched down in anticipation. "Did you find it?"

He held out a slimy, dirty hand. "Here you go."

Naomi winced and recoiled both from the sight and the smell then gingerly accepted the sewage covered necklace. "Thank you," she said politely as he emerged, his suit covered in muck. He looked terrible and smelled even worse, but he'd done what he'd said. "I really appreciate it Mr..."

"Sebastian Scott."

"Thank you Sebastian."

He cleaned his hands on his trouser legs then reached inside his jacket. "I'll give you my card. So I can—"

"Naomi?"

She looked past him and saw her mother waving. She couldn't let her mother see her with this man or the necklace. She offered him a bright smile, snatched the card he held out to her and said, "I'll be in touch," hoping he'd accept her generous reward and she'd never see him again.

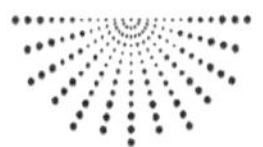

His luck was about to change. Sebastian pumped the air with his fist as he walked into his house and headed for the kitchen. He now had a job with the illustrious Naomi Mensah. It had been worth pulling some strings to make sure he got invited to the wedding of the friend of his second cousin once removed.

"My God, you look awful," his mother said, coming into the room, her cane clicking against the cream tile floor. She'd been staying with him after recovering from hip surgery. She'd improved, but made no move to leave and he didn't want to push her. She'd been lonely since the death of his father five years ago. Although it was past midnight she looked as if she were ready for guests, draped in a silver colored silk robe and her head wrapped in a matching scarf, her mascara and lipstick still in place. But nobody had ever seen Josephine Scott without them.

Sebastian opened the fridge and grabbed an apple. "I met Dr. Naomi Mensah tonight."

"I thought you were going to a wedding."

He washed the apple and then took a bite. "I actually spoke to her and I'm going to be her assistant."

Josephine waved her cane at him. "You smell even worse than you look. At least consider the housekeeper and how much she'll have to clean up after you. You need to get changed right now."

Sebastian rested against the counter and sighed, staring up at the recess lighting that cast a soft light over the marble countertop, amazed by his good fortune. "I can't believe it."

"I'd hoped you would have met someone nice and you come back looking like a toad out of a swamp."

He took another bite of his apple and chewed thoughtfully. "She's better looking in person than her pictures give her credit for. Not that it matters. Hey!" he cried when his mother snatched the apple from him.

"Sebastian!"

He blinked. "What?" He took the apple back from her and frowned. "I'm standing right here, there's no need to shout."

"Did you hear a word I said?"

Nope. He glanced at his watch. "What are you doing up?"

"I couldn't sleep." She stared at his clothes. "What happened to you?"

"I just told you I met Dr. Naomi Mensah."

"Who?"

"Only one of the most brilliant minds in microbiology."

She motioned to his ruined suit with her cane. "You met her looking like that?"

"No, this happened after."

"After what?"

"I got her necklace out of the sewer."

"What was her necklace doing in the sewer?"

"It fell off her neck and I offered to help her and got a job in the process."

"You don't need a job."

That was true, but that was only part of his plan. "It's just the beginning. This will change things for me."

"Have you been drinking?"

"No, this is important. This is amazing. *She* is amazing. Better in person than I thought."

"Is she pretty?"

"I'm not sure, I didn't pay attention."

"You just said she looked better in person than in pictures."

"I was talking about her appearance in general. I wasn't making a specific classification."

Josephine curled her lip in disdain. "I hate when you start to talk like that. Knowing whether a woman is pretty or not does not take a detailed analysis."

"But pretty is relative. Whether I find her pretty or not is irrelevant if you don't think so, therefore I can't give you a factual assessment on a personal preference."

Josephine briefly shut her eyes. "Give me patience." She opened her eyes and spoke slowly. "Do you find her pretty?"

"I think so, but—"

"There is no 'but'. Stay away from her, you always get in trouble with pretty women."

"No, I don't. Besides, I plan to work with her not date her. She's published a number of articles." He paused. "Although, with two of them, I do question the veracity on the calculations used. She may have based her premise on a shaky foundation. However, her article on the—"

Josephine covered her ears and closed her eyes. "Sebastian!"

He took another bite of his apple. "You're shouting again."

She glared at him. "Because you're purposely avoiding the subject."

He frowned. "I am not. I thought the subject was Naomi Mensah."

"It is."

"And I was just telling you about—"

Josephine shook her head and slumped into a seat. "I don't care because I'm not interested. I don't want to see you get hurt again."

"I won't."

Josephine held up her hand and began counting her fingers. "Molly Robb, Kristine Lyle, Barbara Dean—"

He winced. "It's not like that."

His mother didn't need to remind him that he had terrible luck with women. It had started in middle school. That's when he'd first gotten his heart broken by Molly Robb who'd humiliated him in the school courtyard.

He'd been born with extreme clubbed feet that had taken multiple surgeries to fix. He'd spent most of his first eleven years in and out of hospitals so he'd been home schooled, but was thrilled to attend regular school. In middle school, he was in a wheelchair and chubby from lack of exercise and a love of food. He'd eaten to deal with the pain and the isolation, but was happy to be out of the hospital and with other kids.

Molly had been his first crush and she'd acted as if she liked him too with her cupid bow lips and shy smiles, so when she asked to meet him after school, so he could help her with her homework, he'd eagerly agreed.

He should have known when he saw her with her two girlfriends it was a set up. But he realized his mistake too late. They charged him, tipped over his wheelchair and laughed at him as he struggled to get upright. They recorded the event, eventually posting it on an online message board. For the first time in his life he wanted to crawl into the ground and hide, but he didn't. Instead he made it back into his chair and wheeled away determined not to cry.

He didn't know how his parents found out, if his brother had seen the video and told them or someone else, but soon after the incident his father came into his room.

Sebastian remembered not being able to look his father in the eye. He sat at his desk; wearing headphones blasting rap music with foul lyrics that made him feel empowered, pretending to do an equation he'd already figured out.

His father came up beside him, turned off the music and rested a large hand on his shoulder. "I heard about what happened in the courtyard."

Sebastian scribbled some numbers down, wishing he'd go away.

"I'm proud of you. You became a man that day."

Sebastian took off his headphone and stared up at him startled. "What?" He didn't feel like a man. He'd cried like a baby once he was alone in his room and didn't want to have to go to school again. For the past two days he'd stayed home saying he had a cold. He even considered asking his parents to home school him again.

His father squeezed his shoulder. "You made me proud," he said, the island lilt of his words filled with emotion.

Sebastian gritted his teeth. "No, I didn't."

"You didn't get back in that wheelchair and roll away?" his father asked surprised.

"Yes, but—"

"There's no 'but'. That's all life is. It's about getting knocked down and getting back up even when they laugh at you. Even when they hold your hand under their feet." He nodded at Sebastian's surprised expression. "Yes, I saw that too." He motioned to Sebastian's swollen hand where one of Molly's friend, the one with braces and straight black hair, had stood on it. "But you still got up. And you're going to keep getting up by being a success, by using that day as a ladder. As a weapon if you have to."

"A weapon?"

"Yes, a tool that will fuel you past all of them. Keep up your studies and you keep making me proud and you'll own the world. You're going to be taking over my business one day so get used to this."

Sebastian turned away and looked back at his math homework. He didn't look forward to taking over his father's real estate business.

"Do well this semester," his father continued, "and we'll visit your uncle this summer. Think you can do that?"

Sebastian twirled his pencil. He liked his Uncle and would love to visit his home in Trinidad, but he wasn't sure he could face his classmates again.

"You can't have a cold forever. Go to school and shame them with your knowledge."

Sebastian set his pencil down hard, wanting to snap it in two. He hated that advice. He hated his father always talking about the importance of being smart. He loved his father, but could also see how clueless he was. How clueless most adults were. Smart kids weren't liked and didn't make friends. But a summer away would be nice.

He rolled his pencil under his finger, pensive. A summer away with food and sun and beach seemed like a good trade. "Okay," he said and his father's promise galvanized him and helped him ignore the taunts and teasing he endured while he aced every subject.

That summer, the family visited his uncle and Sebastian and his brother, Gregg, got to spend two months in a palm shaded house only yards away from the ocean. His Uncle taught him how to fish and swim, which changed his life.

In the water he was free and powerful. Nothing could stop him and he also became engrossed by what he found in the water. The wildlife drew him in and that's when he knew what his life work would be.

But he still got in trouble with women. Kristine Lyle had been his college mistake. He was the only one who didn't know she was seeing two other guys at the same time and only needed him to help her pass her exams. Barbara had been more serious, he'd nearly married her. Until he found out she also wasn't what she seemed.

He had learned his lesson. His mother didn't need to worry about him. He knew that nothing would happen between him and Naomi. He needed the job to put his plan into action; she was a bridge to something bigger.

After five years, he had a chance at redemption. To reclaim the life he'd once loved. A chance to stand before his father's grave with pride.

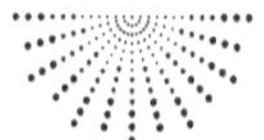

$\mathcal{S}$omeone was at the door.

Naomi glanced at the clock and scowled, she wasn't expecting anyone. She never accepted visitors before noon and she was only home because of a slight cold that she didn't want to pass to others in the lab. She'd been lazing on the couch wearing a pair of worn jeans and a white long sleeved shirt, reading one of her industry journals when she heard the doorbell.

The time on the clock said noon on the dot.

The two other men seeking an afternoon quickie had come around noon time. She really needed to move.

The bell rang again.

"Are you going to get that?" her father called from her bedroom that she now only used as a place to park her computer and extra research materials. He'd come by to make sure that Naomi was safe. Her mother had already hired a crew to clean her place from top to bottom—whispering to her that cucumber seeds could be everywhere!—and didn't want

Naomi left home alone with a cold since she was determined not to stay at her parents' place.

Her father had graciously agreed to look over some data with her and discuss another project she was interested in.

"Yes," she said, then shuffled over to the door. Her scowl increased when she looked through the peephole. Just as she expected. A man. Probably on his lunch break wanting Naomi to put a smile on his face.

She swung the door open and glared up at the large shaggy looking man in his mid-thirties who wore a suit that looked like it had never seen an iron. He had skin the color of roasted peanuts with maroon, square glasses, and nice brown eyes. He needed a haircut and a shave or at least a trim and some semblance of being groomed.

If she were to label him a bacteria it would be the the *lactococcus lactis,* a spherical-shaped bacterium mostly known for use in the production of buttermilk and cheese, but which had most impressed her because it was the first genetically modified organism to be used alive for the treatment of human diseases.

He looked like the kind of man who could both spoil something or improve it, depending on his use. But that didn't matter. He didn't have a delivery package, or a clipboard for her to sign, just a cumbersome looking black bag, possibly filled with sex toys. She couldn't imagine what kind of fantasy he was in the mood for, but she could guess that he'd come to her front door to spoil her day.

He cleared his throat. "Hello, I—"

His voice didn't suit him. His tone was distant but polite, a well modulated baritone as if he were ready to give a presentation, not spend a half hour with a prostitute. Naomi rested her hip on the door and shook her head, interrupting him. "I'm not here to judge you, but you've come to the wrong place. Maya is no longer offering her lunch or afternoon special. So if you could tell the others the same, I'd really appreciate it. Have a nice day." She closed the door and wiped her hands, pleased with herself. When the first two men had arrived, she hadn't been half as nonchalant. She'd shouted at the first one and the second guy—who'd given her a once over and said "You're a bit skinny for my taste with no boobs, but I'll stay if you give a discount"—she'd cursed out, using language she'd invented. So this new guy was lucky.

The doorbell rang again.

Or stupid.

It rang a third time. A fourth time.

Boy, the bastard was insistent. She opened the door.

He adjusted his glasses and cleared his throat. "There must be a mistake."

"There's no mistake. You're not the first to be confused, but you're wasting your time and mine. Now get out of my sight before I call the police." She slammed the door.

Her father poked his head out of the bedroom. "Are you okay?"

"Yes, I'm fine."

"Who was that?"

"No one." She was not going to explain the situation and have him calling her mother. Her mother would try to convince her to move within the next two hours. She didn't want to stay at their house. She loved them to bits, but her mother could nag. Every hour of the day she would be in her space. "Is that all you're going to eat for breakfast?" "Have you washed your hair?" "Are you really going to wear that again?" Naomi shivered at the thought. No, she'd deal with the men until she could find somewhere else to live.

The man rang again and knocked on the door.

"Please, there's been a mistake," he said in a rush when she opened the door. He pulled out his wallet. "I just—"

Naomi's temper snapped, remembering the other man waving cash in her face. "Do you want to go to jail? Do you want me to tell you what I think about men who go out with women behind their wives'..." She glanced at his hand and didn't see a ring... "or girlfriends' backs?"

He sighed and looked pained. "Dr. Mensah."

She froze. He knew her name? And why did his voice suddenly sound familiar?

"I'm here about the job," he continued.

Naomi held up her hand. "That's what I'm trying to tell you. Please listen closely." She leaned towards him and slowed her words, making sure to emphasize every syllable. "I don't do blow jobs or hand jobs or lube jobs. I'm trying to tell you that you've come to the wrong place."

She grabbed the door, but this time he stopped her before she could close it. A shiver of fear coursed through her as she met his hard, dark gaze. His glasses didn't soften his features. He looked large and strong and dangerous. Like a virus invading a cell with the ability to replicate until the cell was destroyed. He could overpower her swiftly and without effort.

She could scream, but she didn't want to put her father's life in danger. This man could easily overtake him. She licked her lips, her mouth dry. She'd make him calm down and then she'd find a weapon. She couldn't show fear.

But something must have registered on her face, because his grip loosened on the door and his expression softened. "I'm not going to hurt you." He held up his wallet to show her his driver's license. "I wanted to show my identification. I'm Sebastian Scott. I'm here to work for you."

She paused. "Me?" Had her mother hired a bodyguard and not told her? He didn't look the part, but his presence would certainly help.

He looked a little rueful. "I guess you forgot."

"Forgot about what?"

"To call me. It's been nearly a week. I'm your new personal assistant."

Naomi furrowed her brows. "I don't need an assistant."

"But you have one now, you promised me the night I retrieved your necklace."

Oh God...the necklace! The man! The sewer! It all came flooding back. Naomi had pushed the memory away as part of an awful dream. He'd even given her his card; it was probably buried deep in her glove compartment where she'd tossed it.

But he was here now and he really wanted to work for her. But he was all wrong. Pete gets a top assistant like Monica and she gets some guy who likes climbing into sewers. Her luck was truly terrible.

"Don't worry," Sebastian said, making his way inside, walking with a distinct stride she'd never seen before. "I'll make your life easy and won't be a bother. You won't regret this." He closed the door behind him, making it clear he didn't plan to leave. "I went to your lab first, and heard you were sick with a cold, so I brought some soup." He patted the black bag beside him. The one she'd imagined carried whips and chains.

"I have a very busy day today," she lied. "Could I call you back, um...?"

"Sebastian," he said patiently. "Sebastian Scott. And I'm ready to get started right now. Where's your kitchen? I'll heat the soup. Have you eaten?"

"No, but—"

Her father came into the room. "Naomi?" he said, his look

and tone unsure, giving her a silent question of whether he should call the police.

"Dad...um this is..."

"Sebastian," the newcomer said, holding out his hand, his face spreading into a warm smile. "And it's an honor to meet you, sir. I attended your lecture in London."

"Thank you. I haven't been doing as much travelling in a while so that must have been quite some time ago."

"Doesn't matter. It was still memorable. Your take on—"

Naomi wrapped an arm around her father's, amazed by the scene of the two men—they looked like a large bear shaking hands with an antelope. "Sebastian, will you excuse us a moment?" she asked, but didn't give him a chance to reply as she led her father into the kitchen.

"He seems like a nice fellow," he said in approval. "That's a relief. I was afraid he was one of—"

Naomi took off her glasses and covered her eyes. "I did too." She let her hand fall and shoved her glasses back in place. "I made a mistake."

"That's okay, I'm sure he'll understand once you explain it."

She shook her head. "No, not about that."

"About what then?"

Naomi paced a moment then paused and rested her hands on her hips. "I promised him a job. I know it sounds crazy, but...I got into a bit of a jam and he helped me and...he's milking a moment of weakness. I'm sure he just wants money. I was going to send him a reward, but I forgot. So now he's here and I'll—"

"He was at my lecture."

Naomi paused and stared at him. "Dad, that has nothing to do with what I just said."

"Yes, it does. You're implying that he's here for dubious reasons. I don't think he is. If you hadn't interrupted him, he would have expanded on what he got from my lecture."

"I'm sure he's just flattering you. It's easy to read up on people nowadays. He knew my name that night. It could be a con."

"What night?"

"At the wedding. He was there. We met in the parking lot."

Her father folded his arms. "And you promised him a job. So you must honor it." He wagged a finger at her. "I brought up children who keep their word."

"Have you looked at him? How can I have a man like that follow me around as my assistant?"

"So you're going back on your promise?"

"It's not that simple."

"Yes, it is." He peeked out the kitchen and glanced at Sebastian sitting in the living room. "I wonder what's in the bag."

"He brought me soup."

"Hmm...I love soup. What kind?"

"I don't know. Probably chicken noodle. He knows I have a cold. But that's—"

"Even better. Tell me when it's ready." He headed for the door. "And you'd better keep your word to that young man or I'm telling your mother you're moving in with us." He flashed a smile then left.

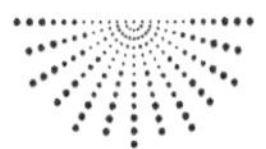

$\mathcal{N}$aomi groaned and walked into the living room like a condemned woman. She sat in front of Sebastian. "We haven't talked salary. I don't—"

He stood. "Is the kitchen free now? You're looking a little peakish."

"Yes, but—" She stopped when he walked past her.

"Did you have breakfast?" he asked, setting the bag on the kitchen table. "Probably not," he said, answering his own question. He unzipped the bag and began to unpack a large container of soup, fresh bread, fruit salad, and a thermos. "Where are your bowls?"

She pointed to one of the cabinets. "But you really don't have to..." She stopped when he opened the lid of the soup, which was still piping hot, steam rising up to the ceiling. The soup wasn't the usual broth with bits of chicken and carrots and noodles. This was Caribbean style heaped with chicken, dumplings, yams, and potatoes and the spicy scent called her forward. It would be a shame to let such a meal go to waste.

Sebastian set the bowl in front of her then lifted an eyebrow. "Bread?"

"Yes, please." She didn't realize how hungry she was until she took the first taste. She'd missed breakfast. He was annoyingly right about that. She usually forgot about meals until someone reminded her, but her empty stomach rejoiced. "This is delicious."

"If you want more, just let me know."

She took another large spoonful. "No, this is fine." She paused then glanced with guilt at the remainder in the container. If Sebastian also ate, there wouldn't be enough for her father. "You gave me a lot. Let me put some of this away."

"I already ate. There's plenty for your father."

"Good," she said in relief.

He leaned back in his chair and studied her. "So what just happened?"

"What?" she said with little interest, solely focused on eating as much of the savory soup as possible. If she could inhale it she would.

"Why did you think I came for a blow job?"

Naomi choked on her soup and coughed.

Sebastian opened the thermos and poured a drink that smelled like lemon and lime. He held it out to her. "Here."

She waved him away. "No, I'm fine," she said then coughed again and changed her mind, taking the drink and gulping it down. She cleared her throat, her cheeks burning from embarrassment. He had a right to bring up her misunderstanding, but she still wished he hadn't. Couldn't he have pretended that she hadn't made an idiot of herself? "I'm really sorry about that. I've had a few unwanted visitors."

"To put it mildly." He folded his arms and leaned back further, tilting the chair to balance on its back legs. She heard the chair groan under his weight. She hoped it would continue to hold him. She'd gotten the kitchen set secondhand and had no idea how old it was. He dwarfed the metal chair, with its curved back and tan cushion, so much so it seemed to disappear beneath him, giving him the eerie appearance of floating in mid-air.

She sighed and returned to her soup, she'd finish it before she sent him on his way. "The truth is I'm really overwhelmed right now. I have to find a new place to live and break my lease and—"

"I'll take care of that for you. Do I need to take care of a spiteful ex as well?"

Her head shot up, the spoon halfway to her mouth. "What?"

"Is there a reason men have been showing up at your door asking for sex?"

She swallowed. He was very straightforward. She liked that in a person, even if it was humiliating.

"My housekeeper." She shook her head. "I mean my *former* housekeeper, invited men here while I was away on business and probably even when I stayed overnight at the lab. And let's just say I work late a lot." Naomi set her spoon down and pushed the bowl away, losing her appetite at the thought of how long or how many men had seen the inside of her apartment. She held her head in her hands. "It's awful."

Sebastian pushed the soup towards her. "It's a problem that can be solved. Eat up."

She picked up the spoon then set it back down. "Not that easily."

He lifted the spoon.

She started to laugh. "Are you planning to feed me?"

"If I have to. You look exhausted."

And she felt it too. She felt as if the weight of her worries were about to crush her.

Sebastian put the spoon in her hand. "Come on. I'm here to help. Let me do my job."

"We haven't even discussed—"

"You can argue while you eat."

Naomi frowned then took a spoonful. Within seconds the warm concoction made her feel like her worries were melting away. Or was it him? His steady, quiet yet forceful presence was oddly comforting. She took another sip.

Sebastian nodded pleased then pulled out his cell phone. "What do you need?"

"What?" She put down her spoon, but when she saw a slight frown touch his lips, she picked it up again. "No, you can't..." She took a spoonful and saw the frown ease. "I mean I can't..." She took another bite and the frown disappeared and he unfolded his arms. "I know what I promised, but I don't have the funds to pay you. Even if it's a stipend, it would be stretch."

He leaned forward, setting the chair down on all four legs with a thud. "That's fine, then I'll be your personal assistant on a volunteer basis."

"But—"

"You haven't touched your bread." He shifted his gaze to his cell phone. "Now just tell me what you need." He stood. "Never mind. I'll be right back."

Moments later her father entered the kitchen with a big grin of his face. "Sebastian told me you'd be here." He grabbed a bowl and spoon. "Does it taste as good as it smells?"

"Where is he?"

Her father ladled soup into his bowl, sat down and began to eat. "Hmm..."

"Dad?"

"What?"

"Where is he?"

"He's just looking around."

"Why?"

"How am I supposed to know that?"

Before Naomi could leave the kitchen to find out what Sebastian was up to, he appeared in the doorway. "You don't appear to need much space or light for that matter."

Her father laughed. "That's true. I sometimes call her my little mushroom."

Naomi winced, that wasn't exactly something she wanted shared, but it was the family joke that she flourished best in dark, damp places. She couldn't remember the last time she looked outside her apartment window and wasn't even sure how many she had.

"Are you doing any university work? Do you want a place within walking distance?"

"No, at least for the next several years. I've won a grant," she said mentioning the project that had been funded by a foreign foundation due to the narrow scope of her research and lack of interest from the greater science community. "But...I'll be looking for another lab location since the present one won't work for what I plan to do."

He nodded. "Done."

She blinked. "What?"

"He said 'done'," her father said.

She shot him a glance. "I know what he said, I want to understand what it means."

"I know the perfect place," Sebastian said. "I can show you when your schedule is free." He held out his hand. "Let me see your phone."

"Why?"

"So I can see your schedule."

Naomi quickly finished her soup and set the bowl and spoon in the sink then left the kitchen. "I don't keep it there," she said as he followed her to the living room. She sat on the couch.

Sebastian sat in front of her. "Fine, then show me your calendar."

She shook her head.

"Your organizer?"

She shook her head again.

He frowned. "Then where do you keep your schedule?"

She tapped the side of her head.

"And how many flights have you missed?"

She paused again surprised by his perception. "Just two. Okay five, but..."

"And conferences?"

"I get to them just fine. Okay," she admitted when he looked doubtful. "So I usually miss the keynote speaker."

"Meetings? Movies? Dinner dates?"

"I don't date."

"Duly noted."

She cleared her throat wondering why she'd felt the need to mention that. It was none of his business, but it still irked her that he didn't seem surprised. She doubted his social life was better than hers.

"What does your girlfriend think about this?" She could have said boyfriend or tried for a neutral term, but decided to go with the law of percentages on the total number of asexuals and homosexuals versus heterosexuals and hazard a guess.

"She's fine."

Bingo. She felt pleased she'd pegged him correctly. Perhaps a little too pleased. She stiffened. It shouldn't matter one way or another. So what if he was smart, detailed, and thoughtful? With a haircut and a pressed suit he wouldn't look half bad. She mentally shook her head. What was she thinking? She'd never thought of a man like this and he was here for a job and probably had a girlfriend who alphabetized her pantry and color coordinated her shoes and purse. "I bet she's organized."

"She would be if she existed." Before she could say anything more, he changed the subject. "So you don't write anything down pertaining to your day-to-day activities?"

Naomi glanced around the sparse room where a bookshelf stacked with textbooks stood next to a dusty green standing lamp. "I have a calendar somewhere."

"That you clearly don't use. Don't worry. What's on the agenda today?"

"I was finishing a project with my father. I just came back from Costa Rica so..."

"Still unpacked from the look of the bags by the door."

She followed his glance. Nearly a week later and she'd practically forgotten about them. It wasn't unusual for a few weeks to pass before she put things away. "Do you want me to take anything to the cleaners?"

"Yes." She shook her head. "No." She held out her hands. "I really appreciate this. You're fast and efficient and I could use some help now that Maya is gone. But I hardly know anything about you."

"That's why I gave you my card." He tapped his leg. "You can look me up right now if you want."

She'd do that later, having him sit there waiting would be too awkward. "Why do you want this job?" she said suddenly feeling like a rattled HR recruiter. "No, first how did you know my name?"

"I saw you at the wedding."

"Yes."

"And I couldn't help overhearing that you might be in need of help."

She cringed. "You heard that?"

"Your mother sounded like you were on the verge of being murdered."

"Yes, well...wait. Then why did you ask me why I said what I said to you at the door?"

He flashed a quick grin. "I wanted to hear you explain it yourself."

Naomi narrowed her eyes and crossed her legs. *Sneaky.* "So you're only here to help."

"Plus, I'm a big fan."

"Fan? I don't have fans. Maybe you have me confused with someone else. I'm..."

"Dr. Naomi Mensah," he said then proceeded to give her a brief description of her academic background and accomplishments as if he were writing her profile for Wikipedia.

She nodded semi-impressed. "You did do your homework."

"I've read your work."

"Then why would you want to be my personal assistant? Since you attended my father's lecture, you must know something about the field. What's your specialty?"

He looked at her for a long moment, his sharp brown gaze both patient and probing. "My name is Sebastian Scott."

"Yes," she said with impatience. "I know. You told me."

"*Dr.* Sebastian Scott."

He waited his probing gaze becoming more intense, as if he expected her to know the answer to a riddle. Was his name supposed to mean something to her? He was at the wedding. Were they family somehow? Distant cousins? No, her father would have known him too or her mother would have mentioned him. *Sebastian Scott.* For some reason his name did sound familiar. She bit her lip and swung her foot. "The only Sebastian Scott I can think of is the disgraced scientist whose lousy research caused BioCorps millions and led to his dismissal under a cloud of shame."

He blinked.

Naomi silently swore as her eyes widened. *Ohhhh...noooo...* "That's you?"

He blinked again.

"But—"

"We can talk about me later. You should probably rest now so you can recover from your cold. I'll be here tomorrow at eight sharp."

"But it's Saturday."

"That's fine." He walked to the door. "We need to find you a new place to stay. It will be a pleasure to work with you." He nodded then left.

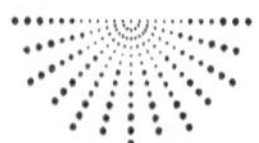

$\mathcal{N}$aomi stormed into the kitchen where her father was finishing his soup with relish. She gestured to the other room. "Did you hear that?" she said with a note of panic in her voice.

He licked his lips. "Is there enough of this soup to take home to your mother?"

"Dad, did you just hear that!"

"Hear what?"

Naomi fell into the chair in front of him. "Dad! That was Sebastian Scott. *The* Sebastian Scott. Dr. Disgrace. Sebastian the—"

"And what do they call you?"

"Besides brilliant?"

"The other name. Isn't it Nutty Naomi?"

She frowned. "I didn't know you knew it too."

"Nicknames have no business in our field, they belong on playgrounds and sometimes not even there. I expect better from you."

"Okay, so I won't call him a name, that doesn't change who he is."

"At least one problem is solved."

"What is that?"

"I wondered why he seemed familiar, and now I know why. He didn't lie about attending a lecture of mine and he would know who you are. So he's not a con or crazy, although he's let himself go a bit."

Naomi's brows shot up. "A bit? He needs to shape his hair and trim his beard and, his clothes don't fit him well and are crumpled. He looks like he's dragged himself out of a cardboard box."

Her father shook his head in regret. "Dr. Scott had such promise. He'd risen faster than most. It's a shame."

It was a shame. There had been such hope in the research he and his team had developed. Their data helped create a synthetic antibiotic against the tuberculosis bacterium. Unfortunately, it had a deleterious effect on the ear and caused impaired hearing. It had been rumored that in a push to produce the antibiotic, results had been doctored or interpreted with lack of care.

"I can't work with him."

"You made—"

"I know what I said, but my reputation is everything. I can't be seen with him. And why would he want this job anyway? He should be teaching high school somewhere. Or selling insurance."

"Insurance?"

She waved her hand in a dismissive gesture. "I couldn't think of something else."

"You can't back out now. He can find you a place."

"So you were listening."

"Only to that part. Your mother is very worried. The sooner you're out of this place, the sooner I can go back to my regular routine."

"You're retired."

"I still have a regular routine. I had to miss playing tennis because of this." He met every week with his close friend Dr. Khan. "And I want to make progress on my book."

"I wonder what he wants?"

"You'll have plenty of time to find out."

Naomi pressed her hands together as if in prayer. "Dad, please, you have to help me get out of this. I can't be seen with him."

"You can and you will. What 'jam' as you call it, did he help you out of?"

She let her hands fall and sank back in her seat. "It's nothing."

He stood and put his bowl in the sink. "Maybe I should ask him."

"No, don't," she said quickly. She sighed resigned. "Fine, I'll work with him." *Until I can find a way to get rid of him.*

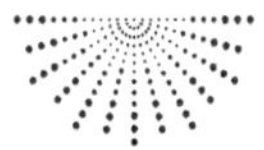

He still couldn't determine whether she was pretty or not. Sebastian tapped a finger on his desk in his study while a grandfather clock ticked in the background. The afternoon sun slipped through the blinds behind him causing striped shadows to fall across the floor.

Sebastian rested his palm flat on the table, perplexed. His mother's question should have been a simple one, but he couldn't answer it yet. Was she pretty?

Dr. Naomi Mensah had arresting, angular features that on their own could be off-putting—a pointed determined chin, sharp cheekbones, short, straight eyelashes—but put together in her oval face he found himself intrigued by her snapping brown eyes and full lower lip. He found himself watching it as she ate, watching her pink tongue sweep across it after a spoonful of soup. That tongue could keep him up at nights.

A knock on the door woke him out of his wandering thoughts. He cleared his throat, trying to ease the heat and tension in his body. "Come in."

His friend and personal secretary, Andre Bremmer,

came in bristling with indignation. Sebastian wasn't surprised, he'd expected the response. "I can't let you do this," Andre said.

Sebastian sighed. "You spoke to Mom."

"She's in a panic. She thinks you've lost your mind."

"I haven't. I've already completed my first assignment."

Andre sat down and waved his hands. "But this doesn't make any sense."

"It makes perfect sense to me. And you know me better than to think I'd do anything irrational."

"I still can't let you do this."

Sebastian smiled, amused. They both knew it was an empty threat. There was nothing Andre could do to stop him. Sebastian was a head taller and fifteen years younger than Andre. A hard looking, greying man with a bulldog face and the tenacity to match. His father had hired him first, eight years ago, but he and Sebastian became fast friends so when his father grew ill, Sebastian hired Andre as his personal secretary. He managed the house and completed other duties for Sebastian and Josephine.

"I'll give you back the money," Andre said.

Sebastian's smile fell. He'd given him an extra bonus to compensate for having to look after his mother while Sebastian put his plan into action. "No you won't. You have a family to support."

"And you've always taken good care of me and my family."

He nodded. "I always will."

"And it's my job to take care of you."

"You don't need to do that for a while. An assistant doesn't need another assistant. It will just look ridiculous. When's the last time you took a vacation? You look like you could use one. I'll get someone to look in on Mom."

"I don't need a vacation, I like what I do. You can't be an assistant to that woman."

Sebastian's patience began to fade. "That woman is a highly respected—"

"I know what she is. But this situation is beneath you."

"You're the only person who thinks so."

"A waste of your genius."

"Again arguable."

"What would your father say?"

Sebastian shrugged. "Considering he's dead. Not very much."

"Why would you do this? You've suffered enough. Why punish yourself even more?"

"This isn't punishment. This is an opportunity."

"How?"

"I have my reasons. But just know this, there are certain variables in place that increase the probability of success."

Andre blinked, confused.

Sebastian adjusted his glasses knowing he needed to speak more plainly. "I know what I am doing."

"We can't ignore the elephant in the room."

"Which is?"

"She looks a little like Barbara."

"She looks nothing like her. The only similarity is that they're both black and wear glasses."

"But you have a type."

Sebastian slid his finger across the table from the left to the right. "See this line? It's best not to cross it."

Andre ignored him. "The moment she entered your life is the moment things went downhill."

Sebastian clasped his hands together in resignation, trying to scare Andre rarely worked. He was one of the few people

Sebastian couldn't intimidate. He clicked his tongue as if to scold him. "That's sloppy logic. You know better than that. Just because it rains the same day you wash your car doesn't mean washing your car caused the rain."

"She went off and married—"

Sebastian couldn't stop a grin. "That just shows she has terrible taste in men," he cut in not wanting to remember how Barbara had left him at a time when his father was dying and his career was at a crossroads, to marry a more established colleague who boosted her career.

Andre frowned. "You're not taking this seriously."

"No," Sebastian said with a laugh, "and I never plan to. It hurt. I got over it. Besides, Dr. Naomi Mensah is different."

"There are rumors."

"I don't listen to rumors."

"She's odd and in your field that's saying a lot. They say she's so focused that a marching band could pass her by with horns blaring and she wouldn't notice. That at almost every meal she uses a straw because her meals come in a thermos."

"I like a little eccentricity."

Andre's frown deepened. "She's not rich enough to be eccentric." He leaned forward. "I know it's been...difficult since your father's passing and having to take care of the business these past several years instead of working on what you want must have been a strain, but you're better off than most. If you hadn't had your father's business to fall back on, who knows where you might have ended up after what happened?"

Sebastian rested his chin in his hand looking bored. "If you have a point, I'd like you to get to it."

"Working with a scientist, isn't the same as being one."

He nodded. "Duly noted."

"And—"

Sebastian held up his hand. "This is where the discussion ends." He let his hand fall and smiled. "I have my reasons so relax. I haven't lost my mind. You worry too much."

"Because you don't worry enough."

"Tell Mom that the company is safe and soon Gregg will be able to take on more duties."

Andre nodded and left, but didn't feel reassured. If there was one thing he did well, it was worry. Growing up he worried where his next meal would come from; he worried about staying out of trouble; he worried about getting kicked around by his father who thought Andre's light brown skin meant his mother had stepped out on him; he worried about keeping his family together. But as he grew older he kept his worrying in check, to the relief of his wife and daughters, but when he did worry it was monumental.

And he was worried now. Sebastian used to trust him, used to confide in him, but he was keeping secrets and that couldn't be good. Andre didn't know what to do.

Josephine met him in the hallway, anxiety shining bright in her eyes. "Well?"

"He said he has his reasons," Andre said, wishing he had better news to tell her.

"Did he tell you what those reasons are?"

"No, but he seems determined. Give him space he may grow bored. Being an assistant isn't easy." He lightly touched her shoulder and offered a smile. "I should know."

Josephine didn't respond to his touch, her gaze growing more anxious. "Should we get his brother involved?"

"There's nothing he can do. The company is stable and Gregg is in a good position now. I don't think Sebastian would have planned something like this otherwise. Come, you shouldn't be standing like this." He led her to her bedroom.

Josephine sat on her chaise lounge chair and set her cane aside. "What do you know about the woman?"

"Everything I told you. Until we can understand his reason for choosing her there's nothing we can do."

"There's always something to do."

Andre shoved his hands in his pockets and rocked on his heels. "Right now, all we can do is wait and see."

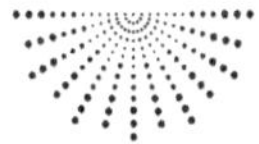

*D*r. Sebastian Scott had clearly lost his mind. Naomi stood in the elegant room not knowing what else to think.

She'd expected a one bedroom apartment, not a suite inside a mansion. That Saturday morning, she'd prepared herself to have Sebastian help her look at a two story walkup or studio apartment on the eighth floor somewhere. When he drove her out of the suburbs to a curved driveway and an expansive home nestled on acres of land that looked as if it were designed for royalty, she had been confused.

Now she stood on the second floor staring at a master suite that could have swallowed her apartment two times over. It boasted high ceilings, large windows—*lots of light!* she could hear her mother squeal with delight—and was meticulously furnished.

"What do you think?" Sebastian asked. "Anything you don't like can be removed."

Naomi stared at the room in awe. "How many others rent here?" She'd counted the bedroom doors and could imagine seven to ten other tenants, but she didn't know what the lower level contained.

"You'd be the only one."

"Has the owner gotten into trouble and needs the ready cash of renters to cover the mortgage?"

"No."

She waited for him to expand further but after a few awkward seconds realized he didn't plan to say anything else. She walked into the full bathroom gaping at the elegant modern design and light effects to create a luxurious experience and then went into the bedroom where a double bed, chaise lounge chair and chandelier greeted her. She met him in the main area shaking her head, dumbfounded that he would even tempt her this way. "I can't afford this. All I need is a simple place to eat and sleep."

"The cost will be comparable to what you were paying for your apartment."

"That's impossible." She walked over to the bookshelf and gasped at the selection of titles—*The Andromeda Strain, Antimicrobial Agents and Chemotherapy*—it was as if the room had been created with her specifically in mind.

"You don't like it?" he asked in an odd tone.

She turned to him. "No."

He nodded. "Duly noted. I'll—"

She spread her arms to the side and threw back her head. "It's divine. I'm in heaven." She let her arms fall and looked at him. "And my sister thinks I have terrible taste, but if she saw me here she'd change her mind. But—" She wagged her finger at him when he opened his mouth. "It's too good to be true. I'm waiting for the other shoe to drop."

She noticed his jaw relax and realized that he'd been worried. How could that be? Who wouldn't love this place?

"Not many people would like that abstract," he said, nodding to a painting on the wall, by an artist who used cell patterns for his creations.

"I'd seen this work before. It's my favorite."

A quick smile came and then went. "Mine too."

She called him over with the crook of her finger.

He bent down. "Yes?"

She cupped his face in her hands. "Why didn't you warn me that you are crazy?"

"Crazy?"

"It's cruel to get a woman's hopes up like this. We aren't sure what the owner is like and whether he or she will even rent to me."

Sebastian clasped his hands behind his back and straightened. "This house is also close to the lab you'll be using."

Her brows shot up. "You found me a lab too?"

He nodded and turned. "Let's go see it."

She grabbed his arm, then quickly let go when he looked at her surprised.

And at that moment a sensuous light passed between them that startled her, causing her heart to beat fast and her gaze to hold his longer than she needed to.

"What do I have to do?" she asked, feeling suddenly breathless.

He frowned. "What?" he asked, his voice sounding deeper than before.

She swallowed and steadied herself. It was nothing. It was the beauty of the room. The light. She'd never been surrounded by so much natural light; it was making her feel heady. "What do I have to do for all this? Everything has a price." She bit her lip. "Things like this don't happen to me."

Sebastian folded his arms and gave her the long, measuring

look that made her skin tingle. She couldn't read his thoughts although it was a look she was starting to get used to. He finally said, "The lab is mine and so is the house so you can stop worrying. You don't have to do anything but focus on your work." He turned.

She grabbed his arm again, but this time when he looked at her, she didn't let go, even though her hands trembled a bit from a mixture of anxiety, excitement and another feeling she couldn't quite place. "What you just said doesn't make any sense to me."

"Which part confused you?"

"All of it." She threw up her hands. "How can you own a lab? How can this be your house when you're—"

"A disgraced scientist who should be living in a boarding house eating canned beans? I'm sorry to disappoint you." He left the room.

She found him heading down the stairs. For a large man, he moved fast. She hurried to catch up. "It's just... Come on, few scientists—let alone ordinary people—live this well. What do you do?"

"I work for you."

"I wish you'd stop saying that."

"Why? It's true."

"That doesn't make any sense either."

"Sebastian is that you?" a female voice called from the hallway.

He halted so suddenly, Naomi bumped into him. She stumbled back catching herself with the railing; he didn't budge.

"Sebastian?"

He sighed then slowly headed down the remainder of the stairs.

"Who is that?" Naomi asked.

"My mother."

Naomi widened her eyes. "You live with your mother?"

"My mother lives with me," he smoothly corrected. "But we won't be in your way. She has a room on the main floor."

"Sebastian!"

His jaw twitched.

Naomi nudged him forward, surprised by his sudden leisurely pace. "She sounds like she really wants you. Maybe she hurt herself."

"No, she always calls me like that when I don't respond the first few times." He proceeded down to the main floor and walked into the sitting room where an attractive older woman sat.

"I thought I heard voices," she said in a pout. "Why didn't you say anything?"

"This is Dr. Naomi Mensah," Sebastian said. "She'll be staying with us for a few months."

His mother's mouth fell open making it clear she'd had no idea of this new arrangement. "And now I'm going to take her to the lab. Andre will be here to take you shopping in twenty minutes." He kissed her on the cheek. "Goodbye." His tone left no room for argument, although Naomi could tell from his mother's expression that she'd have plenty of questions for him when they were alone.

Naomi held out her hand. "It's a pleasure to meet you."

But his mother was too busy staring at her son in stunned silence to notice the gesture, so she took a step back and followed Sebastian outside.

"I knew it was too good to be true," Naomi said once they were in the car.

"My mother won't be a problem."

"She didn't look too pleased to see me."

He checked his rearview mirror looking unperturbed.

"And that doesn't bother you at all," she said in a dry tone.

"I think you're really going to like the lab."

NAOMI ACTUALLY SQUEALED when she saw the lab. It was even more stunning than the house. It was state of the art, simple, clean. It even had a special keypad with the passcode 1872, the year Ferdinand J Cohn contributed to the founding of the science of bacteriology. "You're not my assistant," Naomi said. "You're my fairy godfather."

Sebastian smiled. "That's how I felt the first time I saw it finished."

"But you don't use it."

"I had plans..." he said, letting his sentence drift away, but not before Naomi heard a touch of longing in his voice and saw brief sadness in his eyes.

And at that moment she knew the house and money couldn't replace the loss of a career he'd loved. She wanted to know more. How could he have made such an error? Had he tried to correct it? What had really gone wrong?

Soon she found herself not only wondering about his career, but about the man himself. She suddenly felt drawn to him, noticing his broad shoulders and the elegant slope of his nose. It was the first time she'd seen him unhappy—she'd seen him confused, annoyed, frustrated, but not like this—and she didn't like the expression, so she brightened her tone and smiled and said, "We'll put it to good use. This day has been amazing. The house, the lab. Next you'll be replacing my car—"

His gaze sharpened. "Is your car giving you trouble?"

"No. It was just an example. But it's time we were honest with each other."

He nodded. "I haven't lied to you."

"No, but I don't need an assistant and you clearly don't need a job. Why even volunteer for a position like this?"

That distant, but polite look entered his eyes and she knew he was going to change the topic. He didn't disappoint. He turned and headed outside.

"As you can see," he said once they were through the main doors, "the lab is in an ideal location to walk to eateries and is accessible by bus or train if your researchers don't own cars. There's also a gym nearby, but at the house there's a pool I can show you later."

He had his reasons to avoid her questions and she wouldn't press him. Right now she was getting a better deal than he was. She'd find out his true agenda later. "A swimming pool wouldn't do me much good since I can't swim. I know, I know," she said when an expression of surprise crossed his face. "Graduate with honors from University of Pennsylvania at eighteen but I can't even do a duck paddle. I've put it on my life list to learn one day. What are you doing?" she asked when he started to type something on his cell phone.

"Making a note to find you an instructor. You'll never find time for things you don't schedule."

She rolled her eyes. "You and schedules."

But within two days she was already getting used to him. Actually liking him. She hadn't responded to a man like this in years. Maybe ever. Even in grad school she'd only gone out with Barry out of curiosity. With Sebastian, she was more than curious—she was intrigued. He was like a new specimen she wanted to study. That wasn't good. She could become obsessive about things like that.

He'd helped her solve two major problems, but she didn't need a personal assistant so she'd have to get rid of him on her own.

Josephine hummed as the car sped down the street, finding the spring afternoon bright and beautiful in every way from the dot of clouds in the blue sky to the sight of purple poppies in a garden. She glanced at the back of Andre's head as he sat in the driver's seat, fighting a wild urge to kiss it in relief. She'd never been in such a good mood. So good, she was going to treat herself to a manicure.

"There's nothing to worry about," she told him. "Absolutely nothing at all."

Andre was quiet a few moments then said, "Why the change of heart?"

"I met her. That doctor woman he's been talking about and she's not a threat at all."

"I wouldn't be too sure of that."

"I am. I know my son."

"Then why do you think he chose her?"

Josephine sniffed. "When have I ever understood what my son was about? He's even letting her stay at the house."

"Yes, I know. I had to get the suite prepared." Andre met her eyes in the rearview mirror. "And that doesn't worry you?"

"I told you, I met her. There's no spark between them and she's nothing like Barbara. She's skinny as a twig and pretty enough, but not remarkable. And when I saw him with her, I could tell he wasn't attracted to her like the others. That's when I knew he was up to something. I should have paid more attention when he was talking about her work."

"He might be trying to find a way back into the field."

Josephine nodded. "Agreed. That's my suspicion too, but what could she possibly have that he'd want?"

"You want me to find out even more about her?"

"If it's not too much trouble," she said, which meant 'Find out as much as you can as soon as possible.'

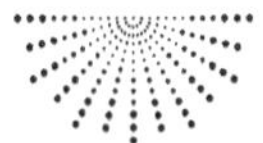

CHAPTER ELEVEN

She couldn't get rid of him.

In the nearly two months they'd been together, Naomi had sent Sebastian on five useless trips to Eastern Shore and Anacostia to get micro-samples she didn't need. He didn't care. He returned and cataloged everything with the precision of a true scientist. Which bothered her. As detailed as he was, how could he have made such a huge error at BioCorps? But she fought to keep her curiosity at bay as she tried to figure out a way to get rid of him so she wouldn't grow attached.

Already she feared she was failing because he made her life easier. In the morning her breakfast was prepared, he took her to the lab where she convened with her research team, having gotten there without having to think about traffic, Sebastian then reminded her about lunch, which he also prepared (before him she'd often forget her lunch at home),then she'd work late into the evening. Her clothes were dry cleaned, he reminded her of a dentist appointment she'd forgotten about and even found a book she'd been searching for for months. He was becoming indispensable.

She couldn't have that. But she didn't mind it either.

Naomi stood in front of the abstract painting in her room, the early summer sun blocked by the velvet drapes she kept closed in order to concentrate. She couldn't understand her warring emotions.

She jumped when her phone rang. She checked the number; a little disappointed it wasn't him, then picked it up and sat on the couch. "Hello?"

"Your father wants to invite Dr. Scott over for dinner."

Naomi adjusted her glasses. "Why?"

"Because you haven't invited us over yet."

Naomi stretched her legs along the couch. "He's my assistant not my boyfriend, you don't need to formally meet him."

"I must thank him for the soup he had delivered to us, and that beautiful place where you're staying."

"He already knows you liked the soup. I had him give me the name of the restaurant, remember? And I'm paying rent, so it's not a complete charity."

"I didn't say it was."

Naomi swung her feet to the ground as a thought hit her. "Oh no, I haven't paid my rent yet." She closed her eyes and pounded her forehead with her fist. "How could I have forgotten that? I used to have it done automatically; I haven't set that up yet." She stood up and paced. "I'll have to tell Sebastian to...wait why didn't he remind me since he owns the place?"

"He's both your personal assistant and your landlord?"

Naomi silently swore. She'd been careful not to tell her mother the connection. When her parents had come to see where she was staying, she'd come up with an elaborate story of a wealthy, elderly woman who'd devoted her life to funding people in the scientific community and on an exclusive basis would let some take up residence in her home for a nominal fee over the course of a year. They'd believed her. "It's a long story."

"I like to hear it. Does he have any food allergies?"

Naomi sighed, her mother could be so stubborn. "I don't know."

"Is he a vegetarian?"

"I don't know."

"What does he like to eat?"

"I don't know."

"You've been with this man all this time and you don't know what he likes to eat?" her mother said sounding appalled.

Naomi felt properly scolded. To her shame she realized that she'd never seen Sebastian eat. He'd always made sure she had her three meals, but now as she looked back, he never ate with her. Why was that? How could she have only noticed that now? *You don't observe the world around you*, her sister had said.

"Call me back when you get the answers," her mother said.

"Don't be surprised if he decides not to come."

Her mother made a sound as if that were an impossibility then said, "We want you over this Saturday around six," before disconnecting.

AT BREAKFAST THE NEXT MORNING, Naomi tucked into spinached eggs and toast reviewing all that she planned to do for the day, wondering what the kidney cancer cells they had on slides would reveal today, when she paused to look across the table at Sebastian who was reading the complete collection of Beatrix Potter, which he did most mornings. She remembered teasing him about it once, and he just shrugged and said "I like the pictures" as if she were the one being childish and she never teased him again, especially after she snuck a peek and saw the artistic detail and skill in every painting and sketch.

But she was getting used to him surprising her and opening her eyes. She remembered the gorgeous bed and breakfast in Pennsylvania he'd found for her to stay in when she had a lecture at the university. The new gold lace red dress he bought her when she accidentally burned the one she was supposed to wear to a charity event with an iron (she'd gotten distracted by a statistics problem she was trying to figure out). When she asked him how much the dress cost, he refused to give her a figure, but she suspected it cost more than her entire wardrobe combined.

However, his generosity didn't end there. When her project funder came into town for a visit, Sebastian scheduled a dinner cruise on the Potomac, something Naomi would never have thought of. In truth, if she hadn't had Sebastian she would have forgotten he was in town entirely. She still remembered the sight of passing by the National Monument at night, while she enjoyed a Mediterranean couscous and chickpea salad and baked ziti pasta. She'd never forget how much she enjoyed finding out more about her funder—what his interests were, how much they had in common—and his wife, for the first time seeing a person behind the foundation.

When the funder went to the dance floor joined by his wife, she remembered that Sebastian stretched his hand out to her.

She looked at him alarmed. "What are you doing?"

"Asking you to dance."

"But I don't dance."

"You will tonight," he said, taking her hand and lifting her to her feet.

"I'm a terrible dancer," she said as he led her to the dance floor.

"That's okay," he said before he drew her into a dancer's embrace.

And in his arms he made it more than okay, within moments she felt as if she were floating on air, the feel of his hand in hers, the heat of the palm of his hand at the small of her back. When she was eight years old, she remembered being caught in a downpour with her father when they'd both gone for a walk. They returned home wet and shivering and as her mother dried her up with a towel, she scolded her father for not paying attention to the weather forecast and at least carrying an umbrella. Then her mother wrapped Naomi in a warm blue blanket and her shivering stopped and she felt secure and safe. She felt that same way now...with a little more heat.

Sebastian moved well and she moved well with him. And for a brief moment Naomi closed her eyes and imagined what it would be like to wake up beside him.

"Naomi," he'd say in a smooth velvet tone. And she'd just sigh and pretend to be asleep. He'd say her name again this time with a question and then he'd say her name a third time, nudging her awake.

She sighed when she felt the featherlike touch of his lips against hers. It felt so real...It took Naomi a second to realize it was. She opened her eyes and looked up at him startled. "Did you just kiss me?"

Her reaction seemed to amuse him. "Yes, I'm trying to wake you out of a dream. I said your name three times."

"Why?"

"Because the song is over."

She looked around and saw others dancing to the upbeat music. She pulled away from him, her facing burning. "I'm sorry."

"It's okay."

Naomi cast a nervous glance around the room to make sure her funder hadn't seen them. She didn't want to look unprofessional. Sebastian was her personal assistant not her boyfriend.

"Don't worry, they didn't see us."

"You didn't have to kiss me," Naomi said, heading back to their table, her lips tingling.

Sebastian pulled out her chair. "It wasn't a real kiss, just a quick peck."

She sat down. "It was a kiss."

He pushed her chair in. "Trust me," he said in a low voice, his breath hot against her ear. "If I were to really kiss you, you'd know the difference."

She swallowed, believing him. He was her personal assistant nothing else and right now he was just teasing her. She couldn't make it mean anything more than that. She pushed the dance and light kiss from her mind and enjoyed the remainder of the evening, indulging in a chocolate cake for dessert and chatting with her funder when he returned to the table. She hadn't paid much attention to Sebastian, determined to pretend he had no affect on her. She didn't even notice if he ate anything or not.

As she studied him now at the breakfast table, it took her a few seconds to notice she was the only one with any food. He didn't even have a cup of coffee or a glass of water.

It was true. She'd never seen him eat before. *Ever.* She didn't even know where his room was. What time did he go to bed? Did he shower in the morning or take a bath at night? She still knew so little about him.

"If you want to make yourself some toast, I don't mind being a little late," she said, her stomach tightening. She hated being late and itched to be in her lab, but she didn't like the thought of being inconsiderate.

Sebastian turned the page. "I already ate."

"What?"

He lifted his head up, surprised. "What?"

Naomi nodded. "Yes, that's what I'm asking you. What did you eat?"

It was the first time he looked at a loss for words. "Food."

"You haven't eaten yet. Why not eat now?"

"There's not enough time. I'll eat later." He nodded to her plate. "Your food's getting cold."

"Do you drink coffee?"

He nodded.

"Tea?"

He nodded again.

"Black, white or herbal?"

He frowned, making it clear he didn't realize there was a difference.

"I'm only asking because my mother has invited you over for dinner and to my shame I don't know what you like to eat or drink."

Sebastian snapped his book closed and stared at her. "Your mother's asked me to dinner?"

"Yes."

"With your father there?"

Naomi paused surprised by his question. "Yes," she said slowly, "my father will be there."

"I admire Dr. Mensah very much."

Naomi couldn't help a smile. "It's not like you've kept that a secret." Her father was one topic he couldn't seem to get bored of. He'd told her again about how much her father's London speech had impressed him, how he'd followed his career and read his papers. And he asked about the book her father was working on.

"Have I come on too strong?"

"No," Naomi said, again not quite sure of the question. Did he think she was jealous of her father? It was understandable, he cast a long shadow. "I'm proud of my father's accomplishments. I'm glad you admire them."

Sebastian nodded looking relieved as he pushed her plate towards her as a reminder to eat.

She took a bite of her toast. "And you made an impression on him too because he's the one extending this invitation. My parents are a little annoyed I haven't had them over here for dinner or lunch or anything for that matter."

"Is that what you want? Do you want to host them here? I can—"

"No, no, no. Let my mother do the cooking, it will be a disaster otherwise."

"I can always hire a—"

"No, it's better this way. Unless you don't want to go."

He looked suddenly alarmed. "That's not it. I just—"

"Then answer my question. What do you like to eat? Do you have allergies or any food preferences?"

"No."

Naomi waited for him to expand then realized he wouldn't. "That's it?"

He nodded. "Your mother can make whatever she wants."

"Baked cow tongue? Pickled pig brain? Crispy chicken feet?"

He nodded again. "That's fine."

She was teasing him, but was surprised to see he didn't even wince. Her mother would never serve unfamiliar foods to new guests. "Okay, I'll let her know."

"What time should we be there?"

"Probably around six."

When he frowned, she knew he found her answer too vague. "Six o'clock sharp, but I'll call to make sure."

"What do they like? Wine? Fruit?"

"You don't need to be formal."

"I can't arrive empty handed."

"Flowers."

"What kind?"

"Any kind. It doesn't matter," she said, not realizing that she'd soon regret not being more specific.

A large bouquet of lush peach roses surrounded by pale yellow mini carnations, with bright red Peruvian lilies and luxurious greens greeted them when Naomi and Sebastian entered the Mensah dining room.

"Thank you for the beautiful gift," her mother said, beaming at him as she gestured to a chair. "I'll have to remove it while we're eating, but I wanted you to see it, Dr. Scott."

"Sebastian, please."

"We hope our simple hospitality will warrant such an extravagant gift," her father said, taking a seat at the head of the table.

"The invitation already has."

Mrs. Mensah set out the food and soon the table was filled with the sight of sautéed Maryland crab cakes, the bright red gaze of Ghanaian jollof rice, the scent of grilled asparagus, and spicy cornbread.

Two more guests joined them, the Mensah cats—one white with a patch of black, the other grey. They sat beside Sebastian's chair and stared up at him with matching green eyes.

"Just ignore Julius and Percy," Naomi said. "They're just curious, but they won't jump on you."

"Julius and Percy, huh?" Sebastian looked down at them and nodded.

"Yes, after Julius Richard Petri and Percy Julian," Naomi explained knowing he'd recognize the name of the creator of the Petri dish and the African American research chemist.

He adjusted his glasses. "I don't know what to do with cats."

"You can pet them later," her father said. "They're very polite. But if they bother you—"

"No, no. It's fine," he said and soon they were talking about his work with Naomi.

But it was several minutes into the meal when it became clear that everything wasn't fine.

"Do you not like the food?" Mrs. Mensah asked him.

All eyes went to Sebastian's still empty plate.

"No, it all looks wonderful," he said, glancing down at Percy and Julius who still sat staring up at him.

"Do you want someone to make up a plate for you?" Before he could reply, she nodded to her daughter. "You're closest to him. Give him something."

"No, really I can—"

But Naomi took his plate before he could protest, sending him a glance that it was best not to argue. The cats walked to the other side of his chair.

"More rice," her mother chided. "Do you want him to be as skinny as you?"

"Like that's even possible," Naomi mumbled as she added another large spoonful.

Her father made a low noise of disapproval, making it clear he'd heard her comment.

She set the now full plate in front of Sebastian. "Enjoy."

"I will."

They waited.

He lifted his fork.

They continued to wait. The cats slowly swished their tails.

Sebastian lifted the fork to his mouth then looked around. "It's delicious."

"You haven't even tasted it yet," Naomi said. "Hurry up." She stiffened her features to mimic a look he usually gave her. "Your food is getting cold."

"Don't rush him," her mother said.

Sebastian took a bite then nodded. "Wonderful." He set his fork down.

"You're not going to finish?"

"I will." He cleared his throat then glanced back down at the cats.

"The cats are making him nervous. Naomi, put them away."

"No, they're fine," Sebastian said, covering Naomi's hand before she could stand, her skin prickled at his touch. "I'm sorry, this is new to me. I usually eat alone." He gestured to their plates. "Just keep talking and eating and pretend that I'm not here."

"That's not how dinner works," Naomi said, half wanting him to remove his hand, half wanting him to leave it there all evening. "You gather with people and talk and eat—together. That's the entire point."

"But if you're feeling awkward," her mother said, "we won't look at you while you eat."

He was no longer just covering her hand; he was absently drawing little circles with his forefinger on the back of her hand. It shouldn't have felt sensuous, but it did. She swallowed and pulled her hand away annoyed at herself and him for making her feel this way. "Mom, that's impossible. Look at the size of him, he's a little hard to ignore."

"Naomi!"

She sent him a firm look. "Eat or I'll feed you myself," she said reminding him of the threat he'd first made when he'd brought the chicken soup.

The corner of his mouth kicked up in a quick grin. "All right," he said, then took another bite. His pace was still slow and a little awkward, but he made his way through the meal until nobody noticed.

At the end of dinner, Naomi and her father sat in the living room and got into a discussion about lymphoproliferation while Mrs. Mensah began to clear the table. Sebastian stood to help her.

"No, I'm fine. Ack, that daughter of mine," she said with a note of frustration and affection as she sent her daughter a look. "She should be helping, but she's oblivious. I blame her father."

"They seem to have a great relationship," he said with a hint of envy.

"They do, heaven help me. What does your father do?"

"He was in the real estate business. He passed away."

"I'm sorry."

"We looked alike, but weren't alike in many ways." He reached for the dishes.

"Please leave me and join them. I can tell that you want to." When she saw him hesitate, she added, "My husband will be disappointed if you don't."

SEBASTIAN TENTATIVELY SAT down across from Naomi and Dr. Mensah amazed by their easy interaction. His father was bold and loud, while Mr. Mensah was quieter and reserved, but firm in his opinions. His father cared and loved him, but also loved to dictate to him rather than listen. As he grew older their conversations became more stilted, especially when he decided not to follow in his father's footsteps. His father couldn't understand Sebastian's career choice and the distance between them became larger. His father was savvy, bright, but thought the ivory tower of academics was for wimps. Sebastian respected him, but couldn't always relate to him.

Many times Sebastian didn't feel as if he could relate to most people. As a child he'd grown used to eating alone, first because he was in the hospital a lot, then at school no one would eat with him, after that he ate alone from the fear of being teased about his size. He remembered in high school one fat girl who only ate salad, loudly complaining that she didn't know why she couldn't lose weight.

He'd wondered the same thing, until he caught her one day sitting alone in a fast food restaurant stuffing her face with cheeseburger and fries like an addict inhaling cocaine. He felt sorry for her and the guilty secret she kept. Another kid, nick-named The Brick, made eating a performance art. He proudly stacked his tray with everything the cafeteria had to offer that day and consumed everything like a giant sinkhole swallowing up a house.

Sebastian wanted to eat in peace. He didn't want to be like the girl and pretend he didn't know why he was overweight, he liked to eat, it was that simple. But he didn't like people watching and commenting either. Even as he grew and slimmed down a little, he'd gotten into the habit of eating alone, except with his family. Eating with others had become awkward. He didn't feel easy with groups anyway and eating with them only made things worse.

But the Mensahs were different. Once he started eating nobody made a big deal of it. They didn't comment when he took another crab cake or a third helping of cornbread. He realized even Naomi's mention of his size didn't bother him. For some reason, with them he didn't feel sensitive about it.

Sebastian glanced down when he felt something nudge against his leg. He looked at one of the cats, Percy he guessed, and bent down to stroke him. Julius nudged his other leg. Sebastian switched his attention and stroked the cat under his chin. He sat back when he felt he'd petted him enough, but both cats wanted more attention. They jumped up on the couch on either side of him and curled up. He stroked one and then the other until they began to purr.

Sebastian would have spent the remainder of the evening just petting the cats and listening to the conversation, if Dr. Mensah hadn't asked him a direct question about his opinion about natural resistance to infection, which he quickly answered. Naomi disagreed with his response and soon the three were involved in a passionate, heated discussion that lasted until Mrs. Mensah had to interrupt them to announce dessert.

For Sebastian, the evening was a success. Even Naomi seemed amazed by how well he and her parents had gotten on. That night he stared at his reflection in the mirror, hardly recognizing the man who stared back at him. *Keep it together Scott. You're close.*

Phase two of his plan was in place.

But it was no longer all he wanted.

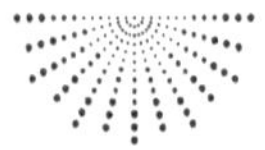

"Who is that?"

Naomi followed Dr. Vera Conklin's cool hazel gaze to where Sebastian sat in the small café. Few things could escape the older woman whose crisp dark suit emphasized her boxy frame. Her sun-washed, blonde hair with streaks of grey was pulled back from her face in a bun and clear framed glasses gave her the appearance of the brilliant woman she was. She'd gotten her doctorate in cell biology and with her former husband, Niklaas, was known in the field for her research into bacterial infections such as listeria. Naomi had asked to meet her mentor for lunch and although she'd given Sebastian the day off, he'd decided to stay three tables away. "He's my new personal assistant."

"I didn't know you needed an assistant."

"Neither did I until he showed up. He's better than he looks."

"Couldn't you have found someone a little more..." She waved her hand searching for words.

"I didn't find him. He found me. It's a long story. Just pretend he's not there."

"That's impossible. He's quite unforgettable. I couldn't believe it when I saw you two coming in together. The way he held the door open for you was almost medieval."

"He's not that bad," Naomi said feeling a little defensive. He was being courteous not medieval. Was it wrong for him to hold the door open for her? And he was hard to ignore, even more so than before. His appearance wasn't as shabby as it had been in the past and he'd gotten his hair cut and his beard trimmed. When had that happened and why hadn't she noticed it sooner? She wasn't the only one to notice his improved appearance, catching the waitress sneaking glances at him.

"I didn't want to say anything," Vera said with a note of caution. "But he looks a little bit like Sebastian Scott."

"Probably because he is."

She stared at Naomi wide-eyed for a few seconds then closed her mouth and shook her head. "Get rid of him immediately."

"You think I haven't tried?" Naomi said with a laugh, even though she didn't want him to leave anymore.

"He can't be on your project."

"He's not."

"What if people find out?"

"How would they? I won't get my funding yanked because of a personal relationship."

"How personal is it?"

"I just told you. He's my assistant. Nothing more." Although she had imagined what it would be like if it became something more, especially that one night only a week after he'd had dinner at her parents, when she'd gone downstairs for a late night snack and found him lying face up on the kitchen floor...

"Oh my God," she cried, racing over to him. "Sebastian, are you okay?" She felt for a pulse.

She heard him mumble something.

"What? Where are you hurt?"

"Stay away from me," he said. "I'm a little drunk."

He was splayed on the cold kitchen floor wearing only his dark blue pajama bottoms. She could guess that he was more than a little drunk, even though she didn't smell much alcohol on him. Was he really that much of a lightweight when it came to drinking?

"Come on," she said. "Let me help you up."

He didn't move. "I don't think I can keep this up. I can't do it anymore."

He was ready to quit? Had she worked him too hard? A part of her heart lifted, then fell and she faced the terrible truth—she didn't want him to.

"You just need to rest," she said, struggling to lift him up. His skin felt hot beneath her fingers and soon her nightgown felt like a flimsy barrier between him and her own nakedness. He fell back against her, his back resting on her breasts, the heat from his skin seeping through the cotton fabric.

"Naomi, I—"

She didn't want to hear him say he wanted to quit. "Don't say anything you'll regret." She tried to push him forward, biting her lip when she felt the urge to press her mouth against the expanse of his back and shoulders.

He sighed then straightened, moving away from her. "I'm sorry." He turned to her, his compelling brown eyes holding her still. "I didn't mean to scare you."

He didn't scare her. He made her heart pound, her hands

tremble, her blood rush. She wanted to feel his skin next to hers. She wanted to feel his lips pressed against hers again, but this time deeper and longer. And he didn't seem drunk—he looked sexy and sober. Or was that just her imagination? She hugged herself to keep herself still. "Are you sure you're not hurt?"

"I'm sure. I do that sometimes. I get hot and like the feel of the cool tiles against my back."

His back. His beautiful, broad back. Oh to be the tiles on the kitchen floor.

Sebastian rose to his feet then held his hand out to lift her up. She didn't move, continuing to stare up at him. "You've lost weight." He'd always been big, but over the past few weeks he'd become more toned and with his shirt off it was easy to notice.

"Hmm."

"Is that a yes?"

He wiggled his fingers with impatience. "Come on. Get up."

She took his hand, but surprised him by pulling him down towards her. Unfortunately, she used more force than she'd planned and he lost his balance and fell on top of her. He lifted his head and his startled gaze met hers and she realized it was the first time she'd seen him without his glasses.

He swore and quickly rolled off of her. "Are you okay?"

Her body still tingled from the feel of his body lying across the length of hers. The contact was brief, but memorable. And for one wild moment she'd wished the kitchen floor was her bed and he was pressing her down into the mattress.

His face appeared above hers, like a prince in a fairytale offering a kiss. "Naomi?"

She blinked and had to resist the urge to pull him down again and press her lips against his. "What?"

"I asked if you were okay."

She quickly sat up, and scrambled backwards when he reached for her. She couldn't trust herself if he touched her. "I'm fine. Are you okay?"

He stared at her for a long moment his eyes unreadable, then gritted his teeth and surged to his feet. "No, I'm not."

"What's wrong?"

He rubbed the back of his neck and said under his breath, "I shouldn't have started this."

"Started what?" she whispered.

His mercurial gaze held her and for a brief, wild moment she saw hunger in his eyes before a shutter dropped down and she knew she wouldn't hear the answer. He opened the fridge. "Do you want me to make you something?"

She stood, desperate to leave. She needed space from him. "No, I'm fine."

"But you came down to get something."

"I changed my mind. Good night."

She'd been awkward around him since that night. He'd also been more quiet than usual and although she tried her best to make his job easy, twice remembering her own lunch, canceling a few impromptu meetings and appointments so he didn't have to scramble to keep her schedule organized, it didn't matter.

"He's still not good for you," Naomi heard Vera say.

She knew that. But it wasn't her reputation she was worried about. Every day she thought about him more and more. What had happened before that night in the kitchen? He hadn't mentioned wanting to quit again, but he didn't seem as happy about the arrangement as he'd once been.

But perhaps she'd been looking at it all wrong. Maybe he missed doing what she did. Maybe seeing her go to the lab brought up memories of what he'd lost.

She wanted to help him, but how? For days she'd wracked her brain for possibilities. What could she offer him? He didn't need money. He discussed her project, but only in passing. It hadn't been his area.

His area. That's when she thought about Vera and knew she could offer him something he couldn't get on his own. Vera's former husband had also worked at BioCorps on the same project with Sebastian. Although divorced, Vera and Niklaas had parted ways on good terms. What if, with her friend's help and her former husband's insight, they could help Naomi uncover what really happened? Perhaps Sebastian could be vindicated and get his reputation back.

"I might be good for him," Naomi said. "I asked you here for a reason."

Vera shook her head. "I don't like that look."

"I need your help in finding out more regarding the BioCorps scandal."

"No."

"Even back then you felt sorry for him."

"I did. We all did. His was a career ended before it even had a chance to begin."

"Your husband knew him."

Vera waved her finger. "Let it go, Naomi. There's nothing to find. You'll only hurt him in the process."

"All I want—"

Vera stood. "I won't help you. No one will. Sebastian Scott is poison and his career is better left buried."

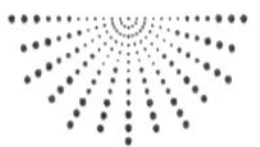

CHAPTER FOURTEEN

He'd miscalculated.

Sebastian let his coffee grow cold as he sat in the café keeping his distance from Naomi and Dr. Conklin.

He'd thought a couple months as Naomi's personal assistant would have been easy, but they'd been hell.

Hell because he was fighting an attraction that he hadn't anticipated and it only grew stronger every day. And if he didn't get it under control, he wouldn't achieve his goal. He'd nearly lost it a week ago when Naomi had found him on the kitchen floor. He hadn't been drunk that night, but he wished he had been.

He'd developed the habit of cooling off on the kitchen floor when his life had imploded five years ago: Discovering that erroneous data in the research that had eventually led to the debacle within BioCorps had kept him up at night. He'd suffered major night sweats and only the cool tiles in the kitchen could give him any relief.

This time it wasn't just his job on the line. It was his heart. Naomi wasn't even his type. Sure, he thought she was pretty...

He inwardly groaned. Even that was wrong. His feelings were subjective and unquantifiable but he thought she was beautiful. He swallowed up the sight of her like a man coming off of a hunger strike. Every look, every glance, he devoured. He couldn't get enough.

When they talked, no matter the subject—microbes, food, world events, movies—his mind felt alive. With her, there were so many things he didn't have to explain, it was a relief to finally be able to converse in the field he'd loved after years of feeling like he'd been in a desert. He'd tired of talking profit, loss, absorption rate and capital gain. He could have talked with her for hours...but then he'd made a mistake and looked at her mouth. And then he couldn't stop looking and wondering and wanting.

He wanted her.

His mother had warned him, but he needed Naomi if he wanted his plan to work. He needed her to like him, to depend on him, but now that was becoming more and more of a goal than a strategy. It wasn't rational to buy a new suit, to start getting his hair trimmed every week. He'd even taken up jogging. He'd never jogged before, but he had energy he had to get rid of because every time she brushed against him, he thought he would burst into flames.

He'd lost fifteen pounds because of it. Because of her.

Because of her determination, her love of science. He liked the fact he had to remind her three times to stop talking and eat before she'd finish a meal. That she could stand for hours, forgetting to pull up a chair, at a microscope without getting fatigued. Even when she sent him on silly errands he didn't care. He liked the look of surprise on her face every time he delivered without complaint. He'd kissed her on the dinner cruise as a small form of revenge, but he'd gotten caught. He couldn't stop thinking about it—about her.

Damn.

Even Andre seemed to have fallen under her spell. Several weeks ago Sebastian had caught Andre looking at his cell phone wiping his eyes in the kitchen.

"Did something happen?" he asked concerned.

Andre quickly rubbed his eyes with the back of his hand and sniffed. "My baby got second prize because of her." He held out his phone and showed a picture of his nine-year-old daughter with a certificate. "She won the science fair. She'd never placed before or even had much interest before Naomi spoke to her."

"Naomi spoke to her? When?"

"A couple of weeks ago. I asked her to help Daphne with an idea. Naomi did five video sessions with her and now science is all that she can talk about. I didn't think she'd have the time."

"You could have asked me."

"You know Daphne clams up whenever you're around. My wife thought a woman would help her open up. Daphne was afraid of looking stupid in front of you and my wife was right." Andre folded his arms. "Naomi's a good woman. I hope you're not going to hurt her."

Sebastian pointed to himself surprised by the accusation. "Why would I do that?"

"I don't know. You're the only one who knows why you want to be her personal assistant."

"I don't break hearts, remember?"

"I think she likes you."

Sebastian felt his heart skip a beat. "You think so?"

"Isn't that part of your plan?"

Sebastian turned and headed to his bedroom.

"Just give me a hint of what you're up to," Andre said following him.

Sebastian kept walking.

"It doesn't have to be big."

Sebastian walked into his bedroom and opened his closet. "I think I need a couple new shirts."

"Don't toy with her."

"And some trousers too." He looked at himself in the full length mirror. "Make an appointment with the tailor."

Andre looked at him stunned. "You haven't seen a tailor in—"

"I know."

Andre couldn't stop a grin. "Should I contact the barber too?"

Sebastian rubbed his chin. "That would be a good idea."

"And the optometrist?"

He turned to him, curious. "Why?"

"You need new frames."

He stared at his reflection again. "Really?"

"Yes, trust me."

He shrugged. "Okay."

"Is she into flowers?"

"No."

"Chocolates?"

"No."

"Jewelry?"

Sebastian thought of the necklace he'd retrieved for her. A soft smile danced on his lips. "Yes."

"Should I book a room?"

His smile fell and he shot his friend a look. "No." He

sighed. He still wanted to keep the relationship professional. "There's nothing going on between us."

But as Sebastian watched Naomi eat with her mentor, he knew he wanted there to be. That night at her parents' house, when he'd covered her hand with his, feeling her soft skin, the delicate bones in her fingers, he knew he was in trouble. Deep trouble.

And he kept sinking.

He glanced up when he heard someone clear their throat. He saw the café waitress, a young black woman with a cute Afro puff and apple round cheeks. "Yes?"

She set a muffin down on the table.

He frowned. "I'm sorry, but I didn't order this."

"I know. I just thought you might like this to go with your coffee." She smiled then left.

He lifted up the muffin and saw she'd scrawled her number on a napkin underneath. He looked at her and saw her watching him. He smiled back, tucking her number inside his jacket pocket so as not to hurt her feelings.

He glanced at Naomi who was having an intense conversation, she probably hadn't even noticed. He had to stop watching her. He had to stop thinking about her.

He pulled out his cell phone and read some news then paused when he heard high heels stop at his table. He looked up and saw an attractive woman in leopard patterned heels, form fitting black dress with a spicy, floral scent. "Could you tell me where the Trust Bank is?"

Sebastian stood and gave her directions, patiently answering questions she could have figured out on her own.

"That sounds complicated," she finally said. "Do you think you could show me?"

He sat back down. "Umm...I'm waiting for someone."

She looked disappointed then placed her card on the table and slid it towards him. "In case they don't show up."

He plastered on a smile, confused. What kind of coffee shop was this? He'd never gotten this kind of attention before. Even at the height of his career, most women looked past him. He glanced down at his shirt. Was it the new clothes? Andre had forced him into dark trousers and a casual dark blue crew neck he'd never tried before and the light rimmed frames were new for him too.

He heard the chair in front of him scrape across the ground and tensed. Was it another woman wanting something? Would she ask him the time or the best place to buy seafood?

He glanced up when he heard a fingernail tap against the table. His tension eased when he saw Naomi.

"Why were you looking down like that?"

Sebastian leaned forward and lowered his voice. "I don't know what's going on. Two women have given me their phone numbers."

"That's no surprise. You're a good looking man."

"Would you give me your number?"

She laughed. "You already have it."

"I mean, if you didn't know me."

She shook her head.

He felt his heart fall.

"I'd feel too shy," she said. "I wouldn't have the boldness."

His heart lifted. Maybe if he played this right, there was a chance... "Naomi—"

She rested her chin in her hand. "I really like these," she said, tapping the frames of her own glasses. "You look more approachable than before."

Approachable? That wasn't exactly a come on. He didn't know what to say so he started to stand.

She covered his hand with hers, stopping him. "We're not leaving yet. There's something I have to say."

He slowly sat back down, his heart racing. She was touching him and looking at him in a way she never had before. Did she feel the attraction too? Did she feel conflicted because he worked for her?

"I want to help you."

His heart fell to the floor and cracked. He'd built up his hopes for nothing. He adjusted his frames, trying to look nonchalant. "W-what?"

"I think I've finally figured out why you wanted to volunteer with me."

Sebastian froze. Did she really know? Could this be the moment he'd been waiting for?

To his relief and regret she pulled her hand away and folded her arms looking pleased with herself. "You want me to find out what really happened with your research."

He felt his throat tighten. This was not good. "I made an error, that's all. I didn't—"

Naomi shook her head, cutting him off. "But you're not the type. You're very fastidious. Over the last couple of months I see how you think. I can see why you rose so fast. Besides, we both know you can't work with me like this forever."

"I like what I do," he said in a hard tone. He didn't want her looking into his past.

"Don't you want more?"

"It's a dead end. Focus on your career."

"You may not know this, but Dr. Vera Conklin is the wife of—"

"Dr. Niklaas Conklin the head researcher at BioCorps, yes I know. Did you talk to her about me?"

"Yes, I thought she could help us—"

"What did she say?"

Naomi hesitated then sighed. "That I should leave it alone."

"Listen to her and never mention this again." He stood. "Are you ready to leave?"

He steeled himself against the look of disappointment on her face. He wouldn't weaken, he couldn't change the past. He looked at the window just as Vera passed, briefly catching her eye and the silent message there.

He had to go forward with his plan fast before Naomi ruined everything.

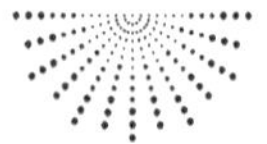

She hadn't meant to make him angry, Naomi thought as she headed up the driveway after a long walk, her skin feeling sticky from the humid air.

For the past week, Sebastian kept their interactions brief. He talked about her father and the lab. That was it. She was going to lose him and she didn't want that.

She didn't want to hurt him, but something about Vera's tone and Sebastian's reaction bothered her. She didn't know why yet. She didn't see the harm in making some simple inquiries into the BioCorps incident. She got her hands on as much public information as possible, but she knew she would need to get more.

Naomi paused when she saw Josephine sitting in the garden, reading a book, a glass of lemonade on the white table beside her. They only nodded greetings to each other, but never spoke. Although she no longer leaned as heavily on her cane as she used to, she made no move to leave and still glanced at Naomi with a look of suspicion. But Naomi wanted to help Sebastian; to know more about him. Josephine was somebody who could help her.

"It's a lovely day," Naomi said, walking up to her.

"Yes," Josephine said, not looking up. "What ridiculous errand are you going to send my son on this week?"

She deserved that, although she'd stopped with that petty revenge weeks ago. "He's a very hard worker."

"That's the problem. My son shouldn't be working. At least not like this. He and his brother inherited a lucrative business from their father. There's no reason he's doing this."

Naomi sat in the other garden chair. "I agree and I'd like to help him."

For a moment, Josephine's face lit up and her eyes softened. "How?"

"I know he's meant for more. He's got a brilliant mind and he could do so much in the field of research."

Josephine's face hardened. "It broke his heart already. I won't see him hurt again. If you truly want to help my son, you'll help him come to his senses."

Naomi inwardly winced at the way Josephine said 'my son' as if Sebastian were a possession or pet she meant to keep close by.

"I don't think he's out of his mind, Mrs. Scott, but that he's searching for something and—"

A cruel smile spread on Josephine face. "Don't delude yourself into thinking you can help him find it."

"I don't."

"Many women think that Sebastian's like other men."

"I would never—"

Josephine closed her book and rested it on her lap. "My husband was the same way. Oh you should have seen the way the women flocked to him. They all thought they were the one for him. Only I knew what he needed. I was—"

"I don't think you know what your son needs."

Josephine grabbed her glass and tossed her lemonade in Naomi's face. "Don't you dare tell me what I know."

Naomi brushed the ice cubes from her lap and wiped her eyes, the cold drink soaking her blouse and stinging her eyes. "I didn't mean—"

"You're an arrogant, stupid woman if you think you know more about him than I do."

Naomi licked her lips, tasting the tart juice on her mouth. "Mrs. Scott I—I only wanted to help Sebastian find his way back to a career he clearly loves."

"And I'm letting you know that he loves his family and his business. The business his father gave to him to keep and pass on for generations to come."

"But if he doesn't want—"

"This isn't about Sebastian, this is what you want. Your selfish desires to trap him back in a life that doesn't suit him. If you have a heart at all, you'll see that." She stood and marched away.

FOR A MOMENT she'd been fooled. Josephine hated being fooled. If only that Mensah woman had wanted to help Sebastian for the right reasons. She likely wanted to use him to advance her career just like Barbara had. Although his reputation was in shambles, she knew he was brilliant. Why did her son have to be so blind to these ambitious women?

But at least this one didn't pretend to be interested in him as a man. But was she really unaware of the effect she had on

Sebastian. Did she pretend not to see the change in him? Or was that all an act?

Josephine marched through the French doors into the cool solarium and took a seat.

She'd lied to Naomi. Sebastian was nothing like his father —a charismatic, boisterous man who could light up a room. Neither of her sons had her husband's ability to both charm and make money. They had those attributes split into two. Gregg could charm; Sebastian could make money. They needed each other and the business needed them both or it would fall apart. Sebastian had to stay and run the company that had been his father's dream.

She still remembered the look on her husband's face when he'd first held Sebastian in the hospital. "He's going to carry on my legacy," he'd said. "My father handed me nothing, but I'm giving this boy the world. He won't have to struggle as I had. He'll take the reins of my company and make it even greater than it is now."

Josephine blinked back tears at the memory. She and her husband had both come from families that had nothing to pass down—except hard work and poverty. Josephine had always dreamed of being part of something bigger. She'd envied those who could trace their roots back generations with a level of pride she could never share. Her husband had come from a small island with nothing, but had made a big impact due to his brains and drive. He'd built a business that could sustain them for generations. Was it wrong to make her sons hold onto something she'd never had? Something their father had never had? Sebastian had to fulfill the destiny his father had set for him, or all his efforts meant nothing.

If only she knew what Sebastian needed from Naomi. That was the key to untangling the chain she held around him.

Josephine gripped her hands around the arm of the white chair. She felt that she was slowly losing him and losing him would be like losing her husband all over again. She couldn't bare that.

She saw Andre passing by and called out to him.

"Yes?" he said, standing in the entryway.

"I need another glass of lemonade. I spilled the last one in the garden," she said, making a vague gesture to it.

He nodded. "Are you sure you haven't gotten too much sun? You look...upset."

"Have you found out anything more about Naomi?"

"Nothing more than I told you. I don't think there's anything to worry about. She seems to be good for him."

The woman even had Andre fooled. "I'm not too sure about that."

"Why not? He's like his old self again."

Josephine gripped one hand into a fist. She couldn't admit that that scared her the most.

Sebastian stared at his cell phone. It was now or never. He had to make the first move to finalize his plan. He started to dial.

"I thought you said you weren't going to hurt her," Andre demanded, storming into Sebastian's study, startling him.

He dropped the phone and swore. He bent down and picked up the phone, glad it was protected in its case. "What is wrong with you?"

Andre jumped in front of him and waved a napkin in his face. "What is this?"

"It looks like a napkin to me. What do you think it is?"

Andre held the napkin between his hands. "I mean this."

Sebastian read the waitress's scrawled phone number. "It's a number."

"I thought I told you not to hurt her."

"I'm not hurting anyone."

"Do you think I helped you so you could pick up other women?"

"I didn't change for her."

When Andre sent him a knowing look he said, "Listen, it wasn't supposed to be like this. You're right. At first I did want to use her. I wanted to use her to get close to her father. I heard he was writing a book and I wanted to help him with the research, but I knew if he knew who I was he wouldn't give me a chance. So I came up with the idea of getting close to his daughter instead. I thought if I got on her good side and he saw what I did; he couldn't help but want to work with me." After hearing Dr. Mensah's lecture in London, Sebastian had kept tabs on him and knew what the proposed book was about, he'd also learned how Dr. Mensah was using his own time and funds to do extensive research. Sebastian knew with his resources he could take Dr. Mensah's project to an entirely different level and by collaborating with Dr. Mensah he would get his name seen in a good light again. "Working with her father was to be my redemption." Sebastian saw Andre's face change and dread slowly covered his heart. He lowered his voice. "Naomi's standing behind me right now, isn't she?"

Andre nodded.

"How close?"

"Close enough."

Sebastian sighed and turned around. "Naomi."

She held out a book to him, her expression neutral. "You said you wanted to read it." She spun away.

He followed her. "Let me explain."

"You just did." She slapped her forehead with the palm of her hand. "How could I have been stupid enough to think you really wanted to work with me?" She shook her head. "Don't worry, you're not the first. I'm a human stepping stone. Monica wanted to work with Pete. Barry preferred to marry my sister." She stopped walking and faced him. "And you...you prefer to work with my father. Fine, I'll put in a good word for you. You'll get the job. We can end this charade now." She headed for her room.

"Naomi—"

"Do I get to keep the lab?"

"Of course."

"Good. I'll start looking for somewhere else to live."

"You don't need to do that." He grabbed her wrist and spun her to him. "Listen, I know I should have been honest from the beginning—"

"Why?" she shot back as tears gathered in her eyes. "That would have defeated your purpose."

"I do enjoy working for you."

"Really? Is that why I found you on the kitchen floor, telling me that you wanted to quit?"

"I didn't say that."

"You said, 'I can't do it anymore.'"

Sebastian shook his head. "That's not what I meant. I—"

She took off her glasses and wiped the tears from her eyes. "I'm such a fool! Why would you want to work with me when you have my father?"

"Naomi," he said softly, her name like a plea on his lips.

"Now everything makes sense." She turned away from him as if the sight of him pained her. "Why you were so eager to impress my parents with the large bouquet. Why you mentioned my father's research every chance you got." She shifted her gaze back to his face, her eyes red but defiant. "You think I don't know how unhappy you've been lately? You've hardly spoken to me these last few weeks."

He sighed heavily, his voice filled with regret. "Naomi, it's not what you think—"

"Do you want to work with my father?"

"Yes, but—"

"Then I'll make it happen." She spun away. "I'm going to change and go to the lab. I have some work I want to do." She sent him a cold glance over her shoulder. "Alone."

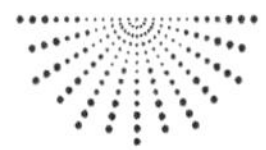

CHAPTER SEVENTEEN

osephine only hated listening to one of the voices on the other ended of the phone, the other was calmer and less prone to panic, but she wasn't surprised by the call. It was bound to happen. She spoke in a low voice as she sat in her bedroom. "You didn't have to call me."

"This shouldn't have happened," the calm voice demanded. "Tell me what went wrong."

"Nothing."

"She has to be stopped," the panicked voice said.

The first voice spoke. "There's nothing to find."

"But what if—"

"She's nobody, there's nothing to worry about."

"If she keeps digging she'll find something."

"What do you want me to do?" Josephine asked, tired of being in between their argument.

"He must have mentioned something," Calm Voice said.

"Sebastian keeps his promises," Josephine said, offended. "This is all her. I knew she was trouble."

"Why is he working with her?"

"I don't know."

"We had a deal."

"I know that," Josephine said in a tight voice.

"If you want us to trust you, you know what to do. We all have something to lose."

The line went dead.

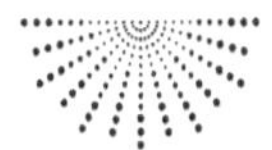

Her father? Her father! All this time Sebastian really wanted to work with her father! How could she have been so stupid? Naomi burned with humiliation as she looked at the samples in her lab.

Stupid. Stupid. Stupid. All the signs had been there, even from the first meeting. The moment he'd seen her father, his expression changed and he'd gushed about her father's lecture. And when he'd brought up her father's work and accomplishments, she'd foolishly thought he was trying to impress her with his knowledge.

The haircut and new clothes had probably been for her father's sake too.

That's why Sebastian had gotten sullen after meeting with her parents. He had gotten bored with her and was eager to pass her by and head to his true goal: the great Abraham Mensah. That's why he had no interest in her helping him with the BioCorps scandal. He had no interest in her.

When she'd broken up with Barry and he'd turned his attention to her sister, it hadn't hurt at all. Not even a twinge.

She liked him, but only as a friend. She truly felt happy for her sister. But her father made her feel jealous. Jealous that he'd soon get to spend time with Sebastian and laugh and discuss topics of interest. She'd come to enjoy his company and she liked him. Very much.

Naomi closed her eyes against gathering tears. She took a deep breath.

Work. She'd focus on work. She was in her favorite place, doing her favorite thing. She didn't need a man like Sebastian. She didn't need any man.

She worked until the next morning, feeling tired and bleary eyed by the time it was close to the arrival of the first researcher of the team. She'd go home and take a quick nap then return in the afternoon. Naomi opened the front door to her lab and gasped when she saw Sebastian standing there.

He didn't say a word, but his expression said "We need to talk" and she knew he wouldn't let her escape him.

CHAPTER NINETEEN

He led her outside, holding onto her arm as if afraid she'd run away. "I want you to listen to me carefully," he said. "I did—do want to work with your father, but that's not the only thing I want—-shit!"

Naomi looked up at him startled, when he suddenly spun them in the other direction. Before she could ask him what was wrong a female voice called out to him.

"Sebastian? Sebastian is that you?"

He groaned and increased his pace. Clearly he wanted to avoid the other woman, but Naomi wasn't in the mood to let him. His shaggy appearance in the past had likely been part of his ploy to get her to pity him. He actually pretended to be surprised in the coffee shop about the women's attention when he was likely used to it. No man could be that clueless to his own appeal.

His mother had told her that he'd inherited his father's successful business; there had likely been plenty of women who'd wanted to get close to him before. She'd stopped herself from being one of them. She was relieved she'd never revealed her feelings; he would have felt sorry for her. She glanced back at the woman and saw she was attractive with cupid bow lips and hair sculpted in a sleek look.

Naomi stopped walking. "Someone appears to be calling you."

"No," he tugged her forward. "It's not like that."

She yanked her arm free. "I'd hate to get in the way of one of your ladies."

He pressed his hands together, his eyes pleading. "Naomi, please let me—"

"Sebastian Scott?" the woman asked, peering up at him when he lowered his head.

He sighed and lifted his head, forcing a smile. "Yes."

She playfully slapped him on the arm. "I thought it was you!" She playfully slapped him again and giggled. "You haven't changed. Well, except for the wheelchair. I'm not used to looking up at you like this. You look great."

He shoved his hands in his pockets. "You too." He turned to Naomi. "This is Dr. Naomi Mensah. Naomi, Molly Robb."

Molly shook Naomi's hand. "Doctor, huh? I've been looking for a new GP. They're so hard to find nowadays."

"I'm afraid I'm not that kind of doctor," Naomi said.

"Oh," Molly said disappointed then smiled again. "So, what did he tell you about me?" She grimaced. "Poor Sebastian. We were so vicious to you back then. Sometimes I can't believe how mean I was. But I guess kids will be kids, right?"

He shrugged nonchalant.

Naomi didn't feel the same way. She didn't like Molly's arrogance that Sebastian would have told her about Molly or the way Molly was looking at him with a superficial embarrassment for her past behavior. Naomi hadn't been around other kids her age long enough to get teased or was too oblivious to notice. She felt a little guilty for forcing Sebastian to face a woman who clearly made him feel uncomfortable. Although she was mad at him, she didn't want him punished like this.

She leaned forward. "I'm sorry, what was your name again?"

"Molly Robb."

"And where did you know each other from?"

"Middle and high school."

Naomi nodded and laughed. "Oh, maybe that's why he's never mentioned you before. I was trying to place you and I just couldn't but now it all makes sense." Naomi linked her arm through his. "It was so long ago and unimportant."

Molly's gaze hardened. "I heard about BioCorps." She made a face. "Poor Sebastian, I read all about it."

"Yes, read and likely didn't understand half of it. The paper can only put so much in layman's terms." Naomi pulled out her phone and squeezed closer to him. "Darling, we'll be late."

Sebastian stiffened whether at the affectionate term or her closeness, Naomi didn't know, but he quickly played along, unlocking their arms and wrapping his around her shoulders. "Right, bye Molly. Like my wife said, it's all forgotten."

It was now Naomi's turn to stiffen in surprise. *Wife?! She was playing his girlfriend.*

Sebastian turned them away from Molly and they walked several steps in silence, Naomi feeling like a tiny sparrow taking shade under a massive oak tree. She'd walked close to him before, but never like this, feeling the warmth and weight of his arm around her shoulders. It felt good. Too good. She had to remember he'd used her.

Naomi looked back. "She's gone." She began to pull away, but he didn't let her. "We don't have to pretend anymore." She released a laugh. "I'm still angry at you, but there was something about the way that woman was talking to you that annoyed me and the nasty tone she used when she mentioned you being in a wheelchair just—"

She stopped when she caught a glimpse of herself in the reflection of a shop window. She looked like a mad scientist! Her hair was springing out of its braid, one collar on her shirt stood up while the other was down, even her glasses were slightly askew. Normally she didn't care, especially after spending all night in the lab, but remembering the sight of Molly's sophisticated appearance she was stunned the other woman didn't laugh in her face. You? His wife? No way.

She straightened and pushed up her glasses. "I can't believe you didn't tell me I looked like this. You—"

Sebastian didn't let her finish. He pulled her into an alley between two buildings, put his arms around her and kissed her. The touch of his lips sent her stomach into a wild swirl, and she reveled in his warm embrace while his slow, soft kiss melted her anger away.

When he finally drew away, his brown eyes studied her face as if in wonder. "That was Molly Robb," he said his hoarse voice barely a whisper.

"I-I know," Naomi stammered, her heart racing so fast she could hardly breathe. She stared up at him stunned. "I'm sorry."

He gently cupped her face in his large hands and kissed her again. "You stood up to Molly Robb for me." He smoothed down her hair, then brushed his knuckles against her cheek, his voice deepening with emotion. "You beautiful, wonderful..." He kissed her again. And again.

Naomi didn't move, not wanting it to end even though she didn't know what was happening.

"No one has ever stood up for me like that," he said, his breath warm against her lips.

"I didn't really do anything," she said unsure.

He rested his hands on the wall behind her, trapping her in the circle of his arms, a sly smile tugging at his mouth. "That was Molly Robb."

"So you've said."

"She made my life hell in middle school. There may still even be a clip of it online. She always loomed so large in my mind, but you made her look so small."

Naomi glanced at the size of one of his arms, positioned near her head. "Compared to you, she is small." She looked up at him perplexed. "Don't you realize how attractive you are?"

He lowered his head embarrassed. "I wish you'd stop saying that."

"I'm not flattering you, it's true." She ducked under one of his arms, feeling her anger returning. She was ready to leave.

He grabbed the back of her shirt, and pulled her back in place, lowering his arm so that it was shoulder level. "It wasn't always true. I was an overweight kid in a wheelchair for many years, then I was a nerd with a rich dad. I don't think anyone's ever found me attractive." A slow smile spread on his face. "Until now."

She turned her face when he bent to kiss her. "I'm sure you just didn't notice."

He pressed his lips against the curve of her neck. "I would have noticed," he mumbled

She pushed him away, determined not to weaken. He could make her knees weak, but only a few hours ago he'd made her cry. "I'm still mad at you."

"I know. I'm sorry." He sighed. "If you don't want me to work with your father, I won't."

She knew how much that admission cost him. She could see in his eyes how much he wanted to. "But you still want to."

He straightened, shoving his hands in his pockets. "Yes."

"Then I'll talk to him," she said, although she'd miss him as her assistant. She knew it had all been too good to be true. "I don't like your methods, but I understand your ambition. There's nothing wrong with going after what you want."

His eyes caught and held hers. "Is there anything wrong with wanting to sleep with you tonight?"

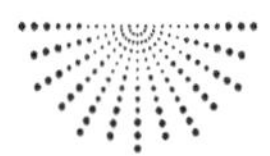

"And you ran away?" Elia said when Naomi told her what had happened.

The two sisters sat in the backyard watching Elia's daughter Susan slide down her play set.

"I didn't know what else to do."

"Given him a date and a time?"

"I panicked."

"What's to panic about? You've been working together for months."

"Working not dating."

"It's been 'Sebastian this' and 'Sebastian that' for weeks."

"I don't sound like that."

"This is the first time you mentioned a man's name without also using microbe inspired gobblygook."

"It's not gobblygook."

"Why did you run?"

Naomi took off her glasses and rubbed her eyes. "Because I needed to get away from him."

"You live in the same house."

Naomi shoved her glasses back on and threw up her hands. "I know!"

"Know what?" Barry asked, coming through the glass doors, having put their younger daughter down for a nap.

"Nothing," Naomi said, sending her sister a look of warning.

"We're just talking about men."

He held out his arms. "I'm an expert, if you need any advice."

"I don't." Naomi nodded towards her niece. "Looks like she wants to be pushed on the swing." Presently Susan was hanging upside down on the jungle gym, but Barry took the hint and went to play with his daughter.

Elia took a deep breath. "I don't understand this. Why do you need to get away from him?"

"Because I'm confused. He's confusing me. I don't know what he wants."

"He's made it quite clear what he wants."

"It doesn't make sense. One moment he wants to use me so that he can work with Dad, the next he wants...you know."

"Sex isn't a dirty word or act." She winked. "Unless you want it to be."

Naomi folded her arms. "I'm going to have to move again." She rested her head back and groaned. "I'll probably have to stay with Mom and Dad until I can find a place."

"If we didn't have guests coming soon, you know we would—"

Naomi stared up at the sky, watching a plane fly overhead. "I know you'd let me stay here."

"But I don't think you have to move."

She sat up. "I'm not going to be used again." She shook her

head. "Not like this. I feel like he's getting a two for one bargain."

Elia folded her arms. "So what?"

Naomi's mouth fell open. "So *what*?"

"Yes, so he likes you and Dad. So he wants to work with Dad and be with you, what's the big deal?"

"The big deal is he's changed so much since the first time I met him that I don't feel like I know who he is. Would you risk your heart on a man like that?"

"So you're in love with him, then?"

"Will you stick to the point?"

"The point is you've got a man you're attracted to who wants to sleep with you and you run to your younger sister like a scardy cat."

"All right I admit it. I'm scared. I'm terrified because I do care about him and I don't want to get hurt."

"But that's not what life's about. You can't hide in your lab forever. You can't stay safe in a neat, sterile environment forever. Life is messy, but it's also wonderful. Didn't you once tell me that you loved science because it was about asking questions and seeking the answers? You said you didn't care if you failed. It was the adventure of experimenting that thrilled you. Love is the same." Elia shook her head in regret. "I don't have all the answers and I don't know him well, but I do know that since you've met him you've been happy in a way I've never seen before."

Her cell phone rang. Naomi looked at the number and froze. "It's him."

"Answer it," Elia said.

"But it's him."

Elia rolled her eyes. "I know. You're lucky he didn't call you right away. Have you forgotten? You ran away from him."

Naomi shook her head. "I can't talk to him."

Her sister reached for the phone. "I can."

Naomi held it out of reach. "But you're not going to."

"You need to talk to him."

"I'll talk to him when I'm ready."

The phone stopped ringing.

"You just lost your chance," Elia said with a sigh. "You could have had a lovely evening instead you're stuck here with me."

The phone alerted her to a text.

She read it. "That's strange."

Elia leaned over to see. "What?"

"He's inviting me to go swimming."

"Say yes."

She hesitated. "But it's not like him to—"

"Naomi, don't over think this. This is your chance. Don't blow it."

Her sister was right. She wouldn't run away again, she did want to see him. She had to face life and all its mysteries. Love was something new to discover. She typed in her reply and hit Send.

CHAPTER TWENTY-ONE

Gregg Scott stared at his older brother who sat across from him in the fast causal restaurant. They'd decided to stop at the American grill type facility for lunch after looking at one of their properties. "Got something on your mind?" he asked as one of the waiters walked past their table with a hot pan of sizzling meat, filled with the scent of jalapeño peppers.

"No, why?"

Gregg nodded to his brother's cup. "Because you just put pepper in your coffee."

Sebastian looked down and swore.

"I know meeting me to look at the Renton property wasn't on your schedule but—"

"It's not that," Sebastian said, lifting his hand to get the attention of one of the wait staff. "I need another coffee," he said when a fresh faced teenager with six earrings approached.

"What is it then?"

"I made a mistake."

"What kind of mistake?"

"With a woman."

"Don't worry," Gregg said with a laugh. "We all make those."

Sebastian thanked the waitress when she set down his coffee and reached for the sugar. "I thought that being honest would fix things, but I think I made things worse."

"What did you say?"

"When should you tell a woman you want to sleep with her?"

Gregg stared at him. "You told a woman you wanted to sleep with her?"

"Yes."

"Just like that?"

"Yes."

His mouth fell open. "Are you out of your mind?"

"Clearly."

"Who is she?"

He hesitated.

Gregg read the expression on his brother's face and groaned. "Don't tell me it's Naomi Mensah." When his brother didn't reply, he swore. "You're lucky you're not really employed or she could sue you for harassment or something."

"I thought she wanted it too."

"What did she do when you said it? Did she slap you?"

Sebastian took a sip of his coffee. "Forget I said anything."

"No way. What did she do?"

Sebastian took another sip then set his cup down. "She ran away."

Gregg looked at him for a long moment then threw his head back and laughed.

Sebastian frowned. "It's not funny."

"How old is she? Fifteen?" He laughed harder.

Sebastian lowered his gaze and slowly turned his cup counter clockwise. "I'll make you stop laughing in a minute."

Gregg quickly sobered. "I'm sorry."

Sebastian lifted his coffee.

"It's just..." Gregg started to laugh again, then quickly covered it with a cough. "I want to help."

"You can't help. I have to find a way to fix this."

"There's no way. You already put it out there. It's like trying to unring a bell. You should have waited until you were more certain of her."

"I know that now."

"Give her time. How long has it been?"

"It happened this morning. She won't return my calls."

"It's not like you don't know where she lives."

That didn't make things any easier. First he'd blundered by letting her overhear that he'd initially used her so that he could get to work with her father and now he'd told her how he'd felt and been rejected. He should have kept his mouth shut. Now he could lose two things he'd wanted.

He returned home that late afternoon in a foul mood.

Andre met him at the door. "What are you doing here?"

Sebastian closed the door behind him. "I live here."

"B-but I thought you were meeting with Naomi."

"Why?"

"I just saw her about fifteen minutes ago. She told me she was meeting you to go swimming. She looked very eager."

"Swimming?"

"Yes, you sent her a text."

Sebastian felt his heart sink to his stomach. "I didn't send her a text." And Naomi couldn't swim.

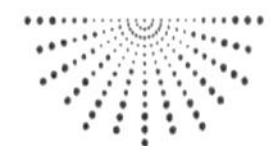

CHAPTER TWENTY-TWO

He found her floating face down in the water.

Sheer, stark terror raced through him. *How could this have happened?* She couldn't be dead. He dove in the water and pulled her out, while Andre called an ambulance.

"Come on Naomi," Sebastian pleaded doing chest compressions on her limp, lifeless body. "Naomi, you came here to meet me and I'm here now. You can't leave me again. Come on, Naomi you can fight this. You're not going to die on me."

But she didn't move, there was no flicker of life left in her.

Please, please, please, he silently prayed. She'd come to him. She'd wanted to see him. To give him a second chance after running away. He couldn't lose her, not like this.

"Let me take over," Andre said.

Sebastian gritted his teeth. "No," he said, continuing to do the steady compressions, until he feared he'd break her ribs. Soon despair swallowed his hope, if she didn't breathe soon her brain would be affected. Just as the crucial time ticked close, she vomited up water. He turned her head and she took a long gasp.

He gathered her in his arms, holding her close, more for his sake than for hers. He needed to feel her body close to his, to feel her cold skin grow warm in his embrace and be certain that she was protected, that nothing could get past him. "It's okay," he said gently. "You're safe now. You're going to be all right."

~

IT WAS ALL STILL A BLUR.

Naomi lay in the hospital bed still trying to understand how she'd ended up there.

She remembered getting Sebastian's text and feeling both anxious and eager to see him again. Her sister had helped her purchase a new suit and swim cap and on the drive there, she practiced what she'd planned to say to him. Was swimming supposed to be foreplay? Did he still want to spend the night with her? She wasn't going to run away this time. If she didn't learn how to swim that night, it would be fine with her.

Then he hadn't been at the pool, which confused her because Sebastian was usually prompt. After that she couldn't remember much else except, hearing echoing footsteps, which she thought was odd since she'd expected him to be barefoot, and then she felt a hard shove at the base of her back.

She hit the water with a splash, panic and fear seizing her as she fought to keep her head above water. Blackness soon followed. The next thing she remembered was Sebastian holding her then being whisked into an ambulance.

Naomi reached for her glasses and saw a figure in the corner. She was about to scream when the figure spoke. "It's me," Sebastian said. "You're safe." He stood and came out of the shadows. "You'll be discharged soon."

"Good."

"You don't remember what happened?"

I have my suspicions, but not enough to share. "Not really. I think I slipped."

Sebastian stood beside her bed, his dark gaze holding hers. "Are you ready to tell me what you've been up to?"

"I don't know what you mean?"

He took her hand and sat on the side of the bed. "Then let me be clearer. Give me a reason why someone would want to kill you."

CHAPTER TWENTY-THREE

"Kill me?" her voice cracked in surprise. "Who would want to kill me?"

"That's what I want to know. How much should the police know?"

"Know about what?"

"Whatever you're not telling me."

"There's no need for the police. Do you think I'm involved in something illegal?"

"No."

Naomi rubbed her forehead. "This is all so strange. I thought that after...I ran off...you'd forgiven me by offering to give me lessons."

"I didn't text you."

Her face burned, she lowered her head embarrassed. Someone had made a fool of her. "Oh."

"I wish I had."

Her head shot up. "Really?"

"Yes," his jaw twitched. "Then this might not have happened. Do you think any of the men that showed up at your former apartment had a grudge? Did you tell someone to get lost in a way that might have made him angry?"

"Yes, but it's been months since then."

Sebastian fell silent then said, "You're hiding something from me."

Yes. "No, I'm not. You know everything about my schedule. I don't have room for any secrets. Unlike some," she said, reminding him of the real reason he'd approached her.

"We're not talking about your father right now. Why did someone attack you?"

"How do you know someone attacked me? I said I slipped—"

"And I said, I didn't send you a text. Now answer my question. Why would someone attack you?"

"I don't know," she said honestly. "I haven't been doing anything except..." She stopped as a thought came to her.

His gaze darkened. "Except what?"

She rested her head back. "I'm sure it's nothing."

"What?"

"I know you hate talking about the past."

"Go on."

"I was looking into the BioCorps case." She held up her hand before he could speak. "But I haven't found anything so I don't see how the two could be connected."

Sebastian's gaze hardened as did his voice. "I told you to leave it alone."

"I was just...I wanted to help. What if it was sabotage? Internal espionage? Maybe you could be vindicated."

He sighed. "Are you really this naïve?"

"What?"

"Do you think I wouldn't have thought about that? Do you

think these past five years I wouldn't have looked at this from many different angles?"

"But I thought with fresh new eyes I could—"

"What?" he said with a sneer. "Restore me to my former glory? Do you have any idea how big this case is?"

"That doesn't frighten me."

"It should and I hope it does now."

Naomi folded her arms. "It makes me angry. If someone tried to hurt me then I'm on the right track."

He stood and looked out the window. "They didn't try to hurt you, they tried to *kill* you. Make an effort to understand the difference."

"A moment of desperation. You must see what we have here."

"I mean it. Let it go."

"You can't walk away from this."

Sebastian spun around with anger in his eyes. "Yes, I can. I have. I can't restore my reputation. I made a choice and I have to live with the consequences. I once got my hopes up that I could..." He shook his head in frustration. "It's too late for me."

"If you had hope once you can have it again. You were alone before. This time I can—"

"No."

"But I believe in you. If we can prove—"

"I said no. Leave this alone. Am I clear?"

"Isn't it worse not knowing?"

Sebastian shook his head and tapped his chest. "I *know* what happened. End of story. I like what I do and now I just—"

"Want to work with my father," Naomi finished in a dry tone. "I get it."

"Do you want me to leave?"

Her voice cracked in surprise. "No."

He pointed at her. "Then stop playing games."

"I'm not."

"Someone tried to kill you and you want me to focus on rebuilding my reputation? Right now all I can think about is how to find the bastard who did this to you and tear him into pieces. Yes, I want to work with your father, but I love you."

Naomi hung her head, trying to process his words. *He loved her?* What did that mean? She knew he wanted to sleep with her, she could accept him liking her, but love? The big L.O.V.E? Would it be wise to believe him or was it another strategy to manipulate her? But he looked genuinely upset as if she meant a lot to him. "I'm sorry," she said still trying to process what he'd said. "I should have listened to you. I won't look into it anymore."

"It's too late now, someone sees you as a threat."

She shook her head, hating the anger and fear in his voice. "No, I'm safe now."

"We'll have the police trace the text, but I'm not too hopeful they'll get anything. We won't pretend that this was done by an amateur. We'll let the police look into it, but I don't have much hope." He walked to the door.

"Sebastian?"

He stopped and turned to her. "What?"

She took a deep breath, her pulse racing. "I love you too."

He closed the space between them, gathered her in his arms and held her as she always dreamed he would and when she whispered 'darling' this time it wasn't pretend.

"I don't know what I'd do if I lost you," he said in a low voice.

"I'm sorry I made you angry."

"All that matters is that you're safe."

She drew away. "You said I can be discharged?"

"Yes, but are you sure you're up to it?"

Naomi nodded, pushing away her sheets. "I want to leave here." She lightly touched his cheek. "And spend the night with you."

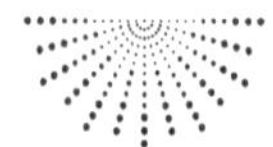

CHAPTER TWENTY-FOUR

They were both eager to reach Naomi's bedroom the moment they got home, but Josephine met them in the foyer. Her lips tightened at the sight of them holding hands. Her gaze shifted to Naomi. "Are you okay?"

"Yes, thank you I—"

She looked at her son. "Sebastian, there's something I need to tell you."

He gritted his teeth. "Not now."

"It's important," she said then walked into the sitting room.

"Maybe we should do this later," Naomi whispered, releasing his hand.

He let out a heavy sigh then said, "I'll join you in a minute."

She blew him a kiss. "I'll be waiting."

Sebastian watched her disappear up the stairs, then walked into the other room. "Whatever you have to say had better be very important."

"What's going on between you two?"

He rubbed his hands together annoyed. "Is that what you wanted to discuss? Because if so, I'm leaving."

"I want to know what's going on," Josephine said in a rush when he turned to leave. "Andre told me you found her in the pool."

The concern on her face softened his irritation. He sat down in front of her. "Naomi was attacked because of me."

"Because of you?"

"She was looking into my research at BioCorps."

Josephine rubbed her hand along the arm of her chair. "Why would she do that?"

"Because, for some reason, she thinks I'm innocent."

"I knew she was trouble," Josephine said with a frown. "This must bring back terrible memories for you. How could she be so careless?"

"Her heart was in the right place, but I'll need to keep her close until I find out what's going on."

"I think you should send her away. I don't want her in this house."

"This is my house," he said in a soft voice.

Josephine's voice rose. "Are you choosing her over me?"

"If you don't want to be here you can leave."

Tears sprung to his mother's eyes. "You're throwing me out?"

"Mom, you know you can stay as long as you need, but you can't run my life. If you don't like to see Naomi you can go back to your place."

"Someone attacked her." She pointed to the ground. "Here on our property. What if something happens to you? How do you think I'll bear it?"

"I can take care of myself. You don't have to worry about me. My only concern is Naomi."

"She's gotten a warning, I'm sure if she stops digging nothing else will happen."

"But I can't let it go."

"Why not? You think she knows something?"

"No."

"Then forget it." She leaned forward, clasping her hands together. "Please listen to me. You don't need this. You don't need her. You'd finally gotten your life in order, but you haven't been the same since she came into our lives."

He leaned back in his chair and studied his mother for a long moment before he said, "No, I'm not. I'm not the same man I once was and I have no regrets. She thinks I'm innocent. She believes in me. Her family welcomed me. She talked to me like an equal, something that hasn't happened in a long time."

Josephine sat down beside him and touched his sleeve with tentative fingers. "I know you miss your career, but this isn't the way to get it back. We made an agreement. Can't you forget this and—"

"Is that the man you raised? Do you think I can just walk away after finding out someone lured somebody precious to me and tried to kill her?"

"Sebastian, I'm sure someone was just trying to frighten her."

His eyes blazed, but his voice remained soft. "They may have frightened her, but they made me angry." He stood and stared down at her his voice filled with venom. "And they're going to pay."

CHAPTER TWENTY-FIVE

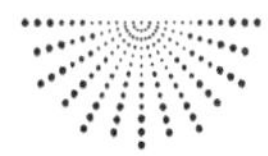

Sebastian knocked on Naomi's door hoping she was still in the mood. The conversation with his mother had taken longer than he'd planned.

The door swung open. He'd hoped to find her wearing something special—a see-through nightgown, a robe and nothing else—but she wore a long sleeved shirt and jeans. Before he could ask if she'd changed her mind she said, "Are you here for a blow job or a hand job?"

He stood still for a moment then remembered when he'd first shown up at her front door. She'd been wearing the same outfit when she'd thought he'd come for sex. Sebastian let his gaze trail the length of her body. Never had jeans and a plain white shirt looked so sexy before.

He swept her into his arms, closing the door behind him with his foot. "I want it all." He headed for the bedroom.

"I don't do lube jobs."

He laid her down on the bed, took off her glasses, and covered her body with his. "Then we'll have to come up with something else," he said also setting his glasses aside.

Naomi slowly unbuttoned her shirt, trying to display a sophistication she didn't feel. She wanted him so bad, the strength of her feelings frightened her. "Do you have anything particular in mind?"

"I like surprises."

"What did your mother want?"

"I didn't come here to talk about her," he said in a low growl.

Wrong topic, she should have known that, but she had been curious. Her mind had been racing as she waited for him to arrive, wondering if he would or if his mother would convince him to change his mind. But he was here with her, she could claim victory. She'd deal with his mother later.

Naomi removed her shirt then wiggled out of her jeans. "Your mother thinks I'm after your money. I wonder if I should tell her the truth."

"Which is?"

She slid a sensuous path down his chest. "I'm after your body."

"Not my mind?"

"That interests me too, but not at the moment."

Sebastian pressed a finger over her lips. "Don't mention her again. I'm not in the mood to talk about her."

"I bet you don't want to talk at all."

"You're starting to read my mind." He covered her mouth with his and she could feel his erection pressing against her thigh.

It wasn't just his mind she was starting to read. She unbuttoned his trousers and pushed them down. She sighed with relief at the sight of his black boxers. "Thank God," she whispered.

"For what?" he asked, burying his face against her throat, his hand searing a slow, sensuous path down her body.

She closed her eyes, letting the heat build within her. "Promise me you'll never wear striped boxers."

"What if I like stripes?" he asked his breath warm against her skin.

"I don't care."

"Okay, I promise," he said before he kissed her again and his hand slipped inside her panties and with his fingers he made her forget about boxers striped or otherwise.

She rose to meet him and he entered her. She wrapped her legs around him, inviting him deeper inside then the image of Maya with the man's brown bottom in the air flashed in her mind. She swore, unlatched her legs and started to move to the side.

"Whoa, whoa, whoa," Sebastian said. "What are you doing?"

"I want to be on top."

"That's fine, but you've got to let me know." He grinned then winked at her. "We're sorta in this together."

"Right."

They shifted positions. "Better?" he asked.

"Much," she breathed, settling down on him. "I'll make it up to you later."

"You can make it up to me now."

Which she did with gusto. With her mouth she made up for not fulfilling her promise to him right away. With her hands she made up for digging into his past. With her body she made up for all the time she'd held herself back from expressing how she felt. And her feelings came like a tidal wave. No part of him was safe—she was hungry for it all.

And Sebastian didn't drown under her passionate assault. Instead he was a boy in the ocean again—wild and free. Free from ridicule, free from obligation. No longer the boy who'd once been in the wheelchair, or the man who'd disappointed his father, or the scientist who'd lost his career. Naomi swept all those memories away and his heart didn't regret being lost to her.

Together their bodies joined in ecstasy.

"Tell me about the scars," Naomi asked, referring to the scars on his legs, as they lay in each other's arms.

"Lots of surgeries. I was born with extreme clubbed feet."

"Yes, I'd wondered about your walk, you have a unique stride, but I hardly noticed it was a limp," she said quickly when his expression changed. "You've come a long way."

He looked a little rueful. "Just not one hundred percent. I'd fooled myself to think I had."

"I don't need a hundred percent, you're perfect just the way you are." She wrapped her arms tighter around him and sighed with pleasure. "This is nice."

"Only nice?" Sebastian said with an edge of disappointment.

"More than nice. I never thought I could be this happy with someone else."

"I didn't want to quit because of your father."

"What?"

"That night you found me on the kitchen floor, when I said I couldn't take it, it was because of this." He drew her body closer to him. "I wanted this."

"Me too. I thought of kissing your back."

"I thought of kissing more than that," Sebastian said with a dirty laugh.

Naomi sighed. "It's a shame really."

"Why?"

"Because now I really can't work with you anymore."

He looked down at her alarmed. "Why?"

"Conflict of interest and all that."

"I'm a volunteer."

"It's still wrong. I can't have you as my lover and my assistant."

"How about as your husband?"

Naomi stared up at him startled. "You're serious?"

He nodded.

She bit her lip.

"It doesn't have to be now," Sebastian said, sensing her hesitation.

"I can't marry you until—"

"I don't expect you to change your name. I know my reputation will be an issue."

She sat up and looked down at him amazed. "You really are clueless."

"About what?"

She affectionately patted his face. "You're like a frog who still thinks he's a tadpole."

"A frog?"

She nodded.

He frowned. "What does that have to do with whether you'll marry me or not? There's something about me—"

"That's my point. If I marry you, I'd have a stellar lab, a beautiful home, a wonderful man, and work I adore... and you think I'm hesitating because of what happened at BioCorps?"

"I'm Dr. Disgrace, remember? You want to know the truth. You want to know the kind of man I really am."

"I told you, I only did it to help you. I will stop looking, I promise."

His frown increased. "If it's not that, then what is it?"

She let her gaze fall. "I have to deal with something else first."

"What?"

"I can't tell you yet."

"Why not?"

"If...if I can't handle it on my own, I'll let you know."

"I don't like you keeping things from me."

"I know, but what if I say 'yes' and then you change your mind?"

"I won't change my mind."

Naomi sighed. "Give me a week and then we'll see."

His face spread into a wide grin. "So you will marry me?"

"Sebastian, I just said--"

"You're worried I'll change my mind." He shook his head. "I won't," he said before he kissed her, giving her no chance to argue.

CHAPTER TWENTY-SIX

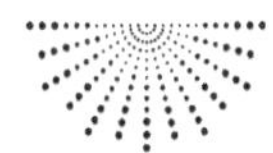

era pinned Naomi with a dark look. "Married?"

They sat in the same café that they had been in weeks before, this time Vera wore a light coat to shield her against the autumn weather settling in, chilling the air and touching the leaves with color.

"Yes."

"When?"

"We haven't discussed it."

"Who?"

"He's also a scientist."

"Didn't I warn you about that? Did the breakup of my marriage teach you nothing? A woman in your position must choose a man from a different field. There's bound to be jealousy when one's career grows faster than another's. What does he do exactly?"

"Right now he's not in the field. But I do see him returning to it."

"Who is he?"

"Sebastian Scott."

"No."

"What?"

"Not only is he not a scientist, he's the lowest sort of man you can attach yourself to."

"I don't think so, although I wasn't able to prove that there might have been a mistake at BioCorps I believe—"

"Are you even listening to yourself? You're already putting your career behind a man who couldn't even handle his own. You made a narrow mistake with Barry. Two kids in three years."

"She's happy."

"Does she have a choice?"

"Of course she does. She wanted a family."

"A man will saddle you down, even the best of them. If it's not children, it's the weight of their career or the delicacy of their ego."

"Not all men."

"A man like Sebastian Scott will drag you down. Don't think I haven't noticed the pretty glass cage he's slowly been putting you in. The house, the lab."

Naomi shook her head. "I didn't—"

"Gifts like that always come with a price. You can only trust your own hard work and effort."

"I do work hard."

"Then why is Pete O'Connell able to get the brightest researchers?"

"Because, through Sebastian, I've learned that our field isn't only about being the brightest and having the most stellar reputation. It's also about being liked and respected. I've had to learn to treat my team better. Give them compliments once in a while." She hadn't done this before Sebastian, she'd taken her researchers for granted and the people who funded her work. She'd been blind to the needs of others, not realizing what a kind gesture or word could do.

"Do you hand out lollipops too?"

Naomi sighed. "I didn't come here to ask for your blessing, I wanted advice."

"And I'm giving it to you. Don't go after a man like a starry eyed teenager. You're a scientist letting your heart rule your head."

"I wanted to know more about Josephine Scott."

"Who?"

"His mother."

"Are you still looking into BioCorps?"

"No, I just wanted to know if—"

"Why would I know anything about her? I've told you this and I'll say it again. Sebastian Scott is poison and that includes those around him. Stay away."

"Why? One man's meat—"

"Is another man's poison," Vera finished in a grave tone. "I don't believe in taking gambles." She stood. "And neither should you."

Naomi finished her coffee disappointed as she watched her friend leave the shop. She'd hoped to be able to get help from Vera, but she would have to face the problem she faced alone.

Naomi found Josephine in her favorite position in the solarium reading.

"I want to marry your son, but I need to understand something first."

"What is that?"

"Why did you try to kill me?"

CHAPTER TWENTY-SEVEN

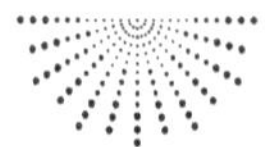

"I don't know what you mean."

"I felt the edge of your cane that night. And I heard the sound of your footsteps. I know it wasn't Andre's and Sebastian's walk is very distinctive. I know it was you."

Josephine sniffed. "You can't prove a thing."

"So you did do it."

Her lips thinned.

"You hate me that much?" When Josephine remained mute, Naomi sighed and said, "If you won't give me any answers, I'll tell Sebastian my suspicions."

"You can't tell him," she demanded. "I wouldn't have let you die. I had no other choice. It was him or you."

"What do you mean?"

"Why must you ask so many questions? Why couldn't you have left things alone?"

"I don't know who you're trying to protect."

"Him. I've always done everything for him. He was happy as things were before you came into our lives."

"No, he wasn't. He wouldn't have sought me out otherwise."

"He had a moment of weakness, nothing more."

"You're not answering my question. Do you hate me that much?"

"Yes, because you're a threat. I need Sebastian here as the head of his father's business. BioCorps nearly destroyed him, I won't see that happen again."

"Mrs. Scott—"

"I'll make you a bargain. I won't interfere with you two as long as you never tell him what happened."

"And why would I do that?"

"Because if you want him to stay with you, you'll keep this a secret."

A secret. *I don't like you not telling me things,* he'd said. But would he believe her if she did?

She could imagine his reaction. He'd deny it at first. Tell her she was mistaken. Force her to provide proof. All she had was her memory. That wouldn't be enough and he'd get angry at her for accusing his mother of something awful. She remembered the rage in his eyes at the hospital when he thought of the person who'd put her there. Would he turn that rage on her? He'd never look at her the same way again.

But if she didn't tell him, he'd never know the depth of his mother's manipulation. How much she hated his love of science. At times, Naomi wondered if Josephine had something to do with the fall of Sebastian's career. But it was all speculation and she had no proof. Vera had warned her that Sebastian was poison and all those around him. Did she know what Josephine was capable of?

But a secret would slowly erode their relationship. Is that what his mother really wanted?

She shook her head. "No, I—"

"Stop pretending," Josephine snapped.

"What?"

"Stop pretending you don't know what happened. Did they put you up to this? Wasn't ruining his career enough for them?"

"Enough for whom? I don't know what you're talking about?"

"You really want me to believe that all this time they haven't mentioned anything? Were they using you to make sure that he didn't say anything?"

"Who are they? I don't understand."

"You keep acting as if you know what he needs when all this time you've been close to the very person who ended Sebastian's career."

"I haven't been close to anyone who could hurt him."

Josephine's lip curled. "Except Vera Conklin."

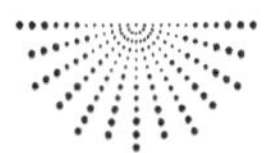

CHAPTER TWENTY-EIGHT

Bad news. He always knew when someone was going to give him bad news and Andre didn't disappoint.

"The jeweler mixed up the order. It won't be ready."

Sebastian hit the steering wheel of his car as he made his way back home after dropping Naomi off at work. She'd been quiet that morning and he'd hoped his gift—a ruby necklace—would have cheered her up when he gave it to her that evening.

"What do you want me to do?"

"They'd better give me a discount, bonus or something impressive if they want to keep my business."

"I'll let them know."

He heard Andre hesitate and knew there was further bad news. "What else?"

"I have to run some errands for your mother, but the security company that you wanted to install cameras around the pool said they'd be coming in an hour."

"I'm almost home, I'll handle it myself."

Moments later, he stormed into the house.

"What are you doing home so early?" his mother asked surprised. "You look upset."

"Because Naomi's—"

"Whatever she told you about me is a lie."

He paused. "Excuse me?"

"Naomi." Josephine nervously licked her lips. "What did she say?"

Naomi hadn't said anything, but from the guilty look on his mother's face, she should have. He folded his arms. "Let me hear it from you."

"I knew she couldn't keep her mouth shut. You know I only did it for you."

He nodded. "Yes, you always try to protect me."

"And she was being dramatic. I was trying to scare her, not kill her."

Sebastian felt his body grow cold. "The pool?"

"Yes, I pushed her, but that hardly qualifies for homicidal intent."

"You're the one who attacked her?"

"Yes," Josephine said suddenly hesitant. "Isn't that what she told you?"

"No," Sebastian said, drawing out the word and narrowing his eyes. "She didn't, but I knew something was wrong." He rested his hands on his hips. "I can't believe what I just heard. You tried to kill her?"

"I didn't try to kill anybody! They said I had to do something."

"Who?"

"You know who. I had to do something so when Andre told me you'd had a fight with Naomi, I took a gamble. I didn't really think it would work to be honest. I spoofed your phone and sent a text to her. I kept waiting for something to go wrong, but it didn't. So when she showed up, I took my chance."

"You left her floating in the pool."

"I wouldn't have let her die, I swear. I was scared of what they would do to you."

"If Vera and Niklaas threatened you, why didn't you come to me?"

"Because you're under her spell, I didn't think you'd listen to me."

Sebastian nodded as the pieces fell into place. "You're the reason she's afraid to marry me." He turned. "I have to talk to her."

Josephine grabbed his hand. "You know I did it for you. Your father dreamed of you running the business—"

"I don't want to run the business! Don't you understand? I never have. I only did it because at the time I felt it was the right choice, but not anymore."

"How can you turn away from all that your father built for you and your brother? How can you cast aside all that he sacrificed?"

"Dad loved what he did. It wasn't a sacrifice for him, it was a pleasure. I don't feel the same, never have." He took a deep steadying breath. "We'll discuss this later. I have to talk to Naomi right now." He turned to the door.

"I told her about Vera Conklin."

Sebastian spun around, stunned that his mother would put Naomi in such a dangerous position. "How much did you tell her?"

Josephine flashed a cruel grin. "Enough to make her curious."

CHAPTER TWENTY-NINE

Naomi had expected a gun or a knife, but the syringe in Vera's hand seemed oddly perfect. She'd left her lab to visit Vera in her office and confront her about what Josephine had shared. Vera had welcomed her into the sleek, minimalist room with the same cool detachment Naomi had grown used to.

She sat at the round table in the corner where two coffee cups sat, prepared to get answers. How could Vera be the reason for Sebastian's dismissal? What had really happened?

But when Vera sat down in front of her and pulled out the syringe, Naomi knew she shouldn't have come. The woman she'd trusted wasn't all that she'd seemed.

"I warned you," she said, when she saw Naomi look at the object in her hand. "You were always so tenacious. Always looking deeper and closer than you should. Why couldn't you have left things as they were?"

"Sebastian knows I'm here," she lied.

"No, he doesn't. He wouldn't have let you come. You came

here all on your own without telling anyone. I know you Naomi. You're one who's proud to depend on herself."

"Sebastian will—"

"I'll deal with Sebastian just as I did all those years ago."

"You don't need to do this. I still don't know what happened."

Vera shrugged. "Your suspicions are enough to make you dangerous."

Suspicions. What did Vera suspect that she knew? How could she be involved? Did it have anything to do with her former husband? She had to keep her talking as she tried to figure a way to get out. "Why did you do it?" she asked, still not knowing what 'it' was.

"I fell under the very spell I warned you about."

"You fell for a man who promised you the world," Naomi guessed. "A man you'd do anything for."

"A man?" Vera said with a note of derision. "It was Niklaas who nearly ruined everything. I had to protect his reputation and mine. What would have happened to me if Niklaas' mistake was uncovered? All the years would have been washed away. Scott had his father's money to fall back on, we had nothing."

"So you made a deal," Naomi guessed.

"That was his mother's idea. Scott had shared his concerns regarding Niklaa's performance with her. He was the one who discovered Niklaas had made a major miscalculation with the data, which would cost BioCorps millions to fix. He told his mother and she helped devise a plan. Josephine used her connections within the media to persuade the public relations division of BioCorps to carefully state what had happened. Scott fell on his sword, so to speak, because he respected Niklaas so much and his father was dying so his mother persuaded him to give up his science career and fulfill his father's wish to head the company he'd built for him and his brother.

"But in the end it had been a waste. Niklaas already had years behind him and had lost his enthusiasm. Scott was the more brilliant scientist. He would have done more in five years than Niklaas could in twenty." She shrugged. "But talking about the past bores me. So—"

Naomi lifted up the table, startling Vera and giving her enough time to try to escape. She ran to the door and struggled to unlock it, but Vera grabbed her before she could. Vera grabbed her arm, dragging her back. Naomi pulled out of her jacket and dove for the door again, her bare arm now exposed.

Vera grabbed her leg, causing Naomi to drop to the ground.

"There's no use trying to fight me," she said, saddling Naomi, effectively pinning her to the ground. She held down Naomi's arm and lifted the syringe.

Naomi slid her other arm free and yanked Vera's earring from her ear, tearing through the flesh. Vera screamed out in shock and pain, giving Naomi enough time to shift Vera's body and knock her to the ground, the syringe scattered to the ground.

They both lunged for it, Vera getting it first. She held it like a knife while Naomi gripped her wrist, her hand trembling as the syringe drew slowly, closer to her skin. Vera was bigger, stronger. Naomi knew she couldn't win by sheer might, she had to use surprise. So she went limp, dropping to the ground, still holding Vera's hand and causing her to stab herself in the thigh.

Vera stared at the needle horrified. "You bitch," she cried, yanking it out.

Naomi surged to her feet and ran, this time managing to open the door before Vera could reach her. She rushed into the hallway and saw Sebastian coming from the other end. "Naomi!"

She ran into his arms.

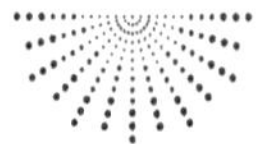

CHAPTER THIRTY

The ruby necklace settled beautifully around Naomi's neck, while the soft sounds of the Caribbean Sea drifted on a wave of a floral scented wind that drifted through their hotel window.

"Do you like it?" Sebastian asked, meeting Naomi's eye in the mirror reflection.

She lightly touched the exquisite piece. "It's beautiful."

After the horror of what had happened in Vera's office she was afraid she'd never feel awe, joy or safe again. Sebastian couldn't seem to hold her close enough to rid her of the feeling. She still shivered with fear at the thought that Vera had tried to kill her; that Josephine had pushed her in the water. In her nightmares, sometimes she was drowning; other times she was being stabbed, every time Sebastian woke her and soothed her back to sleep.

When she learned that Vera survived—barely—she felt a sense of relief. She hadn't wanted to have killed her; the courts would judge her instead and she'd suffer some long lingering effects of the poison. Josephine apologized to Naomi, with

Sebastian's urging, and reluctantly accepted her son's decision to hire someone else to run the company, while he devoted his attention to helping Dr. Mensah with the research for his book.

Naomi remembered the sound of autumn leaves scattering along the ground while she and Sebastian stood in front of his father's grave—a large monument to a life well lived. Sebastian held her hand and solemnly introduced her before he said, "We didn't agree on a lot of things, Dad, but I think you'd agree that I made a good choice. You'd like her." He took a deep breath, blinking back tears. "It was a long time coming, but I'm happy now and I wish you could be here and see me as a man you could be proud of."

Naomi squeezed his hand and said in a soft voice. "I think you were already that man five years ago. You're just finally realizing that now."

A ghost of a smile touched his lips and he nodded. "Your right," he said and the weight she'd sensed he'd been carrying melted away.

But even as she stood in a white organza wedding dress staring up at him as they said their vows, a fear still gripped her—a fear she couldn't shake. She didn't feel safe. She felt she could still lose him somehow.

Now, as she felt the weight of his hands on her shoulders as they stood together in front of the mirror in their honeymoon suite, she finally identified her true fear. "I don't know if I'll ever love you enough." She turned to him, meeting his steady brown gaze. "I haven't changed. I can still be absent-minded. I might miss birthdays or anniversaries, dinner dates and be late for vacations."

He smiled amused. "I'll keep you on schedule."

"But if I forget, I don't want you to be angry with me. My

family is used to me, but...I don't want you to think that I don't—"

He cupped her chin, his voice tender. "I won't get angry about any of that. I love you too much to care."

Naomi felt her anxiety slip away under his warm, gentle gaze. A buoyant joy filled her heart; she could still make mistakes and have him by her side. "Is that a promise?"

"Yes, I promise," he said then sealed it with a kiss.

ABOUT THE AUTHOR

Dara Girard, an award-winning, national bestselling author of more than forty novels, from romance to suspense, loves telling stories.

Born in the US to immigrant parents, Dara enjoys pulling from her Jamaican, British, Nigerian heritage and exposure to various cultures to bring what reviewers and fans call "vivid emotional stories" to life. She is best known for her popular Henson Series, the mysterious Clifton Sisters, and the fun Black Stockings Society.

You can write her at:
contactdara@daragirard.com
or
P.O. Box 10345
Silver Spring, MD 20914
If you'd like to receive a reply, please send a self-addressed stamped envelope.

Visit her website to sign up for her newsletter and get sneak peeks, monthly updates on new releases, and special offers.

For more information visit
www.daragirard.com